M000096457

GRANNIE PANTIES ARE UNDERRATED

GAYLE ERICKSON

MILE HIGH
PUBLISHING HOUSE

ISBN: 0998995908
ISBN 13: 9780998995908
Library of Congress Control Number: 2017906979
Mile High Publishing House Lone Tree, Colorado

For Taylor, who always believed.
Peter Gabriel: "In Your Eyes"

PROLOGUE

May 11, 1994
10:36 a.m.

Thank God Tak had a normal toilet. If not for her boyfriend's obsession with all things American, Elle's face would now be lying in a pool of her own vomit.

Having lived in Tokyo for nearly two years, Elle was accustomed to traditional Japanese-style toilets which didn't have seats and meant users were in for some serious squatting. She was actually a big fan of this system—it seemed much more sanitary (there was no danger of accidentally touching someone else's ass germs), and Elle liked to think she was getting in a good thigh workout every time she used the bathroom. But at this moment, as she desperately hung on to the toilet seat to maintain her balance while heaving out thick, sallow bile, Elle was eternally grateful for the good ol' solid American porcelain bowl.

Highly underrated.

Elle felt like shit. She was in a cold sweat from the sheer physical exertion of throwing up bile, she had a throbbing headache, a severe case of dry mouth, and her left cheek stung—she must have hit it against the toilet seat while puking. Worst of all, a relentless tingling sensation on her upper lip signaled a cold sore was on its way.

Fuck! Fuckity, fuck, fuck, fuck!

And what was that smell? It was sour and warm—the unfortunate result of a combination of undigested sushi and stomach acid. Wanting to remove herself from the source of the nasty odor, Elle gingerly sat up and turned away from the toilet, her back resting against its base. She needed water—her tongue was like an enormous cotton ball in her mouth—but she was too nauseous to stand up and go to the sink.

Completing the utter clusterfuck of her present situation, Nirvana's "Heart-Shaped Box" was reverberating up through the vents from Tak's nightclub, Samantha's, which was directly below the bathroom. Kurt Cobain's howls of despair were like fingernails against a chalkboard—each screech thumped in concert with the throbbing ache in her temples.

Was the club still open? What time was it, and how long had she been in the bathroom? Elle looked around. Daylight peeked through the small window above the toilet. It was definitely morning, probably around ten-thirty, the time Samantha's cleaning staff came in to erase any traces of the previous evening's debauchery. They must be vacuuming, which would explain the blaring music.

If she hadn't been so preoccupied with her hangover, Elle would have realized hearing Nirvana was a bad sign. Kurt Cobain had killed himself in April, so there was that creepiness to contend with. And, as sad as his death was, she didn't really get the appeal of angsty grunge bands anyway. The music was hard to dance to, and greasy-haired guys dressed like lumber-jacks didn't do it for her. Eighties music ruled. Sting, Jon Bon Jovi, and Bruce Springsteen—now those were men worth throwing your panties on stage for.

Irritated, Elle tried to drown out all the noise and focus on how she had ended up in this predicament. What, exactly, had happened the night before?

Think, Elle. Think.

Elle couldn't remember anything. Her brain was scrambled, like the egg splattered in the frying pan on the TV commercial from high school. *"This is your brain on drugs."*

Oh right, drugs . . . there had been the cocaine. That would explain why Elle felt so shitty now—she could drink so much more when she was high. She shouldn't have used again; she had promised her best friend, Mitch, that she was done with all of that. Disgusted by her lack of self-control and ashamed of all the lies, Elle put her head down in her hands and covered her face in shame.

What the fuck is wrong with me?

This wasn't a rookie mistake. It's not like she was a freshman waking up in her dorm bathroom after a night of over-drinking at a frat house kegger. She was a twenty-four-year-old college graduate. She had woken up strung out by coke with her face in a toilet. She was better than this.

Get it together, Elle.

Determined—she'd battled through worse before—Elle carefully stood up and plodded her way over to the sink. As she scooped water into her dry mouth with cupped hands, she heard a door slam and the sound of men talking. Elle immediately recognized her boyfriend Tak's rapid, commanding Japanese. The other voices were likely those of his "bodyguards," Johnny and Mike.

Shit. Tak was the last person she wanted to see.

Elle looked in the mirror. It was bad. Her eyes were red and puffy and her left cheek was swollen and smeared with dried blood from what appeared to be a deep cut—man, she must have really hit the toilet bowl hard. There was a clump of blonde hair (Clairol #59 Platinum) matted against her forehead, and she could see the offending cold sore starting to develop, a third eye on her dry lips.

In anticipation of Tak's arrival, Elle instinctively brushed the matted hair behind an ear and attempted to smooth her miniskirt. Her thong underwear was wedged uncomfortably up her ass, and she pulled at it as Tak stormed in with Johnny and Mike following closely behind.

Despite names indicating otherwise, Johnny and Mike were both Japanese. As equally fixated with America as Tak, they had given themselves Western-sounding nicknames. Elle found it rather absurd, but *whatever.* At least Tak had agreed to drop "Tim," the name he had introduced himself with. *No way* she was going to call him that. She didn't come all the way to Japan to date a guy with the same name as a shoe salesman at Sears.

Elle could tell by the redness of Tak's nose and cheeks that he had been drinking. Her boyfriend couldn't hold his alcohol, and his face betrayed this weakness every time. That he was drunk this early in the day worried her.

"You are okay?" Tak said in heavily accented English. He didn't make eye contact with Elle, which was unusual. Instead, he seemed intently focused on turning the ring on his left pinky finger. The same ring that had been covered in another man's blood a few weeks earlier.

"I'm fine." Elle tried to sound rueful, unsure of where this was headed—Tak's behavior had become increasingly erratic of late. She needed to be careful; he could be a mean drunk. Still, it was hard to play nice—Elle was in no condition to deal with Tak, and the smell of his generously applied Polo aftershave was noxious. She nearly hurled again.

Tak turned his back on Elle and abruptly left the bathroom. Again, his behavior was confusing. Normally, he would stay and take care of her. Regardless, Elle was relieved, pleased even, to see him go. Mitch had been right about her boyfriend—he was bad news and needed to be ditched, right along with all the drugs.

Elle was left with Johnny and Mike and the lingering smell of Polo, which at least masked the warm and sour stench of vomit. Although she didn't particularly like either of Tak's companions, Elle appreciated their presence. She could have them go to the McDonald's down the street and get her a Diet Coke with extra ice. And maybe an Egg McMuffin. Or better yet, a Big Mac and some fries. There really was nothing better than Mickey D's for a hangover. Elle started to place her order when, with an overly dramatic flourish of his arm, Johnny removed a small object from his pocket.

"You know what this is? This yours?" He held out what appeared to be a small square of shiny gold paper. Half of Johnny's front tooth was broken off, and his tongue protruded out through the gap it left when he spoke.

It gave him a slight lisp and made his halting English even more difficult to understand.

Johnny's tone pissed Elle off. Had he forgotten who she was? Hoping to indicate that he was lucky she even acknowledged his question, Elle rolled her eyes and sighed heavily. She didn't need his attitude. Annoyed, Elle strained to see what Johnny was holding. After a few moments, she recognized it as an empty condom wrapper with one corner torn off. "It's a rubber package. So what?" Why was he wasting her time with this?

Johnny scowled. "It yours?"

One long second passed. Then another.

Oh shit.

Reminders of the previous evening came to Elle in quick flashes, like frames from a horror movie. Sensing the magnitude of the situation, her body reacted immediately. Nauseous and light-headed, Elle quickly got down on her knees and grabbed hold of the toilet bowl to steady herself for what was to come. From the nightclub below, she could hear the Red Hot Chili Peppers' "Under the Bridge" playing. This was another bad sign.

Japanese toilet, American toilet—it didn't much matter now. Elle was in trouble. Big trouble.

ONE

JACKSON BROWNE: "RUNNING ON EMPTY"

May 18, 2017
6:47 a.m.

It's going to be a bad day.
Elle was so over it already, and her morning had just begun.

She'd had the nightmare again. The one where she is stuck in a room with no windows or doors, surrounded by a bunch of feral dogs and cats feasting on her used tampons and pads. Elle could never make sense of this bizarre and disgusting dream; she only knew it was messed up. Kind of like she was.

After the nightmare, Elle had fallen back into a fitful sleep only to be woken by a news report, not a song, when her alarm clock radio went off. Something about a recent earthquake in Japan. That Elle hadn't woken to music was ominous enough; more troubling was the first song played after the news report — "Shake It Out" by Florence + the Machine. Music provided Elle with messages, and this song's meaning could be interpreted in two ways: it could prescribe optimism—forget your mistakes and be happy; or it could portend trouble—all that talk about regrets and the devil on your back. Elle hated it when the signs weren't clear. That they weren't was, in and of itself, a bad sign.

And then there was the weight gain. After a few blissful minutes rubbing the belly of her beloved golden retriever, Duke, the first thing Elle did upon waking was to pee and then step on the scale. That morning, "113" had flashed out in bold red, like a Public Service Announcement warning of an impending disaster. *"ATTENTION! ATTENTION! Elle's gained weight. Run for cover!"*

Elle had tried taking off her tank top and drawstring shorts—and even her white cotton underwear—hoping it would make a difference, but suspecting it probably wouldn't. Sure enough, even stark naked, she was still three pounds over her target weight of 110.

Elle berated her lack of self-control at dinner the previous evening. Martin Global Industries, her husband Win's company, had sponsored a fundraiser for the Wounded Warrior Project and there had been a burrito bar. Mexican food was always challenging—all those carbs and so much dairy. Accepting it would be nearly impossible to avoid high, fatty calories, Elle had decided to go for it, loading her plate to the hilt with beans, guacamole, sour cream, and enough cheese to impress even the most jaded Wisconsin dairy farmer.

Regretful over these indulgences, Elle resolved to do better that day— no carbs or sugar—and if that didn't work, she would do another cleanse. Elle hated cleanses. The lemon juice and cayenne pepper mixture tasted horrible and was difficult to swallow, but it was an effective way to quickly lose a few pounds.

Elle needed to get back into her workout routine. She had been finding excuses to cancel sessions with her personal trainer and hadn't gone to Pilates in weeks. She had given up on yoga altogether. Rather than it having the intended effect of calming her racing mind, Elle felt worse after each class, obsessing over whether her bow pose had been good enough. It wasn't supposed to be a competition—that's what everyone said—but Elle knew better. She noticed the other women, smug that they could fit into size 0 lululemon capris, not so discreetly watching each other and making judgments. And hot yoga? Forget it. Elle tried it once but couldn't get past all the sweaty bodies so close to one another.

Finally, there was the matter of the sheets on her bed in the guest room. Elle changed the white Frette hotel linens once a week. *Always.* If she waited any longer, her skin felt itchy. The sheets needed changing, and Elle would have to take care of it herself. Every so often, she could get away with asking her housekeeper, Angela, to do it. Elle would lie and say they had entertained out-of-town visitors—to complete the subterfuge, she would dampen a few towels and washcloths and leave them on the guest-bathroom floor—but if her requests to change the sheets became too frequent, Angela would figure out that either Elle or Win was regularly sleeping in the guest bedroom.

This would be a disaster.

Tantalizing gossip had a habit of spreading quickly, and it wouldn't take long before this news reached Aubrey, the self-appointed social arbitrator for Elle's peer group. Convinced it was her duty to get involved, Aubrey would immediately convene an emergency meeting with their mutual friends to discuss the state of the Martin's marriage. *"Did you hear about Elle & Win?"—dramatic pause—"Her housekeeper and my housekeeper are friends and she claims they sleep in separate beds!" (Gasp!)*

Everyone would set down their skinny lattes, Restylane-plumped lips agape in shock. Forlornly shaking their heads, they would feign concern, hoping to mask their glee that things weren't so perfect in the Martin household after all. *"It wouldn't surprise me if they got a divorce; it's just sooo sad." (Smile. Smile. Ha! Ha!)*

Elle couldn't fathom how a group of women who had so much could take such pleasure in another's misfortune. Wasn't there enough joy for all of them? Apparently not; schadenfreude ran rampant in her crowd, warranting Elle's paranoia about something as seemingly benign as dirty sheets.

Sure, Angela had always been loyal enough, but Elle couldn't take any chances—she knew how things like this worked. Just a few weeks earlier, over lunch at the club after their weekly tennis drill, Aubrey shared that her housekeeper had discovered several scrunched-up, crusty tube socks stuffed behind her teenage son Grayson's bed.

On the surface, Elle found the story highly amusing. Having a sixteen-year-old son herself, she understood all too well the retarded temporal-lobe development of teenage boys which prevented them from realizing that someone would find the soiled socks and figure out what they had been using them for. Or maybe they simply didn't care. The point was, if a housekeeper would sell out a sixteen-year-old to his mom for masturbating, no amount of private information was safe.

Elle looked at the clock—6:53. Her children would be leaving for school soon. Rushed, she stripped the bed and left the dirty sheets in a pile on the floor to be dealt with later. With Duke following loyally behind, Elle darted up the back stairs to the master bedroom, thinking through her schedule for the day. She had a tennis match (it was a big one—if her team won, they would advance to Nationals); a coffee at Jane's to plan an upcoming school fundraiser (she would ignore the baked goods but would allow herself a small bowl of fruit); a tour of her children's private school, Country Day (she hoped the prospective parents wouldn't be the loathsome, pompous type who were convinced their child was a genius. *"Did you know our son speaks Mandarin and read* Moby-Dick *when he was six?"*); a SIDS Alliance board meeting (they were having a guest speaker so she probably wouldn't need to contribute much); and finally, her son Four's high school lacrosse state championship game (this was the one high point, but she was nervous about the outcome—it meant so much to Four to win).

Elle sighed heavily. She wished she didn't have the coffee, or the board meeting, or the tour. Even the tennis match, for that matter. She wasn't in the mood to be perky, and her full schedule meant she had to think about what to wear. As Elle entered her walk-in closet, she looked around at the racks and drawers full of overpriced designer clothes with dread. She didn't want to think about what to wear. It made her tired.

Despite many years attending coffees, cocktail parties, and board meetings, Elle was still anxious, worried about looking the part of Mrs. Winston Ford Martin III. Regardless of the occasion, the women in her peer group always looked *just right*. They seemed to possess an innate sense of what was appropriate, inherited at birth and reinforced by years of observing their mothers. Elle didn't have this luxury. Her own mom, Bobbie, had been a bartender who favored low-cut tops which highlighted her massive watermelon-shaped boobs. (All the easier for drunken men, their hands dirty and calloused from work, to gleefully stuff dollars into.)

Even as a child, Elle had understood that her mom's sartorial choices were often inappropriate, and she learned to take style cues from her classmates and people she saw in magazines and on TV. Determined to fit in, but with limited resources, Elle learned to be creative. When the Izod brand had been all the rage, she had scoured garage sales for affordable items—socks or a hat—with the trademark crocodile on them. She would buy them and then carefully remove the coveted crocodile off and sew it on to one of her secondhand polo shirts. Never mind most of these shirts were stained with another person's sweat. No one needed to know that. Elle was wearing Izod. She belonged. She was One of Them.

At this point, Elle could afford any brand she wanted, but her lack of confidence in how she appeared remained. Likewise, she could easily hire a stylist or personal shopper but refused to do so. It seemed unnecessarily indulgent and would mean she couldn't do it herself. Instead, Elle studied the women around her and tried to quiet the insecure voice in her head telling her that she would trip up. That she would be exposed.

If only she didn't have the stupid coffee first thing that morning. And at Jane's house, of all people. Jane was adept at the art of competitive hostessing. An event at her home would not soon be forgotten. Freshly squeezed juices, homemade scones, muffins, and jam would be served on impeccably decorated tables adorned with flowers from her garden in the crystal vases she "just fell in love with" on her last trip to Milan. As a reminder of her perfect party, Jane would send everyone home with honey from the beehive in her backyard.

It mattered what Elle wore, and she knew it. At the last coffee, a new mom had dared to show up with her hair in a scrunchie, and it had become *the* topic of snarky conversation for several days. "A scrunchie—*can you imagine?"* The mean-spirited gossip stopped only when it was usurped by the more titillating news that the SEC was investigating a former Country Day parent.

Mindful of the time, Elle settled on a fitted navy blazer with the Country Day crest on it, over a crisply starched white tuxedo blouse. After debating whether it was too early in spring to wear white pants, she opted to be safe and selected a pair of dark denim skinny jeans. They were a little tight, which was a good thing—she wouldn't be as tempted to overeat in something snug-fitting.

Although Elle normally wore shoes with a heel to add height to her petite five-foot-one frame, she decided on a pair of nude Tory Burch ballerina flats instead. It was going to be a long enough day already. Why add sore feet into the mix? It would probably help to add a unique accessory— a scarf, a whimsical brooch, or a pair of fabulous statement earrings—but Elle couldn't be bothered. If this wasn't appropriate, she didn't care.

Elle gave herself a once-over in the mirror. For the millionth time, she wished she was from a WASPy gene pool, the kind with naturally thin frames and long patrician legs—oh, to be able to pull off a shift dress without looking pregnant! But no, though she longed to come from an elegant and refined family of aristocrats—Boston Brahmins or Philadelphia Main Liners with names like Topper, Sloan and Pierce—Elle's family tree was decidedly less impressive. That is, of course, unless one considered a bunch of carny-type fat-asses named Jimbo and Bobbie to be the pinnacle of sophistication. *Oh well.* At least she been spared her mom's gigantic rack—one small victory in an otherwise losing battle.

Unable to shake the feeling she was in for a miserable day, as Elle made her way downstairs to see her children off to school, she had to fight an overwhelming urge to crawl back into bed.

TWO

May 18, 2017
7:18 a.m.

Elle loved her kitchen. With its adjacent hearth room, it was the space that felt the coziest and most inviting in her nine-thousand-square-foot home. It had east-facing floor-to-ceiling windows, so the room was always bright and warm with the morning sun. Elle's one regret was that she had caved to the interior designer's recommendation for a stark black-and-white design. Her own instinct had been to paint the walls yellow to match the bright light of the sun, but this suggestion had been met with thinly veiled disdain, so she had given in. (Really, what did she know about interior design?) Still, Elle loved this room, and the sun shining brightly through the large windows temporarily lifted her mood.

There was a bowl of freshly cut fruit on the rectangular farmhouse-style kitchen table, alongside a carafe of orange juice and a tray full of bagels. Angela stood behind the Wolf cooktop, so short her breasts were practically even with the skillet she was making an omelet in.

Seeing her housekeeper, Elle panicked. *Crap!* She had left the dirty bed linens on the floor of the guest bedroom. She would need to take

7

care of them before Angela started her cleaning. What to do with the incriminating sheets? Since Angela did all their washing, Elle couldn't exactly leave them in the laundry room. *Hmmm . . .* She would shove them into the guest linen closet. Yes, that was perfect. Angela would have no reason to look in there.

As Elle settled on her plan, Angela looked up from the skillet. "Good morning, Señora Martin. You want some egg? I come in early to make for Four, for his big game."

"Not for me, thanks. But that was very thoughtful of you. Four will be thrilled." Elle felt a momentary pang of guilt for doubting Angela's integrity. Her housekeeper clearly cared about Four's well-being. Still, she was right to be careful. One could never be sure.

Elle directed her attention toward her teenage daughter, Brynnie, who was casually leaning over the kitchen island, engrossed with something on her iPad. Despite Elle's many attempts to sell her daughter on the flattering skirts and feminine shirts allowed in Country Day's strict dress code, Brynnie wore a pair of ill-fitting chino pants and a baggy men's polo shirt. Much to Elle's chagrin, she had recently cut her striking auburn hair short, and—from the back—one could almost mistake Brynnie for a boy.

Perhaps that was the point. Brynnie eschewed convention. She always had. She was the girl who wanted to take drum—not piano—lessons, preferred karate to the swim team, and insisted on wearing a pantsuit to Cotillion. During her junior year, Brynnie had stopped shaving her legs and armpits and announced that she was a vegan. Her most recent act of rebellion had been turning down her acceptance to Brown in favor of Reed, a college where she would "have a more genuine experience."

Maybe the haircut was yet another challenge: *"What are you going to say about me now?"* Elle suspected there was already chatter regarding Brynnie and her sexuality, and the short tomboyish haircut would only fuel further speculation. Unfortunately, unlike the sheets in the guest bedroom, this was something Elle could not control.

"Good morning, sweetheart." Elle hugged Brynnie and ran her fingers affectionately through her short hair. She stopped herself from complaining about the haircut—what good would it do?—and asked, "Are you ready for your AP Spanish test?"

"*Si. Si.* Angela has been helping me."

"How wonderful." Elle was again ashamed of questioning her housekeeper's trustworthiness. What were the odds someone who resembled a Weeble toy—"*Weebles wobble, but they don't fall down!*"—would conspire to ruin her reputation? Not high, but Elle would remain vigilant. Being sentimental was a trap, an invitation to falter.

Brynnie held out a glassful of thick green liquid toward Elle. "Do you want some kombucha?"

"No, thanks, I'll stick to my coffee."

"I'm not judging you, Mom, but this would be much better for you than drinking a cup of carcinogens. Right, Angela?"

"I no know, Miss Brynnie." Angela shrugged her shoulders and shook her head, smiling.

"I'll take my chances," Elle said, pouring a large cup of coffee. She hoped it would fill her up. The bagels were tempting, but mindful of the extra three pounds on the scale, she was determined not to eat.

"Whatever. Go ahead and enjoy your cup of slave labor. Who cares about the impact on the lives of poor workers in Colombia?"

"That's not true! It's the one you told me to get. It's made in a co-op or something. Look." Elle handed the package of coffee over to Brynnie, hurt that her daughter would question her.

Overcompensating for her own childhood of Swanson Salisbury steak frozen TV dinners microwaved and eaten alone, Elle went out of her way to follow Brynnie's strict regulations on exactly what kind of food was acceptable. She drove forty-five minutes out of her way to get locally grown organic fruits and vegetables at a farmers' market. To accommodate Brynnie's vegan diet, Elle stocked the refrigerator with every type of meat substitute available. Why didn't her daughter appreciate all this?

As Brynnie verified that the coffee would not exploit any underprivileged workers, Four walked in, tossing a ball into a brightly strung lacrosse stick. He was slightly bowlegged and had a bouncy gait, like there were springs under his toes propelling him upward. It was a walk of optimism, the walk of someone who couldn't wait for what he was heading toward.

It was Brynnie who had given Four his unique nickname. His given name was Winston Ford Martin IV, in honor of Win's dad and grandfather. Thinking the name Winston a tad old-fashioned for someone born in the new millennial, they had planned to call him Ford; but Brynnie, who had been a late talker—and taking $75-an-hour speech therapy three times a week—could only manage to call her new baby brother "Four," and the name stuck.

At the time, it seemed cute. He was, after all, the fourth Winston Ford Martin and the fourth member of their family. Over the past few years, however, Elle had become uncomfortable with the name, finding it a bit pretentious. Unfortunately, by the time of this revelation, it was too late to reverse course; everyone already called her son "Four," and he had grown into the name.

Four looked every bit the part of the affluent, privileged, private-school-educated child he was. As it was a game day, he wore the required tie (a red Vineyard Vines one with lacrosse sticks on it) with a red-and-white striped button-down oxford shirt, khaki pants, and Sperry Top-Siders. As was the style with most of his teammates, Four's dirty-blond hair was long, resting just above the collar of his shirt, the acceptable limit for hair length at Country Day. His bangs covered his eyes, and he made a habit of pushing them to the side as he spoke.

Four greeted Elle with an affectionate kiss on the cheek. She was glad he appeared to be in a jovial mood; he had been angry with her the previous evening. Most of the other Country Day parents were allowing their sons to sleep-in and go to school late to ensure that they were well-rested ahead of the big lacrosse game, but she had refused to grant him this same leniency and he had been furious.

Fortunately, this all seemed forgotten now. Seeing the omelet Angela had put on a plate for him, Four grabbed the housekeeper around the waist and playfully spun her around. "Angela, you're the best. Thank you!"

Observing her son's clear fondness for Angela, it was hard for Elle to resist additional guilt, but she refused to feel bad. Weeble wobble or not, protecting her family was Elle's main priority and trumped all else.

Four put his arm around Brynnie's shoulders. "I see you're having some mold again for breakfast, sis."

Brynnie jokingly stuck her tongue out at her brother. Although her children couldn't be more different and frequently argued in the way siblings do, even Brynnie was not immune to Four's charm. "Are you excited for the game?" she asked.

"Well, not so much now that Thatcher is out."

Hearing the name Thatcher, Elle was immediately concerned. There were persistent rumors amongst the Country Day moms that he drank, did drugs, and sold his Adderall to classmates ahead of finals. "What happened? Is he okay?"

"It's so stupid. He got suspended from the team last night."

"Suspended? Why?" Elle set down her coffee cup, thankful that at least Thatcher wasn't hurt—drunk driving had crossed her mind. Still, Country Day didn't routinely suspend its students. Especially one whose parents contributed generously to the endowment fund.

"I don't know. He sent a text to the team late last night." Four took his cell phone out of his back pocket and read, "Coach says I'm a no-go tomorrow. Can't even dress. Not supposed to talk about the deets. I got screwed. Chicks suck. Go get 'em, boys."

"*Chicks suck*? Really? What a misogynist." Brynnie shook her head in disgust. "I suppose I shouldn't expect anything less from a guy who thinks it's original and funny to call public-school kids 'pubies.' Talk about projection—only someone desperately lacking in the pubic hair department would come up with that one."

"Okay, Brynnie, that's enough." Elle turned to Four, sympathetic. She agreed with her daughter's assessment of Thatcher—humility was not his strong point—but he was the team's starting goalie; playing in the lacrosse game would be important to him. "That's such a shame. What do you think happened?"

"Tate said he Snapchatted something 'inappropriate' to Jacinda. He and his parents are going to meet with Headmaster Mason and Ms. Smith today."

Ms. Smith was *The* Country Day's Director of Inclusivity. (Those in the know emphasized "The" when referring to the school, lest it be confused with some other less important institution named Country Day. One that was free and open to the public, like say, a library.) The school had come under fire for being comprised of mainly white, wealthy children and had responded to the criticism by hiring an African-American woman to support Country Day's commitment to equity and diversity.

Brynnie was visibly upset. Jacinda was a friend of hers; they were in the Social Justice Club together. "If the school suspended him, it must have been something really bad. I hope Jacinda is okay."

Four shook his head. "Typical overreaction by Country Day, if you ask me."

Brynnie was incredulous. "What's wrong with you? He was *suspended*. I'm going text Jacinda to make sure she's okay."

Elle worried about Jacinda. She was a sweet young woman, quiet and unassuming, not the type to cause drama. For the school to react so severely, the Snapchat must have been especially offensive. Elle then considered Thatcher's parents. His dad, Arthur, was a prominent attorney. Thatcher was his Golden Child. He would be apoplectic about this. His mom, Kimberly, was on her tennis team. Would she still play in their match?

"I'm telling you, I don't think it was anything major. You know Thatcher, he can be stupid sometimes." Four finished his omelet. "Remember, this is the same kid who thought it was a genius idea to go through the Wendy's drive-through naked."

Brynnie stopped texting and looked up at Four. "Are you kidding me right now? I can't believe you're defending him. What if he had done this to Tabby?"

At the mention of his girlfriend's name, Four shrugged, unconcerned. "She would have just laughed. Tabby has a sense of humor."

"Obviously—she's dating you."

"Hah, hah. You're hilarious. You know how the school is. They make a big deal out of everything. Thatcher's totally a scapegoat for one of their 'teachable moments.' It's ridiculous."

Brynnie stared at Four in disbelief. "Haven't you ever heard of white privilege?"

"Why so salty, sis? Are you on your period or something?"

Brynnie scowled and held up her middle finger to Four, who dramatically feigned injury. "Wait a minute, what was that? Did I just *feel the Bern?*"

"Four!" Elle stepped in, but not soon enough. Brynnie had already shot her a look of utter disappointment.

Elle had seen this look many times recently, and it was over more than just the coffee she bought. She seemed to let her daughter down in every way imaginable. Elle searched for the best way to both correct Four and appease Brynnie, when Win appeared in the kitchen. Seeing him, Elle was relieved. Always calm and centered, her husband could diffuse even the most difficult of situations. He would take control; his children would listen to him.

Win dutifully acknowledged Angela. He kissed Brynnie on the top of her head, asking if she was ready for her test, and then gave Elle a kiss on the cheek. Elle appreciated the gesture. Separate bedrooms or not, she was lucky to have him as a husband.

Win Martin was quite a catch. With his full head of chestnut brown hair—news anchorman kind of hair—he looked like someone you would see on a baseball card or gracing the cover of an outdoor living magazine. He was tall—he had been a standout basketball player at the Naval Academy—and maintained his athletic build. Elle could detect the ripples of his muscular frame beneath his French blue dress shirt.

Although from a solidly working-class family, one that clipped coupons and ate out solely on special occasions, Win's manner projected a lifetime of privilege. Perhaps it was simply the confidence of a man who had been highly successful in his career. Regardless, as his nickname "Win" suggested, Elle's husband was someone you would associate with a derivation of the word "winner."

Everyone loved Win. Yet Elle involuntarily tensed up whenever he touched her. What was wrong with her?

Win rubbed Four's shoulders. "Are you ready for tonight?" He had either failed to sense the tension in the room, or was purposefully ignoring it. Most likely the latter.

Four looked at his sister to discern how mad she still was. Often, the two would engage in a cease-fire of sorts around their father. This morning was no exception. Four didn't bring up the situation with Thatcher. "Yeah, I feel pretty good."

Win grimaced and cocked his head to the side. "It's going be a tough game."

Four chugged his orange juice and set the empty glass down. "I know. We're going to have to stop that really good kid, the one that's going to play football at Alabama. Jareme . . . Jaremeka . . ."

"Unbelievable!" Brynnie was again offended.

"What? I don't know what his name is. It's the African-American guy."

"Seriously? *That's* how you're going to describe him? Holy microaggression!"

Four tugged at his tie. "Yeah, I don't even know what that means."

Brynnie let out a long, exasperated sigh. "Would you describe a white person as 'that Caucasian guy'?"

"Well, yes, Miss Martin, if that was how I thought I could best describe the person I was referring to."

"First of all, it's Ms., not Miss. And *really*? Is it too hard for your tiny brain to find some way other than skin color to describe a person?"

"Okay, you're right. Sorry—" Four paused for emphasis and then added, "We need to find a way to stop the middie with the large Afro."

Elle looked to Win. Why wasn't he saying anything to help? He was distracted—his head was down reading his Blackberry. This grated on Elle; she needed him to be involved in the conversation.

"You're ridiculous," Brynnie exclaimed as she put her iPad into her backpack. She looked disapprovingly at her mom again. Win was forgiven; he always was. It was Elle who had failed her.

As much as Elle loved her daughter, she found her increasing self-righteousness unfair. Everything was black and white to Brynnie; she lacked the life experience to see the gray and was often unapologetically fierce in her judgements. Elle tried to be understanding, but it could be trying. A few weeks earlier, she had told Brynnie that although she didn't necessarily agree with her decision to turn down Brown, she would accept it. All Elle wanted was for Brynnie to be happy, to live her dream.

Brynnie had snapped, "Are *you* happy, Mom? Are you living *your* dream?"

Her daughter hadn't meant to be cruel; Elle was sure of that, but Brynnie's words couldn't have been more biting, their implications all too clear. Elle's life was a joke, not deserving of respect or admiration. This crushed Elle. She was smart and accomplished in her own way. Sure, she had willingly given up her career when Brynnie was born, but it was because she wanted her children to have the kind of childhood she had so desperately longed for. Choosing to stay home was not lack of ambition; it was an act of selflessness. Couldn't her daughter see that?

Brynnie's words had hung uncomfortably in the air for a few minutes before Elle had answered, "Of course I am." It was one of the few times in her life a lie had not come easily to her.

"Brynnie's right. You should be more sensitive about the words you choose, Four. You know better." Elle hoped this was enough, that Brynnie would be placated. She yearned to have her daughter's respect. Their relationship would be different than the one Elle had had with her own mom.

Four put his hands up defensively. "I know, I know. It was just a joke. Relax!"

Brynnie rolled her eyes. Elle understood her daughter's disapproval was directed toward her just as much as it was to Four. Why hadn't Win intervened? Elle looked toward him again; he was still intently reading something on his phone.

Brynnie slung her backpack over her shoulder and turned to Four. "Hurry up, I don't want to be late."

Four grabbed a bagel and tossed it into the head of his lacrosse stick. "Will you bring me a protein shake after school, Mom?"

"Of course." Elle might have to rearrange a few things in her schedule, but she could manage. "Do you need me to bring you something for lunch?"

"Nah, it's alright. Coach is having Chipotle brought in for us."

"He probably needs help wiping his butt, though," Brynnie said, smirking.

Elle pretended not to be hurt by her daughter's sarcasm. She was merely trying to help Four, to be a good mom. She would do the same for Brynnie. Couldn't she recognize that? And didn't she understand just how lucky she was to even *have* a sibling to be annoyed with? Elle would give anything for just one more minute with her own brother, the baby perpetually asleep with his eyes open.

Elle looked again to Win—would it kill him to step in and defend her? His head was still down in his phone. What could he possibly be reading that was so important? Elle was discouraged. Why was it that Duke was the only member of their family that appreciated everything she did for them? Trying to hide her frustration and appear cheerful, Elle hugged her children good-bye. She wished Brynnie good luck on her exam and reminded Four to talk to his advisor about signing up for an ACT test-prep class.

Brynnie blew Win a kiss as she walked past him. "Bye, Dad!"

Win looked up. "Sorry. Are you guys leaving? I was checking to see if the deal I told you about is coming through."

Elle searched her mind trying to remember the deal Win was referring to, but she couldn't think of it. Had he really mentioned it to her? The bulk of their conversations usually regarded their children and their respective schedules.

"Give me one more minute, then I'll walk out with you." Win glanced down again at his phone. After a few moments of reading, he stood up and put his hands above his head like a referee making a signal for a touchdown. "Bonsai and sushi roll. Pack your bags; we're going to Tokyo!"

Tokyo!

Elle's stomach lurched into her throat causing her to choke on her coffee. She remembered the first thing she had heard upon waking. News about the earth caving in on itself and causing widespread destruction in Japan. It had been a warning. And to make sure she got the message, the song "Shake It Out" had come on next. It's meaning was abundantly clear to Elle now. Her experiences in Tokyo could definitely qualify as a devil on her back. One she had spent most of her adult life trying to forget.

Elle suddenly had the taste of metal in her mouth, like the fillings in her teeth had melted. It was an eerie sensation, one she had experienced only one other time: her last day in Tokyo, when she had feared the worst.

As always, the signs had been right. It really was going to be a bad day.

THREE

TOM PETTY: "FREE FALLIN'"

August 30, 1992
7:08 p.m.

What have I gotten myself into?

Elle was tripped out—overcome with sensory overload as she took in the concourse at Tokyo's Narita Airport. All around, there were people—just masses of people. And bright, blaring neon lights. And noise. An unfamiliar, rhythmic noise with a life of its own. Everything seemed a beat off, like the New Orleans funeral parade scene in the James Bond movie *Live and Let Die.* It was spooky.

Elle hadn't bargained for this. Maybe she should have been better prepared.

As it was, Elle hadn't really done any planning at all. She had graduated from college that spring with a liberal arts degree and no idea what to do next. Most of her sorority sisters had the luxury of wealthy parents willing to subsidize them while they took a year off and traveled or went to unpaid internships in art galleries or with fashion magazines. Elle didn't have these options. Bobbie couldn't afford an airline ticket to her daughter's graduation, much less rent on a cute loft in a good neighborhood in

New York or San Francisco. And traveling was completely out of the question; she had zero savings.

No, Elle needed to make money. Although she had hopefully sent out résumé after résumé, she didn't get a single job offer. She could have gone back home and worked at the bar with her mom, but returning to the sad two-bedroom apartment she had grown up in was not something Elle was willing to do. With its potted plants and macramé owls, it was the kind of place you could dust for hours yet still never seemed clean, as though being poor was something that couldn't be wiped away. Elle would do anything but that.

The decision to teach English in Tokyo had come from a sign. She had been in the break room of her summer temp job, microwaving ramen noodles and bemoaning her lack of direction, when she overheard one of her co-workers talking about a friend of a friend who was making loads of money teaching English in Japan. Elle hadn't given it much thought, but when she turned on her Walkman to listen to some music while eating her lunch, the David Bowie song "Changes" had come on. Elle knew this was a sign.

Changes . . . Ramen noodles . . . Japan.

After a few moments, Elle got it. It was a sign telling her the change she was looking for was a move to Japan to teach English. It seemed to be a perfect solution to her state of flux, and she had learned long ago to trust the signs.

The only research Elle had done to prepare for the trip was to check out a book from the library on Japanese culture. Taking to heart the author's observation that the Japanese favored blonde hair, she had purchased some Clairol at a drug store and dyed her mousy-brown hair platinum over the sink in the bathroom she shared with Bobbie. She loved the results. She looked like a whole different person.

Looking around helplessly at the indecipherable Japanese characters on all the billboards at the airport, Elle realized she had bigger concerns than her hair color—why hadn't she thought through the language barrier? She had just sort of assumed everyone would speak English and it would fine.

Elle took a deep breath. There was no going back now; she needed to figure this out.

Surveying her surroundings again, Elle noticed that most signs had an English translation under the Japanese. *Nice.* She could work with that. Elle saw a sign that said Trains to Tokyo with an arrow pointing in the direction of an escalator. She lifted her luggage to head toward the escalator and immediately recognized another failure in planning. She should have invested in a bag with wheels. Instead, Elle had a large army duffle bag stuffed so full that it was heavy and difficult to carry. She could barely take a few steps before her arms got tired and she had to stop, rest, and then start up again.

Elle was vexed by her stupidity. She didn't have time for this.

"Do you need help with your bag?"

Grateful to hear an American-accented voice in the sea of Japanese, Elle looked up to see a college-aged guy removing the earbuds from his Walkman as he approached her.

Wow. He's cute.

"That would be awesome, thanks. I don't know what I was thinking bringing this huge duffle bag."

"No worries. Where ya headed?"

This was something else Elle hadn't really given much thought to ahead of time. She had planned to just sort of wing it and find a cheap hotel once she landed, but she had met some backpackers on the flight who had recommended a hostel. Elle reached into her pocket and pulled out the barf bag she had written its name and address on. "The Ace Inn. It's in Shinjuku."

"Cool. I'm headed to Shinjuku myself."

The stranger grabbed one handle of the duffle bag while Elle held the other. Together, they started toward the train station and Elle had a chance to take a closer look at her Good Samaritan. He was wearing a leather jacket, Doc Martens, and tight black jeans. He was so tall, his long legs looked like licorice sticks in his skinny jeans. He had glistening seafoam-green eyes, made more striking by incredibly long eyelashes, like a woman's. His medium-length brown hair was slicked back on the sides with gel, Duran Duran-style. He was cute for sure, pretty almost, but not someone Elle could see herself hooking up with. He was a little too "New Wave" for her. She preferred a more rugged look; a Mel Gibson to his Simon Le Bon.

Under his leather jacket, which had small silver spikes across the back, he wore a white T-shirt with a picture of the Ramones on it. Elle approved. The Ramones were a great band but not exactly mainstream. This guy knew his music. He must be a musician. He had probably started a band with his college friends and they were trying to scrape up enough cash to record their first single, so he took a gig touring Japan with a Duran Duran cover band to make some easy money. Or maybe he was writing jingles for commercials. Either way, he wasn't selling out. No, he was a solid guy—someone just doing whatever needed to be done to make it happen.

Elle liked to play this game—creating personas for complete strangers. She had invented it as a child as a way to entertain herself during the long days she was left alone while Bobbie tended bar. After years of experience in observing others, Elle believed herself to be somewhat of an expert in human behavior. She saw the subtle clues, she understood what motivated people, and rarely were her instincts wrong. This guy just had to be a musician. She was sure of it.

"I'm Mitch, by the way," he said, extending his free arm to shake her hand. "My name is actually Mitchell, but that's just *waaay* too much for the locals to handle."

Elle looked at him, confused.

"You know, *l*'s are hard for Japanese people to pronounce, so when they try to say 'Mitchell,' it comes out sounding like 'Mitch erre.' It got annoying."

"Oh, okay, got it. I'm Elle . . . or I guess you can call me 'Erre.'" Elle returned Mitch's handshake, realizing that her name would also be difficult to say. Add that to the list of things she hadn't considered.

The truth was, her real name was Michelle. (It was so like Bobbie to pick the same name as nearly every other pregnant woman in 1969.) After seeing the dramatic change with her hair color and how much she liked it, Elle decided a name change was also in order. Why not? *Michelle* was far too common for the person she would be in Tokyo. Her inspiration had been an *Elle* magazine with a platinum-haired model in a kimono on the cover. She had spotted it while returning the book on Japan to the library, and it seemed like another sign. Besides, *Elle* would be the perfect name for her new self. It was chic and original, like the person she wanted to be.

"*Elle*. I like that name. I haven't heard it before."

Elle was pleased by Mitch's reaction; it was just the sort of response she had hoped for. She felt more sophisticated already. "Thanks! And thanks again for your help." Her bag seemed heavier by the minute. It would have taken forever for her to try and drag it by herself.

"No problem. I was just here doing the same thing for a friend going to Hawaii. Apparently, she needed three suitcases for all of her swimsuits."

"That's nice of you. Is she your girlfriend?"

"No, no, nothing like that." Mitch blushed so quickly that Elle guessed he must have a massive crush on the girl. Just as well, he wasn't her type anyway.

As Mitch and Elle reached the platform, a man's voice came over a loud speaker announcing the approach of their train. His Japanese sounded airy and light; it reminded Elle of a lullaby and was reassuring. As the train approached, Mitch and Elle carefully lifted her duffle bag onboard and took seats next to each other.

Mitch sat back and said, "It's about a ninety-minute ride to Shinjuku."

"Okay, cool." Elle pointed her chin toward his Walkman. "What are you listening to?"

"U2's *Joshua Tree*. That whole album just slays me."

Elle perked up. Mitch's interest in U2 was a sign. A good sign. U2 was her all-time favorite band. Their music was synonymous with good luck; it had predicted her high score on the SAT and her full-ride scholarship to college. "Me, too! I love U2. Big time. That album was my favorite in high school."

Mitch sat up on the edge of his seat, energized. "For me, that album *was* high school."

"Totally!" Elle felt the exact same way. *Joshua Tree* took her right back to her senior year of high school, a time of hope and optimism: college was on the horizon. The dark bar and the grimy apartment with its potted plants would soon be behind her.

Elle had been right about Mitch. He was cool.

Mitch rubbed his hands together excitedly. "Alright, since you clearly know your music, I have a game for you. It's called Overrated/Underrated."

"Yeah, yeah, I know it. Bring it on." If this was a test, Elle was ready. Music was a huge part of her life, her greatest love. She would like this game.

"I'll start with something easy. Let's go . . . say, the B-52's."

"Oh, no-brainer. Totally underrated."

"Excellent!" Mitch nodded approvingly. "I see I'll need to make this a little harder."

Elle put up her hand. "Let me save you some time. I'm a big fan of all the music to come out of the eighties, especially all the British New Wave stuff." She paused and nodded at his shirt. "And I love the Ramones— *waaay* underrated."

"I like it, you just went up like four notches on my cool scale. What about Whitney Houston?"

"Aah…" Elle clenched her teeth and grimaced. "She has an amazing voice and maybe if I were like, thirty, I would like her more, but I'm gonna have to go overrated."

Mitch looked at Elle and smiled. It was a curious smile and she wasn't sure what it meant.

She hit him on the knee. "What?"

"I thought I'd catch you on that one."

"Oh really? I see what you did; you slipped it in there like leaving out the Simon Says." Elle was having fun. The conversation was flirtatious, but so natural and easy it was like catching up with an old friend.

"Yeah, you got me. I was pretty sure you were cool, but I had to make sure you knew what you were talking about."

"Fair enough." Elle had a test of her own for Mitch. "How about this: song that even if you are having the worst day ever, you hear it and feel better."

"Easy. U2's 'Bad,'" Mitch answered quickly. "I saw them perform it live at the Amnesty Concert, and I'll never forget it. I mean, I'm not a religious guy, but something extraordinary happened when they played that song. I can't explain it, but I actually almost started crying. It was pretty wild. That song takes me to a totally different place, you know?"

Elle did know. She was not a religious person either—at least not in the traditional sense. She had gone to church a few times growing up with her grandmother and had enjoyed it—it seemed like something normal people did—but then there had been the big fight between her mom and her grandmother. It was right after her brother died and Elle never saw her grandmother nor went to church again. As a result, God, Jesus, and prayer weren't things she gave much thought to. They were for other people.

Music was Elle's religion.

Although it had always been a part of her life—seventies rock was a constant in the bar where she spent most of her time—it was when Elle was in fourth grade that music really began to influence her. One of Bobbie's "regulars" had taken pity on the little girl perpetually alone at a back table and had given Elle a small radio. It transformed her life. Music filled the gaping void in her childhood left by the death of her baby brother. Some people found solace in books or TV, but for Elle it was music. The radio became her constant companion, Casey Kasem her first friend.

Though too young to really understand what most of the songs she listened to were about, Elle escaped her loneliness with the stories they told. She was a guest at the YMCA with the Village People and in a card game with the gambler and Kenny Rogers. She drew pictures of how she imagined the Eagles' Hotel California would look. Elle's portable black Sony AM/FM radio became increasingly important to her daily routine, an integral part of her life.

So much so that, over time, Elle began to believe her relationship to the universe was dictated by lyrics, titles, and band names. In elementary school, if she turned on the radio in the morning and heard Randy Newman's "Short People," she was sure to get chosen last for dodge ball. Donna Summer's "Bad Girls" meant bullying at the hands of the mean girls. Better were the mornings when Elle would hear Gloria Gaynor's "I Will Survive." She would shuffle off to school confident it would be a good day—and more often than not, it was.

This continued throughout junior high. Bobbie wasn't the type of mom who helped with algebra homework or gave advice on how to properly insert a tampon, but Irene Cara's "Flashdance . . . What a Feeling" told Elle to believe in herself and her abilities and Aerosmith's "Dream On" provided her with the strength and determination to keep working hard.

Over time, there were too many moments that seemed foretold through music for Elle to ignore. Michael Jackson's "Beat It" played the morning Justin O'Malley was suspended for getting in a fight with Timmy Schrader; David Bowie's "Let's Dance" came on as she debated asking a boy to Sadie Hawkins; and news of the Space Shuttle *Challenger* disaster reached her by a special report interrupting the Bee Gees' "Tragedy." By the time Elle reached high school, music as a series of omens became her truth.

As such, she completely understood the power of music and accepted without question why Mitch would have such a visceral reaction to "Bad." She *had* cried when she heard the song performed live in concert. She didn't understand the tears, only that she experienced a great sense of belonging, of something bigger than herself that she couldn't quite explain. It had been amazing. Like nothing she had ever experienced before.

If Mitch got that, he got her.

FOUR

The White Stripes: "We're Going to Be Friends"

August 30, 1992
9:29 p.m.

Elle and Mitch continued to talk animatedly during the train ride to Shinjuku, bonding over their shared musical tastes. She had been wrong about him being a musician. Mitch confessed that although he would have given anything to be in a band, he lacked any musical talent, whatsoever. (Excepting, of course, his ability to whistle "Happy Birthday" in one long breath.) Elle sympathized with him; she was also utterly devoid of any musical aptitude—at least he could whistle.

Though not a musician, Elle was satisfied that her instincts about Mitch had been correct; he was definitely a good guy. To date, the only person she had ever misread had been her dad. For a brief period, she thought he might actually care about her.

Elle didn't know her dad, not really; like her grandmother, he had disappeared shortly after her brother's death. But one day when she was around seven years old, he had unexpectedly shown up at the bar where Bobbie worked. (Elle remembered it was spring because she'd had a terrible sunburn. It had been field day at school and her mom hadn't thought to provide her with sunscreen.) He had enthusiastically greeted her with a big bear hug—it had felt like sandpaper scraping against her burning red shoulders—and invited her to sit next to him at the bar. This was huge—Elle was never allowed to sit in one of the high stools with maroon seats that could swivel.

He had then directed her mom to make her a Shirley Temple and to give her a glass filled to the top with maraschino cherries. (This second request had required a fair amount of coaxing on his part; Bobbie had initially objected—she didn't want her daughter to be spoiled.) Along with these treats, he had placed a large stack of quarters in front of her to play slot poker with on the machine at the end of the bar. Elle didn't understand the game, but she had a great time putting the quarters in the machine and pulling down on the handle. Between sips of his drink and puffs on his cigarette, her dad had looked at her proudly, especially when quarters came pouring out of the machine. He ruffled her hair and told her she was good luck.

Elle had been thrilled and took these as signs her dad loved her. He was giving her money, smiling at her, and she was at the bar! It was so much better than playing with paper dolls at a table in the back by herself. Elle couldn't wait to see her dad again, and for the next few weeks she looked up hopefully every time the door to the bar opened.

But he never showed up again, and Elle realized the unhappy truth that her father's attention that day had not been out of love; it was simply a way to keep her occupied so he could drink.

She had been crushed. How could she have been so wrong? She vowed to be more careful, to pay more attention. She would never make the same mistake again. And she hadn't. In terms of detecting scumbags, Elle was now batting a thousand and she intended to keep it that way.

Mitch was different, and she knew it. On the train ride, Elle discovered they had many other things in common besides their love of music: they were both English Lit majors, yellow was their favorite color, mashed potatoes their favorite food, and they agreed that it was essential to eat all the marshmallows out of the Lucky Charms cereal box first.

As far as things they found overrated? People who stood in the middle of escalators blocking the way for those in a hurry, acid wash cut-off jeans, corn dogs, and mall rats that wore parachute pants and roach clips. Roach clips were the worst, especially the ones with the added piece of dangling hair. Lame. A look for total posers.

Too bad I'm not attracted to him.

Mitch was cool. And good-looking. But Elle knew from experience she was either into a guy or she wasn't, and she just wasn't feeling it with Mitch, which kind of sucked. They would make a good couple.

Mitch told Elle he had used his college graduation gift money to buy a one-way ticket to Tokyo and had been living there since June. He had a job teaching English for a company called English First. "They're a chain, and are everywhere. They're popular because they're the most affordable schools around—kinda like the Wal-Mart of English-language schools." He said he was sure he could help her get a job. "Obviously, if they hired me, their standards aren't very high."

Elle was grateful—she hadn't yet sorted out the finer details of securing a job.

Mitch also convinced her to stay at the same place he was living, a hostel for *gaijin*—the Japanese word for "foreigner"—called the Zen House. It was a complete shithole, but the owner had a thing for blondes and Mitch was sure she would be able to negotiate a cheap rate with him.

This was another offer Elle was happy to accept. What did she have to lose? Besides, it couldn't be any worse than the shithole she had grown up in.

Dragging her duffle bag into the Zen House, Elle could immediately see Mitch had not been exaggerating in his description of the place. There wasn't anything the least bit Zen about it. Paint was peeling off the walls, the linoleum floors were stained, and a rank smell permeated the air. Elle wasn't sure what the source of the odor was, but it was gnarly.

"That would be the kimchi," Mitch explained. "It's a Korean thing. Fermented vegetables or something. You'll get used to it."

Elle tried to smile gamely. It would be fine.

The two walked in past the main living area. It was full of men of varying age, size and nationality. Several of them were crammed together uncomfortably on a couch, while others were sprawled out on the dirty floor in front of a small TV. Elle was unnerved—she didn't see a single other woman in the room. What had Mitch gotten her into?

Perhaps sensing her nervousness, Mitch set down Elle's duffle bag and reached for her hand. He led her past the common room and down a hallway, where he peeked in through a half-closed door. "Watanabe-san, may I come in?"

"Ah so. Mitch-san. Yes, yes. Come in, please."

Elle followed Mitch into what was an office with a rather small, middle-aged Japanese man sitting behind a large oak desk, smoking a cigarette. The man's fingers were slightly discolored, and his fingernails were longer than a man's ought to be.

Mitch protectively put one arm around Elle's shoulder and gestured toward her with his free hand. "Watanabe-san, this is Elle. She is a very good friend of mine and needs a room."

Watanabe stood and bowed enthusiastically toward Elle, looking her over as he did. "Nice meet you, Erre-san. Welcome-o Zen House." Watanabe's eyes lingered a little too long on Elle's breasts. It made her uncomfortable.

Mitch noticed Elle's unease and stepped in front of her, blocking Watanabe's view. "Here's the thing. She needs to be in the same room as me."

"Yes. Yes. So, your room, one week is ten thousand yen." Watanabe nodded agreeably, but also reached out his hand indicating he was expecting payment up front.

Elle tried to do the math on how much this was in American dollars. Bobbie had refused to cosign for her on a credit card application, so all she had was the $300 she had saved working as a temp over the summer. One U.S. dollar equaled approximately one hundred Japanese yen, so the charge for a week was around a hundred dollars. This seemed reasonable, although it was a full third of her funds—she would need to start working right away. Elle reached for her pocketbook, but Mitch stopped her.

"So, the thing is, Elle doesn't have a job yet. Is there anything you can do to make it more affordable for her to stay here? Say—five thousand yen a week?"

"You funny man, Mitch-san." Watanabe furrowed his brow and looked over Elle once more. He deliberated for a few minutes and then said, "Okay, special favor for you, one week—eight thousand yen."

Elle looked over at Mitch. He nodded *okay* to her, and even though not entirely convinced it wasn't a mistake, she carefully counted out eight 1,000-yen notes and handed them to Watanabe. "Do you have a key for me?"

Watanabe laughed, exposing a set of horribly crooked and coffee-stained teeth. "You no need key. This Japan."

No key? Elle's stomach tightened. Nervous, she looked to Mitch again.

He was reassuring. "It's cool. You really don't need a key."

Elle smiled wanly. What else could she do? It was too late to try and drag her duffle bag anywhere else. She would trust Mitch.

Elle bowed awkwardly to Watanabe and followed Mitch out of his office and back into the common room where they grabbed her duffle bag.

"Thanks again for your help." Although ambivalent about the Zen House, Elle *did* appreciate Mitch's kindness.

"Well, you might want to hold off on the thanks until after you see the room."

Oh no. How much worse can it get?

Mitch led Elle further down the hallway and stopped in front of a red door damaged with scratches, like those from an animal clawing to get in. He paused and explained that they had two other roommates, brothers from Iran who worked in some sort of electronics factory. "They're alright, and they work the night shift, so you won't even see them all that much."

Mitch opened the door and gestured for Elle to enter first. She took a few steps in and surveyed the room with dismay. The Spartan room was shocking, even by her working-class standards. It was really nothing more than a ten-by-ten-foot space with two sets of bunk beds. In place of mattresses, there were incredibly thin futons on each bed frame and even thinner light-blue floral-patterned comforters. They looked old. And very used. *Yuck.* Elle tried not to think about all the other people who had slept under them.

Mitch nodded his head upward. "Better for you to have the top bunk. I'll move my stuff." He stood on his toes and grabbed his belongings in one fell swoop, the way only a tall person with a large arm span could, and dropped them haphazardly onto the lower futon. He then lifted her duffle bag and shoved it up toward the end of the top bunk. "You'll have to keep your bag up here; there isn't room for it anywhere else."

It wasn't ideal, but Elle was so tired she didn't much care. "Yeah, that's fine."

Mitch placed a hand on her shoulder. "Look, I'm sure you're beat. Let me show you the bathroom and then you can get some shut-eye. The best part of teaching at English First is that it doesn't open until one o'clock, so I can help you out some more in the morning."

Mitch guided Elle out of the room and back down the hall, stopping in front of another red door, this one free from scratches. "The good news is, there aren't any other women who live here, so the women's bathroom should always be open. The bad news is, I'm fairly sure guys go in there if the men's room is taken." He rapped on the door with the back of his hand several times. "You're gonna want to knock loudly before going in. Trust me." When no one responded, Mitch turned to Elle and said, "It's all yours. I'll leave you to it. I'll be in the living room if you need anything else. If not, I'll see you in the morning." He turned to leave, adding, "Welcome to Tokyo."

Elle opened the door and was immediately struck by a strong urine odor—Mitch was right about men using the bathroom. Elle had read about Japanese-style squat toilets, but she was still surprised by what looked like a small porcelain babies' bathtub on the floor. It was stained and there were clear indications that some users had missed the toilet hole altogether.

Unsure of what to do, Elle looked around for something to hold onto but couldn't find anything. Above the toilet there was a sign in both Japanese and English: How to Use a Japanese Toilet. There were three illustrations, two of which had big red Xs marked over them indicating what not to do. It was a funny sign and made Elle laugh—like anyone would be stupid enough to plant their ass in the disgusting urinal like the stick figure in the first picture with an X on it.

Elle pulled down her jeans and underwear and set about squatting, mimicking the picture with the green sign above it. *It's just like camping.* Never mind that she loathed the outdoors. If Elle was going to make this work, she needed to have a positive attitude. She was on an adventure.

Elle peed without incident. *That was easy.* Going number two might be more challenging, but she would worry about that later. She walked back to her room and was relieved to find it empty. Elle trusted Mitch but wasn't so sure about sharing the space with two other strange men. She rummaged through her bag and found a sweatshirt and a pair of sweat-pants with her sorority letters embroidered across the back. She changed into them, hoping they would keep her warm. She wanted to avoid use of the nasty floral comforter at all costs.

Elle flopped down on the futon, exhausted. Normally, she fell asleep to music—it was comforting to listen for a final sign, and it helped to quell her night terrors over her dead baby brother. But tonight, it seemed like too much effort to get her Walkman. Elle could detect the faint sound of U2 coming from the room Mitch had gone to—that was good enough. She drifted off into a deep sleep, confident she didn't need to listen for any further signs.

I got this.

FIVE

JOY DIVISION: "ISOLATION"

May 18, 2017
10:11 a.m.

Elle jumped up and down a few times at the baseline, trying to ready herself to return serve. She wasn't in the mood to play tennis. As feared, her day had continued to be a total nightmare.

The metallic taste in her mouth and its reminder of a time and place she had no desire to revisit had lasted a full hour after Win's sudden announcement about his business deal in Tokyo. The only way Elle could finally rid herself of the offensive taste was by summoning all her resolve to not think about what a return to Japan would mean. Luckily, she had plenty of experience with ignoring the unpleasant truths of her life.

But what Elle *did* have to think about that day was not much better. The coffee at Jane's was as tedious as expected. Thatcher's situation had been discussed ad nauseam. What would the ramifications be beyond his suspension from the team? Thatcher had been accepted to Princeton. Was that now in jeopardy?

Elle understood everyone's concern. It wasn't like it had been in the eighties, when getting caught misbehaving meant a trip to the principal's office for a talking to or a slap on the wrist from a sympathetic police officer. No, that's not the way it worked anymore. Conduct which was once considered to be the mostly benign naughtiness of normal teenagers was now viewed through an entirely different lens.

Especially at Country Day, where the reputation of the school's student body meant everything: Ivy League acceptances—good; drug busts on campus—bad. While administrators liked to tout the value of children experiencing *"teachable moments"* within the *"safe environment"* of the school, consequences for poor choices were, nonetheless, severe. Country Day enforced a strict Zero Tolerance policy for substance infractions, physical altercations, and bullying—a beer at a football game, a fight in the locker room, or an offensive text were all grounds for automatic expulsion.

And that was just Country Day's punishment; if the police got involved, matters quickly became much more serious. Teepeeing a house could mean charges of trespassing or criminal mischief. Being at a party where beer was served could result in an MIP ticket, even for minors not drinking. Having a fake ID was a felony. Cyber bullying could lead to both criminal and civil charges. For children under eighteen, the sending of a naked "selfie" on a cell phone was considered distribution of child pornography and could necessitate registration as a sexual offender. While defending against any of these charges was time-consuming and expensive, it was a conviction that parents feared most. Guilty pleas required reporting on college applications, and Yale didn't likely accept felons.

This explained why Elle and all the other Country Day moms hovered so neurotically over their children. Why they micromanaged every aspect of their teenagers' lives from the maniacal reading of their texts, to the stalking of their social media accounts, to the placing of tracking devices in their cars. Students couldn't even go to the movies without an interrogation from their parents akin to the Spanish Inquisition. *"Who are you going with? What are you seeing? What time will you be home?"*

The perception was that even one slip-up was unacceptable, so parents kept their children in bubbles, like they were veal to keep tender, to protect them from making what they perceived to be life-altering mistakes.

Thus, Thatcher's situation had been rehashed with unrelenting intrigue. Every detail was poured over to be brought up as fodder for dinner-table conversation—there being no better way to dissuade poor behavior than by scaring the shit out of your kids. *"Thatcher got slapped with a harassment charge, and Jacinda's family is suing. There goes Princeton! Do you want that to happen to you?"*

After exhausting the subject of Thatcher's suspension, and before getting down to the important business of how best to raise funds for a new climbing wall for their children, the women at Jane's coffee had then spent twenty more minutes debating whether it would be better for Maggie to order a navy with beige interior or a silver with black interior Range Rover.

Once this had been decided with an overwhelming vote for navy with beige, they reached consensus on a gourmet hot dog bar for the fundraiser—crepe stations being so 2016. The group had gone on to have a spirited discussion over the merits of raising additional funds by selling $100 raffle tickets for the chance to win a three-day rental of a Bentley. Some women thought it rather gauche to expect their children to *sell* tickets, but Aubrey, whose husband had offered to donate the Bentley, argued that parents could buy the tickets themselves and give them to members of their staff. It might even be tax deductible.

With everyone in agreement that this was a brilliant idea—wouldn't their gardeners and nannies and housekeepers *just love* the chance to drive a Bentley?—business was concluded. Before saying their good-byes, Jane had proudly shown sketches of her daughter's deb gown to a fawning audience. The women all feigned enthusiasm while secretly taking note of everything they didn't approve of to be discussed later. *"Bell sleeves? Puulease!"* Jane's scones had been admired, but not eaten. Instead of honey, guests had all been gifted homemade beeswax candles. Just what they needed.

As exasperating as all that had been, it paled in comparison to the aggravation caused by Elle's current hunger. She had limited herself to just coffee at Jane's and was now starving. To cap it all off, her period had come early. (Perhaps this helped to explain the bizarre nightmare about the animals eating her feminine hygiene products.) Besides having terrible cramps, Elle was deathly afraid she would bleed through her tennis bloomers. She wished she would just go through menopause already. Not having her period would mean one less thing to worry about.

Elle had considered getting out of the tennis match by claiming to be sick, but Thatcher's mom, unwilling to face all the inevitable questions, had wisely already canceled. If Elle didn't play, their team would have to forfeit the court and risk losing the match and not qualifying for Nationals. This simply wasn't an option. To her team, winning tennis matches was Very Important. Right up there with placing the winning bid for a coveted seat next to the headmaster at the Country Day Winter Fest Celebration.

Previously known as the Christmas Program, the Winter Fest Celebration was an opportunity for Elle's friends to show off a new Badgley Mischka or Diane von Furstenberg dress while ostensibly listening to their children sing songs about snowflakes and hot chocolate. Santa, Hanukkah, and even Kwanzaa references weren't allowed. The Director of Inclusivity didn't want to offend anyone.

As it was, Elle's lack of interest in the tennis match was apparent. She and her doubles partner, Kit, had lost the first set, 1–6, due in large part to Elle's inconsistent play. This irritated Kit, who tried to hide her frustration by giving Elle peevish pep talks between each point. Realizing somewhere in the second set that she didn't really care one way or the other how the match ended, Elle relaxed and her game improved. Kit became more energized the better Elle played, high-fiving her after each winning shot. The two were now a point away from taking the second set and getting to a third set tiebreak for the match.

Kit approached Elle while their opponents strategized at the baseline. "I think Liz is getting mental. When you return serve, try hitting it right at her—*hard!*"

So Liz was the player at net and Heather was the server. They had introduced themselves at the beginning of the match, but Elle couldn't remember which one was which. They both wore identical lime green Lily Pulitzer tennis dresses and were equally thin and tan, with blonde ponytails and large, fake boobs. The crow's feet around their eyes had been so heavily Botoxed that each appeared to be in a state of perpetual surprise.

Elle wasn't judging. Not really. She also got Botox treatments, but just once a year and only sparingly. She didn't want to look plastic and had to be careful Brynnie wouldn't find out. Her daughter wouldn't approve, and Elle didn't want to be lectured. *"Wrinkles are a sign of the wisdom that comes with aging. Stretch marks are a badge of honor. You should embrace them all as signs of feminine power."* Yada, yada, yada. Easy for a teenager with nary a laugh line to say.

Still, Elle didn't want to provide Brynnie with any more reasons to be disappointed in her, so despite her need for more fillers, she abstained. Elle had also often debated getting a boob job—after breastfeeding two children, her boobs were saggy and rather sad— but she would never be able to hide an actual surgery from Brynnie. Instead, she made it a point to scrutinize other women's breasts, often with envy.

Elle could always tell those who had had work done. The top of recon- structed breasts, even the tastefully done small ones, had a slight curve and fullness that was simply not possible with age. In this case, it was obvi- ous that Liz and Heather had fake boobs; small women with slight frames didn't have DDs. It went against nature.

Although she didn't necessarily plan to follow Kit's advice, Elle nodded that she understood. Liz took her place at the net while Heather intently bounced the ball with her left hand at the baseline. After thirteen such bounces, she threw the ball high in the air and let out a guttural grunt as she served. It wasn't a hard serve (certainly not one worthy of the dramatic groan), and Elle could have easily drilled the ball directly at Liz as Kit had directed. Instead, she opted to return a high lob.

Heather let out a loud, dismayed "ugh" as she ran to get the ball. Lob shots were thought to be "lame" and reserved only for those who didn't have much skill or were over the age of sixty-five. *Real* tennis players, like they were, hit the ball hard and with pace. Yep, they were all just one step away from playing Wimbledon, not a bunch of forty-something housewives who had taken up the game within the past few years "for fun."

Unable to get a good shot off Elle's lob—maybe because she had exerted so much energy complaining about it—Heather hit back a weak floater, warning Liz, "Short!"

Kit crashed the net and hit the high-floating ball hard, directly at the head of Liz, where it landed against her sunglasses with a loud *whap*.

"Ow!" Liz immediately dropped her racquet and reached up protectively to her face. Heather rushed to her partner as Elle and Kit approached the net.

Kit spoke first, "Are you okay? I didn't mean to hit you in the face."

Liz's Prada sunglasses had broken and a red welt was developing under her eye.

Heather angrily confronted Kit. "I can't believe you hit her right in the face. What's wrong with you?"

"I didn't mean to hit her in the face." Kit was adamant, adding for emphasis, "Trust me, I'm not good enough to know where I'm going to hit the ball." She looked to Elle for confirmation, but Elle wasn't inclined to protect her. Was it passive-aggressive payback for the way, in the beginning, Kit had pretended not to know Elle even though they had been introduced to each other on numerous occasions? Perhaps, but there was also that Kit wasn't telling the truth—she was certainly experienced enough to *not* hit the ball right at someone's head. And hadn't she instructed Elle to take the same exact shot?

Elle put her hand on Liz's back. "Are you okay? Do you want to sit down for a minute?"

Liz looked at her sunglasses and then back at Kit. "You broke my sunglasses! What were you thinking? That's so rude!"

Kit crossed her arms in anger. "Whoa! Wait a minute. I said I didn't mean to hit you!" She sounded indignant, though she had yet to apologize.

Heather's voice rose to a near squeal. "You aimed the ball right at her and you've been doing it the entire match."

The women on the court next to them stopped playing and looked over, trying to figure out what was going on. Elle was sure Aubrey would be there any minute.

Kit shrugged her shoulders, unconcerned. "If you're afraid of getting hit at the net, you should stand back at the baseline. Getting hit is a risk you take at the net. If you don't like it, don't play tennis."

Seriously? That was Kit's response?

Something flipped in Elle. She couldn't take this. If it had happened a few weeks before, she would have gotten right into it with Kit and the other ladies, her high ponytail shaking violently with each insulting remark the same as the rest of them. But not today. Elle didn't have it in her. Three grown women, their perky 350cc boobs bursting out of their overpriced dresses, arguing over a tennis match. It was ridiculous.

"Are you happy, Mom? Are you living your dream?"

Elle needed to leave.

She walked over to the bench on the side of the court and made a show of taking her iPhone out of her Birkin tote. As expected, Aubrey and the rest of the team had gathered around the women who were still arguing loudly.

"Let's all calm down a minute!" A tournament official, an older gentleman with a stooped back, had entered and was trying to maintain some order. "Can someone go get this young lady some ice for her eye?"

"That's right. I need *ice* for my injury," Liz snarled at Kit. She was so upset that, despite all the Botox, her forehead visibly crinkled in anger.

"Okay. Tell me what happened. One at a time." Aubrey was in the center of the argument taking over.

Elle reentered the group. "Hey, I'm really sorry. I just checked my phone and I have an emergency. I need to leave."

"Leave?" Kit and Aubrey expressed their shock in unison.

"I'm so sorry. It can't be helped; I really have to go." Elle was feeling far from apologetic, but her desire to leave was growing more urgent by the minute.

"But we won the second set. If we win the tie-break, we will advance." Kit crinkled her eyes as if confused by Elle's willingness to disregard this important fact.

"Elle? What is it?" Aubrey's tone expressed concern, but by the slight upturn of her mouth, Elle suspected she was enjoying the moment. She lived for drama.

Elle ignored her teammates, and turned to Liz with an outstretched hand. "I'm sorry you were hurt. Really, I am. Good luck with the rest of the tournament."

Before anyone could say anything else, Elle turned and quickly exited the court. She walked to the parking lot and got into her white Tesla. (A car chosen, in part, to gain her daughter's approval. Brynnie wouldn't abide a gas-guzzling SUV.) Elle was proud that she had refrained from engaging in the petty argument. Even though all the signs had pointed to an abysmal day, maybe her luck was changing. That happened sometimes.

Elle decided to test it—the song that was playing when she turned the radio on would be a sign about the rest of her day. As she backed out of the parking lot, Elle turned the dial on—a love song was playing. Love songs didn't count; Elle had discounted their significance after getting married. They no longer applied to her.

Elle could either wait for the next song or change the channel.

She decided to wait for the next song. Her stomach rumbled with hunger. *French fries.* She hadn't eaten a potato, let alone French fries, in longer than she could remember but nothing sounded better than a nice salty pack of fries. Leaving the match early meant Elle had some extra time before her board meeting. She was driving right by a bunch of fast food restaurants—should she pull into a drive-through?

No, she shouldn't give in to the temptation; she would regret it later. Elle settled on treating herself to a nonfat latte with hazelnut flavoring. That would have to be enough. She grabbed her phone to ask Siri where the closest Starbucks was when a new song came on the radio.

"Sweet Baby James" by James Taylor.

Elle forget about her hunger. She was five years old again, and it was a dark winter morning. She had woken up early, excited because her mom had promised to take her and her brother, Jimmy, to the mall to get their picture taken with Santa Claus. Wearing only a sleeveless pink Cinderella nightgown made of thin polyester, Elle was cold. She reached for Jimmy. He was cold, too.

Honk! Honk!

The light Elle was stopped at had turned green. Startled, she put her foot on the gas, drove through the intersection and pulled over.

"Sweet Baby James."

Depending on her mood, Elle interpreted this song in one of two ways: it could provide an endearing memory of her beloved brother, or a devastating reminder of her role in his death. Elle put her head against the steering wheel and cried. After the day she was having, hearing this song could only mean one thing.

A bad day, indeed. The question was, just what was next?

SIX

PHILLIP PHILLIPS: "HOME"

September 1, 1992
9:13 a.m.

This has got to be the worst fucking shower ever.

Elle had woken up eager to see what her first full day in Tokyo would bring, but her excitement was quickly replaced with irritation.

First, her room smelled like ass. The Iranian brothers had returned from their night shift and stunk up the entire space with their BO. Elle couldn't get out of the room fast enough. Gagging, she had hurried into the bathroom only to discover that there was a coin slot in the shower door. Apparently, you had to pay to take a shower. *Seriously?*

Elle didn't have any Japanese coins and Mitch was still asleep, so she had no choice but to slog her way into Watanabe's office and ask him for change. She hadn't thought to put a bra on first, and Watanabe had inappropriately ogled at her breasts for several long minutes before finally handing her a 250-yen coin. *What a pervert.*

Making matters worse, there was little water pressure in the shower and what was dripping out was lukewarm. Shivering, Elle tried in vain to increase the water temperature. When that didn't work, she settled on washing her hair as quickly as possible. Although thankful there was a dispenser with soap and shampoo in it—Elle hadn't thought to pack those things—there was no conditioner, so she would have to deal with impossible tangles in her long hair.

FUUUCK!

Elle was cold, rankled, and in desperate need of a cup of coffee.

Suddenly, the shower door opened and she saw one of the men she shared a room with lewdly staring at her. "Aah!" Elle screamed, crossing her legs and simultaneously trying to cover her boobs and pubic area with her hands.

Her roommate licked his lips in such a crude and vulgar way that Elle was momentarily scared into silence. Regaining her senses, she turned her back to him and yelled, "Get out!"

Within seconds, Mitch arrived. "Leave her alone!" He clutched the perpetrator's hair from behind, turned him around, and awkwardly hit him on the jaw with a clenched fist.

As her roommate fell to the ground from the impact of Mitch's punch, Elle hurriedly grabbed the towel she had put over the shower door and covered herself with it.

By this time, Watanabe was in the bathroom. "What going on?" He looked around, confused.

"This fucking pervert was spying on my friend." Mitch cradled his hand as though it hurt.

"You very bad man. I get police." Watanabe made a dramatic show of kicking the man on the floor.

"Come on." Mitch reached out his hand and led a shaking Elle out of the bathroom. Curious about the commotion, a crowd of residents had gathered in the hall. A few of them whistled as Elle walked by. She felt vulnerable and more than a little afraid. Maybe she had been wrong. Misinterpreted the signs. Had coming to Japan been a colossal mistake?

SEVEN

THE CARS: "GOOD TIMES ROLL"

September 1, 1992
9:53 p.m.

"It probably doesn't feel this way now, but it will be a great story some-day," Mitch said, taking a sip of his beer. "Trust me. A classic. One for the books."

"Maybe for you, Mr. Tough Guy Hero. You weren't the one standing buck naked in the shower." Elle took a long drag from a cigarette. She had always considered smoking somewhat white-trashy, a reminder of her mom and their dismal smoke-filled apartment, but considering her morn-ing, Elle had gladly accepted Mitch's offer of a cigarette. *Why not?*

It was a clove cigarette. Elle liked the smell and the way it made her lips tingle. It complemented her buzz from the beer.

"The crazy thing is, that's the first time I've gone to fisticuffs. Like, ever." Mitch paused before adding, "My dad would be so proud."

Elle sensed bitter irony in Mitch's tone. She wanted to explore this subject more but didn't want to be a killjoy. "Really? You seemed rather experienced at it to me."

"Nope, I was a fight virgin." Mitch held up his mug of beer and clinked it against Elle's. "Here's to popping my violent-tendencies cherry with you. I wouldn't have wanted it to be with anyone else."

"I'm happy to oblige. I hope your hand will be okay."

Mitch rubbed at his right hand which was slightly swollen and bruised. "A small price to pay to protect your honor." He turned serious. "All joking aside, are you alright?"

Elle thought for a few moments. She *had* been pretty freaked out, but now, a few beers in, she had a little different perspective. It hadn't been *that* scary, and Mitch was right: it would make for a good story. "I'm not gonna lie, it was a little nerve-racking, but you know, no harm, no foul. Plus, I'm thinking the silver lining of this whole thing can't be overlooked."

As promised, Watanabe had called the police. As the crime was in a gaijin house, a unit specializing in immigration had been sent in. After arresting the peeping Tom, officers had checked everyone's paperwork and discovered nearly all the residents of the Zen House were in the country illegally, working without the proper visas. One-by-one, the police had roughly escorted them all out in handcuffs.

In contrast to the other foreigners, the police had treated Elle and Mitch with polite deference. They weren't asked to show their passports (much to Mitch's relief—his work visa had yet to be approved) and through the muddled translation of Watanabe, the head officer had apologized profusely to them, bowing respectfully several times.

Bizarrely, he had even asked for permission to take photos with Elle and Mitch. They had agreed, finding it highly amusing that their picture would be passed around to this strangers' friends and family like they were the main attraction at a zoo. *"Here I am with a panda, and a lion, and oh, look at this! Here I am with two Americans."*

When all was said and done, except for a pair of elderly Chinese men, Elle and Mitch were the only two left in the Zen House. Remorseful over the incident and unwilling to lose his new blonde tenant, Watanabe had offered to let them both stay on at the Zen House free of charge for two months. As a further gesture of goodwill, he had also given Elle her rent money back.

As a result, Elle and Mitch had the Zen House almost all to themselves for free. A silver lining, indeed. They had even been left with a fully stocked refrigerator, although most of the food in it seemed rather dodgy.

Not wanting to leave Elle alone after everything that had happened, Mitch had called in sick at work. They decided to celebrate their unexpected financial windfall by going out for drinks. Tokyo had an active bar scene, and there were beer halls serving cheap drinks and food on almost every corner. Mitch had taken Elle to his regular haunt, a place called Tangu, which was on the ground floor of a high-rise full of offices and a favorite of all the young businessmen who occupied cubicles in the building. The bar contained rows of several long, wooden tables where similarly dressed twenty-something men in dark pants, white shirts, and skinny ties sat, community-style.

The men had all looked up with surprise and pleasure when Elle had walked in with Mitch. She enjoyed the attention. Even more, Elle liked how the waiter kept bringing them beers and pointing to one group or another of Japanese men, explaining in halting English that they had bought the drinks for them.

Mitch was impressed. "Going to a bar with a hot blonde—underrated! This is outta control. I'm bringing you with me every time I go out!"

Dying her hair platinum had been a good call. Free drinks! That was well worth the hassle of touching up her roots every few weeks.

Mitch set down his beer empty mug and waved his hand around the room. "So, I know it's less than forty-eight hours since you've been in Japan, and there was that unfortunate bit this morning, but tell me, day two, Tokyo—overrated/underrated?"

Elle considered Mitch's question. Yes, things had gotten off to a bit of rocky start. Still, it wasn't *all* bad. "Honestly, the verdict is still out, but considering all the free drinks, I'm going to have to go underrated."

"*Niiice!* What is this, our fourth free round?"

Elle had lost count, but she was definitely shit-faced—she usually limited herself to just a drink or two. Elle was so drunk, she couldn't help but ask about Mitch's dad. She was too curious about what his situation was. "So, tell me about your family."

Mitch took a long drag of his cigarette and blew the smoke out methodically. He looked quizzically at Elle, like he was trying to decide something very important.

Elle waited.

Mitch exhaled loudly. "I'm from Iowa. My dad is a master electrician who hunts. My mom sells Avon and does hair out of our kitchen, and my older brother was the star wrestler at my high school. He has a mullet and 'dude' is his favorite word." He looked thoughtfully at Elle. "Does that paint enough of a picture for you?"

Elle nodded her head knowingly. So they both came from family situations they didn't fit into. The difference was, Mitch was willing to own up to it right away. He didn't try to pretend to be something else. He was braver than she was.

Even so, Elle knew it was best to make fun of what Mitch had revealed, to let him see she couldn't care less about his background. "I think I'm getting it, yeah . . ." Elle pursed her lips in mock contemplation. "Let's see, does your dad chew?"

"Duh, that would be Skoal Long Cut, which he charmingly spits into an empty Budweiser can."

"Uh-huh. And your mom, does she religiously watch a soap opera?"

"Right again! That'd be *General Hospital*. And don't ask what happens if the VCR doesn't work and she misses an episode. That's some serious shit." Mitch nodded toward Elle. "What about you, my dear—what's your story?"

Elle wasn't sure how to answer this question. She was embarrassed by her upbringing and preferred not to talk about it, but she liked Mitch. He was different. She should be honest with him.

Elle wasn't ready. Instead, she deflected the question asking, "What do you think?"

"Hmmm . . . I suppose you would like me to think your dad's some sort of professional—let's say a lawyer. Your mom doesn't work, but she loves to garden. She's especially proud of her Lady Diana roses. I'm not at all getting a homecoming queen vibe, but perhaps you were . . . say, editor of the school newspaper?" Here Mitch paused. "The only thing is—and correct me if I'm wrong here—people with résumés like that wouldn't find the need to dye their hair platinum and run off to Japan."

"How do you know this isn't my natural hair color?" Elle was surprised. She thought her hair looked pretty good.

"Honey, did you forget the part about my mom being a hairdresser?"

"Oh, right!" Elle nodded, smiling. She would have to be honest with Mitch; he was too smart to fool. Besides, she trusted him. "I guess all you need to know about me is I lived in a crappy apartment, in a crappy town whose name sounds like that of a venereal disease. My mom—she goes by Bobbie—is a bartender in a place that's always dark and where the drink of choice is Jack Daniels with a draft beer chaser. Bobbie calls her regulars 'hon' and smells like the perfume section in a department store. Oh, and let's not forget her tattoo."

Mitch sat up straight. "Wait! Let me guess. It's of angel wings . . . or maybe a butterfly?" Mitch sucked in his breath, narrowing his eyes. "I'm going to go butterfly. On the inside of her wrist."

"Close. Angel wings on the back of her neck." Elle wouldn't mention the name of her dead brother, Jimmy, above the angel wings. That could wait. The thought of him, blue-lipped and cold, momentarily sobered Elle. Hoping Mitch didn't notice her brief sadness, she continued on, "And my dad, well . . . let's just say I haven't seen him since I was like, seven. I'm sure he's very happy in a trailer park somewhere."

It felt good for Elle to tell the truth. She looked at Mitch to see if his face registered shock or disapproval and was grateful to see it didn't, although she somehow knew it wouldn't.

Mitch nodded like he understood. "So, tell me this, does Bobbie have big tits?"

"Ginormous! And she's very proud of them."

"Well, naturally. As well she should be. I'm sure they look fabulous in a strapless bandeau with some cutoff jeans."

"Oh my God, do you know my mother?" Elle was blown away. Mitch was as adept at this game as she was.

"I'm getting a Stevie Nicks sort of vibe."

Elle shook her head. "Yeah, not so much. I could work with that."

"Well, even so. You're lucky. I would take that crappy apartment, that dark bar. You probably got left alone a lot."

Lucky? Elle had never thought of herself as lucky before. That seemed ridiculous. "I think I might make that trade."

"Well, my dad would absolutely love you. You'll see when he comes here to visit me, which will be—*never.*" Mitch leaned forward. "Here's the thing. The beauty of all this"—he pointed to the tables full of Japanese men drinking—"is we can be whoever the fuck we want to be."

Elle understood this better than anyone. It was the very reason she had dyed her hair and changed her name. To be something other than what she really was.

Mitch lit another cigarette. "When my students ask, I say I'm from San Francisco and that my mom is an artist who specializes in making casts of pregnant women's bellies."

"Original. What about your dad?"

"No dad in the picture, but I do have an older sister—we're extremely close. And I most definitely have a cat. A Persian named Queeny." Mitch sat back, relaxed. "What, my darling, would you like your story to be?"

The shameful reality was Elle had already gone through this exercise. Not content to be known as the working-class girl on a full-ride scholarship, she entered college with an intricate story she would intimate about herself to others. "My dad is a pediatrician, a very popular one. All the kids love him. He keeps a bowl full of candy at the reception desk. My mom is a nurse who works in his office twice a week. I grew up in a red brick house with black shutters. My room has pink gingham curtains and a window seat where, as a child, I sat and read *Little House on the Prairie.*"

"Alright, I see you've thought about this already. Are you an only child?"

Elle hated this question, it was too complicated to answer. Although Mitch was asking about a family that didn't exist, she was compelled to somehow acknowledge Jimmy, the sweet baby whose eyes she had closed so he could go back to sleep. "I have an adorable little brother and lots of pets: two dogs, a hamster, and a turtle. Oh, and a horse. I just adore my horse."

"Well, of course, what girl doesn't?" Mitch raised his beer. "Let's drink to our lovely families." Mitch and Elle clinked their mugs together again. "Kampeii!"

Elle considered the Japanese music playing in the background. The words were nonsensical, but the song had a good beat. "We should go dancing!"

"Yes! Let's do it!" Mitch slammed his hands against the table.

Elle finished her beer and stood to leave. The room spun a little, and the faces of all the Japanese men blurred together. She experienced the same surreal sensation as when she had first arrived at the airport. So many odd sounds, the cadence and rhythm of the Japanese language still unfamiliar to her. Dancing would be good; it would help sober her up.

Then again, who cared about being drunk? Elle was having a great time. She looked Mitch over. He really was cool. *And* good-looking. Could she be into him? A little make-out session might be nice. Although Elle had only had sex with one guy—her college boyfriend, a preppy from Boston who loved the Red Sox more than he loved her—she was a notorious flirt who found kissing boys to be innocent fun. There really was nothing better than beer breath on a cute guy.

As Mitch escorted Elle out, he protectively placed his hand on her lower back. It felt brotherly, not the least bit sexual, and Elle knew they would never be more than just friends. There just wasn't any physical chemistry there. *Bummer.* There would be no make-out session after all.

As they stepped outside, Mitch suddenly stopped walking and turned serious. "I gotta tell you something. Mitchell is my middle name. My real name is actually Wayne."

Elle burst into laughter. She grabbed Mitch's arm and hunched over, still laughing. "Oh shit, I think I just peed in my pants a little!"

Mitch looked hurt. "Look, I know it's a dumb-ass name, but it's not *that* funny!"

"No, no . . . you don't get it!" Elle held her hands against Mitch's shoulders. "My real name isn't Elle. It's Michelle!"

"No shit! Are you serious?"

"As serious as a heart attack." Elle tried to compose herself, but she couldn't stop laughing. If she were sober, it probably wouldn't have struck her as all that funny, but many beers in, it seemed hysterical. And the name Wayne? *Hilarious.*

"Please, just promise me you will never, under any circumstance, call me Wayne. Seriously. I fucking hate that name."

"It's a deal." Elle and Mitch high-fived, pleased with themselves and their capacity for reinvention. Elle was happy. She realized that not once that night had she listened or looked for a sign. Perhaps she didn't need to. Maybe Mitch was the sign telling her that coming to Japan was the right decision.

Yep, if Elle hadn't been entirely sure of it before, she was now. Tokyo: underrated, big time.

EIGHT

QUEEN: "THE SHOW MUST GO ON"

May 18, 2017
6:12 p.m.

Elle was behind an endless line of cars waiting to pass through the "Welcome Center" of The Country Day School. The lacrosse state championship game was going to start in less than an hour, and people were already lining up to get in. "Welcome Center" was a euphemism. It was a security gate, plain and simple; Country Day regulated entrance into the school grounds.

Usually there was not a line to get onto campus. Expensive European cars and SUVs were quickly ushered in, one after the other, their drivers recognized by the security staff. As there were so many unfamiliar visitors this evening, the process was taking longer.

Elle's terrible, horrible, no good, very bad day had yet to improve, although the SIDS Alliance board meeting had at least been uneventful. The guest speaker had prattled on and on as Elle tried to recover from the agonizing reminder of her role in Sweet Baby James' heartbreaking death.

But then there had been the school tour. The couple Elle had been assigned to take around campus had been *that* type of parents. Within minutes of walking out of the admissions office, they had proudly shared that their seven-year-old held a patent for a creation made with detergent boxes during Imagination Station in first grade. A *patent,* they had said, smiling at each other, self-righteous in their ability to raise such a remarkably talented child. If Elle had eaten at all that day, she would have vomited in her mouth.

But Elle *hadn't* eaten all day and the abject hunger in her empty stomach made her day from hell complete. To stop thinking about how much she wanted to down a slice of cheese pizza, Elle touched the extra skin popping out above the waist of her snug jeans. It was soft and jiggly like Jell-O, and feeling it gave Elle the extra determination she needed to not eat anything.

As she took a piece of sugar-free gum out of her purse and put it in her mouth, Elle looked at the car in front of her. It was an older model Ford sedan, packed full of teenagers bouncing around in the back seat to loud music. Elle guessed they were students from the other team—the only American cars Country Day students drove were Suburbans and Jeeps. Her suspicions were confirmed when the driver honked the horn and yelled "Go Kennedy!" through an open window. This display of innocent and unbridled joy, coupled with the satisfying sensation of chewing, made Elle smile and she temporarily forgot about being hungry.

A moment later, a golf cart decorated with red and navy streamers and full of Country Day middle-schoolers zipped by on the shoulder of the road. They waved mockingly to the Kennedy students in the Ford as they passed ahead of them—and all the other cars waiting in line—and entered the school grounds unchecked. Elle was embarrassed by their arrogance and wished she could apologize to the visiting Kennedy students for their behavior.

As she inched her way toward the Welcome Center, Elle's phone rang and she didn't need to look at the name on her dashboard to know it would be Aubrey—she had already called multiple times since the tennis match. This wasn't surprising. It was of paramount importance to Aubrey's position as social arbitrator that *she* be the one to relay to their social circle why Elle had left the match early. Elle had ignored her previous calls—withholding information was the only way to exert power over Aubrey—and besides, she had needed time to come up with a plausible story.

At first, Elle had considered saying Four had forgotten his iPad and she needed to run it over to Country Day. Coming to the rescue of one's child was always an acceptable excuse and would be met with nods of sympathetic understanding. *"Sorry I'm late. Lockton wanted his presentation laminated and I had to go to three different Kinkos before I could find one that had navy blue cover paper!"*

Ultimately, Elle had abandoned this as too risky. Aubrey might say something to Four. Instead, she decided to make up an emergency involving her gardener. There were two upsides to this explanation: Aubrey didn't know her gardener so there would be no way to check the veracity of the story; and Elle, not Aubrey, would be the hero—the person needed to swoop in and fix the problem. As Aubrey wouldn't repeat something that was, frankly, not only boring—an emergency with the staff? *Yawn!*—but also didn't make her look good, the whole episode would die down quickly.

Knowing she wouldn't be able to put Aubrey off any longer, Elle pushed the answer button on her steering wheel. "Hello?" Elle spoke more loudly than was necessary. She was a little nervous—Aubrey would be irritated she hadn't returned her earlier calls.

"Oh my gosh, Elle. I've been trying to reach you *all afternoon.*" Aubrey couldn't get the words out fast enough. "I've been *sooo* worried about you. Are you okay?" (*"Please, please tell me you're not."*)

"Oh, thanks. I'm sorry I haven't been in touch; it's just been so crazy," Elle paused, sensing Aubrey's anticipation for the reveal of the Big Crisis. What could possibly have been so urgent that she would leave such an important tennis match? Cheating? Injury? Death? "My gardener had a family emergency, and he couldn't think of anyone but me to call for help."

"Oh no! That's terrible. I'm so sorry to hear that. What can I do to help?" Though Aubrey masked it well—she *was* good at all this—Elle could sense her disappointment. There would be no juicy story to tell after all. *Darn. Too bad.*

This was all as Elle had anticipated. Aubrey would express concern and then find a way to insert herself into the drama. Elle had prepared for this, and her confidence grew. "Oh, thanks. It'll be fine . . . Is Kit upset we had to forfeit?"

Elle already knew the answer to this question. There was no way Kit was fine with forfeiting. It would affect her standing. Women from other clubs would look up her record and see the match recorded as a loss. *Totally unacceptable.* Still, she had to ask.

"No, not at all. She was just worried about you. We all were. When you didn't return my calls, I was just frantic."

And just like that, Aubrey made the entire situation about her. She really was a pro.

There was an awkward silence. Elle was supposed to apologize for not considering how her own personal crisis (make-believe or not) had affected Aubrey's feelings. Elle refused to say sorry, but she couldn't stand the uncomfortable quiet. "Well, I hope the team . . ."

"That's my contractor on the other line. I've got to get this," Aubrey curtly interrupted Elle. "I'm *so pissed.* They put walnut stain on the hardwood floors in the lake house. I told them *ebony*, not walnut. Gotta go— I'll see you at the game."

With that, Aubrey hung up, the pressing needs of the remodel on her second home trumping, at least temporarily, the drama on the tennis court. Or perhaps she was just angry that she didn't get her apology. Either way, Elle was pleased with how she had handled the call. It was a good performance.

Waved through the Welcome Center by a security guard, Elle slowed as a group of teenagers she recognized as Country Day students walked across the road directly in front of her. The students didn't pause, look up at Elle, or make any gesture indicating thanks that she had yielded to them. They simply continued looking down at their phones as though traffic *should* stop for them.

Elle wasn't surprised by this display of entitlement. These teens were, after all, members of a generation who regularly received "participation" trophies at competitions (rewarding just the winners was not inclusive and hurt feelings) and had lavish parties thrown in their honor for accomplishments as banal as successfully completing fifth grade. These were the same children for whom the local police shut down an entire city street during the middle of a busy workday, just so they could cross over and walk to a frozen-yogurt shop on a fourth-grade field trip. It was no wonder they didn't feel the need to be appreciative. The rules did not apply to them. They were *special.*

Elle wished she had listened with a more open mind to Brynnie when she'd expressed a desire to leave Country Day after eighth grade and go to their local public high school. At the time, it didn't seem to make any sense. Country Day was A Very Good School. Why would Brynnie want to leave? Elle had sought the counsel of other Country Day parents and they each had convincing arguments for why Brynnie should stay.

"Central has only six AP courses, and they don't even offer Mandarin!"

"Our son visited, and he was completely bored in all the classes. Country Day covered the same material in seventh grade!"

"Central's valedictorian didn't get into one single Ivy. The counselors at Country Day have much better connections."

Elle had listened to her peers and convinced Win, who in turn convinced Brynnie, to stay and graduate from Country Day. It was the last time the two of them had successfully imposed their will on their daughter, and Elle now recognized it had been a mistake.

Who could blame them? Elle had believed what all the other Country Day parents needed to believe to justify the over $30,000 in annual tuition: they were providing their children with a significantly better experience, a leg up. Why settle for anything less? As one mom said, *"I told Carter, public school is NOT an option."* She had said it with such vitriol, as if going to public school was the equivalent of not feeding your child. Or in this mom's case, akin to—*gasp!*—letting your kids eat foods containing processed white flour.

In this way, the private-school business model thrived, feeding off affluent parents' fears that their perfectly perfect child would not lead a perfectly perfect life. At Country Day they could all relax, smug in the knowledge they were giving their kids The Very Best. From the free-range chicken served at lunch, to the locker rooms stocked with Aveda products, to the spring trip to the Cayman Islands for underwater photography class.

Elle's peer group had expressed great relief when Brynnie stayed on. *"Whew."* A disaster had been averted—imagine sending your child off to a school that didn't have a dander-free golden doodle as a therapy dog available for playing with between classes. *"Disgraceful!"* And besides, everyone knew a public-school education provided nothing more than a one-way ticket to a university with "state" in its name—a surefire path to a life of mediocrity.

Acknowledgement that students could excel outside the confines of a private school would diminish the significant financial investment of the Country Day parents, so those few who did leave we rarely mentioned and their achievements always came with some sort of caveat.

"Everyone knows it's easy to get an A at a public school. The academics at Country Day are so much more rigorous."

"She was the valedictorian with only a 4.1—a 4.1!"

"Of course she got in to Middlebury—her uncle donated a building."

It was much more satisfying for Country Day parents to talk about the very few students who left the school and later regretted it. *"Tsk. Tsk. We knew. We warned them."*

Elle circled around the lot, looking for a place to park. There were few open spots, all the large SUVs took up slightly more than one space, leaving little room for anyone else. She saw Brynnie's Prius and was pleased. Given the argument with Four earlier, she had been unsure if her daughter would come to the game. Maybe things with Jacinda hadn't been so bad after all.

Elle carefully parked her Tesla in a tight space between a Hummer and a Mercedes Jeep. She couldn't understand the appeal of these types of cars when you lived in a metropolitan area. What was the point? On your way to Saks you might suddenly need to go off-road and traverse through rugged terrain? Or was it case you needed to drive over a Kia to get to the front of the line at the Starbucks' drive-through?

Hearing the beep of an incoming text, Elle checked her phone. It was from Win: *Depart Tokyo 6/1 return 6/8. Ok for you and kids? At game. See you soon.*

Ugh. Japan. Not again. Elle had successfully blocked thoughts of a trip back to Tokyo for the better part of the day. She didn't want to start thinking about it now.

Elle was exhausted, completely drained. She wanted nothing more than to escape. To go home, get into her pajamas, cuddle with Duke, and lose herself listening to some U2. Sure, Elle was excited for Four, but she didn't want to go to this game, to talk about tennis, about what Thatcher had or hadn't done. To smile and act like everything was perfectly fine.

"Are you happy, Mom? Are you living your dream?"

Elle put her head against the backseat of her car and held onto the steering wheel with both arms extended, willing herself strength. She needed to get it together. It was an important night for her son. She pictured Jimmy, not asleep with his eyes open, but smiling at her as she held his head up. *He* would have come to Four's game, the proud uncle.

Elle could do it. She had to.

Determined, Elle checked her hair in the rearview mirror and applied some pale-pink lip gloss. The signs had rightly predicted a bad day for her, but maybe it would be different for Four. She would listen for a sign. Elle turned up the radio. Heart's "Magic Man" was just ending. On the surface, it was a love song and didn't count. But then again, the lyrics talked about a man with magic hands. This could be interpreted as a message that Four was going to play well—everyone always said he had "soft, magical hands." Yes, that must be what it meant. It was a good sign.

Elle wasn't convinced. She would listen for *one more* song, just to make sure. She changed the channel. Queen's "We Are the Champions" came through her stereo. Elle smiled; she loved it when the signs were so clear and direct. Her mood greatly improved, Elle turned the volume up and sang along. Four's team would win the game; she was sure of it.

NINE

WEEZER: "MY BEST FRIEND"

October 16, 1992
11:43 a.m.

Making coffee wrapped only in a towel and with dripping wet hair, Elle was grateful for the privacy afforded by the new apartment she and Mitch had recently moved into. It was a small studio, nothing more than a tiny square room with two futons for sleeping, a small kitchen, and a bathroom. Still, they were thrilled to get it. Although Elle and Mitch had enjoyed the relative calm of an empty Zen House for one blissful month after the immigration raid, Watanabe had soon filled it again with other laborers. More people meant more odd smells, noises, and longer wait times for the shower and toilet. The situation was becoming unbearable for them both, but they had few options.

It was incredibly difficult for foreigners to rent apartments in Tokyo. The rents themselves were exorbitantly high, and Japanese landlords had a system of requiring *reikin* or "key money" to secure an apartment. Key money was a sort of gift to the landlord, and it usually meant anywhere from three to six months' rent in advance. Even though Elle was now working with Mitch at English First and they had good salaries, it would take them months of saving to come up with both the rent and key money. And even then, it could still be challenging to find a landlord willing to rent to gaijins.

Luckily for Elle and Mitch, one of their students at English First had been accepted to graduate school in America and had offered to sublet his apartment to them. This was a real coup as the studio came furnished, and they gladly accepted the offer.

That Elle and Mitch would live together was a given. They had become fast friends, spending every day together since their first meeting at Narita six weeks earlier. Free from sexual tension, they enjoyed an easy, uncomplicated relationship, and like an old married couple, they had established a routine.

Both required caffeine immediately upon waking, so they took turns waking up early and making coffee. If they were unusually tired or hungover and needed an extra boost of caffeine, on their way to work they would make a quick stop at McDonald's for two large drinks—Coke for Mitch and Diet Coke with extra ice for Elle.

Today was Elle's turn to wake up first. She poured two cups of coffee and walked toward a still sleeping Mitch. She hated to disturb him. He looked so content lying sprawled out on his stomach, one arm and a leg lazily stretched out, spilling onto Elle's adjacent futon.

"Okay, sleepyhead. Time to make the donuts." Elle set down one cup of coffee and gently shook Mitch's shoulder with her free hand.

"Five more minutes," Mitch pleaded, turning his back to Elle.

"Two and a half or we won't have time to go to McDonald's." It had been a particularly late night—they would definitely need extra caffeine that day.

Elle took a sip of coffee and turned on the TV. She had been taking Japanese language classes twice a week, and her teacher had recommended watching cartoons as a good way to pick up new words. Mitch had studied Japanese in college and was so proficient in the language that he often translated for her. Elle was determined to catch up with him.

She set her mug of coffee on top of the TV and began to blow-dry her hair. Elle tried to follow along with the cartoon, but she was too hung-over and couldn't concentrate on the unfamiliar words. She turned the TV off and flipped on the radio, certain Mitch would scold her laziness.

Hair nearly dry, Elle rustled Mitch again. "Wakey, wakey."

"Aaaah . . ." Mitch stretched out. "What time did we get home?"

"I'm not really sure. Maybe around four?" Elle had a flash of the previous evening. "Oh no! Don't tell me I mooned those guys from Datsun!"

Mitch sat up and ran his fingers through his hair. "Oh yeah, that's right. You did. At one point, I thought you were going to go all full-frontal *Basic Instinct* on them."

"Oh no! Really?" Elle grimaced. That would have been a bit much, even for her.

Elle's drinking had taken on new dimensions since her arrival in Tokyo. Sure, she had partied like everyone else in college, drinking her fair share of Everclear-spiked punch from a red Solo cup. Having spent the better part of her childhood in bars, Elle was right at home in frat houses and was often sought out for her skills at darts, pool, and quarters. But whereas in college, Elle limited herself to just a few drinks on week-ends, she partied hard almost every night now and her drunken behavior had become increasingly outrageous.

Mooning Japanese businessmen was Elle's most recent party trick. She found the looks of shocked delight on her unsuspecting victims to be hilarious. It was harder to understand the humor in her behavior when sober, and Elle often regretted her late-night antics the next morning.

Still, Elle didn't question why she was partying more. Every young person in Tokyo seemed to be doing the exact same thing. And besides, she was having a blast. For the first time, Elle was completely free from the undercurrent of anxiety that always seemed to accompany her. Gone was her sense of trying, *always trying*. Elle was relaxed. Nothing seemed to worry her. It was amazing.

"Aaaah." Mitch turned his head in a slow circle and then stood, his impossibly long, lean frame filling up the small room. "Did you happen to look at the schedule yesterday? I think my first class today is with Mrs. Tadahari."

"Oh, joy." Elle curled her hair in soft ringlets away from her face. "With my luck, I'll get that skeevy Adahiro."

Although most of their students at English First were pleasant enough—young, engaging college kids, sweet, giggly housewives, and serious businessmen—there were a few students Elle and Mitch couldn't stand. Mrs. Tadahari and Mr. Adahiro were two of them.

Mrs. Tadahari was a know-it-all and tight-ass, the kind of person who never let their gas meter get below a half a tank and who brought their own popcorn to the movies to save money. She took pleasure in correcting her teachers on useless grammatical pedagogy. Really, did it matter what a dangling modifier was? *Who cares?* Mr. Adahiro spent the better part of his lessons trying to make physical contact with Elle. He was a total pervert who made no effort to hide his obsession with pornographic anime magazines. *Gross.*

Even so, all said, teaching at English First was a good gig. Being well paid and not having to be at work until one o'clock weren't the only perks of the job. As all Japanese children learned to read and write English beginning in grade school, the work itself was easy—they didn't so much "teach" as offer encouragement and correct pronunciation. A typical work day for Elle and Mitch consisted of five individual classes, followed by an hour off for dinner (and a beer, sometimes two, if they had time), and then ended in the "Conversation Room"—easily the best part of their day.

Designed to look like a typical living room in a suburban American home, the Conversation Room served as a non-threatening place for English First students to improve their fluency by engaging in "Free Talk" with teachers. The only restrictions were to avoid political and religious dialogue. Given this freedom, and encouraged by their drinks at dinner, Elle and Mitch had made it a game to see which of them could out-shock the other with innuendo or double entendre which the Japanese students wouldn't understand. The more outrageous the comment, the better.

"So, Mrs. Yamamoto, would you like to tea bag Mitch?"

"Do you like to mow your wife's grass, Mr. Yadashi?"

"Did he make you wet, Ayumi?"

The Japanese students were so sweetly naive in their confusion at these statements that sometimes Mitch and Elle were remorseful over their puerile jokes. But only a little. Yes, it may have been immature and inappropriate, but it wasn't malicious. Mostly, they were pleased with themselves and how clever they were. Mitch had even introduced his Overrated/Underrated game to the Conversation Room. It proved to be quite popular.

Mitch winced as he got up. "Middle-aged Japanese man trying to cop a feel. Yeah, highly overrated." He popped two aspirin into his mouth, washing them down with a large swig of coffee. "But I'd rather Mrs. Tadahari—who, by the way, is butt-fuck ugly—make a play for me than listen to her annoying, high-pitched voice. *'Mitch-san, isn't that a double negative?'"*

"I'm going to wear a baggy shirt, just in case." Elle rummaged through her dresser, looking for a bra.

"Well, if Adahari knew what kind of underwear you wore, he'd be less inclined to flirt with you."

Elle groaned. "Not *that* again. If you had any idea how uncomfortable it was to have a thong up your ass, you'd be more appreciative of my underwear." Elle held up a pair of her large white cotton underwear. "Grannie panties are *totally* underrated."

"I'm telling you, a girl should always be prepared." Mitch shook his head as he made his way to the shower. "I don't get saving your sexy underwear for special occasions. One should always assume something hot is about to happen."

"Don't even get me started on *your* underwear. Tighty-whities? What are you, eighty? Boxers are much sexier. Especially the plaid ones. Maybe I'll get you a pair."

"And maybe I'll change my name to Chip, put some pennies in my loafers, and move to the Vineyard—NOT!" Mitch stepped out of his Fruit of the Looms, one leg at a time. Naked, he opened the door to the bathroom. Before stepping in, he turned back to Elle. "Make sure I'm out by noon, will ya? I definitely need a Coke to survive Mrs. Tadahari."

As Mitch closed the door to the bathroom, Elle was overcome with an excruciating sadness and nostalgia for her brother. This is what her relationship with him would have been like.

Elle had almost told Mitch about Jimmy the previous evening. Things had taken a serious turn, the way they sometimes do when you are drunk, free of inhibition, and staid with emotion.

Mitch had admitted to having a difficult relationship with his dad, a belligerent drinker. He told Elle of the time his father had, in a drunken rage, called Mitch a pussy and smacked him hard across the face. His brother had laughed in the corner while his mom attempted to put a cold washcloth over his bleeding nose. All this because Mitch had refused to try out for the wrestling team.

Impressed by his brutal honesty, Elle had been compelled to share her demons. To talk about Jimmy, about the shame and the guilt, but she couldn't. It was too painful.

Still, Elle had to let Mitch know that she understood—that she, too, knew degradation. She had followed his confession with the story of Mrs. Whannel.

Mrs. Whannel was the mother of a classmate who volunteered in the cafeteria at her elementary school. One day when Elle was in second grade, she had announced loudly and in front of all the other students in the lunch line, that Elle didn't have any more punches left on her lunch card. The government-issued free-lunch card she qualified for because her mom couldn't afford to pay for her meals.

Wearing a denim bell bottom pantsuit, maroon boots, and large gold hoop earrings, Mrs. Whannel had placed her hands on her hips, smacked her gum, and told Elle—and everyone around her—that she would need to go to the school office to get another lunch card. She couldn't afford lunch on her own.

Elle had been horrified, but too proud to cop to her embarrassment. Instead of going to the office as directed, she had announced indignantly that she wasn't hungry and would rather go to recess. Shoulders back, Elle had stormed outside to the swing set where, ignoring the rumblings of hunger in her stomach, she pushed her legs back and forth as hard as she could, determined to go higher than any other second-grader ever had.

"It was horrible," Elle had told Mitch. "At the same time, maybe it was one of the best things that could have happened to me. I was so angry, so hurt, I vowed never to give some bitch like her power over me again. I would work hard. My life would be different."

After twenty-two years of pretending, sharing the truth gave Elle a certain lightness and she had the courage to admit, "I guess in the end, I'm afraid I won't ever be good enough."

Mitch was generally the first to break a serious moment with a wry comment, a droll anecdote, but not this time. Instead, he had reached over and hugged Elle, commiserating, "Look, I get it. I do. More than you could know." He had then taken a long, slow sip of beer, and Elle had been certain he was going to confide something important to her. Something she had guessed within weeks of getting to know him.

But before Mitch could say anything, they were interrupted by a boisterous group of drunken young men gifting them with shots. A night out with Americans seemed to be a rite of passage into manhood for many Japanese young men, so there was no point in trying to reject them; they would be insistent. Mitch and Elle had gamely done the shots and had their pictures taken with the businessmen.

The moment had been lost.

Did Mitch remember their conversation? Was he in the shower thinking about it right now? Elle hoped he knew he could tell her his secret, that she could be trusted. She loved Mitch. He was her first true friend, the brother she had failed to protect. Elle wouldn't let that happen again. She would help Mitch. But how?

TEN

ALPHAVILLE: "BIG IN JAPAN"

October 31, 1992
7:41 p.m.

In preparation for a big night out with her English First coworkers at a karaoke bar, Elle sang along to Queen's "Bohemian Rhapsody" as she teased up the bangs on her blonde wig and took a drink of champagne. It was Halloween, and she was dressed as Garth from *Wayne's World*. In addition to the wig, she wore a pair of large, chunky black glasses and a plaid shirt open over a white Black Sabbath T-shirt and jeans.

Mitch had lobbied hard for the two to go as Madonna, but Elle had convinced him that it would be a cliché to sing songs by the Material Girl at a karaoke bar in Japan—it would be much more original to perform something from the *Wayne's World* soundtrack.

Mitch had begrudgingly acquiesced and was wearing a trucker hat and a black T-shirt. As a form of protest, he decided to add a little extra flare to his costume and had stuffed a sock into his jeans, giving the desired effect of a rather large package. Mitch pointed to his crotch and asked Elle, "Are you sure it's not too much? I don't want to scare any Japanese girls."

Should Elle take this opening and drop a hint about what she sus-pected Mitch was going to reveal about himself? No, she wouldn't say anything. It would be better for Mitch to tell her himself, when he was ready. "Cheeuh, are you kidding me? It's Halloween. Go for it."

"Okay, then . . . *Schwing!*" Mitch thrust his pelvis in the air. "I still say I would have made a fabulous Virgin bride."

Mitch adored Madonna. She was the one subject the two disagreed upon. Elle found her music highly overrated. "Like A Virgin"—*seriously?* As much as Elle wanted to please Mitch, she had drawn the line at his suggestion that she don lace gloves and crucifixes. "Get over it already! Trust me, you're going to see about a thousand Japanese school girls in wedding dresses tonight."

"Fine, but we should at least toast my girl Madonna, she did pay for this most excellent Dom."

Madonna's *Sex* book had recently been released in the States. As it was banned in Japan, Mitch had seen a great opportunity to make some cash off it. He had friends from America mail him copies of the book, which he then sold to an eager Japanese audience at an exorbitant profit. He'd made the equivalent of $500 selling the contraband books.

Mitch had taken a portion of the proceeds and splurged on the bottle of Dom Pérignon they were now enjoying. He put the rest of the money into the "Mitch & Elle's Adventure Jar" on top of the TV. This, too, had been his idea. He and Elle each put a portion of their salary and any extra change into the jar, hoping to collect enough to pay for an extravagant trip to Europe—a trip like all their wealthy college friends could go on. They would stay at fancy hotels, order room service, and go shopping.

"Yeah, sure. Why not?" Although not particularly a fan of her music, Elle had no problem drinking to Madonna—their Adventure Jar had an extra $450 in it, thanks to her. Elle reached for the bottle of Dom. It was empty. "Ooh, we're out."

"Already? Wow. That was quick. Do want a Kirin? Or maybe a shot?" Mitch twisted his head to the side in contemplation. "It's 'liquor before beer, you're in the clear,' right?"

"Yeah, that's right. 'Beer before liquor, never sicker' so we should be okay." Elle considered the wisdom of another drink. They had a long night ahead of them. Maybe she should slow down. Or at least eat something. She wanted to maintain her buzz but didn't want to get too drunk too early. "Actually, I'm good."

"You sure?"

"Yeah, but I'd take a smoke"

"Roger that." Mitch took a pack of Camel Lights out of his pocket and put two cigarettes into his mouth. He lit them both saying, "Matches—totally underrated. Is there anything in the world more satisfying than the sound a match makes when it strikes? And the smell, I love that just-lighted match smell." He handed a lit cigarette to Elle.

"Thanks." Elle took a puff of the proffered cigarette, conveniently refusing to acknowledge how much she hated that her own mother smoked. What she was doing was different. It's not like she woke up and had a cigarette; she only smoked when she drank. Anyway, who cared? This was Japan. Everyone smoked. "We need to pace ourselves; we should eat something. It could be a long night."

"You're right. Tonight could be a complete shitshow."

Mitch and Elle were justified in their concern over spending the evening out with their English First coworkers. They were a bizarre assortment of characters.

Simon was a twenty-something arrogant pseudo-intellectual who started every conversation with "Well, in Canada . . ." As if being an authority on Canada mattered to anyone. He dressed in the nerdy and academic way of a college professor and smoked cigars. His ultimate goal was to impress everyone with his extensive vocabulary. Not hard to accomplish in a country where English was everyone's second language.

Stewart was a half-Japanese, half-Caucasian New Zealander who desperately wanted to be cool, but he didn't quite fit in with either his fellow teachers or the Japanese locals. It seemed his dual race left him stuck between a chasm he couldn't figure out how to reconcile. Elle and Mitch were sympathetic and tried to include him, but he was just so awkward, inserting himself into conversations with non-sequiturs and anachronistic comments. *"Do you prefer pens with black ink or blue ink? I can't decide which is better."* It was too exhausting to try to engage with him.

Mary, the wife of a midlevel British diplomat, was older than the others—in her mid-thirties, they guessed. She had a glass eye, which made talking to her a challenge. Conversations were fine if you kept your focus on her one good eye. If you made the mistake of looking into the glass eye, things got dicey. Mary was sweet enough. She worked because she was bored, lonely, and desperate for company. She treated all the other, younger teachers as if they were her children, inviting them to British Embassy events, to church, to supper at her home. Mitch and Elle always bowed out of these opportunities. *Too weird.*

Shane was a young Australian who had come to Japan because he had a hard-on for Asian women. Within weeks of arriving in Tokyo, he had knocked up a Japanese girl and had done the honorable thing and married her. His expectations of the carefree bachelor life banging Japanese women dashed by his own carelessness, he was bitter and abrasive. Not at all a fun person to be around.

Rupert, another Australian—whom Elle was initially attracted to, until she saw his excessively hairy back—was teaching English to make money until he could land a lucrative job with a large Japanese company. He was smart and could be quite witty, but he was a bit too macho, too "matey" for Elle and Mitch. He slapped men on the shoulders and referred to women as "Sheilas."

All told, none of the teachers at English First had anything in common. The only thing thinly binding them together was their work—and a shared desire to leave their home countries. In search of what, they could only guess of the others.

"A shitshow is right. What do you think the over/under is on Stewart awkwardly hitting on a waitress?" Elle adjusted her chunky Garth glasses. They were uncomfortable and made her think she should be more appreciative of her good vision—one bonus in an otherwise worthless gene pool.

"That's too easy, you gotta give me something more to work with than that." Mitch put out his cigarette. "You're right about food. Why don't we grab some roadies and get a curry bowl at the station?"

"Sounds like a plan." Elle and Mitch headed toward the stairs where they kept their shoes. (In keeping with Japanese tradition, they removed their shoes before stepping onto the tatami mats in their apartment.) Converse high-tops on, they walked out past the grocery shop where they bought their milk, coffee, and beer. They spotted the elderly couple who lived in the apartment beneath them out for their evening walk.

Elle was sure their neighbors must be confused by their costumes. Even so, the older couple bowed politely to them and smiled the smile of two people benevolently befuddled. Elle felt a rush of warmth. She liked this couple. She liked their neighborhood of Nakameguro. She liked Tokyo. She liked Japan.

No longer was it the strange, pulsating place she had first encountered at the airport. Elle had quickly adapted to Tokyo's energy. She found the city intoxicating and the people kind, considerate, and accommodating. She and Mitch had become accepted and welcomed faces in Nakameguro. Elle relished this sense of belonging. It was like being Norm walking into the bar in *Cheers*.

Mitch and Elle smiled and waved to all the curious Japanese onlookers as they walked into Nakameguro station. They were used to this sort of attention by now and milked it for all it was worth. They rode the escalator down to the platform on the Hibiya line, where a train would take them into Roppongi. Roppongi was Tokyo's entertainment district, famous for its vibrant nightlife. It was a popular area for foreigners to party in, so they weren't surprised it was where their coworkers wanted to meet. Mitch and Elle preferred drinking in bars off the beaten track, but they often ended up in Roppongi, as that's where most of the good dance clubs were located.

As they reached the platform, Elle saw a group of Japanese women all dressed in blonde wigs and wedding gowns. She pointed toward them. "Dressing up as Madonna for Halloween—overrated/underrated?"

"What a totally amazing, excellent discovery. Not!" Mitch smirked as he escorted Elle to the curry stand along the platform. It was one of their favorite spots for grabbing a quick bite. The service was fast and the rice bowls were filling and cheap.

Elle turned to Mitch while they waited in line. "So what is our word gonna be?"

Elle and Mitch had a system. They picked a word they would casually drop in case one of them wanted to make an exit from a situation they found uncomfortable, or if they were simply bored and wanted to move on.

"You know how I feel about karaoke. If I volunteer to sing it will be time to leave."

Elle nudged him affectionately in the side. "Oh, c'mon! I'm thinking you have a little 'Greatest Love of All' in you."

"Oh dear God. This is going to be gruesome enough already. If anyone sings that, I will scream. Really. I'm not kidding." Mitch led Elle by the arm to the front of the line. "*Why?*—that's the perfect word for tonight."

ELEVEN

BILL WITHERS: "LEAN ON ME"

November 1, 1992
1:19 a.m.

Mitch and Elle had been pleasantly surprised that besides the other teachers, several of the young women who worked as office girls at English First were also at the karaoke bar. Yumiko, Ayumi, Mariko, and Koko were a bit daft, but they were good-natured and easy targets for the type of absurdity Mitch and Elle relished in. Adding them to the equation made the whole evening *way* more interesting, and despite their initial misgivings, Mitch and Elle were having fun.

The group had their own private room, and they sat around a rectangular table which was too small to accommodate them all comfortably. With everyone shoved in tightly next to each other, it felt a bit like being on the subway during rush hour. Elle was accustomed to this; Tokyo seemed perpetually overstuffed.

The alcohol had been flowing freely all night, and they were all massively drunk. Mary, emboldened by a belly full of sake, was making her way through a rousing, if not quite in key, version of "The Rose." Mitch was at the far side of the table holding court over the office girls. They were a rapt audience, giggling encouragingly at everything he said.

Shane was openly flirting with Koko and had his hand on her leg. Her cheeks were flush from the attention. She had brought along a friend, and Shane had his free arm possessively around her back. Koko's friend had an unusual name, one that was hard to pronounce, so Mitch had decided to call her Trixie. She looked like a Trixie.

Elle was sitting next to Rupert, who had dressed up as Gandhi—an unconventional choice, but that was Rupert. Along with Stewart, they were discussing American politics. Elle and Mitch had received their absentee ballots for the upcoming presidential election a few days prior, and Rupert, a conservative and politico, was captivated by the race.

"Do you really think Clinton can be trusted after all that nonsense with the Flowers woman?"

"Pshaw!" Elle waved her hand. "It's 1992! His sex life is a non-issue."

"Well, in Canada—" Simon began.

"Oh, for fuck's sake, Simon, quit being such a twat!" Mitch chimed in, irritated. "No one gives a rat's ass what Canadians think about the next U.S. president."

Elle was surprised by Mitch's tone. It was out of character for him to be so openly belligerent. He was generally a happy drunk.

"Oh, excuse me, I forgot. America is the center of the universe. Please forgive me." Simon scowled at Mitch.

Mitch ignored him, turning his attention to the office girls at the table. "Now, who's ready for another shot? Let's have a show of hands." He turned to his left. "Yumiko, you in?"

Several of the office workers raised their hands. Mitch counted them and then called the waitress with a loud. *"Sumimasen!"*

A pretty, nubile woman dressed as a Playboy Bunny appeared at the table.

"Jägermeister *no nine chotto kudasai.*" The Japanese words came easily to Mitch.

Although still not fluent, Elle's hard work in language class was beginning to pay off, and she could now speak and understand conversational Japanese. Hearing Mitch's request, she shook her head in objection. "No, not Jäger. I can't!" The room was already spinning a bit, and what sense Elle had left told her Jäger would not be such a good idea. That stuff could really mess her up.

"C'mon, why not?" Mitch slurred.

"How about some Sex on the Beaches?" Elle queried the group of women next to Mitch, hoping they would agree.

"Yes, yes. Sex on Beach. Good." Yumiko clapped her hands together excitedly, a habit amongst Japanese women Elle found insufferable. It's not as if they were five years old and at a birthday party with a clown performing tricks.

"Oh, fine," Mitch conceded. "You're all a bunch of pussies."

"Hey, watch it there, mate." Shane removed his arm from the back of Trixie.

Koko, looking slightly perplexed, turned to Yumiko and asked her in Japanese to explain what "pussy" meant.

Mitch waved his hand. "Whatever, I don't care. Order what you want. I'm going to sing!" He stood up, somewhat dramatically. Noting the looks of confusion on the office girls' faces, he pointed to Shane and said, by way of explanation, "Shane—pussy."

Thinking it was a term indicating affection, Yumiko and Mariko clapped their hands and repeated, "Shane, pussy!"

"You're a fucking arsehole." Shane pushed against the table and abruptly stood up.

Mitch jutted his chin forward defiantly. "Take a chill pill, mate."

"Go fuck yourself. I'm out of here." Shane turned to the women next to him. "Koko, Trixie, you coming with me?"

"Going to take the girls home with you, I see. That's brilliant. I'm sure your wife and kid will be thrilled to make their acquaintances."

Mitch's unbridled sarcasm made Elle nervous. It was so unlike him.

Shane moved closer to Mitch. "So you want to take this outside, do you?"

Worried things could get ugly, Elle quickly interceded, "C'mon, everyone. Let's all just relax."

"Whatever, I don't have time for this shit." Shane motioned for Koko and Trixie to follow him. As he left, he flipped the bird over his shoulder, adding, "See you arseholes tomorrow."

The waitress returned, carefully balancing a tray with nine shot glasses filled with a pink liquid. Elle was thankful the shots were the Sex on the Beaches she had requested. Mitch was antagonistic enough already, Jäger would only make things worse.

"Good, leave. It just means more for us." Mitch waved Shane off and greedily grabbed two of the glasses from the tray. Throwing his head back, he quickly drank one shot after the other.

The waitress smiled widely, exposing a crooked eyetooth. It was higher than the rest of her teeth and looked like a fang. For reasons neither Mitch nor Elle could understand, the Japanese found these "snaggleteeth" desirable. They were considered cute.

Mitch set the empty shot glasses down and put his arm around the waitress. "Oh, honey, you really should get that fixed."

Elle was again shocked by Mitch's attitude. Why was he being such an ass?

Luckily, the waitress seemed unsure of what Mitch meant and smiled agreeably, like she had been given a compliment.

Mitch did another shot and announced, "Alright, I'm going to sing!" He clumsily pushed his way to the microphone and started looking through the song list.

Elle was sure this wasn't a good idea. Mitch was too wasted. He hated to sing. She needed to stop him. "Wait, Mitch—*why*?"

Mitch looked up. "Because I want to."

"No, Mitch—*why*?" Elle tried to get across she was using their safe word. The word that meant she wanted to leave.

Mitch nodded he got it. "Fine. One song then we'll go. I have the perfect one in mind." Mitch plugged numbers into the karaoke machine and appeared to steady himself, his eyes fixed on the screen where the song lyrics would appear.

The music began, "Da err . . ."

Elle immediately recognized The Smiths' "How Soon Is Now," a song about a gay man bemoaning his father's inability to love him for who he was. So she had been right about Mitch, but that wasn't the least bit important to her now. This was bad. What should she do?

The office workers were encouraging Mitch as he swayed drunkenly to the music and sang the opening lines. He seemed okay. Still, Elle held her breath. She knew better.

Mitch came to the part of the song about being human and needing to be loved. Elle stood and began to walk toward him, instinctively recognizing she needed to be near him. Her fears were confirmed. Mitch suddenly stopped singing and looked helplessly at the table. Everyone quieted, looking back at him in eager anticipation of what he would do next. Mitch was the life of the party. What outrageous behavior would follow?

Mitch dropped the microphone, turned, and ran out of the room. Elle followed and caught up with him outside on the street. He was trying to light a cigarette, but his hand was shaking too much. "Fuck!"

Elle gently took the cigarette from Mitch's hand, lit it, and handed it back to him. She lit another for herself. "You alright?"

Mitch took a long, protracted drag from the cigarette and then waved his hand in the air. "So there it is. Newsflash: Wayne is gay. A fag, a fairy, a flamer, a poof . . ."

Elle reached out. "Mitch, it's okay."

Mitch moved his arm away. "No, it's not okay, Elle. It's not fucking okay."

Elle wasn't sure what to say or what to do. How could she let Mitch know this news didn't matter to her, that she accepted him for exactly who he was? All she could think to do was hug him. He tried to resist, but she wouldn't let go.

"Oh fuck!" Mitch collapsed in Elle's arms, tears streaming down his face.

They stood this way for several minutes, Elle occasionally looking around to make sure no one from their group came out to check on them. Luckily, most of them assumed Mitch and Elle were a couple—something the two did nothing to discourage—and likely figured they wanted to be alone.

Mitch brushed his arm across his nose and reached for another cigarette. "Did you know?" The intensity of the situation had sobered them both.

"Yeah, I guessed as much." Elle ran her fingers gently through his hair. "A cat named Queeny? I mean, c'mon!"

Mitch's lips turned up ever so slightly. It wasn't quite a smile, yet Elle was encouraged. "And then there's the fact that you have somehow managed to resist my amazing breasts."

"The left one is a little bigger, you know."

Thank goodness! Mitch had his sense of humor back. He would be okay. "So really, my tits do nothing for you?"

"Let me put it this way: one time in college some friends insisted on taking me to a strip joint for my birthday. This girl with a rocking hard body is dancing naked right in front of me—I mean, her bush was literally in my face. All the other guys were freaking out, getting hard-ons, and all I could think was 'I like your shoes!'"

Elle laughed. It would be safe to ask a more serious question. "Have you told anyone else?"

Mitch shook his head. "Do you remember when you told me your greatest fear was you wouldn't be good enough?" Fresh tears formed in his eyes. "Well, that would be me. I'm *not* good enough, not for my parents at least. If I'm honest with them about this, they'll disown me."

"Mitch, I'm so sorry." Elle hugged him close again. Sure, she had demons of her own, but mainstream society didn't shame her for something wholly out of her control. Elle couldn't imagine how difficult that would be, how terrible it would feel. "I think you're incredibly brave."

"Brave? That's rich. I'm so brave I had to move halfway across the world so I wouldn't have to face the truth. So I could pretend it didn't exist." Mitch tossed his finished cigarette on the ground and stomped on it with his foot. "You can see how well that's working out for me."

Elle rubbed Mitch's back. "I'm running away, too. We all are."

As if on cue, always interrupting when he shouldn't, Stewart appeared. "Hi, guys! Whatcha doing?"

Really? He had to show up now?

"Nothing. We just wanted to be alone." Elle tried to be nice, hoping Stewart would take the hint to leave.

No such luck.

Stewart continued, "I just love Halloween. Well, Christmas is my favorite holiday. What do you want for Christmas?"

What the fuck? He was so mental.

"Actually, Elle was getting ready to suck my dick, so can you please leave us alone?"

"Oh, right. Geez, okay. I'll see you guys in a minute." Stewart nodded knowingly and winked at Mitch, like he'd had lots of blow jobs outside bars before.

"It'll take more than a minute." Elle smiled sweetly.

Stewart's face reddened as he walked away. "Yeah, okay . . . See you later."

Mitch watched Stewart leave. "Do you ever wish you could be like him?"

"Like Stewart? Umm . . . no! Why do you ask?"

"I don't know. I think it would be a relief to be one of those people who doesn't know any better, someone who is happy with their mediocre little life. I mean, take Yumiko, Ayumi—all of them. Do you think they are tortured by the endless possibilities of what is ahead of them? No, they go home, have their cup of tea, watch TV, and wake up content to do it all over again. Don't you think that would be nice?"

"Only every minute of every day." Elle knew exactly what Mitch meant. It was like her mom, somehow perfectly content in her pathetic little life. She accepted the dismal fate she had been handed and never wanted nor expected more. For all the things her mother was not, like the Japanese girls in the karaoke bar, she was satisfied. She hopefully bought a lotto ticket every week and was never disappointed when she didn't win.

Not Elle. Her every waking moment was colored by guilt, shame, resentment and an unrelenting need for something more. Something better. She put her arm around Mitch. "What's wrong with us?"

"Fuck if I know, but it sucks. Sometimes it really fucking sucks. I'd happily give up fifty IQ points to live in blissful ignorance of my potential."

"Don't say that!" Elle was emphatic. "I wouldn't like you nearly as much if you weren't exactly who you are."

Mitch put his head down. "Sometimes I don't think I can take it."

What did he mean? Elle was concerned. Mitch needed her. She had to help him. Elle put her arm around Mitch's shoulders. "I think you're perfect."

Mitch rubbed his hand across his face to dry his tears. He seemed intent on regaining his composure. "Running from the truth—overrated/underrated?"

"That's easy. Overrated. Most definitely overrated."

"Agreed. You've got to help me get laid."

"Yes! Totally!" Elle was glad the conversation had become light again. She couldn't bear to see Mitch so distraught. "So what's your type, Mitch Carpenter?"

"Well, I once had a rather lurid dream about Gopher from *The Love Boat* which involved bondage. And then there was a slightly less X-rated, yet nonetheless satisfying one with Donny Osmond, but I suppose I would have to say I'm mostly attracted to creative, pretty, slightly feminine guys. David Bowie in his Thin White Duke faze, that sort of look. Having George Michael sing 'Father Figure' to me naked would fulfill a major fantasy."

"Alright, I can work with that. I'm on it!" Elle paused and added, "You need to hook me up as well. It's not like I'm beating men off with a stick."

"Well, you've certainly had more action than me."

"True, but considering the one guy I've ever had sex with is someone who regularly wore plaid pants and bow ties, I'm not exactly qualified to discuss the finer arts of the Kama Sutra."

Mitch grimaced. "Ugh, I guess you do have a point. Okay then, let's make a pact. We both need to score. Soon." Mitch stuck out his hand and they shook on it.

Elle didn't release her hand. Instead, she took both of Mitch's hands and held them to her lips. He could joke all he wanted, but she needed him to understand he shouldn't be ashamed. "You deserve to be loved for who you are, Mitch—and you are. I love you. You're my best friend and I wouldn't change a single thing about you. Not one thing."

"You wouldn't add an inch or two to my johnson? I sure would."

"Nah. Not even that." Elle circled her arm in Mitch's. "Now, getting a Taco Bell in Tokyo—there's something to change. How amazing would a Burrito Supreme be right about now?"

"Yes! The Double-Decker Taco is possibly the greatest invention ever. Highly underrated. Maybe after our trip to Europe we should come back here and open a T-Bell franchise. Seriously, we could become zillionaires."

Arm in arm, Elle and Mitch walked toward Roppongi Station to a train that would take them home. Elle was glad Mitch had confided in her. She had meant what she said. Mitch was her best friend; she loved him. He was safe with her. Elle would make up for what had happened with Jimmy. She would protect and take care of Mitch. No matter what.

TWELVE

The All-American Rejects: "Move Along"

.

May 18, 2017
6:39 p.m.

"Hi, Mrs. Martin!" Tabby waved enthusiastically to Elle. *Smiley face, smiley face.* Four's girlfriend spoke with such animated emotion, it seemed like everything she said ended with a corresponding emoticon.

Elle waved back as she walked into the crowded stadium. She liked Tabby. She was a genuinely sweet and perpetually happy girl. She hand-painted fairies and flowers onto children's clothing and sold them at the Junior League Holiday Bazaar, donating the proceeds to St. Jude's. Tabby was also pretty in the lithe, wholesome, horseback-riding, patrician sort of way Elle so admired. She would go to a good college, major in art history or French, study abroad, and get an internship at a trendy gallery in the city before marrying.

Tabby would always know what to wear.

She was perfect for Four and just the kind of girl Win should have married.

Tabby skipped toward Elle. Along with the de rigueur out-of-school Country Day uniform for females of black lululemon yoga pants and Ugg boots, she wore Four's #4 away jersey. She hugged Elle, careful to avoid smudging the 4 she had painted in red on her cheek. "It's so good to see you!" *Row of pink hearts.* Tabby stepped away from Elle and frowned. "My mom told me about your tennis match. Is everything okay?" *Furrowed brow emoji.*

Elle wasn't surprised that news of the argument at the tennis match had already made the rounds. She ran in a small social circle; it had been Tabby's mom who had sought advice on the color scheme for her Range Rover at Jane's house that morning.

Although sure Tabby's concern was genuine, Elle didn't have it in her to talk about all the bickering. It seemed pointless. She swatted her hand in the air casually. "Oh, it's fine. Nothing to worry about."

"Oh, good!" *Smiley face.* Tabby looked around and then lowered her voice asking, "Did you hear about Thatcher? It's *such* a *huge* bummer." *Frowny face, frowny face, face with a tear drop.*

Thatcher's suspension was another issue Elle had no interest in discussing, so she didn't answer. Instead, knowing Tabby was easily distracted and not the type to dwell on anything negative, she changed the subject. "Aren't you glad the weather is so nice?"

"Yes! I'm so glad it didn't rain! But still, I'm *sooo* nervous for Four!" *Wide eye emoji.* Thatcher's fate temporarily forgotten, Tabby jumped up and down, rubbing her hands along Elle's arms. "They can do it, right?" *Nervous face, hands in prayer.*

"Yes! They can. I have a good feeling about this game." Elle was confident; she had heard "We Are the Champions"—there couldn't have been a clearer sign predicting victory. She patted Tabby on the arm reassuringly. "Go on ahead with your friends. I'll see you after the game."

"Okay. My stomach is just in knots!" *Face with tongue sticking out.* Tabby offered Elle another quick hug, waved good-bye, and ran to catch up with her friends. Just like the women on the tennis court earlier that day, Tabby wore her blonde hair in a high ponytail. Adorned with navy and red ribbons, it bounced with youthful optimism as she ran off.

Yes, Tabby was a happy girl. How lucky for her. She would continue to make dream boards and end every text to Four with smiley face and heart emojis. In a few years' time, she would be debating the merits of varying color schemes for a new European car of her own.

Could Elle be happy in the same way Tabby was? If she had grown up in a house with a pediatrician dad and a nurse mom, would she have been one of those girls who used a red sharpie to decorate white boxer underwear with hearts for her boyfriend? If Jimmy hadn't died and her dad hadn't left, would she have spent her free time making mixed tapes for friends with each song title written in a different-colored pastel pen?

It didn't matter, not anymore. What was important was that Elle's children wouldn't look back at their own childhoods and wish they had had more.

Elle continued into the stadium and saw Regina Moore, one of Brynnie's favorite teachers. Elle often sought out Regina's company at school events. She was kind, smart, and interesting to talk to.

"Hi, Regina, it's so nice of you to come tonight." Elle was impressed that Brynnie's teacher had made the effort to come to the game. She couldn't imagine that Regina was an avid sports fan. She was too earthy, too academic—someone who didn't own a TV and spent her weekends reading the classics with a steamy cup of Earl Grey tea.

"Well, I admit I don't know much about lacrosse, but I wanted to be here to support my students."

Of course. Elle knew there was a good reason why she was drawn to Regina. She was genuine; a person who actually gave a shit about others.

Regina took in the atmosphere. "What a glorious evening it is."

"Yes, it is!" Elle nodded in agreement. Wanting to demonstrate a sincere gratitude, she placed her hand in Regina's and said, "I've been meaning to tell you how much Brynnie is enjoying your class on postmodern feminism in fiction. She was really moved by . . ."

"Hey." Elle was interrupted by a gruff voice. Ward Johnson, her tennis partner Kit's husband, entered the conversation, nodding his head slightly toward Regina and half-hugging Elle, his hands otherwise occupied with a hamburger and a soft drink.

Oh, great.

Elle couldn't stand Ward. He was an ass. An unapologetic social climber and pompous blowhard who thought he knew everything. He was the type of guy who took his job as president of the Homeowner Association for his gated community very seriously. He walked around with a clipboard and sanctimoniously noted every errant weed and every trashcan left on the curb overnight. Ward had fat sausage fingers, and seeing the hamburger in his chunky hands momentarily reminded Elle of her empty stomach and how hungry she was.

Ward lifted his drink in the air and talked with his mouth full. "I can't believe this situation with Thatcher. It's ridiculous! I was on the phone with the headmaster all afternoon. He wouldn't budge."

Not for the first time, Elle wondered if Ward suffered from some sort of disability which stymied his ability to read social situations. How else to explain his habit of blurting out inappropriate comments? Did he honestly think it was acceptable to bring the situation with Thatcher up in front of a teacher? What did he expect her to say? Strange how a man with an MBA from Harvard could lack such tact.

Elle was unsure how to respond. She offered a half-hearted smile—seeing Ward's mouth full of hamburger had at least killed her appetite. Regina said nothing.

Oblivious to the awkward position he had put them both in—or maybe he knew and just didn't care—Ward took another bite of his hamburger and directed his attention toward Regina. "I want to talk to you about Easton's grade on his paper—a C? C'mon! I read that paper. It was an A paper."

There it was again; something really must be wrong with him. Elle fidgeted uncomfortably.

Regina seemed slightly taken aback by Ward's abruptness but rebounded quickly. "If Easton wants to make an appointment, I'd be happy to go over it with him."

90

Still chewing with his mouth open, Ward shook his head. "Here's the thing: he needs an A on that paper."

Elle was sorry for Regina and the ambush. She should try to diffuse the conversation, to help Regina out somehow, but she couldn't. As strongly as she had wanted to flee the tennis court earlier, Elle needed to get out of there. Quickly.

"Oh, I see Brynnie. I need to go talk to her," Elle lied.

Ward, still focused on Regina and clearly unconcerned with Elle, waved his fat sausage-fingered hand dismissively toward her and continued, "Seriously, he deserves an A."

Elle mouthed the word "sorry" to Regina as she turned to leave. Regina gave her a nod indicating everything was fine and turned toward Ward with a conciliatory gaze.

Elle didn't know how Regina, or any of the other teachers, abided such poor behavior. Country Day parents could be total nightmares.

Earlier that week, Aubrey had complained to the headmaster about a math teacher after Grayson had failed his latest calculus test. It simply wasn't possible for her son to get an F; either it wasn't a fair test or the teacher hadn't properly explained the concepts. Aubrey had first talked to the teacher, and when she wasn't satisfied with the answer he gave—something along the lines of "Perhaps Grayson should have rechecked his work for mistakes"—she decided to go above the teacher's head, straight to the headmaster. Aubrey would be heard. Grayson would be allowed to retake the test.

Although Elle could—and did—helicopter parent with the best of them, Four's and Brynnie's grades were not among her neurosis. She didn't obsessively track her children's progress online, fretting over each assignment that wasn't given an A. Elle trusted the Country Day teachers to be fair and refused to indulge any complaints regarding the types of assignments given or their resulting grades. Given all that her children had, it seemed rather trite and petty to complain.

Elle was considering the possibility that she liked the teachers more than the parents at Country Day when she spotted Brynnie in the concession line with a group of friends. She waved her over, and Elle was surprised to see that her daughter also had a 4 painted on her cheek. Tabby must have been behind this—Brynnie wasn't one for unabashed displays of school spirit.

As if to temper her nod to convention with the face paint, Brynnie eschewed the navy and red logoed Country Day shirts of her classmates in favor of a purple T-shirt with three sets of stick figures on it. The first was a man, a woman, and a child; the second, two men and a child; and the third, two women and a child. In bright rainbow-colored letters across the top it read: "There are all types of families: Love is Love."

Elle gave her daughter an earnest hug. Normally, she would be worried over what people would say about Brynnie and the statement she was making with the T-shirt, but not tonight. Tonight, Elle was proud of her daughter's courage, her indifference to what others thought, and her commitment to what she believed. "Hi, sweetie! I'm so glad you're here."

"Of course I'm here. Why wouldn't I be?"

"I wasn't so sure after your argument with Four this morning."

"That kid makes me crazy sometimes—he can be so ignorant—but I still love him. And besides, I'm quite looking forward to this spectacle."

Elle was relieved. It gave her hope that Brynnie had also forgiven her. "Have you talked to Jacinda? Is she okay?"

Before Brynnie could answer, Aubrey approached, marching purposefully, like she had an agenda.

First Ward, now Aubrey. Elle couldn't escape.

Except for her white jeans—apparently, it *wasn't* too early to wear white—Aubrey was dressed almost identically to Elle. This should have been incredibly satisfying—it meant Elle had chosen her outfit correctly—but all she could feel at this moment was dread.

Aubrey removed her sunglasses and placed them on top of her head. She reached for Elle's hands. "Elle! I'm so glad to see you. Are you sure everything is okay? Can I help?"

"Everything's fine." Elle's tone was short. She didn't feel like playing along.

Aubrey freed her hands and slowly tilted her head from side to side, silently considering Elle for several drawn-out seconds. Without speaking, she turned toward Brynnie and looked over her T-shirt with disdain—or was it confusion?

Brynnie placed her hand soothingly along Aubrey's arm, the way one would if comforting a child, and explained, "It's to honor gay rights. I'm sure you've read about how the Supreme Court ruled in favor of marriage equality."

Aubrey didn't respond. Instead, she twirled at the platinum medallions—each bearing the name of one of her four children—on the necklace that hung near her chest. Was this some sort of power play? A subtle reminder that she was superior? She had borne four children. She could afford private school tuition, first-class plane tickets, tutors, and nannies—four times over.

After several uncomfortable seconds, Aubrey finally spoke to Brynnie through a strained smile, "Read? I don't have time to read!"

"Of course not!" Brynnie put her hands up against her cheeks. "How silly of me! I forgot how busy you are. You had a tennis match today, right?"

Holy shit!

Elle was impressed by Brynnie's quick retort, yet as much as she admired her daughter's courage, Elle was apprehensive. Aubrey wasn't one to be crossed.

Sure enough, Aubrey's retaliation was swift. She cocked her head to the side and pursed her lips. "So, sweetheart, remind me—who is your date to prom?"

Elle's stomach tightened. Brynnie had never had a boyfriend, let alone a date. Everyone knew that. Was Aubrey implying Brynnie was gay? Elle wanted to say something to protect her daughter, but what?

Brynnie didn't seem the least bit bothered by the question. "I'm choosing to go alone. I'm independent like that—kind of a modern-day Elizabeth Bennet . . ." She paused, then condescendingly patted Aubrey on the back. "Oh, sorry. How silly of me—since you don't read, you couldn't possibly understand the *Pride and Prejudice* reference."

Elle tried to contain her laughter. *Good for Brynnie.*

Aubrey stood speechless, like she had been scolded by a stranger for failing to pick up her dog's massive dump on the playground—*"Aren't there people for that?"*

Smiling, Brynnie kissed Elle on the cheek. "See you after the game!" She walked away, waving her arms high in the air with feigned enthusiasm. "Go, Country Day!"

Aubrey turned toward Elle, eyes squinted in anger. Ignoring phone calls was one thing. Elle had really crossed a line now. Aubrey expected an explanation. An apology.

Elle refused to give in. Let Aubrey say and do whatever she wanted. She no longer cared. Elle offered Aubrey a quick and insincere hug good-bye saying, "I should go. I need to catch up with Win. He's just closed a major international deal and we have loads to discuss."

Aubrey's mouth dropped in shock. She'd have to pick the poop up herself.

Elle walked away, satisfied. She had done it. She had stood up to Aubrey and it was exhilarating.

Still, Elle knew better than to celebrate too much. There would be consequences for her actions; Aubrey would make her pay. She just didn't yet know how.

THIRTEEN

THE WAITRESSES: "I KNOW WHAT BOYS LIKE"

October 24, 1993
7:18 p.m.

Elle lifted first her left breast, then her right one, pushing them up in her body-hugging red strapless dress—her goal was to show *just enough* of the tops of her boobs. She wanted sexy but not slutty. Elle didn't like the dress—it reminded her of something a pageant contestant would wear—but had to admit Mitch had been right to talk her into getting it. It was ideal for her job in the hostess bar. The Japanese clients would appreciate how it accentuated her curvy, petite figure. She would make loads of money tonight in this Miss America gown.

Hostess bars were a phenomenon unique to Japan. A modern version of the geisha establishments of old, the concept was a private club where wealthy Japanese executives paid hefty sums to have attractive women attend to their needs. The hostesses flirted with them, poured their drinks, lit their cigarettes, and made them feel important. As one of the few non-Japanese hostesses, Elle was a rarity, and her company was highly sought after. With her platinum-blonde hair, light-colored eyes, and voluptuous figure, she represented the fantasy of the ideal American woman, the one Japanese men saw in movies and on magazine covers.

And why shouldn't Elle give them what they wanted? It's not like she was getting attention from any other men. Most Japanese guys were shy and intimidated by her. Elle couldn't get anyone to flirt with her, let alone ask her on a date. She had even less luck with the American, Australian, and British expats living in Tokyo. Like the Japanese men in the hostess bar, they sought out what was different. Many of them had come to Tokyo specifically because they preferred Japanese women. They weren't the least bit interested in Elle. There were plenty of girls like her back home.

Things were worse for Mitch. As much as Elle had wanted to make good on her Halloween promise to get him laid, it had proven to be a challenge. Despite Tokyo being a cosmopolitan city, homosexuality was still frowned upon by many Japanese and few men were openly out. Those who were seemed as equally reluctant as their straight counterparts to engage with an American.

So it had been a very, *very* long dating dry spell for the two, one they hoped to remedy. Elle missed kissing cute boys and Mitch was anxious to explore his sexuality with a man.

Elle looked in the mirror, debating whether the bright blue eyeliner and blue mascara were too much. Mitch assured her they highlighted the blue in her eyes, but Elle wasn't so sure. With her platinum-blonde hair worn down straight, it was all a little too . . . too red, white, and blue.

"Ladies and gentleman, presenting for your viewing pleasure: Elle, the American flag."

Elle stretched her arms outright. She nearly knocked over an open bottle of Chardonnay on the vanity, catching it only at the last minute. The bottle was light in her hands. Had she really finished it all off? Funny, she didn't feel drunk.

Elle again considered the blue eyeliner and decided it was fine. Satisfied, she made her way from the dressing room into the main area of the Big New York Apple Club. Elle and Mitch loved this name and found it hilarious—such a classic example of the Japanese tendency to misuse English. Tokyo was filled with places and things with similarly ridiculous names: the drugstore Let's Wellness, which sold "Moistage Essence Lotion," and the restaurant Eat Me, with "Mouth Watered Chicken" on the menu. Although Elle and Mitch appreciated the humor in the club's name, it was a mouthful to get out, so they had taken to calling it simply "The Big YAC."

Elle surveyed the room. Several customers were already enjoying whiskey at the bar, while others sat in olive-green swivel chairs around small oak tables over gold shag carpet. The Big YAC's décor had a distinct seventies vibe, like the Regal Beagle in *Three's Company*. Elle imagined Mae-san, the club's owner and madam, had watched too many reruns of the sitcom and thought it was the epitome of American cool.

But as with the club's name, Mae-san hadn't gotten it all quite right. Inexplicably, along with the seventies look, the Big YAC was also part Italian pizzeria, with posters from *The Godfather* and of famous Italian-Americans, like Frank Sinatra, hanging on the walls. The first night they discovered the place, Mitch and Elle placed bets on who would walk in first: Mrs. Roper in a kaftan or Sonny Corleone smoking a cigar.

Elle considered the men sitting at the bar and around the tables. Who did she want to spend the next few hours drinking with? The men who frequented the club were all rather the same: older, successful, married executives longing for the attention of their ideal woman. Elle's job was to figure out what this ideal was and to become her: the giggly, easily impressed schoolgirl who found everything they said highly clever; the smart, savvy professional who could intelligently discuss their business; or the sassy, ribald woman who told racy jokes.

It didn't matter. Elle could be whomever they wanted. After a lifetime of never quite fitting in, she had mastered the ability to read those around her. Within minutes of meeting new people, Elle could adapt her posture and tone to imitate those she was with, effortlessly morphing into the person best suited for almost any situation. Especially after she had a few drinks in her. It was really easy when liquored up.

Elle already had a good buzz going, so it should be an easy night. The question was, who did she think would give her the biggest "gift" at the end of the evening? The Japanese didn't tip per se, but cash as a thank-you to a hostess for a job well done was commonplace. Having recently been fired from English First, Elle needed the money, and her desire to quickly fill up the Mitch & Elle's Adventure Jar had been her main rationale for accepting the hostess job.

She wasn't proud of being fired but accepted it as inevitable. After a year at English First, teaching had become tedious, and to compensate for their boredom, Elle and Mitch had started drinking more and more on their dinner breaks. Their usual one or two beers had turned into three or four, often with a shot thrown in. After one such alcohol-infused dinner, Elle had come back to work completely smashed and was in the Conversation Room with Shane when he referred to the AIDS crisis as God's way of eliminating "dirty fags." Offended, Elle had hit him several times on the chest, called him a homophobic asshole, and told him to fuck off. Unfortunately, her rage played out in front of a group of astonished high school girls.

"You leave us with no choice," management had said.

Mitch didn't want to stay at English First one minute without Elle, so the next day he brought a flask with vodka in it to work, drank it all, and proceeded to teach a group of beginner students that the American slang word for "cheers" was "suck my dick." Mary had walked in on him and an entire group of housewives in the Conversation Room enthusiastically clinking their cans of Dr. Pepper together, reciting, "Suck my dick!" Full of shock and indignation, Mary had reported this transgression and Mitch was also promptly fired.

Mitch had seen the end coming and had wisely already started collecting the phone numbers of his students, offering them private lessons at a discounted rated. Elle could have done the same thing, but she wanted to try something new. So it had been lucky when, after a night out of drinking, she and Mitch had stumbled upon the Big New York Apple Club. Mae-san had taken one look at Elle and offered her a job—an astonishingly high-paying job.

It seemed to be a good deal, an easy way to make money, but Elle was hesitant. *A hostess?* Wasn't that a little too close to a call girl? Mitch and Elle discussed the opportunity in sober earnestness the next day.

"Well, it's not like you're going to sleep with anyone," Mitch pointed out. "I would look at it like a kind of acting job—all you have to do is pretend a bunch of old pervs are interesting."

Elle had still been wary, but agreed to try it for one night—*why not?*—with the condition that Mitch could accompany her. Mae-san had agreed; having an attractive Caucasian male in her club was a welcome addition—another American prop.

Despite her initial fears, Elle quickly discovered Mitch had been right; there was no reason to be worried. She spent the evening drinking champagne and talking to some very boring businessmen. There had not been a single insinuation of anything the least bit sexual. It was just like being in the Conversation Room—only she was wearing a tight dress, and the consumption of alcohol was encouraged. Best of all, Elle received a 50,000-yen note as a "present" at the end of her first night. *Not bad.* She decided it was an effortless way to make lots of money and accepted the job.

This evening, with a big tip in mind, Elle settled on joining Mitsuya-san, the president of a large international electronics company, who traveled frequently to America. In addition to being exceedingly generous, Mitsuya was smart and interesting so conversation with him was easy. It would be a pleasant way for her to pass the time until Mitch arrived.

With their new jobs, Elle and Mitch had quickly settled into a new routine. Mitch taught his private lessons in the evenings, and when he was finished, he joined Elle at the Big YAC. Mae-san found Mitch charming and he was welcomed as a regular at the club.

This arrangement suited Mitch just fine. In another ode to Americana, the Big YAC had a Ms. Pac-Man game table off to the side. Mitch had loved this game as a tween; while all the other boys went to the town's arcade and played Tetris, he had been obsessed with trying to advance to the point in Ms. Pac-Man where Sue and Blinky got married. As such, Mitch was more than content to spend his evenings waiting for Elle to finish work by drinking whiskey and chasing dots with his old friend Pinky. After closing time, the two would leave and hit a dance club, scamming for the ever-elusive men who could put an end to their dating dry spells.

Elle had finding hot guys on her mind as she approached Mitsuya. Maybe she and Mitch would have better luck later that night. Or Mitch at least. They were planning to go to a new club, one rumored to be frequented by gay men.

"Hello, Miss Elle-san. Please sit." Mitsuya rose as Elle approached. "You look very, very beautiful tonight. What would you like to drink?"

"Thanks. I'm so glad you're here. I've missed seeing you." Elle sat down, wondering if her words sounded as insincere as they were. Sure, she enjoyed Mitsuya's company, but it was an overstatement to suggest she had missed him. "How about some champagne?"

"Of course. Dom Pérignon? Your favorite?"

"Sounds perfect, thank you." Elle would have preferred to stick to white wine, but as she made a commission off alcohol sales, it was key to order the most expensive drinks available.

Mitsuya motioned for Mae-san to approach. As he ordered a bottle of Dom, Mae-san nodded approvingly. Elle was good at her job. She kept the clients entertained and she could drink. Men always felt the need to keep up with her, ordering one expensive bottle after another, all night long. *Cha-ching.*

Elle was easily making over four times the amount she had at English First, and that didn't include the gifts of perfume, jewelry, and dresses. She supposed some clients hoped that by giving her these things, she would be enticed to engage in more than a professional relationship with them. Elle had no intention of crossing that line. Instead, she was appreciative of the gifts, yet unmoved, often selling them for cash and putting the proceeds into the Mitch & Elle's Adventure Jar.

When the bottle of Dom arrived, Elle leaned forward and poured a glass for Mitsuya. She was relaxed, happy even, thinking of the money she would make. The Adventure Jar was getting fuller by the day. At this rate, she and Mitch would have enough to finance their much-anticipated trip to Europe by summer.

Mitsuya drank the champagne in one big swig, motioned for her to pour him another glass, and said, "I wanted to talk to you about the most interesting story I heard. About a Mr. John Wayne Bobbitt getting his penis cut off by his wife. Do you know this story?"

Elle smiled and took a large sip of champagne. She had been right to choose Mitsuya. It was going to be an easy night.

◆ ◆ ◆

10:52 p.m.

Elle stood at the bar smoking a cigarette, pleased with herself. With her encouragement, in addition to the Dom, Mitsuya had ordered a bottle of The Macallan 40-Year-Old Scotch—she was in for a hefty commission. Even better, as she had helped him into a taxi, he had handed her a thick wad of yen in thanks. All told, she had made almost a grand. She couldn't wait to tell Mitch.

Elle looked at the clock—10:52. Mitch would be there soon, and then there would be only one more hour to kill before they could go out. Elle had the perfect buzz going and predicted they would have a very good night.

There was a flurry of activity at the front door. Elle turned to see what was going on. A group of five or six Japanese twenty-somethings had walked in. Although smartly dressed, they were too young for the Big New York Apple Club. Elle saw Mae-san approach them and assumed she would ask them to leave, to come back after they'd made their first million and grown tired of their young wives.

So Elle was surprised when Mae-san led the men toward a table and waved at her to join them. Although in her early sixties, the madam was still stunning and Elle noticed the young men admiring her as they sat down. Mae-san was also very good at her job—the ideal combination of savvy and sweet.

Elle guessed she had been a very famous geisha back in her day, well-known for her grace and beauty. She had fallen in love with one of her wealthy clients and was set to marry him, but then he had been in a horrible accident, one too cruel to make sense of. Distraught and convinced she would never again find true love, she had settled on opening a club of her own.

At least this is what Elle liked to think. The truth was, she had no idea what Mae-san's background was. Like most Japanese, she gave little away and was hard to read. Regardless of her story, Elle held Mae-san in high regard. She answered to no one.

Elle put her cigarette out in the red glass ashtray on the bar and approached the group.

Mae-san held her hand out to the man closest to her. "Tak-chan, this Erre-san."

The young man stood and bowed politely to Elle. He was tall and his black hair was slicked back in a neat, short pony-tail, which highlighted a strong jaw and rugged, angular features.

Holy shit! He was hot.

Tak wore a diamond earring in his right ear and was dressed in a rather showy black striped suit with an eggplant-colored shirt and matching skinny tie. He was far from the preppy, conservative guys Elle had liked in college, yet she was inexplicably drawn to him.

Elle held out her hand, full of anticipation. "It's a pleasure to meet you."

"Nice meet you. Please. Sit."

By his heavily accented and halting English, Elle knew that Tak's grasp of the language wasn't very strong, but she didn't care. She was attracted to him in a way she hadn't ever experienced before and was flustered by it.

As Elle sat down next to him, she was overcome with the smell of Polo cologne. This would normally be a deal breaker—it was too reminiscent of all the guys she went to high school with—but on Tak, it didn't bother her. Elle's leg brushed against his and she felt a powerful magnetic energy, like an electric shock. It made her dizzy with excitement.

"I know Tak-chan father, Akimoto-san," Mae-san explained.

So that's why they were allowed in. His dad was someone important.

Elle turned toward Tak and noted with approval that he had perfectly straight teeth and a well-defined, muscular body, with incredibly broad shoulders. He had a confident swagger Elle found particularly appealing. Finally, someone she actually *wanted* to flirt with!

Tak looked at Elle with a directness and confidence unusual for a Japanese man. Especially a young one. "You call me Tim."

Tim? Really? That wouldn't do. "I like the name Tak much better. Is it okay if I call you Tak?" As she spoke, Elle rested her hand against Tak's arm and felt another titillating burst of energy. She couldn't deny the chemistry. Did he feel it, too?

Tak took Elle's hand in his and kissed it. It was a bold move—the Japanese were typically not physically demonstrative. "Yes, okay. Sure." He moved her hand away from his face, but didn't let go of his grip.

It was a little presumptuous, yet Elle's cheeks flushed and a tingling sensation raced down the back of her spine. She liked the contact. She liked him.

"Tak it is." Elle gently extracted her hand from his. She didn't necessarily want to remove herself from his touch, but it was imperative to give the impression that she was in control. She put Tak's hand next to the top of her thigh and noticed that he was wearing a large diamond-encrusted gold ring on his pinkie finger. Again, this was something that would normally be a turn-off—the ring was rather garish—but on Tak, it seemed masculine and necessary.

Tak looked intently at Elle. She became light-headed. It felt deliriously intimate, like the room had shrunk, and they were the only two people who existed. He placed his hand on Elle's thigh and they spent the next hour intently trying to communicate with one another.

Elle had been right about Tak's English—it wasn't very good. He could understand everything she said if she spoke slowly and deliberately, but it was hard for him to find the English words to respond with. Elle could have made it easier for him by speaking in Japanese, but there seemed to be something incredibly romantic about the way he was trying so hard in English. She decided to keep her knowledge of Japanese a secret.

Elle was so engrossed in conversation with Tak, she completely missed it when Mitch came in. She only noticed him later, happily sitting at his regular spot playing Ms. Pac-Man. When they made eye contact, Mitch gave her an approving thumbs-up.

Elle was confident Tak was the leader of the group—he paid the others little to no attention, yet one of them was always ready to pour him more beer and to light his cigarettes. At closing time it was one of Tak's companions—Elle thought he had said his name was Johnny—who discreetly paid Mae-san.

Tak's focus never left Elle. When it was time to leave, he cupped his hands under her chin and said, "You are coming with me." It wasn't a question as much as a forgone conclusion.

Tak was so sure of himself, cocky even, that Elle should have been put off—but she wasn't. Quite the opposite. Elle wanted nothing more than to go with him. Still, she wondered whether it was a good idea. Technically he *was* a client. She hadn't planned to go there. Elle excused herself for a minute. She would go see what Mitch thought.

Elle sat down at the Ms. Pac-Man table across from Mitch. "He wants me to go with him. What do you think?"

"Cheeuh! Are you kidding me? Go!"

"I don't know—I mean, I said I wouldn't go out with customers."

"Elle, come on. It's not like he's some sketchy old man. He's hot. Go for it."

"Yeah, but . . ." Elle was still not convinced. She had been out of the dating game for too long. Maybe she should listen for a sign. Over the course of the past year, Elle had stopped taking direction from music. It hadn't been a conscious decision; it just didn't seem necessary anymore.

Elle was having too much fun. But this was a big deal. She should listen for a sign.

Elle concentrated on the music in the background of the Big YAC, expecting to hear something by Elvis Presley. He was Mae-san's favorite pop star and "Love Me Tender" and "Can't Help Falling in Love" seemed to be on an endless loop in the club. To her surprise, instead of Elvis Presley, something from a Japanese band was playing. Elle didn't recognize the song and couldn't decipher the lyrics. She decided this was a sign that a sign wasn't necessary. Elle knew what she was doing.

"Okay. It's just like meeting a guy at a bar, right?" Remembering they had plans to go dancing, Elle felt guilty bailing on Mitch. "Do you want to come with us?"

"As intriguing as a threesome sounds, I'll pass. Besides, I know what kind of underwear you're wearing."

Elle thought about her underwear: plain, white, boring grannie panties. She lifted both hands over her mouth in horror. "Oh no! Shit!"

Mitch shook his head in mock dismay. "How many times have I told you? A girl should always be prepared. Wearing sexy underwear—hello!—underrated."

"You're right. What should I do?"

Mitch took a drag of his cigarette and smiled. "You gotta ditch the grannie panties."

"Really? You think they're that bad?"

"Honey, I love you, but you don't have to be straight to see they're a total boner-kill. Ditch 'em, or forget about playing hide the salami with your new friend."

Elle was shocked by Mitch's suggestion. "I'm not planning on sleeping with him!"

"Why the hell not?"

Because I'm not that kind of girl. A full-on make-out session and some dry-humping was one thing, but sex with a guy on the same night you met him at a bar? *No way.* That was a total slut move. "I don't know, don't you think that's a little rushed?"

"Elle, please don't tell me you're going to go all Puritanical on me now. You've only had sex with one person and that was way back in college. You've finally met a guy you're into. For God's sake, do him!"

Mitch was right. Elle hadn't met a man she was interested in in a very long time and she might not have this chance again. Besides, she was in Tokyo. No one knew her here. Who cared what she did? And Tak was hot. Really hot.

Elle would go with him. It would be fun.

Now, if she could just figure out where to ditch her grannie panties . . .

FOURTEEN

ECHOSMITH: "COOL KIDS"

May 18, 2017
6:54 p.m.

Elle looked around for Win and was relieved to see he was, as was his preference at games, alone and off to the side of the field. This was perfect. Elle didn't want run-ins with anyone else. She had no interest in rehashing the details of the tennis match smack down or hearing more about Thatcher's suspension. She would forgo her usual spot in the stadium next to Aubrey and stand with Win. He would be calm. Centered. He always was. Elle put her head down and pretended to read something Very Important on her phone as she walked toward him.

Win must have come straight from the gym—he was wearing athletic shorts and a T-shirt from a charity half marathon they had run together in. It would be so like him to get in a quick workout before the game. Elle envied him this. No one would disparage his lack of shower, his bad hair, or the ratty old shorts from his Navy days. He was *Win Martin*; he could wear and do whatever he wanted. It was much harder to be his wife, the one who could easily be replaced.

As Elle approached, Win smiled and gave her a warm hug and kiss on top of the head. He smelled musky in a good and masculine way which would have made her melt with desire a decade ago. Why did his touch make her uncomfortable now? What had changed?

Although irritated with him earlier in the morning for not intervening in their children's argument, Elle was now thankful for her husband. He was safe. A place of refuge. Yes, she was lucky to have him. She would try harder.

"Did you get my text about the dates for Tokyo? Amber needs to make all the travel arrangements."

Elle stiffened as an enormous knot tightened in her empty stomach. She had resolved not to think about Japan. This was Four's night. "Yes, I'll call her tomorrow."

Win smiled. "I bet you're excited to go back to Tokyo."

"Yes! I am," Elle lied, and then felt guilty about lying. Win was so earnest, so sure he had done something to please her. If only he knew.

Eager to direct conversation away from their upcoming trip, Elle pointed to Four's team. "How do they look?"

"Good, but this is going to be a tougher game than the boys think."

Elle turned her attention toward the scene on the field.

There were swarms of Country Day players. They looked like ants in their matching warm-up suits, helmets, gloves, and cleats. Their identical equipment bags were all placed neatly along the sidelines next to the home bench, which was protected from the elements by a large canopy emblazoned with the school's crest. There were five or six coaches clad in navy polos and khaki pants leading drills, while two similarly dressed team managers filled bottles with water and Gatorade. Other staff members set up cameras to tape the game, readied laptops for player stats to be entered in, and tested the stadium's state-of-the-art sound system. "Hello! Welcome!"

It was all very impressive. Once upon a time, Elle would have looked upon it with envy and longing. How different it seemed now that she was a part of it all.

"Which one is the player Four was talking about this morning? The one they need to watch out for?"

Win nodded toward the field. "Guess."

Elle looked at the Kennedy players; there were far fewer of them. Although all their shorts were black, they weren't identical, and they didn't have jerseys. Instead, they wore white T-shirts under simple mesh pinnies. Elle was immediately drawn to a player double the size of the others. He was running the length the field, his thigh muscles bulging with each long stride. Despite being so physically large, he moved with an amazing grace, like a gazelle. Elle pointed to him and laughed. "I'm thinking that's him there—#21."

"Yeah. He's going to be tough to stop. They all are. They came to play."

Win was right. Kennedy's success that season had been a Cinderella story: a team of football players who had picked up lacrosse to keep in shape during the off-season. Led by a young and inspiring coach, they had surprised the high school lacrosse community by beating teams with more experience and talent with their athleticism and sheer will.

Still, Elle was convinced Country Day would win. There had been the signs.

There was also the fair weather to consider. As Regina had noted, it was a lovely evening, clear and warm—perfect conditions for the Country Day players to display their superior stick skills, honed after years of attending the best camps money could buy. If it were raining or cold, Elle might be more concerned. It was when things got uncomfortable for Country Day kids that their weaknesses began to show. They would work hard, but there was a limit.

It wasn't as if *they* were expected to get dirty in the muck of life with everyone else. At a certain level of discomfort, Country Day players decided it simply wasn't worth it—why step in the mud and fight for a ground ball? They were somehow above it all, because they could be. The Kennedy students would expect life to be difficult, for things to be hard, and they would play as if every moment counted.

As the game had all the makings of a John Hughes 1980s movie—rich prep-school kids versus fledgling public-school program—there was more press in attendance than was usual for a high school game. Elle noticed a cameraman from a local TV station seemed to have his lens focused on Four. She could understand why. With his boyish good-looks, he was TV-ready.

Jimmy would have looked just like Four. Elle was sure of it. Would her brother have also played lacrosse? No, he wouldn't have been into sports. He would have been artsy and musical. He would have started a band.

Elle wondered if Four was nervous. If so, he certainly he gave no indication of it. He appeared confident and wholly at ease, casually stretching with another player. Elle was excited for him, for this opportunity, yet she recognized he, too, was weak in the same way as all the other Country Day players.

What could she have done differently for Four? What should she do for him now?

Elle looked back toward the field and saw Ward pacing along the sidelines with two other dads, Charles and Westin.

The Three Wise Men. They epitomized the out-of-control competitiveness at Country Day Elle found so tiresome. They were the male equivalents to the women on the tennis court earlier that day.

Ward was a father living through his child. His chubby little sausage fingers had certainly never held a lacrosse stick, so it was imperative to him that his own son, Easton, excel. He pandered to the Country Day coaches like a desperate, sycophantic schoolboy jockeying for a spot at the cool kids' table, shamelessly kissing ass to promote his son. Not only would Easton get all A's, he'd also be the star of the team.

Charles was vested solely in the success of his own child, Cord, the only player he actively cheered for. Believing his experience as a high school football player qualified him to understand the subtleties of lacrosse better than anyone else, Charles was quick to point out the many mistakes he saw Country Day players make. But never Cord's. Cord didn't make mistakes—any penalties he received were all "bullshit calls." Opponents who played physically, but within the confines of the rules were "hacks" and "cheap." There wasn't a game where Charles didn't exchange heated words with a parent on the opposing team.

Westin had been a standout lacrosse player at a small DIII school and couldn't let go of his glory days. He knew the game and wouldn't let you forget it. When his son didn't make the best club team, he financed his own league. A firm believer in "daddy ball," Westin never subbed his son out, padded his stats, and nominated him, over other more talented players, for the All-Star games. Because he was an expert, he also believed it was his responsibility to complain loudly and frequently to the referees about their calls. "C'mon, learn the game" was Westin's go-to phrase as he shook his head and kicked the ground in disgust. If only everyone knew as much as he did.

Their wives were no better. They complained if their sons weren't starting or didn't get as many shifts as the other players. Some even used stopwatches to time how long their sons were on the field. (It was helpful to have supporting data when complaining to a coach.) A gaggle of menopausal-aged women mistaking themselves for high school cheerleaders, they fervently waved signs with enlarged pictures of their sons' heads on them during games. In between shrieks of praise, they bragged about how talented and athletic their prodigies were.

Elle was embarrassed by their vulgar display of . . . of what? Superiority? Is that what it was? *"Look at us! Look at out how wonderful we are!"*

No wonder everyone loved to hate Country Day.

The one thing all three men and their wives had in common was their unwavering desire to have their sons recruited to play Division I lacrosse. This meant everything. The ultimate status symbol. The most impressive piece of news to casually drop at a cocktail party.

To this end, Country Day families spent thousands of dollars on club teams, camps, recruiting showcases, and private lessons. Most players had personal trainers, nutritionists, speed and agility coaches, sports psychologists, and chiropractors. And because recruiting for top college programs began as early as the summer before high school started,

Country Day parents also routinely held their sons back in eighth grade so they would be bigger, stronger and faster than their contemporaries and the ones to catch the eyes of coaches. If players still didn't get picked up by the end of their freshman year, another common strategy to get recruited was for students to "reclassify" to a later high school graduating class than the one they were in. (Lacrosse teams were formed based on graduation year, not age, so a 2018 graduate could reclassify as a 2019 graduate and become eligible to play on teams with players a full year younger than they were, once again gaining an advantage.)

There was just one little hitch with this approach. Reclassified players needed to spend the year after their high school graduation as a "post-graduate" at prep school. Luckily, this wasn't a problem for Country Day students. $60,000 in "PG" tuition was thought to be a reasonable sum to ensure a verbal commitment to a good DI school. It wasn't cheating; it was a wise investment.

As such, almost all the Country Day players had either been held back or reclassified. Ward's son had done both. Easton was a nineteen-year-old senior with an additional PG year of high school ahead of him. Never mind that he would graduate from college as a twenty-four-year-old man. He was committed to Johns Hopkins. *Johns Hopkins!*

Elle couldn't understand the hysteria around playing a sport for which there was limited scholarship money and little to no financial gain post-collegiately. It wasn't equivalent to football, basketball, or baseball, where the best players could go on to earn millions in high-paying contracts and endorsements. Most professional lacrosse players needed second jobs and made far less than the annual tuition at the schools where post-grad years were spent.

Perhaps that was the point. Country Day players didn't need to worry about expensive tuitions, getting into exclusive colleges, or ensuring financial security after graduation. Success was a given for people like them. When all your peers were expected to do well, being a good lacrosse player was the best way to distinguish yourself. To be better than.

Elle found it all exhausting.

Then there was Win. Elle hugged her husband close, reminding herself again what a good man he was. If anyone had reason to be an unhinged sports dad, to seek the best for his son, it was Win. Yes, he had been a stand-out basketball player at the Naval Academy, but he had also turned down a chance to play for Georgetown, the school he had wanted to go to ever since he was a young boy.

Georgetown had offered Win only a partial scholarship and he didn't want to burden his parents with private-school tuition, not with his three younger sisters to consider. Win concluded going to the Naval Academy and getting a free education would be the best decision for his family, so off he went to a mediocre Navy team while Georgetown went on to win two NCAA Division I Basketball Championships.

Never once did Win express regret or bitterness at this cruel fate. He never brought it up at all. Instead, he volunteered to coach what-ever sports his children showed interested in. When Four wanted to play hockey over basketball, Win learned how to ice skate.

Sure, Win was proud of both of his children's athletic achievements—he was particularly pleased when the Navy lacrosse coach expressed inter-est in recruiting Four—yet he was perfectly content to stand by himself during games and observe the competitions calmly and with remarkable perspective.

That was the kind of man her husband was.

Elle wrapped her arm around Win's. She was lucky. She could be mar-ried to someone like Ward, or Charles, or Westin. Elle would make it work. She had to.

Warm-ups over, both teams stood along the sidelines. There was a palpable, electric energy in the air. The Country Day players huddled together, jumping up and down, firing themselves up for the biggest game of the year.

Elle was excited for Four. She was. Yet as she looked over at the Kennedy bench, then back to the Country Day players, and then to Ward, Charles, and Westin, a part of her—a rather large part—suddenly and unexpectedly wanted the Kennedy players to win the game.

It would mean more to them.

Win or lose, the Country Day players would go home to their sport courts, their media rooms, their finished basements with wine cellars, granite bars, pool tables, and sports memorabilia signed by professional athletes hanging on the walls. They would still attend expensive camps, get new gear, and go on to elite colleges. Sure, holding the state championship title would make them happy, proud even, but it was somehow expected.

Elle looked at the Three Wise Men again. With their manicured hands, they leaned against lacrosse sticks of their own, as if at any minute they might be called in to play. In their bespoke suits and Ferragamo shoes—*they* hadn't gone to the gym first—they seemed entirely out of place standing near the raw and athletic Kennedy players.

Yes, Elle wanted Kennedy to win. To absolutely crush the Three Wise Men's massive egos. Could she really feel this way? Wasn't it wrong to root against her own son? And what about all the signs pointing to a Country Day victory?

As the whistle blew and the game began, Elle was confused. Had she somehow misinterpreted the signs?

FIFTEEN

BØRNS: "ELECTRIC LOVE"

January 28, 1994
6:45 p.m.

"I would think your boyfriend could have come up with a more original name for his club. 'Samantha's' is a bit uninspired, wouldn't you agree?" Mitch swirled around in the white leather and chrome barstool at Tak's nightclub while Elle helped herself to a beer behind the bar. Opening time wasn't until nine o'clock, so save a bartender who had gone to the stockroom to check inventory, they were the only two there.

"Not for someone whose first exposure to American culture was the TV show *Bewitched*. And c'mon, everyone loved Samantha. Even *I* had a crush on her." Elle tried to be positive even though Mitch was being disingenuous—before meeting Tak, Samantha's had been one of his favorite clubs. The drinks were cheap, good dance music was played, and—in another nod to Tak's infatuation with American TV—it had been fashioned in the mold of *Miami Vice*: pastels, fake palm trees, and bouncers dressed like Sonny and Rico. Mitch loved how over-the-top cheesy it was and had originally been thrilled to learn Tak was the club's owner. "He has a big dick, *and* owns a nightclub where we can drink for free. Score!"

Mitch's initial enthusiasm for Tak had waned, however, once his status with Elle had progressed from that of an occasional hookup to boyfriend. A few booty calls now and again were one thing, but Elle's relationship with Tak was beginning to interfere with her and Mitch's routine and that was not okay.

Elle got it. She didn't blame Mitch. She'd probably be just as jealous if he suddenly had a boyfriend around. They had a good thing going, and the introduction of Tak into the equation altered their balance. Elle didn't want things with Mitch to change. She was trying hard to maintain both relationships, but it was becoming more and more difficult.

The problem was, as much as Elle loved Mitch and valued their friendship, she had never been as physically attracted to a man as she was to Tak. He was so confident, always in charge, always in control. His overt masculinity turned her on. And Tak was the first man who had ever put Elle on pedestal. He showered her with compliments and gave her thoughtful gifts every few days: a U2 bootleg cassette; a box of chocolates; a bouquet of her favorite flowers, yellow Gerber daisies. Who wouldn't like that?

Mitch remained unimpressed. What did they even talk about? Tak could barely speak English and the only thing he ever seemed interested in discussing was soccer. He was increasingly territorial over Elle, had no sense of humor, and no real friends. His only companions, Mike and Johnny, were paid employees—bodyguards for a little rich kid pretending to be a tough guy. Mitch worried he was trouble.

It was true that Elle and Tak didn't engage in much deep and meaningful discussion. He could understand most of what she said; that was enough. She found the quiet a welcome break from all the inane babbling at the Big YAC. Elle could always speak to Tak in Japanese if she needed to, but she had kept her knowledge of the language a secret. Being privy to conversations others believed she couldn't understand had its benefits.

Yes, things suited Elle just fine the way they were and she wished Mitch could be more supportive. To appease him, she teased, "Well, Captain Nelson was also pretty easy on the eyes. We could always call it by that name."

"Meh. I still say he could have done better." Mitch looked around the bar. "Where is Mr. Pink, anyway?"

Mitch was really gunning for a fight now; he knew Elle didn't like it when he referred to Tak with this nickname. (He had come up with it shortly after they had all gone to see the movie *Reservoir Dogs* together—whereas Tak loved the movie, Mitch found it distasteful, too gratuitous in its violence and a perfect metaphor for everything he disliked about Tak.)

Still, Elle refused to take the bait. She didn't have it in her to argue. The late nights drinking at the Big YAC and then the after-partying at Samantha's were taking a toll on her. She wanted nothing more than a mellow, drama-free evening. "He's upstairs, in his office. He had some work to do. Why don't we call it a night and go back to the apartment and veg out? I went to the video store yesterday; we could get caught up on *Twin Peaks*."

"Umm, how about 'Things I don't want to hear for two hundred dollars.'" Mitch shook his head. "Seriously, Elle, that's weak. It's been ages since we've had a proper adventure."

Although it went against every fiber in her being, Elle knew she had to rally. Mitch was her best friend. If a night out with her would make him feel better, she would do it. If only she weren't so tired . . .

"You're right, I'm in!" Elle tried to sound excited. She pointed to the stacks of alcohol on the shelves behind her in the bar. "What's your pleasure? A brewski? Perhaps a shot?"

"I'd take another Kirin."

"You got it!" As Elle drew Kirin from a tap, she had a flash of her mom doing the exact same thing in the dark bar from her childhood. Elle shivered uncomfortably and got goose bumps, but rationalized what *she* was doing was different. It's not like she was going to spend the rest of her life working at a bar. Elle was just having fun. She and Mitch were smart. They were going to do cool, interesting things. This was simply a little pause before hitting play on their real lives.

Elle didn't often think of her mom. Their last contact had been in December when Elle had sent her a Christmas card with two 10,000-yen notes inside. It was as impractical a gesture as it was impersonal. What would Bobbie do with Japanese yen? Maybe it was Elle's subconscious way of proving her success; she could toss around $200, no problem.

In return, her mom had sent a tiny red bear. Like Elle would want a stuffed animal called a Beanie Baby. It was a lame gift, but she didn't expect anything more. Bobbie simply didn't get her, nor had she ever tried to.

Whatever.

Elle didn't want to think about her mom. It would inevitably lead to thoughts of Jimmy. No, she needed to focus on having fun with Mitch and she could sense from his body language he was still in a pissy mood. She should change it up. "So where should we go? Do you want to try someplace new?"

Mitch ignored her question. "What exactly is it that Johnny and Mike do for Mr. Pink, anyway? I mean, don't you think it's odd the way they follow him around like two lost little puppy dogs?"

"I don't know," Elle answered truthfully. She hadn't ever given it much thought. Maybe their relationship with Tak *was* strange, but who cared? If the evening was going to be saved, Elle needed to get Mitch out of his funk. She tried another approach, asking, "What do you think about the bartender, Kenji—he's cute, no?"

Elle had noticed the way Mitch lingered around the bar when Kenji was working and suspected there was something there. Kenji was his type—lithe and pretty—and he seemed flattered by Mitch's attention.

"He's sweet, but I don't think he plays for my team."

"You don't think so? I get the feeling he kind of likes you."

"Well, maybe, but I'm not so sure this would be the right place to test the theory. I don't think your boyfriend would approve."

Oh, so that's what this is all about. Mitch was upset she hadn't told Tak he was gay. Maybe he had a right to be. "I'm going to tell him. Really. It just hasn't come up yet, that's all. I can go tell him right now if you want."

Mitch shook his head. "I wouldn't want to interrupt his . . . working." He emphasized the word *working,* putting quotation marks with his hands around it. "Seriously, why would a guy with an MBA from the University of Tokyo own a nightclub? Shouldn't he have some big-time job?"

Elle sighed. She really didn't want to fight. "Tak's dad is high up at Sony, so he has a ton of pressure on him. He just wants to take some time off before starting an office job." Elle wanted to add "kind of like us" but thought better of it.

Mitch smirked. "How nice. Lucky Mr. Pink."

Elle was annoyed. She was doing her bit, why couldn't Mitch? Maybe they should leave. Being at Tak's place wasn't a good idea. "Let's chug these and bolt."

"Alrighty." Mitch started to put his mug to his lips, but set it down when he saw Kenji approach, carrying several cases of beer. "Do you need some help?"

"I okay!" Kenji tried a half bow, which caused the heavy cases to shift unsteadily in his arms.

"Here, let me help you." Mitch stood and lifted a case of beer out of Kenji's arms.

"Ah . . . thank you!"

Elle saw this as a perfect opportunity to leave Mitch and Kenji alone to talk. "I'm going to go say good-bye to Tak, then we can go, okay?"

Mitch nodded. "Yeah, sure."

Elle hoped getting his flirt on with Kenji would kill the bug up Mitch's ass. If not, it was going to be a long night. She walked past the dance floor and up a long stairway to Tak's office. As the room also had a futon and a small bathroom with a shower in it, her boyfriend often crashed there when he was too tired or too drunk to go home.

Elle was trying not to think about all the drunken girls Tak had likely entertained on his office futon when two young Japanese men suddenly bolted down the stairs past her, nearly knocking her over. *WTF?* She made a mental note to tell Tak; he would make sure it didn't happen again. Elle reached the top of the stairs and Tak's office. The door was closed. She knocked. When no one answered, she knocked again. "Tak, it's me, Elle."

Johnny opened the door, then quickly stepped into the hallway, shutting the door behind him. He bowed deferentially to Elle and asked her to wait a minute. As he spoke, his tongue protruded out from behind a broken front tooth. It reminded Elle of a snake preparing to strike. She wondered why he wouldn't get this fixed. It wasn't a good look. Maybe he thought it made him look tough.

Elle was irritated. "Let me in."

"*Hai. Hai.*" Johnny nodded but stood in front of the door, blocking Elle's entry.

"Seriously, Johnny. I'm not in the mood for this." Elle was being bitchy and taking her frustration with Mitch out on Johnny, but she couldn't help it. This was pissing her off. "I'm going in!" Elle pushed her way past Johnny and opened the door.

As she entered, there was a bit of commotion. Clearly, Elle had walked in on something; she just wasn't sure what.

Tak hastily shut his desk drawer. "Blondie!"

This was another nickname Elle didn't like—talk about uninspiring. Even worse, with Tak's heavy accent, it came out sounding more like "Brondie," but Elle chose not to complain—there were worse things than a stupid pet name. Her college boyfriend had referred to her as "babe" which had been equally as clichéd.

"You are okay?" Tak seemed surprised, yet pleased, to see her. He turned to Mike and told him to leave—he would meet up with him and Johnny in a little bit. Mike nodded and bowed politely to Elle before exiting.

"Yeah, I'm fine. What's going on?" Elle surveyed the room, looking for evidence of what she had interrupted.

"Nothing. Everything good." Tak cupped Elle's face gently in his hands. She loved it when he did this. It felt protective, like he would do anything to keep her safe.

Elle put her head against his shoulder. "I wish we could just go back to your place. I'm exhausted."

"Ah so . . . we can." Tak brushed his hands through Elle's hair, pausing to admire it.

"No, I need to spend some time with Mitch. We haven't hung out much lately. Besides, you have to work."

"So . . . Maybe I have idea for you."

Elle looked at him expectantly.

Tak backtracked. "Maybe you get angry?"

"Angry? Why would I get angry?"

Tak tilted his head to the side, like he was skeptical of saying more.

"Tell me! I won't get angry, I promise."

"Ah so, okay." Tak walked behind his desk, opened the top drawer, and carefully took out a mirror with lines of white powder on it. "This help you, no more tired."

Cocaine.

So *that's* what they had been doing when she knocked on the door. The guys who raced past her on the stairs must have delivered the drug. Elle should have guessed as much. Tak was not much of a drinker; his cheeks would turn a bright red after a single beer and this embarrassed him. He probably used coke because it was a good way to hide being high.

Elle had never done drugs before. Well, not really. She had once smoked pot from a large bong with her college boyfriend in his fraternity house but didn't like it. Her lungs ached from the burn of the drug and she became paranoid, worried everyone would know what she had done. Having no desire to experience that type of paralyzing anxiety again, Elle had thereafter always politely declined when joints were handed out at parties. Many of her sorority sisters had encouraged her to experiment with ecstasy and mushrooms, but she always passed on those offers as well. Nancy Reagan's "Just Say No" campaign had been effective; Elle was convinced drugs presented too much of a risk.

Perhaps sensing her hesitation, Tak put his arms around Elle and reassured her. "It's very safe one, Blondie. No worry. Just little bit, you no more tired."

Elle considered the choice before her. Many times in the past year she had made decisions which at other points in her life she would have never considered. To smoke cigarettes. To get drunk at work. To take a job as a hostess. To have sex with someone she had just met at a bar. Unfathomable actions in a different time and place, but it all seemed different while living in Tokyo. It wasn't real. Elle was in a pretend life, one in which there were no consequences.

If Mitch knew she was flirting with the idea of doing coke, he would be livid. He had known too many people who abused the drug. The high was too good; once experienced, it was too hard to pass up. But Elle was so tired. And she needed to rally. Having a good night out with Mitch was necessary to get their friendship back on track. Elle looked at the white powder. It reminded her of snow. *How bad can it be?*

"Okay, I'll do a little—but not too much."

Tak smiled and led Elle to the desk. He picked up a rolled yen note and held it against the right side of his nose. Putting a finger against his left nostril, he leaned over the mirror and snorted. "Just breathing in, like this."

Tak handed Elle the yen note and she mimicked his actions, bending her head over the mirror. Afterwards, she sniffled—it felt a little like she needed to blow her nose—but that was it. It wasn't such a big deal.

Tak wiped his finger across the mirror and rubbed the residue along Elle's lips. Her mouth tingled, similar to the first time she had smoked a clove cigarette. It was nice, a little daring and exciting.

Tak kissed her. It was a hard kiss. An urgent one. He pushed her back against the wall and put his hand up her skirt, deftly reaching under her pantyhose. He pulled her G-string to the side. Elle was glad she had finally taken Mitch's advice and ditched her grannie panties in favor of sexy thongs. She moaned with pleasure and anticipation as Tak explored her with his fingers. She didn't know if she was extra turned on from the coke, but this felt good. She wanted Tak.

He tried to move her toward the futon. Elle imagined all the girls he had brought up to his office. No, she wouldn't go to the futon. They would do it right there, against the wall. Elle returned Tak's kiss; her tongue was tingly now, too. She reached down to undo his belt and unzip his pants, wondering why she had been so afraid to try cocaine. She could handle it.

◆ ◆ ◆

8:29 p.m.

Elle bounced down the stairs from Tak's apartment. She was no longer tired—far from it. She was invigorated, alive. Sex with Tak had been incredible. She'd had such an intense orgasm, her toes had gone numb. It was insane. In the afterglow, the two had celebrated by doing another line. *Why not?* Tak was right. It wasn't dangerous, and Elle felt great. Fucking incredible, actually.

Up ahead at the bar, Elle saw Mitch and Kenji engaged in animated conversation. Mitch was gesticulating wildly and Kenji was smiling, nodding his head agreeably. This was good, very good. Elle almost hated to interrupt them but figured she could help as Mitch's wingman. She approached the two of them and put her hand on Mitch's shoulder. "Hi, guys."

Mitch turned in his stool. "Why, hello there, doll."

Nice. He was back in his happy place. Her plan had worked.

Mitch eyed Elle as she sat down next to him, as if studying her for clues. She panicked, worried he might correctly guess what she had been up to.

Mitch winked at her. "So, a quickie in the office—overrated/underrated?"

Phew! He didn't know about the cocaine—only the sex. "Underrated. Most definitely underrated. How are things here?"

Mitch raised his eyebrows and nodded. "I've got to go underrated as well. Very pleasantly, surprisingly underrated."

Elle smiled. God, she felt good. Clearheaded in a way she had never experienced before. Everything made sense. Elle had *the best, the most interesting* ideas running through her head. She couldn't wait to get them all out. To share them with Mitch. And she had so much energy. She needed to dance. Elle turned toward Kenji.

"You gotta do a shot with us. I think we're in for an epic night."

It *was* going to be a good night. She and Mitch would have a blast together, just like old times. *Definitely, for sure.* And then there was Kenji. She could help Mitch with him, follow through on her Halloween promise to hook him up. Wouldn't that be something! Once they were both in romantic relationships, all would be well again. Maybe they could even double date. Try all those restaurants they wanted to. They could even go skiing. She had always wanted to ski. Or to Hong Kong! She could buy some clothes made of silk. That would be awesome.

Yes, after tonight, order would be restored to Elle's universe. She could feel it.

SIXTEEN

The Who: "Behind Blue Eyes"

May 18, 2017
8:40 p.m.

At the end of regulation, the game was tied, 11–11. As Win predicted, the Kennedy players had come out determined, like they had something to prove. They played physically, sending a message with each hit that they weren't going to go down without a fight. Kennedy also had the support of a partisan crowd, thoroughly on the side of the underdogs. Fans cheered wildly every time #21 ran through the Country Day players unimpeded, warding them off like they were nothing more than annoying little pests. *He* didn't need to repeat a grade to look impressive.

For their part, the Country Day team played with discipline and patience, their advanced stick skills on full display. Their sophisticated offense was also difficult to defend against, and they were able to take advantage of Kennedy penalties and score on man-up opportunities. It had been a close game all along, and throughout the first four quarters there was never more than a one-point differential.

Elle was conflicted. She was happy for the Kennedy players; they were playing out of their heads, beyond their abilities. The Country Day parents and players were duly humbled, which was satisfying. Yet each time Four was hit—and it had been often that game: big, tough, punishing hits—Elle's enthusiasm for a Kennedy win waned.

Now, with the game tied and going into overtime, maternal love ruled. Elle decided she did, in fact, want Four's team to win. She gripped Win's arm tightly—despite all the signs pointing to a Country Day victory, she was still nervous for Four.

The crowd cheered wildly as the players ran onto the field and lined up for the face-off. It was sudden death. The first team to score would win.

The referee dropped the ball and two face-off middies crouched down and fought for its possession. An intense battle ensued, with the Kennedy player losing his footing and the ball popping loose. In one swift, impressive movement, Cord ran in and scooped the ground ball into his long stick.

"That's what I'm talking about. Ya!" Charles fist pumped into the air.

Cord quickly ran down the field and passed the ball to Easton.

"Let's go E!" Ward yelled, cupping his hands around his mouth in the shape of a megaphone.

Easton tried a quick dodge to the right but couldn't get past the large and intimidating defender covering him. Undeterred, he turned rapidly in a quick half circle and fired a low, hockey-style shot. It wasn't a strong shot, and the Kennedy goalie made an easy save.

The Kennedy sideline burst in excitement as their goalie looked for a player to pass the ball to. Under pressure, he rushed and made a high, looping throw to a defender covered by Four. Seeing the bad pass, Four moved in front of the goalie's intended target, jumped in the air and intercepted the ball. Within seconds, he was in front of the net and the startled goalie. Four lifted his stick high above the goalie's head, then swiftly moved it down low, and then back up again, shooting the ball in the corner of the net before the Kennedy goalie had time to react.

GOAL!

Country Day had won the state championship.

There was a loud roar in the stadium. Elle realized she had been holding her breath. She exhaled and allowed herself to feel joy. The signs had been right, as they always were. Why, after all these years, had Elle bothered to question them? She knew better.

Elle and Win joined the celebration of players, students, and parents on the field, congratulating other fans along the way.

Ward held his hand out to Win. "What a great game! How lucky was it that their goalie made that terrible clear?"

"Lucky?!" What an asshole. Ward couldn't even give Four any credit for his interception or his shot? If Easton had been the one to score, Ward would have arranged a parade in his honor.

"You're right, it was a great break for the team." Unfailingly gracious, Win shook Ward's hand.

How can he be so nice?

Ward turned to Elle. "Can you believe that whack-a-doodle Regina? I can't believe she gave Easton a C on that paper. I know that was an A paper. You know why? Because I wrote it! Easton didn't have time with the game coming up. He got a C because she's a feminist cow and didn't agree with my argument that Title IX is no longer necessary." Ward waved his fat fingers dismissively. "Unbelievable!"

For the third time that day, Elle was uncomfortable and wanted to run away. She was considering how she could best excuse herself when Four approached; a beaming Tabby wrapped around his arm.

"Congratulations, honey. What a great game!" Elle hugged Four. She was genuinely happy for him. Jimmy would have been so excited, he would have lifted him up the air.

Win put his arm around Four and shook his hand. "Great job, my man. I knew you had him beat after the second fake."

"Thanks. I wasn't so sure. He was so good up high all game."

Elle observed her son and husband and their obvious love for one another. Yes, she was lucky. Very lucky.

Tabby turned to Elle, the 4 on her cheek smeared from tears of joy. "Oh my gosh! I totally thought I was going to throw up! I was sooo nervous!" *Face with gritted teeth.*

"Nice work, bro!" Brynnie arrived on the field.

Registering the 4 on Brynnie's cheek with surprise and then gratitude, Four extended his arms toward his sister. "Thanks so much for coming."

Elle's children hugged. It was a nice and genuine moment, like something taken straight out of an after-school special on TV. Elle was grateful for this, for her family, yet . . . why didn't she feel happier?

What's wrong with me?

"Excuse me. Neil Burton—I'm with Channel 9 News. I'm wondering if I could have a word with this young man."

"Yes, of course." Win stepped aside to make room for the reporter and the cameraman accompanying him.

Tabby's eyes widened in a combination of astonishment and pride. "My boyfriend. Being interviewed for TV. OMG!" *Smiley face, smiley face, smiley face! #howcoolisthis?*

Tabby grabbed Elle's arm. "Did you know he had four goals? Four, #4, four goals! Isn't that *so awesome*?" *A whole row of smiley faces, a thumbs-up, and several pink hearts.*

Elle watched Four as he was interviewed on camera. He was incredibly poised and confident, like he understood that this was what was expected of someone like him and he was prepared for it.

Elle was filled with a surge of pride, yet something about the scene made her uncomfortable. Was she confusing her son's calm demeanor with what she hoped it wasn't—an innate sense of superiority?

Is my son one of them?

Elle saw Ward and Kit behind Four. They were talking with Aubrey and their attention appeared directed toward the Martin family. Aubrey waved to Elle and then turned to Kit, her hand covering her mouth conspiratorially as she spoke to her.

And . . . BOOM!

There it was. Little Miss Schadenfreude busy at work.

Elle knew exactly what Aubrey had whispered to Kit. She was giving life to the hushed talk, the whispers and innuendo regarding Brynnie's sexual preferences. Elle should have known better. She should have apologized for her and Brynnie's behavior. Aubrey would not cede her position as Queen Bee.

No, Aubrey would go after Elle with everything she had. She would make it personal. She would make sure it hurt.

And so what if Brynnie is a lesbian? Much the same as the karate lessons, the short haircut, and attending Reed over Brown, it wouldn't be what Elle would choose for her daughter. But still, in that moment of Aubrey's abject cruelty, Elle knew without a doubt she loved Brynnie unconditionally. Gay or straight, it didn't matter. Elle cared more about her daughter's happiness than she cared about what others thought. She only regretted her inability to protect Brynnie from the vicious insinuations, the snickers, and the disapproval. Brown acceptance, state lacrosse title, international business deal—so what? Brynnie is a lesbian; things *aren't* so perfect for the Martins after all.

Fuck them. Fuck all of them. Aubrey's whispers behind a covered mouth revealed the truth. These people were not Elle's friends. Not really.

They all simply played their parts as friends exceedingly well. A luminous, fun-loving group going to dinner parties, on ski trips, playdates, and charity events together. Living the life. Elle had to admit she enjoyed these times and was flattered to be included, to belong. So she had willingly played along, ignoring the underlying tension, the weariness and the competition. Everything was fine if they were all doing equally well. It was when someone was perceived as doing better or having more—that's when jealousy and envy emerged in full swing.

Elle looked around, taking in the group celebrating on the field. What a perfect picture they presented. All smiles and happiness, they were a virtual Ralph Lauren advertisement of the American dream. Winners, one and all, smug in the satisfying glow of their own success. They *did* have it all.

Or so they wanted everyone to think.

Elle knew better. She had ample experience in reading people. She watched and listened carefully and saw the cracks in their facades of perfection. The cheating, the anxiety attacks, the living beyond their means. It was all there if you looked closely enough and paid attention to the clues: body language, comments made after one too many drinks, what was left unsaid. Elle was simply more careful. More guarded. But she couldn't control everything. How could she best protect Brynnie?

"Elle, come here. We're getting a picture!" Aubrey waved excitedly to Elle, just as a good friend would. A friend who was genuinely thrilled for her son's success, not one plotting and scheming to cause her misery.

Elle dutifully entered the group and stood next to Win, Brynnie, and Tabby. The lacrosse team spread out in front of them, holding their large championship trophy. The photographer made a cheesy joke that he didn't need to instruct anyone to smile before taking the picture, yet it took all of Elle's resolve to smile convincingly.

"Are you happy, Mom? Are you living your dream?"

Elle wanted to cry out in despair, but she wouldn't give Aubrey the satisfaction. Instead, she focused on the one bit of knowledge that would make her smile genuine. Yes, Aubrey could order wine in perfect French, mastered after a year abroad in Paris; she knew the monogram on her cotton paper stationary should be engraved, not flat-printed; and she was so thin that she wore her clothes like a coat hanger. But Aubrey would have no idea what the word *schadenfreude* meant. Elle was smarter than she was. She had that.

Click.

The photographer got his shot. A group terrifically proud, celebrating their undeniable superiority with a happiness that teetered obnoxiously close to gloating. The picture would be on the Country Day website within the hour. Admissions would go up and alumni donations would come pouring in. People liked winners. It was good for business.

SEVENTEEN

February 21, 1994
6:45 p.m.

I look like shit.
Elle leaned over the sink and scrutinized her reflection in the mirror. Her face looked puffy. Had she gained weight? Elle turned and looked at her backside. Her ass still looked good in the hot-pink gown Tak had bought for her. She hadn't gained weight; maybe she was just PMSing.

Yes, that was probably it. Elle always got bloated right before her period. When was she due next? It was hard to say for sure because she had misplaced her birth control pills and her cycle was off. It was a pain in the ass to get the pill in Japan, but Elle needed to get a new supply soon. She and Tak had been having unprotected sex over the past few weeks and it worried her. She would insist he wear a rubber until she got back on the pill.

The door to the bathroom was ajar, and Elle could hear Tak in the other room with Mike and Johnny. She leaned in closer to hear what they were saying, glad they all remained unaware of her ability to speak Japanese. From bits and pieces of conversations she wasn't meant to understand,

131

Elle had discovered two important pieces of information: Tak was dealing drugs—the young men she had seen charging down the stairs had actually been customers, and he was running an illegal gambling business out of Samantha's—he sponsored high-stakes games for preferred clients with a buy-in of a million yen.

These revelations didn't bother Elle in the least. It wasn't as though Tak was peddling crack to school kids. He only sold blow, and just to people he knew—Samantha's regulars looking to have a good time. And the gambling operation? It was more intriguing than anything else. Elle was anxious for the opportunity to peek in on one of the games to see what it was all about.

Elle knew better than to mention either of these things to Mitch. Despite her efforts to make their friendship a priority, he was still prickly about her relationship with Tak. This news would only confirm Mitch's opinion of her boyfriend—he was nothing more than a rich kid playing the part of a two-bit thug. And so what if he was? They were all pretending to be something other than what they were.

From the tone of his voice, Elle could tell Tak was pissed off. She had learned he had a short temper and often took it out on Mike and Johnny. Here again, Elle wasn't concerned. Tak was always sweet and accommodating with her, and she didn't blame him for getting angry with those two. They got on her nerves as well. Especially Johnny. Elle didn't trust him and sensed that behind his broken-toothed smile lay a seething resentment of her. She had taken to treating them both as nothing more than Tak's employees at her disposal to order around like errand boys. Elle often had them bring her dinner, drop off her dry cleaning, and give her rides in Tak's Mercedes.

Speaking rapidly and in a higher pitch than normal, Tak was complaining about being taken advantage of. He referenced the stockroom several times. Curious to hear more, Elle stepped out of the bathroom. Tak looked up as she entered and his posture softened. He eyed her approvingly. "You looking very beautiful, Blondie."

"Thanks." Elle smiled appreciatively, even though she didn't like the dress. In addition to its shocking pink color, it was strapless and covered in sparkly sequins which made it garish and loud, like something a freshman would pick for their first prom. Even so, Elle wouldn't complain. She would indulge Tak in the same way she did with his use of the stupid name Blondie. What did it matter what she wore?

Elle approached Tak and kissed him, ignoring both Mike and Johnny. It was spiteful not to acknowledge them, but she didn't care. She rubbed her thumb and forefinger affectionately along Tak's cheek, asking, "Is everything okay?"

"Yes, fine." Tak kissed the back of her neck, putting his hand territorially on her ass.

Elle was not placated. What was going on in the stockroom? Was there a game? Convinced Tak would be more forthcoming if Johnny and Mike weren't in the room, Elle was going to ask them to go fetch her a cold drink when, in commanding Japanese, Tak ordered them to go to the stockroom and wait for him.

Something was definitely up. Elle was intrigued. "What's going on?"

Tak ran his fingers through her long blonde hair. "Nothing, Blondie. You no worry." He drew her close and they kissed for a few minutes before he abruptly pulled her away. "I wish you no more work hostess. It no good."

Elle's job had become a sore subject with Tak. He was jealous she spent so much time with other men and wanted her to quit, but Elle wasn't ready to leave the Big YAC just yet. She was making good money and the Mitch & Elle's Adventure Jar was filling up quickly. Soon, she and Mitch would be able to afford their trip to Europe.

Elle rubbed Tak's back sweetly. "Don't worry, I'll be back early . . ."

Tak frowned.

"And I can stay with you tonight," Elle offered, knowing it would only cause more problems—Mitch was expecting her to go out with him after she got off work. But what else could she do? Elle didn't want to argue with Tak. He and Mitch's demands on her time were exhausting. It was a constant juggling act to try to keep them both happy.

"I no like, better you quit."

"I don't have to be at work for another hour." Elle started to kiss Tak again. Maybe if they had sex it would reassure him he had nothing to worry about.

Tak pulled away. "I no time."

Elle was surprised—and hurt. Tak had never turned her down before. Something really serious must be going on. "Are you sure everything is okay?"

"Yes. Yes." Tak adjusted his tie, walked over to his desk, and pointed to a mirror with a few lines of cocaine on it. "You want?"

"Yeah, sure, why not?" Elle leaned over the mirror and snorted a line. She had never intended to regularly use cocaine, but she couldn't see any downside to it. Conversation flowed easily when she was high, so nights at the Big YAC practically flew by. Better yet, Elle could drink like a fish when amped up on coke and more drinking equaled more money in commissions. It was a win-win.

Tak reached into his desk drawer and took out a baggy full of white powder. He handed it to Elle. "So . . . you keep. You need at work, you have. I see you back here. Midnight." Tak kissed Elle, a little dismissively she thought, and walked out without saying more.

Disappointed by her boyfriend's brush off, Elle sat on his desk and looked at the baggy. It made her nervous to think about taking cocaine into the Big YAC. She was having a hard-enough time hiding her habit from Mitch. What if Mae-san found out?

Elle heard the door to the office open. She quickly put the baggie in her purse and looked up to see Kenji. He was holding a case of Tak's favorite rum.

Seeing her, Kenji jumped back, startled. He bowed awkwardly with the case still in his hands, apologizing, "I very sorry. I no think you here."

Elle waived her hand. "It's fine; don't worry. I'm happy to see you."

Elle *was* glad to see him; she was convinced there was something between Kenji and Mitch. Knowing neither of them would ever make the first move—Mitch was afraid of rejection and Kenji was incredibly shy—she was determined to set them up. It would be perfect: once Mitch was having sex of his own, he'd lighten up about her relationship with Tak.

Elle's plan was to move slowly, first gaining Kenji's trust. Once that was accomplished, she would arrange a date for the two of them in time for Mitch's birthday in May. It would be the perfect gift. She smiled at Kenji. "It's so nice of you to bring that up here for Tak. I hope you know he appreciates everything you do."

Kenji set down the case of rum. "Thank you. Tak-san good boss."

"Yes, he is, but he can be tough. If you ever have any problems with him, you come to me, okay?"

"Yes, yes. Thank you." Kenji nodded his head in quick half bows.

"We should all go out sometime . . . I bet Mitch would love to join us."

At the mention of Mitch's name, Kenji's cheeks turned a bright, hot red. "Yes, yes. I very much like. Thank you."

Elle was pleased by Tak's reaction—she *knew* there was something there. "Great, I'll work on putting something together." That was enough for now. She didn't want to make Kenji uncomfortable. There was still plenty of time. "Do you know where Tak went?"

"I'm no sure, maybe he stockroom?"

"Okay, thanks. I think I'll go check on him." Elle grabbed her purse—the cocaine still in it—and walked down the stairs into Samantha's, eager to see what Tak was up to. What could possibly be more compelling than sex with her?

The TV behind the bar was on, showing a broadcast from the Winter Olympics in Lillehammer. Elle didn't particularly care about sports—or the Olympics, for that matter—but the story of Nancy Kerrigan and Tonya Harding had captured her attention. She stopped to see if the figure skating competition was on.

Elle hoped Nancy Kerrigan would win the gold medal. It would be the appropriate karmic reward for what she had been through, and she deserved it. Although everything about the figure skater—the way she looked, talked, and moved with such grace and ease—gave the appearance of someone born into wealth and privilege, she was actually from a modest background. Nancy Kerrigan had *earned* her success. She had been determined, she had paid attention, and she had made it happen. Elle was inspired by her example.

An alpine skiing event was on and nothing about figure skating, so Elle grabbed a bottle of beer from behind the bar—*why not?*—and walked down the hallway to the stockroom. It was cold, and she shivered involuntarily as she drank the beer. The door to the stockroom was closed; she put her ear against it, hoping to hear something.

Nothing.

Elle considered knocking but decided against it. She was Tak's girlfriend; she could do whatever she wanted. She opened the heavy steel door and walked in, unnoticed. Tak, Johnny, and Mike were all standing with their backs toward the door, huddled around a young man tied to the back of a chair. Elle couldn't be sure, but he looked like one of the guys who had almost knocked her over on the stairs a few weeks ago. It was hard to tell; the man's face was purple and bleeding and both of his eyes were swollen shut. He yelled out in agony as Tak punched him in the face. Shocked, Elle dropped her beer bottle on the concrete floor. What had she walked in on?

The sound of glass shattering got Tak's attention. He turned and looked blankly at Elle, like he didn't recognize her. Strands of hair had come out of his ponytail and he was sweating. He pushed the stray hairs away from his face with a bloody hand. His pinky ring was covered with a thick, deep red.

For several minutes, no one said anything. The only sound in the room was a low whimper from the beaten man in the chair. Elle was too stunned to move.

Finally, Tak approached her. "Sorry, Blondie. You no see this." He put his arm around her and led her out the door, apologizing again, "Sorry you see."

Elle stood in the hall with Tak. Through the open door she could see Johnny repeatedly shove his knee into the beaten man's face. She turned her head away, ashamed of the violence. Were they beating him up because she had complained about him almost knocking her over?

No, it couldn't be that. Elle had been distracted by the cocaine in Tak's office that day and had forgotten to mention what had happened. Still, what could this guy possibly have done to deserve this treatment? He couldn't have been more than eighteen or nineteen years old. Elle should go help him. Tell Johnny to leave him alone.

Tak took Elle's face in his hands. They were warm and smelled like metal. Was that the odor of blood? "It's okay now, Blondie. You no worry." Tak gently kissed Elle behind the neck.

Elle smelled beer on Tak's breath and felt his hair, warm and damp from sweat, brush against her cheek. As he leaned in and kissed her open-mouthed with his tongue, she tasted salt. Tak stared intently into Elle's eyes as he explored her body with his hands. He whispered in her ear, "I love you."

He loves me.

Elle was horrified by what she had seen, offended and disgusted by the violence, yet she couldn't deny an overwhelming feeling of arousal. She wanted Tak. All her senses yearned for him.

How could that be? Was it the cocaine?

It didn't matter. Elle couldn't resist.

He loves me.

She gave in, pulling Tak close and kissing him passionately. Tak returned her kiss and lifted her arms above her head, holding them up with one hand. With his other hand, he reached under her dress and deftly pulled her G-string off.

With the door to the stockroom still open, Elle knew Johnny and Mike and the beaten man could see what she and Tak were doing. She didn't care. In fact, she kind of liked it.

He loves me.

She helped Tak remove her thong and unbuckled his pants. Elle felt him, hard and ready. Tak lifted her off the ground and she wrapped her legs tightly around him. He pressed her back to the wall and entered her with a single deep thrust.

Elle closed her eyes and moaned with pleasure. For a split second, she remembered the misplaced birth control pills—she should make Tak wear a rubber—but she couldn't stop him now; it felt too amazing. As Tak rocked rhythmically inside her, the small of Elle's back began to ache with tension. She tightened her legs around him and tried to push him into her even deeper.

Elle wanted to scream—the pressure building inside her was almost too much to bear. As she opened her eyes and saw Mike and Johnny watching, Elle climaxed. The release was so intense, so gratifying, she shivered uncontrollably for several minutes.

Holy shit.

Never in her life had Elle felt so good. She wanted more.

EIGHTEEN

THE KILLERS: "ALL THESE THINGS THAT I'VE DONE"

May 19, 2017
12:07 a.m.

Why did I eat those enchiladas?
Elle loaded a dirty plate and fork into the dishwasher, full of disgust over her lack of self-control. Despite Four's win, it truly had been the penultimate bad day, just as she had known it would be when she woke up that morning to the news about the earthquake and the song about past regrets. The signs were never wrong.

Consumed with worry over Aubrey's decision to target Brynnie's sexuality, despondent over the sad reminder of Jimmy, and disturbed by Win's announcement about the trip to Tokyo, Elle had been restless and unable to sleep. She had decided to get up and get something cold to drink. While getting a bottle of Evian out of her Sub-Zero refrigerator, she had seen a dish of Angela's homemade enchiladas on the shelf and was tempted. Elle hadn't eaten all day and was starving. *Just a bite*, she had told herself.

The one bite was delicious. Still hungry, Elle had given herself permission to eat one full enchilada. *Just one.* She scarfed it down greedily. Still not sated, she had continued eating until the entire pan of cheese and tortillas was gone.

Elle now wished she could throw up—it would be such an effective way to counteract the binging. But it wouldn't work; Elle had tried making herself vomit many times before after overeating and could never quite bring herself to do it. She understood why so many of her friends took their kid's Adderall. How blissful to never feel hungry.

Always petite and curvy, Elle remembered the exact moment when she had become concerned about her weight. It was shortly after she had started dating Win. He was retiring from the Navy, and she had accompanied him to Nordstrom to purchase clothes for his first civilian job. After looking around separately, Elle had approached Win with some ties she had picked out. He had responded by affectionately putting his arm around her—she didn't recoil from his touch back then—and kissing her on top of the head.

There had been a preternaturally pretty, slim, and long-legged salesgirl helping Win. The kind of girl guys would turn their heads to look at again. When it registered with the salesgirl that the very good-looking man she had been helping and trying to flirt with was with Elle, a look of surprise had passed over her face. The look had been subtle and ever so brief. Most people, lacking Elle's acute ability to read others, wouldn't have given it a second thought. But Elle had seen it and recognized what it implied. *"He's with her? That can't be. He should be with someone like me."*

Once again, Elle was Not Good Enough. She was the girl in the school cafeteria who couldn't afford lunch.

Elle was humiliated but refused to feel less than. It became another challenge. She couldn't change her physical attributes, but she *could* do more. Get rid of the platinum hair and bright lipstick, to start with. Outside of Japan, their stark shades seemed too brash. And then there was her weight—she could control that, and maybe she *was* a little chubby. So began the dieting, the obsessive calorie counting and weighing in. Within a month, she had lost ten pounds. By the time she was married six months later, Elle had gone from a healthy and curvy 125 pounds to a 1994-Kate Moss-like heroin-chic 100 pounds.

Win didn't seem to care or notice one way or the other how much she weighed, but Elle loved being so thin. She enjoyed the feeling of going to bed hungry. She was empowered, strong from her self-control. Hungry, but like the little girl on the swing set, it was on her own terms.

Shutting the dishwasher, Elle was annoyed with Angela. Why had she made the enchiladas? Elle hadn't asked her to. If the enchiladas hadn't been in the fridge, she wouldn't be in this predicament.

Elle really wouldn't be able to sleep now. She should have taken an Ambien right away when she couldn't fall asleep. She had debated it, but she only had three pills left and couldn't possibly ask her doctor for a refill yet—he had warned her the last time that she was relying on the Ambien too much. She needed to save her limited supply for the trip to Tokyo.

Tokyo! Win's stupid business trip to Japan was a driving force behind Elle's inability to sleep in the first place. And there was no getting out of it. Win was so excited, so sure she would welcome the opportunity to return. And why shouldn't he feel that way? Elle had spent the past twenty years painting a rosy picture of her life in Japan. She had been an English teacher at a fabulous school with fabulous students. It had been great fun. She had loved it. Elle had told this version of her story so many times, she had almost begun to believe it herself.

How could she return to Tokyo without acknowledging the truth?

Elle leaned over and rubbed Duke's ears. Ever loyal, he had followed her from the bedroom into the kitchen. God, how she loved that dog. If only everything in Elle's life could be as uncomplicated as her relationship with him. Never mind what you wear or how you look. Forget your demons, your past mistakes. Take care of me, and I will love you back unconditionally. What a concept.

Duke nuzzled next to Elle's leg and licked her bare knee. She had put on an old T-shirt of Win's to wear to bed. She wasn't sure why, but it seemed to be the right thing to do, like maybe by wearing her husband's clothes she would feel closer to him. Elle really was trying. Maybe she should start wearing sexy lingerie again. Would Win notice?

Sexy lingerie reminded Elle of her old friend Mitch. He would be disappointed to learn that after years of seductive Cosabella bikini briefs and racy animal-print G-strings, Elle had reverted to the large white cotton panties she had worn when they first met. Who could blame her? They were more comfortable and way more practical—no need for all that hand-washing. Besides, no one saw her underwear anyway.

Thinking of Mitch made Elle smile. He was one happy memory of Japan, maybe the only part of her life in Tokyo she cared to remember.

Elle looked into Duke's eyes as she scratched behind his ears. Mitch had been her Duke in Tokyo, the one person who understood and accepted her without question. Her confidante. Her playmate. Her best friend. Even his name suggested a symmetry between them—*Mitchell:* Mitch and Elle, two parts who together made a whole.

What would Mitch think of me now?

He would be sorely disappointed and not just by the underwear she wore. They had made a habit of making fun of people just like the one she had become: a housewife with two kids who waxed poetic about her dog. Elle might not drive a minivan or wear mom jeans, but she couldn't deny her willing entrance into all the other banalities of her ordinary life: the McMansion, the $50 goodie bags for each attendee at her child's fifth birthday party, the requisite white-polo-and-khaki-shorts family beach picture, the $3,500 Christmas lights installations . . . the blah-blah, blah-blah, blah. She could vomit them all. Each and every last blah, blah, blah.

No, this wasn't how it was supposed to be. The two of them were *different.* They were going to go to Europe and do great things. The Mitch & Elle's Adventure Jar had almost $10,000 in it when she left Tokyo—an enormous sum to her back then. Elle hoped Mitch had taken the money and gone on the Grand Adventure they had planned together. She hoped he was doing something fabulous. One of them should be.

Elle regretted that she had lost touch with Mitch. Although not in contact, she thought of him often over the years: when watching *Friends*—he would have insisted she get the Rachel haircut; when new U2 music was released—they would have joyously dissected each song; when *Wayne's World* was replayed on cable; and even while at the grocery store—Mitch would have despised self-serve check-out lanes in supermarkets just as much as she did. Really, who had time to type in the code for bananas?

But it was during headier moments that Elle most keenly felt Mitch's absence. He was the man meant to give her away on her wedding day and the Godfather her children should have had. He was the first person she worried about on 9/11, frantically looking through the list of those who perished, terrified she would find his name.

If only Elle had been able to say good-bye to him . . .

Was it possible Mitch was still living in Tokyo? The thought of seeing him again would at least give her something to look forward to regarding Japan.

Yes, that's it. Instead of worrying, Elle would focus on the possibility of reuniting with her best friend. Forget about the enchiladas, she was on a mission now. With Duke in tow, Elle made her way into her office. She turned on the lights, sat down at her desk, and typed "Mitchell Carpenter" into the Google search screen.

A long list of names came up—a dentist, a CPA, and a noted historian—but nothing about the Mitchell Carpenter she was looking for; the creative, smart, funny boy. The one who was going to Do Things. Elle typed in "Mitchell Carpenter Japan" and "Mitchell Carpenter English teacher" with no luck. Refusing to give up hope, she tried "Wayne Carpenter" and even "Wayne Mitchell Carpenter." Still nothing.

Out of curiosity, Elle Googled herself. A little to her surprise, a long list of items came up: articles highlighting her philanthropic work, nods in society columns, pictures from charity events. Elle cringed at one particularly unflattering photo. She looked old. *Really old.* Where did all those wrinkles on her forehead come from? And the bags under her eyes— *yikes!* They weren't your dainty bathroom-trash-can-type bags. No, they were Hefty strong sacks, the ones designed for heavy yard work. Elle needed more Botox and maybe even some Restylane. She would make an appointment with her aesthetician in the morning. Brynnie wouldn't notice, Elle would be conservative. It's not like she wanted plumped-up duck lips.

It bothered Elle that she had no control over the unflattering photo being out there for the world to see; modern technology wasn't always such a good thing. Sure, if texting had existed in 1994 she wouldn't have lost contact with Mitch, but if there had been cell phones with cameras back then, Elle would be in trouble. She had, after all, gone through a phase of drunkenly mooning people. How would that play out now? The ass of the wife of Win Martin, CEO of Martin Global, all over the internet?

No, Elle was lucky. It was best there was no record of her life in Tokyo.

Elle considered Thatcher's poor judgement and subsequent suspension. It had come out that he had Snapchatted Jacinda a picture of two unwrapped Hershey's kisses, compared them to her "milky brown" breasts, and told her how much he wanted to lick them. Thatcher had bragged about how funny it was to anyone who would listen. Not seeing the humor in story, another student had called Safe2Tell and reported it.

At first, Elle had retained a bit of sympathy for Thatcher. His Snapchat was completely inappropriate and he should absolutely take responsibility for his actions and accept the consequences. But still, weren't young people supposed to make mistakes? Wasn't that part of the process of growing up? Hadn't Elle been equally as stupid when she was young? Mooning people? Like that was smart?

The difference was, Elle had learned from her mistakes.

This wasn't the case with Thatcher. His parents had been conspicuous in their absence from the lacrosse game, their anger and pride outweighing support for their son's close friends and teammates. Instead, Thatcher's father, Arthur, drafted a threatening letter to Country Day from the highly-esteemed law firm where he was a partner. He argued Thatcher had done absolutely nothing wrong. As proof, he offered signed statements from both Jacinda and her mom indicating they were not offended by Thatcher's comments. Quite the contrary, they understood unequivo-cally that the entire conversation was a joke the two students were both in on.

Arthur went on to contend that culpability for the incident fell with Country Day. The Snapchat had been sent during lunch on school grounds—the Country Day staff had not lived up to its responsibilities in providing a cell-phone-free environment. It was *the school's* fault Thatcher had been allowed to use his phone. *He* was the real victim. Country Day had failed Thatcher and the punishment was unfair; he had earned the right to play in the state championship game.

Elle was appalled by this reaction. The signed statements were a trav-esty. Jacinda was the first person in her family to attend high school, let alone be on a full-ride scholarship to a school as prestigious as Country Day. Her mom was an immigrant from Mexico and didn't have full command of the English language. Country Day was Jacinda's golden ticket. Of course she and her mom would sign anything to make the situation go away.

Worse was Arthur's flagrant disregard for his son's responsibility in what had happened. His steadfast refusal to acknowledge that Thatcher had acted inappropriately and that this was an opportunity for self-reflec-tion and growth was insulting. Rather than consider the effects of his son's actions on a sixteen-year-old young woman, Arthur chose to be defensive and indignant—it was all about Thatcher and how hurt *he* had been.

The only life lesson Thatcher was going to get was affirmation that he was free to behave badly. Nothing would be his fault. His dad would make sure of that.

At least Elle had learned from her mistakes—or had she?

Elle looked back at the computer screen. How could there be so much information available about her yet nothing about Mitch? It didn't make sense. He was so outgoing, so determined. He had plans.

A Google search was the limit of Elle's technological sophistication. She wasn't interested in social media. She didn't have a Facebook page, Instagram, or Twitter (or Twatter, or whatever it was). She didn't "pin" things, Skype, or understand what it meant to be on fleek.

Elle also failed to see the point of Snapchat. It seemed incredibly narcissistic. "Here I am at the kitchen table doing homework!" 'Here I am driving in the car with my mom!" *Who cares?* Elle didn't get it, but she figured it was a generational thing. Her own mom never understood Elle's excitement over finally getting an answering machine. Or call waiting, for that matter.

In any case, notwithstanding Mitch, Elle was in contact with everyone from her past she wanted to be. If she wasn't in touch with someone, it was for a reason. She didn't welcome the idea of some unwanted person from her past suddenly showing up in her life. Maybe Mitch felt the same way. How else could it be that Mitchell Carpenter seemed to no longer exist?

Elle would ask Brynnie to search for him on Facebook in the morning. Maybe she would have more luck. Were there any other ways she could track Mitch down? Elle decided it might be worth going through some of her things from the time she lived in Japan. She left her office and walked down the basement stairs with Duke trailing behind.

It was cold in the basement. Elle shivered as she entered the storage room. Behind their Christmas decorations, some old paintings, and Win's comic book collection, Elle found what she was looking for: a cardboard box with the words "Elle—high school/college/Japan" written across the side with a black sharpie pen in her neat elementary school teacher-like handwriting. Everything she had brought to her marriage was in this container.

As it was at the bottom of a stack of old tax returns and financial documents, it took considerable effort for Elle to get to the box. By the time she sat down to go through its contents, she had warmed up. She dusted off the box and began her search.

At first, Elle was surprised by how little there was to go through, but then she remembered how she had been forced to leave Tokyo in such a hurry, she hadn't had time to pack. Two years of her life was reduced to little more than a subway pass, some Japanese coins, and a stack of photos.

Elle looked through the pictures. They had been taken at a birthday party for one of her previous students at English First. Elle's face appeared fuller in youth than it was now. (Or was it just bloated from all her heavy drinking?) She was wearing a bright turquoise silk blouse with large shoulder pads, and her platinum-blonde bangs were teased up straight with hair spray. She wore bright red lipstick and blue mascara. Elle shook her head in disbelief. She couldn't believe she had thought this was a good look.

Mitch was also in most of the pictures. He wore a leather jacket and, like Elle, had a fair amount of product in his New Wave-styled hair. Elle had forgotten how handsome he was. And funny. You could see a sparkly mischievousness in his eyes.

Elle was fond of looking at pictures and dissecting the subtext—the clearly fake smiles, the body language which hinted at people's true feelings. In all the photos from the party, she was smiling widely and comfortably leaning into Mitch, who had his arm around her. They looked like a couple, relaxed and at ease with each other. As ridiculous as she looked, at least Elle had been happy then.

Given the chance, what would Elle say to the girl in the photo? What would the girl in the photo say to her adult self? To the person she had become?

Elle didn't want to think about it.

Although it had been fun to see the pictures, she was discouraged there wasn't anything more in the box that might help her find Mitch. As Elle carefully returned the photos, she noticed something white and scrunched up toward the side of the box. Taking it out, she laughed. It was a purse in the shape of a Hello Kitty head. Had she really carried that around? It was worse than the blue mascara!

Elle looked inside the purse. There was a red butterfly hair clip, round red plastic earrings, and a tube of bright red lipstick. She remembered how, in the early nineties, she had thought it looked good to be matchy-matchy—to have your earrings match your purse, and your headband, and your belt, and your shoes. *Ugh. What was I thinking?*

Inside the purse, Elle also found a box of matches and a nearly empty pack of Camel Lights. That she smoked while living in Japan was another detail Elle had conveniently chosen to forget. Finally, there was the key to the tiny apartment in Shinjuku she had lived in with Mitch. Elle rubbed her fingers across it. It probably wouldn't help her search—it seemed highly unlikely Mitch still lived there—but she was pleased to have found it. It was a tangible reminder of Mitch and brought back happy memories of all the fun they had had together in the apartment.

Elle put the key next to her on the floor and returned everything else to the purse. She felt something hard in the small zipped pocket inside; it seemed about the same size and shape as a tampon. She opened the zipper and pulled out a clear plastic tube. Elle looked at it, confused.

Then she remembered.

The disturbing taste of metal in her mouth returned. Duke sensed something was wrong and started licking her arm. It didn't help her feel better. Nothing would.

How could Elle go back to Tokyo? She didn't want to confront this past. It didn't matter that she had only three Ambien left—Elle would take one. She had to. Otherwise she'd never sleep that night.

NINETEEN

FUN.: "SOME NIGHTS"

April 28, 1994
8:50 p.m.

What the fuck? Am I seriously being fired from another job?
"I think better you go," Mae-san was staid, speaking calmly and without emotion.

Did she mean Elle should leave for that night only, or something more permanent? Elle looked intently at Mae-san, searching for clues, but the madam sat expressionless and quiet.

It had been a bad call to come to work so fucked up. If she weren't so high, she might be able to better read the subtext. As it was, Elle had done a few lines with Tak and members of the Japanese rock band Sugar Puss before work, and she was having a hard time focusing on the situation at hand.

Perhaps sensing Elle's confusion, Mae-san made her intentions clear. She placed a stack of yen on the table and stood to leave. "Here your final pay. You go now."

High or not, this wasn't difficult to interpret. She *was* being fired.

Elle was ashamed. For twenty-four years she had been the model of responsibility, a consummate pleaser intent on proving her worth to class-mates, teachers, employers—everyone, really. And now she was being fired for the second time in six months? *Unbelievable.* Elle's humility quickly turned to anger. *How dare she fire me?*

Elle was good at her job. She had made Mae-san tons of money. And how did the madam even know about the cocaine? She had been very discreet.

It must have been Sato, the lawyer Elle had met a few evenings ago and sold a few grams to. He wasn't a regular. Maybe he had hoped to score brownie points with Mae-san by selling her out.

What a jack-ass.

Elle should have known better than to trust someone she didn't know. Still, it's not like she had been dealing *that* much coke at the Big YAC. Elle had been careful, bringing in just enough for a few lines to help her get through the night. If customers wanted to partake with her, what was the big deal? Mae-san should thank her. Everyone could drink so much more when high.

Whatever.

Elle was sick of the job, anyway. And Tak would be pleased, he had wanted her to quit for some time now.

Elle considered the money on the table. From what she could tell by the stacks of yen notes, it was the equivalent of at least $2,000, maybe more. Should she take it? Elle wasn't sure. This was all such bullshit.

What would be better? To take the money, or to leave it on the table and storm out, indignant? Elle decided to take the money. She had earned it.

As Elle stood and reached for the yen, she became light-headed. She teetered in her high heels and needed to hold onto the table for balance. Funny, she didn't think she was *that* high. Elle searched for the right words to say. Before she could think of anything, Mae-san held her arm out in the direction of the door, inviting—no, commanding—her to leave.

Elle was again humbled. She dropped her shoulders, her bravado weakened by the realization she had disappointed Mae-san. It was important to Elle that the madam approve of her and she had let her down. She wasn't worthy.

For a moment, Mae-san seemed to be moved. She softened a tad, touching Elle's shoulders. "You smart girl. You be careful."

Elle fought a strong urge to hug Mae-san. To thank her. To explain. But it was too late. The moment had passed. Mae-san pulled her shoulders back and, again, pointed to the door.

Elle bowed to Mae-san, a final gesture of respect. She became dizzy as she stood back up. When she turned to leave, she wasn't sure where to direct her gaze. She couldn't face the other hostesses in the club. It was too humiliating. Instead, Elle focused her attention on the poster next to the door. It was of Al Pacino as Michael Corleone. This made her feel worse. Michael Corleone was sitting in a chair, pensive, staring back at her with stern judgment in his eyes. *"How disappointing your behavior is. What a failure you are."*

Elle opened the door and tried her best not to cry as she left the Big YAC for the last time.

◆ ◆ ◆

9:01 p.m.

Elle sat on the curb outside of the Big YAC smoking a cigarette. She needed a few minutes to get it together. Japanese women walking by averted their eyes, pretending not to look at her; Elle's low-cut gown and stiletto heels made her profession obvious. Men were less successful at hiding their curiosity and most eyed her with varying degrees of intrigue and desire. Elle usually enjoyed the attention, but not now.

It had been a fucked-up day, right from the start. She should have expected something like this.

It had all started back at the apartment Elle shared with Mitch. She was spending most of her free time with Tak now and needed a change of clothes. Unwilling to face Mitch, she had returned to the apartment at a time she knew he wouldn't be home. It was a shitty thing to do. Elle knew she hadn't been—and wasn't being—a good friend to Mitch, but she rationalized it was okay. She was going to make it up to him on his birthday. She had a plan.

Back in their apartment, Elle's unslept-in futon was still hopefully pushed up next to Mitch's. It was a sad reminder of how much their relationship had changed, so she tried to avoid looking at it. Rummaging around for some clean clothes, Elle saw a light blue envelope with red and blue stripes and the words AIR MAIL/PAR AVON on it. Intrigued, she reached over to inspect it. The letter was addressed to her.

Michelle Simpson. Elle didn't like to see her real name. She preferred not to think about the bad memories associated with that person.

Elle didn't recognize the handwriting. Curious, she opened the envelope and two 10,000-yen notes fell out onto the floor. Elle found this odd but ignored the money; she was anxious to read the letter. The writing was in the large, loopy handwriting of a child, or perhaps someone who was old and had a hard time holding a pen.

Dear Michelle,
   This is your Grandma Jean.

Her grandmother! Elle hadn't seen or heard from her since she was a little girl.

I hope this letter finds you. We had a terrible time trying to figure out where you were at.

Elle chafed at this sentence. Her mom frequently made the same grammatical mistake, ending a sentence with "at." It was embarrassing, a reminder of her mom's lack of education and sophistication, like the way she mispronounced "hors d'oeuvres" and thought that wine came in only two varieties: "the red or the white kind." Slightly put off, Elle continued reading.

We finally seen the Christmas card you had sent your mom and it had this address on it. Lord knows if this will ever reach you. Why you would want to go halfway around the world, I'll never know, but I suppose you are trying to find yourself or something.

Elle found this remark a little snarky and backhanded, especially coming from someone stupid enough to write "we finally seen," but then again, what did she expect? She barely remembered her grandmother.

As you probably know, your mom and me didn't always get on the best. She never did forgive me for thinking that her and your dad had something to do with little Jimmy's death. How could you blame me? He was a no-good drunk, and in my day, no one had ever heard anything about this Sudden Infant Death Syndrome.

At the mention of her little brother, Elle became angry with her grandmother. *What a bitch.* What did she know about Jimmy? Her instinct was to throw the letter away, but Elle decided to continue reading. It would be satisfying to keep track of all the grammatical mistakes and take note of what a dumbfuck Grandma Jean was.

Anyways, I tried many times to work it out but she wouldn't have nothing to do with me. I would sometimes hear about her through people in town and she seemed to be real happy. She was seeing Candy Lynn's nephew Bruce, who everyone said was a real nice man. I don't know how to tell you this, so I'll come right out with it. Your mom and Bruce was in a motorcycle accident. It was on March 19th (Three days before her 43rd birthday). It had rained real hard that night and Bruce must have lost control of the bike. Anyhow, they hit a tree on Main Street. We were told she died instantly, so know that she wasn't in any pain. (Bruce died two days later in the hospital. He never did come to.)

Wait, what? Elle had to reread this section several times. Her mom had been in an accident and was killed?

Elle couldn't believe it. It wasn't possible.

She skipped through the rest of the letter quickly. It talked about the funeral, presided over by Pastor Bob; about how her mom was reunited in heaven with little Jimmy; about how she was returning the Japanese money; and how she wished she knew Michelle more—she would keep her in her prayers.

Elle sat down on the futon, numb. Shouldn't she feel something? Sure, she had never been particularly close to her mom, yet this news was gut-wrenching. Why was she not crying?

Elle picked up the two 10,000-yen notes and looked them over. Had her mom touched them? Shown them to Bruce? Bragged to him about her successful daughter living in Japan? She placed the money against her cheek, her hand involuntarily shaking.

"*. . . In my day, no one had ever heard anything about this Sudden Infant Death Syndrome.*"

Sudden Infant Death Syndrome. SIDS.

It had been Elle who, lonely and wanting company, had gotten up in the middle of the night and taken Jimmy out of his crib. *She* been the one who put him in bed next to her and surrounded him with stuffed animals. *She* had been the one to place her pink blanket over him so he wouldn't get cold. *She* had been the one who let him sleep on his tummy. *She* had been the one who had done all the things that were risk factors for SIDS.

If only she had left Jimmy in his crib. Or turned him over on his back and taken away the pink blanket and all the stuffed animals. But she hadn't, and he had died.

And now her mom was dead, just like he was.

Elle stood, closed her eyes, and vigorously shook her head. She didn't want to think about any of this. Not now. She couldn't.

Resolute, Elle took the letter and the yen notes and stuffed them into her large green army duffle bag. She picked up her change of clothes and left the apartment. She would go back to Samantha's for a few hours before she had to go to work. Partying with Tak and the band Sugar Puss would be just the distraction she needed.

It was amazing, really, Elle's ability to not think about things she didn't want to deal with. She seemed to be getting even better at it since living in Tokyo. Perhaps it was because the Japanese seemed to have already perfected this skill. They were adept at hiding their emotions and were impossible to read—you certainly wouldn't find any of them blabbering about their issues on a couch to Oprah. Was Japanese stoicism rubbing off on her? Elle hoped so; she didn't want anyone to recognize what she was hiding.

Now, hours later, smoking on the street after being fired from the Big YAC, Elle still didn't want to think about her mom's death. But she wasn't Japanese enough. With all the traffic whizzing by, she couldn't *not* think of her mom.

Her mom on a motorcycle.

Bobbie wouldn't have worn a helmet and her lemon-yellow hair would have flown wildly around her face. She would have been in high spirits, enjoying herself. She loved motorcycles and the men who rode them. Elle imagined Bobbie clasping her arms around Bruce, leaning in to him tightly with every turn. Maybe she was even laughing her deep, throaty laugh.

Then, her mom hitting a tree. Her mom dead on Main Street.

Elle hoped that Bruce had been hopelessly in love with her mom. She hoped that there hadn't been too much blood, and that the ambulance had arrived quickly. She hoped that her mom had had been wearing long pants and a coat. Elle wasn't sure why, but it seemed crucial that she be covered.

Tears welled in her eyes. She didn't want to think of her mom sprawled out, dead on hard black asphalt. She had never understood Bobbie. She had resented her inability to provide her with the life she thought deserved, but Grandma Jean's letter had provided clarity. Elle had only ever considered how Jimmy's death had affected *her*. She hadn't ever considered her mom's feelings.

Bobbie had lost a child. Only twenty-three years old herself, she had accompanied her still baby in an ambulance, desperately hopeful even when the driver had turned the sirens off. She had come home from the hospital and taken her son's unwrapped presents from under the Christmas tree and given them to the pregnant woman in the apartment next door. She had purchased a teeny tiny casket, arranged a funeral, and watched with despair as her sweet, innocent, beautiful baby boy was buried in the cold December ground.

It all made sense now. The emotional distance, the lack of interest or involvement in her daughter's life. Elle was nothing but a bitter reminder to Bobbie of everything she had lost. Perhaps she even blamed Elle for Jimmy's death, just as Grandma Jean had blamed her.

It was no wonder her mother couldn't love her.

Elle couldn't fault her; she would have reacted in the same exact way. It was, after all, in her bed, on her watch, that Jimmy had died.

Elle rubbed her hands against her eyes to stop the tears. She was on the verge of a complete breakdown, perilously close to turning into a heaping mess of tears and snot. She couldn't let that happen.

No. Elle would get it together. She would be Japanese.

"Erre-san!"

Elle looked up and saw Sato, the lawyer she had done the blow with a few nights before, waving his hand to her through the open window of a black town car. Elle pretended she didn't hear him and made a show of searching through her purse. She wasn't in the mood to deal with Sato. She needed to get to Samantha's.

"Erre-san!" Sato emerged out of the car, still waving.

Shit. She wouldn't be able to ignore him now.

Elle tried to appear casual, nonchalantly pulling out a tube of red lipstick from her purse and carefully applying it to her lips. Although she had worn light-colored lip gloss in college, on Tak's suggestion, Elle had taken to wearing brightly colored, bold lipsticks in Japan. Fire engine red and hot pink.

"Erre-san. I so happy see you." Sato extended his hand to help Elle stand up off the curb. "You go work now?"

"No, I'm not working here anymore."

"Ah . . . so . . . you no work here anymore?" Sato dropped his shoulders. "I many sad, I come here see you."

Elle debated bringing up the coke. She was sure Sato had said something about it to Mae-san, even if inadvertently. She considered the lawyer. Although he wasn't what she would call handsome, he was well put together in the way of someone with money. Perfectly tailored suit, expensive haircut. He wasn't as old as the other clients at the Big YAC, and his teeth weren't too bad.

Elle decided it wasn't worth mentioning. Perhaps Sato could give her a ride to Samantha's. It would be worth saving the taxi fare. She nodded her head toward the town car. "Could you do me a huge favor and give me ride into Roppongi? I need to meet some friends."

"*Hai. Hai.*"

Why was it the Japanese insisted on saying yes twice? Elle got it the first time. She tried to hide her irritation as Sato guided her into the town car with outstretched hands.

As they sat down, Sato scooted over, his thigh touching Elle's. It made her uncomfortable, so she leaned forward and away from him as she gave the driver directions to Samantha's. Traffic was still heavy, so it would be at least a thirty-minute ride, maybe longer.

"Ah . . . so, I have present for you." Sato reached into his suit pocket and took out a small red silk purse, similar to something jewelry would be put in.

Elle was receptive—it wasn't unusual to for clients to buy her jewelry. She held out her hand expectantly. She hoped it would be earrings. Pearl ones. They would be easy to sell.

Instead of handing her the purse, Sato opened it, revealing a baggy full cocaine. "You want share?"

Elle wasn't disappointed there was no jewelry. Some coke was precisely what she needed. It would help erase her shitty day. She crouched down and snorted a line over Sato's lap. As the drug entered her system, Elle's mind became free. She forgot about her guilt over letting Mae-san down. Over letting her mom down. Over letting down her helpless baby brother.

Thank God.

Elle wanted to tell the driver to turn up the music, but Sato had asked him to put up the partition. Satisfied with the effects of the first line, she leaned across Sato to do another one. As Elle finished, he gently pushed the back of her head down into his lap. Her nose touched against his dick. It was hard.

Elle tried to lift her head, but Sato pressed down on it again. Not exactly forcefully, but he certainly wanted to keep her head in the general area of his crotch. He reached into his pocket, took out several 100,000-yen notes and placed them on his lap.

Elle should have been outraged, incensed by his proposition, but for the second time that day, she felt nothing. The numbness had returned. Elle lifted her head, looked Sato in the eye, and shook her head no. She should have protested more, but it didn't seem worth the effort.

Sato returned her gaze. He didn't seem angry or even disappointed. His eyes conveyed acceptance, maybe even a hint of understanding, like he knew Elle was fragile and should be handled with care. Sato pulled her close to him and kissed the top of her head in an avuncular sort of way, more paternal than sexual. Elle rested her head back against him, relieved. He did understand.

They drove this way for several minutes. Elle waited anxiously for the second line to kick in, for her feeling of contentment to be heightened. Instead, she had an image of her mom dead on the street. And then Jimmy, eyes open and cold next to her in bed.

Elle shook her head. She needed this to stop. It would be better once she got to Samantha's. The band would be playing and she could lose herself in the music and dancing.

The town car stopped. They were stuck in heavy traffic. Should she get out and walk the rest of the way? Elle turned her head to the window to see how much farther they had to go. Sato took her hand and led it to the bulge in his pants. He moved his legs apart and gently rubbed her hand against his stiff penis.

Once again, Elle should have been offended. She should have objected violently, but she couldn't. She couldn't do anything but close her eyes and hope the excruciating visions of her dead family would disappear. Paralyzed, Elle didn't move her hand away. Not even when Sato unzipped his very expensive pants and led her hand through the opening in his silky underwear. She held his dick, throbbing and hard in her hand. Still, Elle felt nothing. All she could think was how different Sato's penis was from Tak's. It was smaller, chubbier. Sato turned toward her and reached his hand between her legs. Elle didn't resist. It just didn't seem to matter. Any of it.

TWENTY

SUM 41: "OVER MY HEAD (BETTER OFF DEAD)"

April 28, 1994
9:34 p.m.

As Sato's town car slowly wound itself like a deliberate snake back into the crowded Roppongi traffic, Elle double-checked her nose in a compact mirror for any stray white-powder residue. To stop the harrowing images of her dead mom and brother, Elle had done two more lines before getting out of the limo. It had been successful. She felt better already.

Elle couldn't accept what had just taken place. She wouldn't. It hadn't been real. *Nothing happened in the limo. Absolutely nothing.* She would never think about it again.

Elle considered the stash of yen notes stuffed in her purse. *They* were certainly real. She wasn't sure of the exact amount, but figured she must have at least the equivalent of $7,000. So much money. . .

It's all from Mae-san. Yes, that was it. The money was her severance package.

Fuck Mae-san. Fuck the Big YAC. Fuck it all.

None of it meant anything to Elle. All that mattered was her trip to Europe with Mitch, and she now had more than enough money to pay for plane tickets and a room at a nice hotel for them both. Getting fired was for the best. She would be able to spend more time with Tak. And Mitch.

Mitch . . . What would he think? Elle wouldn't tell him the truth about getting fired. Or Tak, for that matter. Instead, she would tell them both she had quit. That was reasonable. They knew she was tiring of the job.

Satisfied with her story, Elle put the compact back in her purse, pulled her strapless gown up, and entered Samantha's. The Rolling Stones' "Sympathy for the Devil" was playing in the background. Elle didn't give a second thought to the song's meaning or what it could symbolize. Over the course of the last two years, though her love of music hadn't waned, Elle had stopped using songs as signs altogether. It no longer seemed important.

"Blondie!" Elle was greeted with enthusiasm by members of the band Sugar Puss, who were sitting at the bar with their girlfriends. She could forgive members of the band for calling her Blondie—she had fun partying with this group. They were cool. Elle was looking forward to joining them on their private jet for a scuba diving vacation the upcoming weekend.

"You want drink?" Kenji was behind the bar. Elle had finally gained his full confidence and he had admitted to being very interested in Mitch. The two had recently finalized her plan to surprise Mitch on his birthday by gifting him a very willing Kenji. It would be perfect. She couldn't wait.

"Sure. I'll have a Kirin." Elle went behind the bar and furiously washed her hands in the sink. Three times. Then once more. She looked around for Tak but didn't see him. "Is Tak in his office?"

Kenji nodded as he handed Elle a beer.

"Thanks." Elle took the drink and smiled at Kenji. She was glad she had done the extra lines. She was amped up in a good way. "Is everything all set for Mitch's birthday next week? We'll get here from dinner around eleven o'clock."

Kenji's face reddened as he bowed enthusiastically. "Yes, yes. I be here and off work midnight"

"Excellent!" Elle was pleased. Mitch was absolutely going to die. She put her finger to her lips as she turned to go find Tak. "And don't worry; it will be our little secret." Kenji was terrified of Tak or anyone else at the club finding out he preferred the company of men. She would honor his desire to keep it quiet.

Elle drank her beer as she glided up the stairs to Tak's office. The blow had really kicked in now. She was practically floating. Whereas only a few hours ago she hadn't been able to feel a thing, she now felt incredible. What a difference the cocaine made.

Elle walked into Tak's office feeling hopeful. Yes, her day had absolutely sucked, but that was all behind her. She was finally going to get her best friend laid. She could pay for their trip to Europe. All was well.

Tak stood when Elle entered his office. She loved how he did this unfailingly. How it meant he was always eager to see her. It made her feel special and appreciated. As usual, Johnny and Mike were also in the room. Elle wanted them to leave. She wanted to be alone with Tak. She was safe with him. Tak would gently run his fingers through her hair and protectively cup her chin in his hands. Elle had a sudden and desperate need to be kissed.

She turned toward Johnny and Mike and demanded, more rudely than was necessary, "Go!"

The two men abruptly turned to leave. By now, they were accustomed to taking orders from Elle. Johnny exited, turning back to look at her. Was that a sneer on his face? *Asshole.* Elle ignore him and started to kiss Tak longingly.

He pulled away. "Wait. First, I have something show you. Something you take with us on airplane this weekend." Tak reached into his desk drawer and pulled out two small, clear containers. They looked like tampons made of glass or plastic.

"What are those?" Elle was hurt. This was the second time Tak had rejected her advances.

"They for you to bring on airplane for scuba trip. You put cocaine inside, take with you, we have cocaine for party."

"What do you mean?" Elle was confused. Maybe she had done too much blow. She couldn't think clearly and her heart was pounding.

Tak motioned to her crotch. "So, you put in there, take inside you. Sugar Puss girlfriends do many time."

What? What was he thinking? "No way. That's gross! And dangerous. What about security?" Elle wished her heart would stop beating so fast. Was she going to have a heart attack?

"No worry, we on private airplane, no one check. You do this, Blondie. You see, it good."

"No, that's too much." Elle needed to sit down. Drink some water.

Tak ran his fingers through her hair. "It fine. I promise." He kissed Elle behind the ear, a little roughly. He hadn't shaved—he was trying to grow a goatee—and the stubble scratched at her skin and hurt.

Tak pulled Elle's arms above her head and held them together tightly with one hand while his other hand reached between her legs. She usually loved it when Tak took her in this way, the same way he took everything he wanted. But it didn't feel right. Not now. Elle couldn't enjoy nor return Tak's passion. His grip was too tight. Her head was spinning. Her heart was racing. She couldn't breathe.

Tak pushed Elle toward the wall, fumbling to get his pants off. As he forcefully entered her, Elle closed her eyes and resisted the urge to cry. For only the second time since arriving in Japan—the first time being her encounter with the pervert while showering at the Zen House—Elle was scared. Terrified, actually.

TWENTY-ONE

IMAGINE DRAGONS: "ROOTS"

June 1, 2017
11:40 a.m.

Within of moments of sitting down in an espresso-brown leather recliner on the Martin Global private jet, a steward approached Elle asking if she would care for anything to drink. She ordered a sparkling water and took in her luxurious surroundings. It was remarkable just how far she had come from being the girl with the government-issued lunch card, the one who scoured thrift stores for Izod socks. Sure, like generations before them, Elle and Win had wanted more for their children than they themselves had had growing up, but not necessarily All This.

A private jet hadn't really been a part of their master plan; they had been happy in their simple life. After leaving the Navy, Win had become enormously successful as a medical device sales rep, the kind doctors trusted and nurses and office workers looked forward to flirting with. Elle went back to school, got her master's degree in social work, started volunteering with the SIDS Alliance, and took a job at a women's shelter. The work was meaningful and fulfilling, and she was good at it. Unlike most of her coworkers—earnest trust-funders whose biggest mistake from their teen years had been weekly trips to tanning booths—Elle could relate to her clients. She understood regret. She was personally acquainted with shame.

After a few years, Win and Elle had saved up enough to buy their first home, a modest brick ranch in an up-and-coming neighborhood. Soon after moving in, Elle had become pregnant with Brynnie. They were thrilled. *They had it made.*

Then Win had come up with his first Big Idea. During sales calls to doctors' offices, he noticed how inefficient the ordering process was. To make his job easier, he developed a software program to streamline the tracking of medical devices and pharmaceutical products. It was a genius solution, and Win had an offer to buy his program around the time Brynnie was born.

Overwhelmed with caring for a new baby and terrified she would find Brynnie unresponsive and cold like she had her brother, Elle never knew how much Win had profited from the deal. She only understood that she would never again need to worry about money. *Jackpot!*

At first, not much changed. Elle upgraded Brynnie's wardrobe from Target's Circo brand to Baby Gap. She started treating herself to regular manicures and pedicures and bought some furniture for their house from Pottery Barn, astonished and delighted by her good fortune.

Over time, one seemingly small decision after another, their lives began to change. Four was born, and they decided to buy a larger home. Why not look in a more expensive neighborhood? It made sense to join the nearby country club, Brynnie and Four needed a place to take swim lessons and Elle could learn how to play tennis. Private school? Why not? It's what everyone else was doing. A second home on the lake followed; it was cheaper and more convenient than renting a place in the summer.

Not one to stay idle, Win continued working on new innovations, each more successful than the last. He started Martin Global, and on and on it went, until they found themselves at the place they were now: in a private jet headed to Tokyo for one of the largest international deals ever.

Were they Greenwich-hedge-fund-director, Silicon-Valley-dot-com, or Hollywood-movie-star rich? No, they were more your standard Middle America new money, the opposite of old and unassuming wealth. The loud, proud type who bought all the requisite toys associated with their new status: the convertible Porsche, and the boat, and the house in Vail. Still, it had been a mind-numbingly quick hop, skip, and jump from T.J. Maxx to Ann Taylor to boutiques with exposed brick walls where someone with a name like Chandra offered you cucumber water or champagne, whichever you preferred.

As Elle's children boarded the plane and took seats in leather recliners of their own, she wondered if they realized how lucky they were. Brynnie, yes; she had spent every summer since ninth grade volunteering in a Third World country. But Four? Did he realize this was not the way most people lived?

Probably not. How could he? Sure, Country Day required all its students to complete service work, but did picking up litter on the campus of your private school for three hours really count? As much as Elle tried to instill a sense of gratitude in Four, he had still learned how to drive in a $90,000 car. He had tutors, trainers, and every other sort of professional at his disposal to ensure his success. Could her son understand anything less?

Maybe, but certainly not at that moment. Four was too busy feeling sorry for himself. He didn't want to go to Tokyo. It meant he couldn't play in two lacrosse tournaments, and he didn't want to be away from Tabby. He had asked if his girlfriend could accompany them on the trip, but Elle didn't think it was a good idea. As much as she approved of Tabby, she was concerned that Four was getting too serious about her. Although certain the teens were not yet having sex, Elle wasn't prepared to add that headache to her already long list of worries.

Sulking, Four sat down then stood up again abruptly. "Wait, do they have Ebola in Japan?"

Brynnie was incredulous. "Are you kidding me? Seriously?"

"What? Is it so wrong of me to want to know if I'm headed to a country where I might catch a disease that makes blood come out of my butthole? I think that's some *preeetty* important information."

Elle sighed. How could her children be so different? Hadn't she raised them in the same way? Perhaps she had been easier on Four. But why? Was she that afraid of having to shut the eyes of another dead little boy?

Elle tried to be patient, explaining, "There is no Ebola in Japan."

Four tilted his head. "What about that Zika thing?"

Brynnie shook her head in disbelief. "That's South America. When's the last time you read the news, genius?"

Four pulled an issue of *Inside Lacrosse* out of his jacket. "Cover to cover, baby!" He tapped on the magazine with pride. "That's forty-eight pages!"

"Congratulations. I'll be sure to come visit you when you're thirty and living in Mom and Dad's basement, making $10 an hour stringing sticks at Lax World."

"Savage!" Four flopped down in a recliner and leaned back lazily. "What you don't realize is that people pay top dollar for my stringing."

To Elle's relief, Win stepped in. "Alright, you two. Simmer down—"

"*Konnichiwa!*" Win was interrupted by an astonishingly glamorous woman in her twenties waving to them as she entered the jet. She was tall—of course she would be—and looked like an advertisement for Prada in her black leather pencil skirt, open-toed booties, and crepe bodysuit, which exposed the outline of two incredibly perky breasts. She had blonde hair, the same shade as Carolyn Bessette-Kennedy, and it was up in a messy bun, the kind meant to imply it had been casually thrown together, when in fact, it had taken twenty minutes to achieve. She had full lips and a toothy smile. Elle immediately disliked her.

"Oh, hello, Ainsley!" Win smiled and introduced the Prada model to his family. All Elle could manage was an icy, distrustful nod. *Ainsley?* She would have a name like that.

Brynnie was only slightly more enthusiastic, offering a skeptical smile. Four seemed the most pleased to meet Ainsley. His eyes widened in surprised delight, like he had discovered it was a snow day and school was cancelled.

Ainsley's toothy smile made a repeat appearance. "It's lovely to meet you all."

Lovely. That's just the sort of thing someone named Ainsley would say.

Perhaps sensing everyone's confusion over her sudden appearance, Win explained, "Ainsley is the producer of the documentary team who will be filming our negotiations in Tokyo. There was a problem with her ticket, so I offered to have her join us."

A problem with her ticket. Yeah, right.

Win could be so naïve. Elle really despised Ainsley now and was irritated with her husband. Why did he always have to be so nice? Didn't he see what was going on? There was not a single reason Ainsley couldn't have traveled with the rest of her team on a commercial flight.

As it was, Win had decided to make a documentary covering the deal Martin Global was making with the Japanese company Tsugunai. The technology that his company was funding and that they would be introducing together was groundbreaking. Win believed the deal was an important process to document, not out of arrogance—he didn't do things to feed his ego. No, Win wanted to provide young business people with tangible insight into the complicated workings of a large international deal.

Elle could hardly argue with his rationale. Still, she didn't relish the idea of having a camera crew around. Elle had watched enough reality TV—much to Brynnie's chagrin, the ones about the housewives were a guilty pleasure of hers—to understand the inherent dangers of letting cameras into your life. She suspected the people in these shows set out creating the persona they wanted to portray: "sweet ingénue," "hardworking, driven career girl," "sassy troublemaker." It always worked initially, but then the cast members inevitably got cocky and faltered, revealing their true nature. One simply couldn't hide the truth from the cameras for that long.

Of course, this sort of worry wouldn't enter Win's mind; he was completely free of guile. His behavior wouldn't change one bit, camera or not.

Elle was in an entirely different situation. Horrified by the idea of being filmed and somehow exposed, she had convinced Win that as the point of the documentary was to detail Martin Global's deal with Tsugunai, their family didn't need to be very involved. Win had agreed. The film crew would be with them only for brief periods of time, just enough to get footage giving the documentary some context. The bulk of the filming would be done during the business meetings.

Introductions made, Ainsley asked, "Win, where would you like me to sit?"

Elle bristled at Ainsley's use of her husband's first name. It seemed too personal.

"Wherever you like." Win motioned around the jet with his arm and took a seat next to Elle, who took this as a small victory. She was back in high school and the star quarterback had just sat next to her instead of the head cheerleader. He picked *me*.

"There's a spot here," Four offered, pointing to the empty seat next to him.

"Win, is that okay with you?" Ainsley asked.

There was his first name again. *What's up with that?* And why was Ainsley asking his permission? Elle was suspicious and looked at Win, searching for clues that would suggest anything other than a professional interest in the young producer.

Nothing. In fact, Win seemed genuinely taken aback by the question. "Sure, whatever you like."

Elle was temporarily relieved.

As Ainsley took her seat next to Four, Elle couldn't help but admire the young producer's breasts. It was like driving by a car accident—she didn't want to see it, knew it would only upset her, yet she still looked. Yes, Ainsley had perfect tits. Had Elle's ever looked that good? She looked down at her chest and took stock. Even in an expensive bra with ample support, her boobs resembled two deflated balloons. They had given up, relegated to the sad realization they were no longer of use—the party was long over.

Discouraged, Elle reconsidered a boob job. Why shouldn't she get one? Just a lift, something to keep them from sagging. Was that so terrible? After seeing the unflattering picture of herself online, in addition to her usual Botox, Elle had gotten some Restylane. Only a little under her eyes and in the laugh lines around her mouth. She had been pleased with the results; Win and Angela had both commented on how rested she looked. Brynnie hadn't said anything, so Elle was sure she didn't suspect the truth. So why not get a boob job, and even a tummy tuck? Her stomach got flabbier by the day, no matter how many sit-ups she did. Brynnie wouldn't need to know. She could do it in the fall, when her daughter was away at college. Yes, that's what she would do.

"How's your speech coming along?" Win leaned across Elle and placed his hand on her lap, distracting her from thoughts of the perfect body.

Upon Win's suggestion, Elle was going to give the opening remarks at the press conference announcing Martin Global's partnership with Tsugunai. He thought it was a great idea; Elle had, after all, lived in Japan and could speak the language—why not show off a little?

Elle had been reluctant—it had been a long time since she had spoken Japanese—but Win was so clearly excited by this idea, so proud to have his wife speak, she could hardly say no. It was wonderful to be so appreciated by Win. Elle still tensed up, as if by a defensive reflex, when her husband touched her, but it was getting better. She was trying.

Of equal importance, Brynnie also seemed impressed that her mom would be addressing the crowd in Japanese. Elle was determined to make her daughter proud, and if speaking in Japanese at a press conference would help, she would do it.

"I'm almost done. Would you care to see what I have so far?" Elle opened her laptop.

Ainsley leaned over the back of her seat. "I'm sorry to interrupt, but did I hear you say Mrs. Martin is giving a speech?"

So Ainsley was on a first name basis with Win, but she was *Mrs. Martin*. Elle wanted to claw her eyes out.

"Yes. She'll be opening the press conference. She used to live in Tokyo and can speak Japanese. Isn't that great?" Win smiled proudly at Elle.

Take that, Princess.

"How wonderful. I just wish I had known; it would have been good to get a shot of her working on the speech for the documentary. Maybe we can get it at the hotel?"

"That would be *lovely,* but I don't think it's necessary." Elle couldn't imagine anything worse. She wanted as little to do with the documentary as possible. She looked to Win for his support.

"That's right. Let's limit the cameras to our team's interactions with the Tsugunai staff, though I do want Elle's opening remarks to be filmed." Win smiled at his wife. It was a dagger to the heart—she didn't deserve him.

Ainsley pouted, her plumped-up lips downturned sadly, like a five-year-old who didn't win at Pin the Tail on the Donkey. "Okay, but think about it. It would *really* add to the story we're telling."

Story? Ainsley had no idea what she was talking about. She was chronicling a business deal—that was all. Elle was the one with a story to maintain.

Irritated, Elle put her head back against the recliner. If only she could have brought Duke along. Win had tried to gain permission, but Japanese laws were firm. Their dog would have been forced to stay quarantined in a kennel for the duration of the trip.

Elle tried to get comfortable. The last few weeks had been challenging. Her disturbing nightmares with the rabid animals had returned with alarming frequency. Even worse, Aubrey had been relentless in her revenge against Brynnie, and Elle had yet to come up with an effective strategy for dealing with her unwarranted insinuations. She wouldn't have cared so much if she were the subject of all the gossip, but it grieved Elle to know Brynnie was being scrutinized. Time away from that situation was the only positive thing about a return to Japan.

That and the possibility of finding Mitch again. Elle had resolved to spend some time looking for him while she was in Tokyo and had brought along the key to their old apartment with her. It wouldn't likely be helpful, but it gave Elle comfort to have the reminder of Mitch with her.

Everything else regarding her return to Japan filled Elle with trepidation. She was convinced some sort of reconciliation with her past was inevitable. There had been too many signs pointing to it for her to ignore. Even though her children were far too old to be obsessed with the Disney movie *Frozen*, Elle could not escape its theme song "Let It Go." It seemed to be everywhere; she heard its message of confronting an uncomfortable past every time she went into any retail store. Nauseating as the song could be, Elle's constantly hearing it had to mean something.

And even if she didn't count "Let It Go" as a sign, there was the Florence + the Machine song "Shake It Out" to consider. It had come on the very morning of Win's announcement regarding Japan, and it seemed to be on the radio all the time now. The song's lyrics about a devil on your back and not being able to leave the past behind certainly portended trouble.

Elle wasn't sure exactly what all these signs meant, but she knew the danger of not taking them seriously. She had made that mistake once before with disastrous results. She would pay close attention. Still, it couldn't be *that* bad. Elle tried to be logical; it had been over twenty years since she lived in Tokyo. It was a huge city with millions of people in it. No one would remember her. What could possibly happen?

Elle's initial plan had been to take an Ambien and sleep during the flight. At her request, Win got a prescription of his own ahead of the trip, so she no longer needed to ration her supply. Between worrying about Tokyo and Aubrey, and the return of her nightmares, Elle hadn't had a good night's sleep in weeks and was looking forward to a nice long siesta. But having Ainsley on board fucked everything up. As if she didn't have enough on her mind already, Elle now had to deal with Gwyneth Paltrow flirting with her husband for the next thirteen hours. She considered the Ambien and the reason she had been so desperate to get more of it and was ashamed.

The truth was, Elle was nervous about the prospect of sharing a hotel bed with Win. She loved, respected, and even liked her husband, yet Elle dreaded sex with him. At some point along the way—perhaps around the time she reverted to wearing her grannie panties—sex had become a chore. It was like going to the DMV to renew your driver's license, an act that wasn't looked forward to but needed to be done.

Like her explanation for why she preferred to sleep in the guest room—she was a light sleeper and Win snored—Elle could use the Ambien as an excuse to avoid sex by saying she was exhausted from jet lag and needed the drug to help her sleep.

But how could Elle deny her husband sex with a more than willing Ainsley eager to step in and take her place? Ainsley wouldn't flinch when Win touched her. She definitely still wore sexy underwear or none at all. And those lips? Those lips were made to give blow jobs.

Elle couldn't remember the last time she had French-kissed Win, let alone engaged in oral sex with him. What had happened to the girl who wore the sexy underwear? When had she become so frigid?

There was no way Elle could take an Ambien as planned. No, for Ainsley's benefit, as well as her own, she would stay awake and be the model attentive wife, spending the plane ride trying to learn more from Win about the deal he was brokering. It was for the best. Sex notwithstanding, Elle truly was trying harder to make her marriage work. And she was sincerely interested in the company Martin Global was working with. Its name "Tsugunai" was the Japanese word for atonement. Somehow, this seemed symbolic. A hopeful sign bobbing in a rough sea of otherwise distressing signs.

Signs. Elle needed one. Something to tell her she didn't need to worry about the trip—or Ainsley. She would listen for one and then direct her full attention toward Win. Elle put in her earbuds and turned on her iPod. She pushed play, hoping something good would come on. Maybe a U2 song. That would be the best.

Instead, it was "Love The One You're With" by Stephen Stills. This had been one of her mom's favorite songs. For a moment, Elle was once again the young girl at the bar watching Bobbie sing along to the song with her throaty voice and jiggly boobs while serving drinks to men in baseball caps smoking Marlboros with their dirty fingers.

Elle could now smile at the reminder of her mom, but she couldn't see how the song applied to her current situation. The *next* song would *absolutely* be the one that told her what to expect.

Elle waited. Florence + the Machine's "Shake It Out" came on.

Shit.

There was no denying it. A confrontation with her past was inevitable. But when? And how? Elle didn't want to deal with it. Ainsley and her perky boobs be damned. She would take an Ambien now.

TWENTY-TWO

BRUNO MARS: "COUNT ON ME"

May 10, 1994
8:41 p.m.

"Suck my dick!" Mitch smiled gregariously as he raised his small glass high in the air toward the businessmen who had sent over the expensive sake. He turned to Elle, laughing. "That line might have gotten me fired, but I still love it. I mean, truly, can you think of a better way to say 'cheers'?"

"Nothing immediately comes to mind." Elle clinked her glass against Mitch's. "Here's to the birthday boy."

Elle and Mitch each threw their heads back and drank their sake in one large gulp. The warm rice wine tasted sweet in Elle's mouth. She and Mitch were both pretty buzzed; they were at a sushi bar in downtown Ginza, and the clientele had been exceedingly generous in plying them with free drinks all night.

Although Tak had to use his connections to get them a table at the popular restaurant, he was unable to join them. An avid soccer fan, he was hosting a party at Samantha's for the Japanese national team, which had scrimmaged a team from Brazil earlier in the day. Without Tak's presence, it was like old times between the two friends. They were joking, laughing, and thoroughly enjoying themselves.

It was all going according to Elle's plan.

She reached down between her legs for her purse, which had Mitch's birthday present in it. Elle needed to be careful. Inside was one of the plastic containers filled with cocaine Tak had given her. She didn't want to risk Mitch seeing it.

"Oh dear God, no!" Mitch shook his head with disapproval as he spied Elle's purse. It was in the shape of a Hello Kitty head. "That might be the most ridiculous thing I have ever seen."

"I know!" Elle agreed. "I have no clue why a smiling cat with a pink bow is all the rage here. Tak gave it to me a few days ago. My plan is to 'lose it' in the very near future."

"Or you could give it me. It would make a good dart board."

Elle reached carefully into the purse and pulled out a small square box gift-wrapped in brown construction paper with a bright yellow bow. She hoped Mitch would appreciate that she remembered yellow was his favorite color. She handed the package to him. "Happy Birthday!"

Mitch admired the present. "Your wrapping job is very Japanese. Well done. Nice touch with the yellow bow."

Elle smiled; he *had* noticed.

Mitch began to unwrap the gift, then stopped. "Oh, I totally forgot. You got a letter from the States. It was at the apartment. Did you get it?"

Elle's stomach tightened. She wanted to tell Mitch about her mom, but not tonight. Tonight was all about fun and setting him up with Kenji. "Yeah, I got it. It was from my grandma. No biggie."

"Grandma? You never mentioned a grandmother . . ."

"Seriously, you're going to talk about my grandma when you have that amazing present in your lap? Don't you want to know what it is?"

"Yeah, you're right." Mitch enthusiastically tore the wrapping off the gift and opened the box, revealing two plane tickets to London. Elle had splurged and upgraded the tickets to first class. *Why not?* She could still afford to pay for a nice hotel—one with room service and a doorman—and there was plenty of cash in the Mitch & Elle's Adventure Jar for spending money. It was the ideal time to take their trip. She hoped Mitch would be pleased.

Mitch surveyed the tickets, eyes wide in surprise. "Are you serious?"

"As serious as a heart attack. What do you think?"

"I think it's fucking awesome!" Mitch seemed excited, but then he paused, squinting his eyes ever so slightly. "How could you afford these? First class? They must have cost a fortune."

"Let's just say I got a good severance package when I quit the Big YAC." It was imperative that Mitch accept this explanation without question. Elle wasn't sure she could convincingly lie to him about where the money for the tickets had really come from.

Mitch pursed his lips and looked at her quizzically. Elle sensed he was debating whether to push her for more information. If so, he decided against it and changed the subject. "How does Mr. Pink feel about this trip?"

"Don't worry about him." Elle casually waved her hand.

"Really? You think he's going to be okay with this?"

"It doesn't matter what he thinks. I'm going to break up with him."

"Is that so?" Mitch perked up, leaning forward against the table. "Do tell."

Elle wasn't sure what to say. The scuba-diving trip she had taken the past weekend with Tak and Sugar Puss had been horrible. Tak was moody and increasingly controlling. He was easily angered and snapped at her the way he did with Johnny and Mike. Elle no longer had the upper hand in the relationship and it scared her.

And all the drug use had gotten out of control. Elle hadn't wanted to carry the cocaine in the plastic tube inside her on the plane; it was a reckless thing to do. She had resisted right up to the very end, but Tak had been so cruelly insistent, she had finally acquiesced—it was easier than arguing with him. Elle had been so ashamed of her weakness, she had gotten terrifically drunk on the plane ride and passed out.

The rest of the trip had been a total disaster. Elle didn't want to be there, didn't want to party, and didn't want Tak to touch her. She went as far as to lie and say she had her period as an excuse to avoid having sex with him. Tak was so enraged by this news that he had thrown a beer bottle against a wall. Frightened, Elle claimed she had a fever and spent the rest of the weekend alone in her hotel room.

This self-imposed sobriety had given Elle a chance to assess her situation. Mitch had been right all along. Tak was bad news, and she was in over her head. It was time to stop all the blow and end it with Tak—*after* Mitch's birthday. It was critical she get through that first.

Elle hadn't been a good friend to Mitch and he deserved more. To assure she would be a fun partner for his birthday celebration, she had kept one of the unused plastic containers of cocaine Tak had given her. She had done a line before dinner, reasoning that once this supply was gone, she would quit using altogether.

But Elle couldn't tell Mitch any of this; he would freak. Instead, she demurred, "I don't know. It's run its course. Besides, I miss hanging out with you." This, at least, was true.

"Well, I can't say I'm sorry. You know how I feel about Mr. Pink." Mitch looked intently at Elle. "I do think it's for the best. I worry about you. He's a bad dude and you're doing way too much blow with him."

Elle stiffened. How could Mitch know? Had he somehow seen the coke in her purse? "What are you talking about?" Elle was a skilled liar, but this sounded insincere, even to her.

"Oh, c'mon, Elle. I could tell the first time you did it up in Tak's office when I was talking to Kenji at the bar."

Elle should have known as much. Mitch was as highly perceptive as she was, and he *did* know her better than anyone. It wouldn't do any good to try to lie to him. "Okay, you're right, I have done it with him a few times," she looked down at her drink, afraid to make eye contact, "but I'm not doing it anymore."

"Bullshit flag! You're high right now."

How does he know? Was she acting that differently? Elle thought she seemed fine.

Elle looked directly at Mitch with confidence. What she was going to say wasn't a lie, she *was* going to stop. She would dump what was left of the cocaine down the toilet. "No honestly, I'm not doing it anymore."

"Here's the thing, Elle. You know I party just as much as the next guy, and drinking, the occasional joint, that's one thing. But coke, ecstasy, heroin—those synthetic drugs are a whole different deal. They're not for people like us. They're too addicting. We aren't designed for the self-control needed to say no to that kind of pleasure." Mitch took Elle's hand in his. "Trust me."

"I know. I'm done with the coke. And Tak. Really. I am."

Mitch rubbed the top of Elle's hand. "Good." He took a long drag from his cigarette. "Look, if you're going to give Tak the Heisman—as much as I would love to see that—I don't think it's such a good idea for us to go to Samantha's tonight."

Elle agreed—the last person she wanted to see was Tak—but going to Samantha's was essential to her plan. Once Kenji's bartending shift was over, he was going to present Mitch with the keys to a love hotel. Elle had picked out the room—it had an absurd and kitschy aquatic theme; Mitch would love it.

"The thing is, I have a little birthday surprise and it is waiting for you at Samantha's."

"What are you up to, Miss Kitty?"

"Well, someone I know has had several conversations with a certain sexy bartender, and me thinks he's very interested in seeing you at Samantha's tonight."

Mitch slammed his hand down in disbelief. "Shut up!"

"I will not!"

"No shit? He's gay?"

"I shit you not, my friend. He's gay *and* interested."

Mitch leaned back and rubbed his hands together in delight. "Holy fuckballs!"

Elle smiled. She was thrilled to help Mitch. "You just might say that turning twenty-four is highly underrated."

"Well, it *would* be appropriate for me to end the evening in my birthday suit. Are you sure you don't mind seeing Tak again?"

"Not at all. I can handle him." Elle was lying again. She wasn't at all convinced she would know what to do when she saw Tak, but she had been such a shitty friend to Mitch, it was the least she could do. "Tonight is all about you."

Mitch reached for Elle's hand. "Thank you, Elle. I know I've been a bit of a prick lately, but it's only because I miss you."

"Don't you dare apologize! I'm the one that's been the asshole. You're my best friend. I've missed you more than you can know."

"You're aces, kid. Let's drink to that. Best friends!" Mitch struck his bottle against Elle's.

"Yes, best friends going to London. Whoop! Whoop!"

"London! I can't wait. What do you say we rock and roll Cleveland? Apparently, I've got an appointment with a hot young Japanese man."

"Yes, perfect. Let's go!"

It *was* perfect. Elle had made a mess of things, but she would right her wrongs. Tak and the hard partying would soon be things of the past. She would spend more time with Mitch. Europe was going to be amazing.

Elle was excited for Mitch and excited for them. Good times were ahead; she was sure of it.

TWENTY-THREE

THE ENGLISH BEAT: "MIRROR IN THE BATHROOM"

May 10, 1994
11:15 p.m.

Mitch and Elle ignored the interminably long line of party-goers waiting to get in to Samantha's and went straight to the front door, where they were immediately ushered in by two bouncers dressed in white blazers over pastel T-shirts.

Entering the club, Elle was relieved to see that the table where Tak liked to hold court was blissfully empty. *So far, so good.* She guessed he was up in his office, supplying soccer players with cocaine. Hopefully, he would stay there. Kenji would be off work soon, and once he was with Mitch, she could leave.

It was loud in the club. Elle had to raise her voice to be heard. "Do you see Kenji?"

Mitch shook his head. "Let's head to the bar."

News that the Japanese national soccer team was at Samantha's must have gotten out. The club was teeming with young women provocatively dressed and angling to meet the players. Mitch pushed his way through the mass of young people, leading Elle by the hand.

Mitch suddenly stopped and pointed toward the bar. "Holy shit. Brazilian soccer players—overrated/underrated?"

Elle had been blindly following Mitch's lead. She looked up.

Mama mia!

Ahead of them, surrounded by a circle of Japanese women, was a group of the visiting Brazilian national team. Although they were all attractive, it was the one in the middle who most caught Elle's eye. With his icy blue eyes and blonde hair that cascaded down to his shoulders, he stood out amongst the other players. He was tall and his dress shirt, the same striking blue as his eyes, was unbuttoned nearly to his naval, showing off a large gold chain around a perfectly toned and hairless chest.

Elle's mouth dropped. "Underrated. He's hot! Let's go talk to them." Kenji could wait a few minutes. This would be fun.

The crowd of Japanese women made room for Mitch and Elle to join them. Elle introduced herself to the Adonis soccer player. "Hi, I'm Elle. What do you think of Japan?"

He responded with a smile, eyeing Elle approvingly. "Oh! So much better now." He held her hand to his lips. "I'm Gustavo. Can I get you a drink?"

"Sure!" Elle was impressed by the feel of Gustavo's hand—it was rough and strong, not manicured and soft like Tak's. Elle also liked his accent. It was earthier and more masculine than the singsong Japanese one she had become accustomed to.

"What's your pleasure?" Gustavo bent down to speak directly into Elle's ear so he could be heard above the noise in the crowded club. The warmth of his breath tickled her ear and made her tingle.

Elle couldn't think. "Beer . . . anything. Whatever you're having."

"Alright, I'll get us two beers." Gustavo rubbed her back. "You're the most beautiful girl I've seen since I've been in this country."

Elle's stomach fluttered. She was flattered and felt especially feminine next to Gustavo's massive broad shoulders. She was anxious to continue talking to him but desperately needed to pee. "I'm just going to run to the bathroom. I'll be right back, okay?"

Gustavo nodded and turned toward the bar to order their drinks. He towered over the other bar patrons, and everyone seemed small and insignificant in his presence. Elle started toward the bathroom and saw Mitch talking to another group of soccer players. She stopped and tapped him on the shoulder to get his attention.

"Oh my God, he's so fucking hot."

"That he is."

"I'm going to pee. I'll be right back."

"Okay." Mitch pointed to the other Brazilians. "These guys are all straight as an arrow. I'm going to go look for Kenji."

"Yes, you should, birthday boy! I'll catch up with you in a little bit."

As Elle turned her back to leave, Mitch grabbed her by the shoulder. "Elle—wait."

"Yeah?"

"Be careful, okay?"

"Don't worry. I'm just flirting a little." She hugged Mitch and added encouragingly, "Now go get Kenji!"

There was a long line for the bathroom, but the regular customers, recognizing Elle as Tak's girlfriend, let her pass to the front. She was appreciative and proud—she was important.

Elle lit a cigarette as she squatted down to pee. Although Tak had an American-style toilet retrofitted for his office, he had kept the traditional Japanese-style ones in the bathrooms at Samantha's. By now, Elle had perfected the squat and was proud that she had mastered the ability to both pee and smoke at the same time. Elle looked at the Hello Kitty purse she had put to the side on the floor and considered the cocaine in it. There was just a teeny tiny bit left, enough for maybe one last line. Earlier, she had vowed to flush it down the toilet.

Should she do that now? No, she would hold-off until she had made sure Mitch was all set with Kenji. *Tomorrow* she would absolutely get rid of it.

Elle finished peeing and quickly washed her hands. She wanted to get back to Gustavo. It was fun to flirt with someone new. It was so over with

Tak. She couldn't possibly be with him anymore. Still, Elle dreaded the conversation they would need to have; she had no desire to talk to him. It sucked they needed to go to Samantha's to see Kenji. It would have been better for her not to be there.

Shit. What if she saw Tak? What would she say? Elle thought of the coke in her purse, of how much it would help her get through the night. She would do just one last line; she needed it in case she ran into Tak. But that would be the end of it. *Really.* She would *never* do coke again.

Elle looked around the bathroom. It would be rude of her to cut back in line and go into a stall again. She decided to snort the line right there. She could be discreet. No one would care. Besides, Elle was in a hurry. Gustavo was waiting.

TWENTY-FOUR

4 NON BLONDES: "WHAT'S UP?"

May 11, 1994
12:11 a.m.

Elle was so fucked up, it seemed like the floor was moving beneath her feet. She shouldn't have done that last line of coke in the bathroom, and she definitely shouldn't have drunk so much with Gustavo. That last shot of Jäger had really put her over the edge.

Elle watched with dizzy satisfaction as Kenji got off work behind the bar and approached Mitch. *Mission accomplished!* She could leave now—and not a moment too soon. It was fun to flirt with Gustavo, but Tak could show up any minute.

If only she weren't so drunk. Elle wanted to lie down—everything was spinning. She needed to go home, to call it a night. She should try to get a taxi . . . she couldn't do it. It was too much of an effort. Better to just go up to Tak's office and crash there. Yes, that was the best thing to do.

Still, Elle hated to leave Gustavo. Before saying good-bye, she got the name and room number of the hotel where he was staying. She would call him tomorrow when she was officially single again.

As Elle staggered up the stairs to Tak's office, she had to stop several times to get her bearings. Everything was blurry and unclear. *Why wasn't there bread at Japanese restaurants?* If she had eaten bread at dinner, she wouldn't feel so fucked up now. Elle hoped Tak wouldn't be in his office. It would be better to deal with him sober. If he *was* there, she would just ignore him and head straight to the futon—the new one she insisted he get so she wouldn't have to think about all the other women he had been with.

Elle stumbled into Tak's apartment. He was sitting on the edge of his desk. Mike and Johnny were on the futon.

Shit! Why did they all have to be there?

Elle approached the futon. She needed to lie down. "Get off, you assholes."

Mike and Johnny looked at each other.

Hadn't she been clear? Elle tried again, this time speaking more deliberately. "Get *off!*" She pushed against Johnny's chest. "Leave . . . GO!"

The two stood—a bit reluctantly, Elle thought—and she waved them off with a dismissive "Buh-bye!" Elle had no reason to be such a bitch, but she couldn't help it. The Jäger had totally jacked her up.

As Mike and Johnny left the room, Tak considered his girlfriend. "You very drunk."

"Yeah, so?" The room was really spinning now. Should she try to make herself throw up?

"I no like. Mitch bad for you."

Elle knew better than to engage with Tak. She was too wasted, yet she couldn't abide his talking shit about her best friend. Mitch was none of Tak's business, and she didn't appreciate being told what to do. "It has nothing to do with Mitch. I don't know why you can't be nicer about him. You know he's my best friend."

"Man best friend, no good. I say many time, you need girlfriend."

Elle wasn't in the mood for this conversation. "Whatever, Tak. Just shut the fuck up and leave me alone." Elle was surprised by her aggression but didn't regret it. Tak was being a dick, and she could always blame it on the Jäger. That stuff was evil.

Tak's face turned bright red. He grabbed Elle by the shoulders. "I say, no more Mitch. He bad."

Elle squirmed away from Tak's grip. Who did he think he was? She stood up unsteadily. "No more Mitch? I don't think so."

"I SAY NO MORE MITCH." Tak shook his head so violently, Elle worried it might spin off like a top. He leaned forward and tried to grab her again.

Elle moved away. She was really pissed off now. "You know what there will be no more of? Me, carrying drugs for you." Elle looked around for her Hello Kitty purse. Where was it? She wanted to get the plastic container out, to throw it at Tak, to see it break into a thousand tiny pieces. To make it go away.

"Drugs for me?" Tak shook his head. "Drugs for you!" He pointed his finger in Elle's chest. The slight force made her lose her balance. She had to catch herself from falling.

"For you, for me, who cares? It was wrong." Tak was being such an asshole. Elle didn't deserve this. "And I'm not doing coke anymore. I'm done with that."

Tak laughed. "You high now."

"No, I'm not," Elle lied. Why had she done that last bit of coke? She should have flushed it down the toilet like she had intended. She was too wasted. She needed to get it together. "I'm done with you—with all of this. I'm leaving." Elle turned to go, again looking for her purse. How could she not see a Hello Kitty purse?

"You no go. You do I say. No more Mitch!" Tak squeezed her by the shoulders again, this time more firmly. It hurt, and Elle winced in pain.

"Get your hands off me. I'll see whoever I want." Elle no longer cared about the Hello Kitty purse. She needed to get out of there. She pulled herself away yelling, "Fuck you! I'm leaving!"

Elle hadn't meant to go that far, but there it was.

Her words hung uncomfortably in the air for a few moments, suspended in time as Tak took them in. Elle was satisfied by his silence and turned to leave. As she did, Tak yanked her hair with one hand, causing her head to whip back. With his free hand, he hit her across the face. A hard, punishing backhand that caused her head to recoil.

Elle fell to the ground. *Fuck! That hurt.* Tak's pinkie ring—the same one she had seen covered in blood a few weeks ago—had dug into her cheek. Elle reached her hand up to her face. Had he really hit her? Is that what this had come to?

Tak paced around the room, his fists clenched at his side. "Why you make me do? Stupid girl."

Elle gingerly stood up, cradling her cheek in her hand. Tak was right about one thing. She *was* a stupid girl. Incredibly stupid and she had been for a long time now. She should have listened to Mitch.

Dazed, Elle spotted her Hello Kitty purse on the ground. Her instinct was to flee before Tak could say or do anything else, so she reached for the purse and quickly ran out of the apartment, slamming the door as she left.

Elle walked unsteadily down the stairs into the club. Unfortunately, the argument had done nothing to sober her up. Things were even fuzzier than before. It was too noisy, too crowded; Elle couldn't think. She needed to find Mitch—he would know what to do. Elle hoped he was still at the bar and headed in its direction. As she tried to make her way past a large group of giggling Japanese women, she made eye contact with Gustavo.

He raised his glass toward her. "Elle, come here. I missed you."

Elle waved back to him weakly. Her cheek throbbed. Where was Mitch?

Gustavo took several steps toward Elle. The crowd parted in his wake. He was so strong, so damn hot. He reached his hand out to hers. "Come— dance with me!"

Elle grabbed onto his hand to steady herself. Was there a mark on her cheek? Would Gustavo be able to see she had been hit? Nothing made sense, not even the music in the background. Elle couldn't hear the song, only felt its loudness. She became light-headed and tripped. Gustavo reflexively caught her, lifting her up with both hands.

"Are you okay?" His embrace was secure, safe.

"Blondie!" Above the noise of the crowd, Elle heard Tak. She turned to see how close he was and saw the group of giggling women making way for him to get through.

Fucking dick.

Elle looked back up at Gustavo. "I'm good." She took his hand. "Follow me."

Gustavo obliged, first taking a large gulp of his beer. "Yeah, sure. Let's go."

What was she doing? Elle wasn't sure of anything but her need to keep ahold of Gustavo's hand, at least until she found Mitch. She loved the feel of his hands. They were solid. Masculine. Gustavo had the hands of a real man.

Elle spotted Kenji by the cloakroom. This was good, it meant Mitch would be nearby.

"Erre!" It was Tak again. He had given up on 'Blondie' and was now like a scolding parent using a child's full name. He was getting closer.

Elle turned and looked at Tak. He was urgently waving to her, his eyes expressing sorrow. He mouthed the words "so sorry."

Elle held his gaze for a few moments. He was *sorry*? As if that nullified what he had done. No, he hurt her—now it was his turn to suffer.

Elle turned toward Gustavo. He was so tall she had to stand on her tippy toes as she pulled his head down and cupped both her hands around his mouth, the way Tak did with her. She kissed him passionately. Gustavo placed both hands around Elle's ass, leaned into her, and returned her kiss.

How do you like that, asshole?

Elle and Gustavo made out for what must have been several minutes—surely long enough for Tak to see them. Elle came up for air, holding on to Gustavo's face for balance. Everything was hazy, everything but Gustavo's eyes. They were clear. Icy blue and clear. Elle needed those eyes; his gaze steadied her.

She took Gustavo by his strong, reassuring hands and led him into the cloakroom. Elle didn't dare look around. Tak was likely close behind, and she was afraid to make eye contact with him. Off to the side, she saw Kenji watching her.

Good. He'll go get Mitch.

Gustavo shut the door to the cloakroom. It was spring and warm, so the racks were barren except for a few empty hangers. Gustavo and Elle kissed again, his hands slowly and purposefully exploring her body. She loved those hands, the feel of his rugged, manly touch. Elle wanted him; she wanted to submit to his strength and masculinity. She was safe with him.

Gustavo continued kissing Elle and reached into his pants pocket. With one hand he pulled out a gold square condom package. He stopped kissing Elle long enough to tear the package open with his teeth. He then took the condom out and gently held Elle's face in his hands. He looked her in the eye. His expression was earnest, like he wanted to make sure what was about to happen was wanted.

Where his icy blue eyes had been clear and piercing a few moments ago, they now seemed cloudy. Elle tried to focus on them, but everything was spinning. She held onto Gustavo and tried to get her bearings.

This is wrong. She was still Tak's girlfriend. If he would hit her for mouthing off, what would he do when he found her in a room alone with Gustavo?

Elle was afraid to find out. She pushed Gustavo away. "No, wait. Stop—I can't." Before he could protest, Elle ran out of the room. She was going to throw up.

TWENTY-FIVE

HOZIER: "TAKE ME TO CHURCH"

May 11, 1994
11:06 a.m.

Mitch

*S*ex—*overrated/underrated?*
More specifically, sex with a man.
Underrated. Most definitely underrated.

Mitch considered Kenji's dark ruffled hair and smooth skin. He had never seen, let alone felt, skin so soft, so perfect. Mitch was happy. Complete.

It's about fucking time.

Mitch chuckled. *Fucking time.* Given the circumstances, that was a funny way to think of it. He'd have to share that little nugget with Elle. She'd appreciate the humor. Mitch couldn't wait to talk to her. *Finally,* he could have a real conversation about sex! Elle would savor every last detail with him.

Mitch looked around, and for the first time, took in the details of the love hotel room. He had been too drunk and too horny the night before to notice anything other than Kenji's slender hips.

Although he and Elle had often talked about renting a love hotel room just to see what they were all about, it was Mitch's first time in one. Like hostess clubs, love hotels were a singularly Japanese idea—rooms could be rented by the hour with complete anonymity. Patrons simply put yen in a slot in exchange for a room key. Higher-end love hotels, such as this one, were often extravagantly decorated.

This room had an "Under the Sea" theme. There was a large aquarium filled with colorful fish making up an entire wall. Paintings of more fish and other sea life adorned the adjacent walls and ceiling. Elle had done a perfect job in choosing this room. It was brilliant in its tackiness.

Mitch looked over at Kenji—he was curled up in a ball, still sleeping soundly. He looked adorable. Mitch wanted to kiss him. Was that appropriate? He wasn't sure. This was his first rodeo.

Should I wake him?

Mitch leaned over and gently ran his fingers through Kenji's hair. Kenji stirred from sleep and sat up, rubbing his eyes.

Unsure of what to do, Mitch patted Kenji on the head, immediately regretting it as a lame move. Kenji wasn't a cat.

Kenji didn't seem offended. He snuggled up affectionately next to Mitch.

Oh, man. This is great.

Should he say something? What? Mitch was rarely at a loss for words, but he was in uncharted territory. This was terrifying. Delicious and wonderful, but terrifying. Mitch realized he had no game. Flustered, he blurted out, "Did you have fun last night?"

Did you have fun last night? Seriously? What a moronic thing to say. He might as well have said, "How was I?" Kenji would surely know this was his first time.

Kenji brushed his hand along Mitch's cheek and looked at him earnestly. "Yes. I'm many funny."

This wasn't quite the response Mitch was expecting, but he loved it all the same. Everything about Kenji was perfect. Mitch could melt in his chestnut brown eyes. *Oh, to make out with him again.* He should go brush his teeth.

Kenji scratched at his head and furrowed his brow, like he had just thought of something unpleasant.

Fuck! My breath must be rank. Mitch covered his mouth with his hand, embarrassed.

"You remember last night I tell you Erre?" Kenji looked solemn.

"About Elle? No . . ." Mitch didn't know what he was talking about. He had been incredibly shit-faced the night before, and all he could think of was being alone with Kenji.

"I see her last night. She is kissing tall man from Brazil."

Mitch abruptly sat up, immediately concerned. "What? Elle was kissing one of the soccer players?"

"*Hai. Hai.* I think she very drunk."

Shit. This could be really bad. "Was Tak there?"

Kenji nodded his head and nervously bit his lower lip.

Shit. Shit. Shit.

Mitch sprang out of bed and reached around frantically for his clothes, dressing as quickly as he could. Even if Elle refused to acknowledge it, Mitch saw the truth about Mr. Pink: he was a full-on scumbag. Mitch suspected he was dealing and had a strong inkling there was even more bad shit that went down in the back rooms of Samantha's. How could Elle have been so fucking stupid as to make out with another guy in his club? Tak's ego was too big to let this go.

Fuck!

Mitch sat on the edge of the bed, tied the shoelaces on his favorite pair of Chuck Taylors, and looked over at Kenji, who had also gotten up and was getting dressed. *Damn, he was pretty.*

Mitch dreaded leaving him, but he had no choice. He loved Elle. She was his best friend, and she was in trouble. He had to go help her.

Mitch allowed himself one more luxurious moment to admire Kenji and the small of his back as he put his shirt on. Wanting to etch this moment in his memory, he gave the room—every last gaudy detail of it—a final look-over.

Mitch stood, gave Kenji an awkward kiss, and promised, "I'll call you when I get back from seeing Elle. We can have dinner."

Kenji nodded, adding as Mitch left the room, "Good luck!"

Elle was the one needing luck. *How am I going to get her out of this mess?*

TWENTY-SIX

THE OH HELLOS: "HELLO MY OLD HEART"

June 4, 2017
7:52 p.m.

Within moments of arriving back in Tokyo, Elle's worst fears were confirmed. It *was* going to be a horrible trip. Despite taking the Ambien,
she'd once again had the nightmare with all the feral animals gnawing at
her tampons. And then, not long after landing, Four had run to the bathroom, complaining his stomach hurt. Along with the security officer sent
by Tsugunai to escort them through customs, the Martins and Ainsley had
waited over twenty minutes for Four to come out. Elle wasn't sure if her
son had been vomiting or had diarrhea. Either way, she dreaded taking
care of a sick child on top of everything else. Rattled by these bad signs,
Elle spent the entire limo ride to the hotel panicked, worried about what
would go wrong next.

Fortunately, Four had quickly rallied, and the Martins thoroughly
enjoyed spending their first few days in Tokyo visiting all the usual tour-
ist spots. Cognizant that Four's patience would be tried with too many
cultural outings—he couldn't hide his boredom while visiting the shrine

at Meiji Jingu—Elle had been sure to include activities he would enjoy: a professional baseball game and a sumo match.

It had been an easy, fun vacation. There was little bickering or eye rolling. Elle's fears over sharing a bed with Win had even been unfounded. Although they hadn't had sex—they were both exhausted by the end of their busy days—they had snuggled a bit and it was fine. Actually, it was better than fine. It was *nice*. Why had Elle been so worried? Everything was going so well. The sights, the sounds, the unique cadence of Japan, all of it felt welcoming to her.

Elle had spent so much time trying to forget the aspects of her life in Japan she regretted, she had forgotten all the good memories. She had absolutely loved the people and the culture in Japan. And Tokyo? It was an amazing city, vibrant and alive.

The neon signs, the noise, the people, all of them were reassuring in their familiarity and Elle felt a comfortable ease—like finding her favorite pair of Levi 501 jeans from high school still fit. For someone in a place she had tried so hard to forget, Elle felt a remarkably keen sense of homecoming in Japan.

As Win promised, the film crew had not been overly invasive and had spent very little time with the Martins. Still, Elle had watched Ainsley carefully. Her paranoia over the possibility that the producer had a thing for her husband further fueled Elle's efforts to be a better wife. She was making a conscious effort to be extra engaged, to listen, and to ask more questions. She had even started reaching out for Win's hand and affectionately rubbing his back. It wasn't hard. In fact, she rather liked it.

Tonight was the Martins' final chance to enjoy their family trip. Win's business meetings with the Tsugunai executives would begin in earnest the next morning, and he would be less available. Elle wanted to end their last night together on a high note.

"Okay, what did you think? Pretty good, right?" Elle looked expectantly toward her family. They were at a restaurant in Ginza, trying one of Elle's favorite Japanese meals, *shabu-shabu*—thinly sliced beef cooked tableside with vegetables in a pot of boiling water.

"Well, besides the part where you kept saying 'shabu-shabu' every time you moved the meat around in the water, I have to say it wasn't bad." Four pushed his nearly empty plate away.

"I enjoyed it. This was a good choice." Win smiled and lightly rubbed Elle's back.

"Yeah, I agree; it was good, although I didn't love the green tea ice cream." Brynnie, who had volunteered to be more flexible with her usual dietary restrictions on the trip, scrunched her nose in distaste.

"Yeah," Four agreed, "that stuff sucked ass."

"Four!" Elle scolded her son, then admitted with a smile, "Actually, I never much cared for it either."

A young waitress appeared with the check, smiling flirtatiously at Four. Win took the bill and excused himself to go pay it. The waitress lingered at their table in an awkward silence for a few minutes.

After she finally left, Elle teased Four, "I think she might like you."

"Yeah, chicks dig me. What can I say?"

Brynnie rolled her eyes and shook her head. "Since we're on vacation, I'm going to ignore that you just called that woman a 'chick.'" She leaned forward in her chair. "More interestingly, did you notice her makeup? How she had rouge on under her eyes? I've noticed it on others and asked the hotel concierge about it. Apparently, it's a popular trend—it's called 'uru-uru.' The idea is to purposefully make yourself look sick."

Elle was intrigued. "Really? Why would anyone want to look sick?"

"I think it's tied to a desire to seem vulnerable, in need of rescuing. Maybe they think that's what men want."

"Not me." Four brushed his hair to the side. "I'm not feeling the whole Asian thing."

Brynnie hit her brother on the arm. "Seriously, Four? I'm trying to engage in an intelligent conversation, and all you can do is denigrate women?"

"I'm just saying, they don't do it for me, sick-looking or not. I can't get past the crooked teeth. That's just nasty."

Elle sighed. Their vacation had been going so well. She didn't want her children to start bickering now. Still, she needed to say something. "Four, Brynnie's correct. It's disrespectful to categorize women."

"Sorry!" Four looked at his sister. "Why does everything have to be some sort of trigger for you to turn into a cause. Can't you just chill?"

Win returned to the table asking, "Is everyone ready?"

As always, Elle was relieved by her husband's presence. She didn't want to argue, not tonight. They were having so much fun. "I have an idea. Since we are in Ginza, I thought it might be fun to go to a karaoke bar."

"That's a terrible idea." Four moaned.

Elle pressed on, undeterred by his lack of enthusiasm. "C'mon, hashtag YOLO."

Four put both hands to his face and shook his head. "No, Mom, just no! Please!"

Brynnie winced. "Yeah, Mom, that was bad."

"I'm not giving up! You can't come all the way to Tokyo and not go to a karaoke bar."

Win stepped in with his support. "Your mom is right. I think it's a great idea. Let's ask the waitress if she knows of a good place."

"Seriously?" Four was still not convinced.

Brynnie was more game. "Fine, but if you two break out into anything from *Titanic* by Céline Dion, I'm leaving. Really. I'm not kidding."

Brynnie's words reminded Elle of the time Mitch had said the same thing about a Whitney Houston song. It was the night they had gone to a karaoke bar with their English First coworkers. The same night he had told her he was gay. Elle was planning to spend the next afternoon looking for Mitch. So far, the trip had been a success and she was optimistic that she would find her old friend.

"It's a deal. Let's go." Elle was in a great mood. Everything was going so much better than she had expected. It was fun to be back in Japan. She was reconnecting with Win and things with Brynnie were also improving.

Maybe Elle had overanalyzed the signs, worried too much. Perhaps her return to Tokyo wasn't anything to be worried about after all.

TWENTY-SEVEN

THE ROLLING STONES: "UNDER MY THUMB"

May 11, 1994
12:52 p.m.

Elle stepped out of the bathroom, a large towel wrapped around her freshly showered torso. Once she had finished vomiting in Tak's bathroom in response to the condom wrapper, Johnny and Mike had forcefully escorted her back to the studio apartment she shared with Mitch. Elle was thankful they had allowed her to take a shower. Although her cheek still hurt and the cold sore on her lip throbbed painfully, the hot, steamy water had diminished her nausea.

The shower had also allowed Elle to clear her head and fill in the blanks from the night before. She could vaguely remember Tak helping her up the stairs to his office. She didn't remember him scolding her, but Elle was sure he was furious with her. Why else would he have left her alone, passed out on the floor overnight.

The question was, just how pissed off was he? Tak was a proud man with a huge ego, and Elle had embarrassed him in front of his employees and an entire club of partygoers. He needed to save face. She would have to pay somehow. Elle put her hand up against her injured cheek, still sore from the impact of the back of Tak's hand and his pinkie ring. Was this just the beginning? Would she, too, end up bloody and beaten in the stockroom?

What have I done?

Elle hoped Mitch's night with Kenji had been amazing, but she needed him to get home. He would know how to help her.

The phone in the apartment rang. Johnny seemed to be expecting the call; after just one ring, he answered, "*Hai! Hai!*"

Johnny bowed as he spoke, as if upon reflex, and Elle knew it was Tak on the line. Understanding her boyfriend was the one person able to grant her reprieve, she lurched toward Johnny and the phone. "Let me talk to him!" If she could assure Tak that nothing had happened with Gustavo beyond kissing, maybe she could get out of trouble.

Mike immediately stepped forward and blocked Elle, while Johnny kept his attention on the phone call.

"Please, Johnny! I can explain everything." Elle pushed against Mike, trying to move past him. In the commotion, the towel that had been draped around her fell to the ground, leaving her naked and exposed. Mike, somewhat taken aback by the sight of Elle's nude body, stepped away from her. She reached for the towel, but Johnny had hung up the phone and swiftly stepped on it, preventing her from picking it up.

Johnny opened his mouth and laughed, his tongue visible through his broken tooth. Elle desperately tried to cover herself with her hands, just as she had when spied on in the shower at the Zen House, acutely aware that, this time, Mitch wasn't there to protect her.

"Nice!" Johnny surveyed Elle's naked body approvingly. He stepped forward and roughly pried her forearm away from her chest. Cupping his hand under one breast, he said with a lecherous enthusiasm, "Pink! Japanese girl, brown." Johnny rubbed his forefinger over Elle's nipple. "Pink, nice." He looked at Mike. "You like?"

Elle turned her head away in shame. She tried to remove Johnny's hand, but he grabbed her and turned her naked body close to his own. His grip was tight, and she couldn't move. Elle felt a hardness in his pants.

Her body turned cold and numb, like it sensed something horrible was about to happen and didn't want to feel it.

So this was it. Her final humiliation. Johnny was going to have his way with her. And maybe even Mike, too. Retribution in one final, violent act of dominance for all the times she had been such a world-class bitch to them both. Maybe it was fitting. Perhaps she deserved it.

Flight was not an option. Elle had nowhere to run. Would she have it in her to fight?

Mike's face was flushed red and he avoided eye contact with Elle.

Maybe it will only be Johnny. At least he wouldn't try to kiss her, not with the huge cold sore on her lip. Elle's heart was racing, yet she was paralyzed, unable to move. Time stood still. The only thing Elle was aware of was a strange metallic taste in her mouth, as if the fillings in her teeth had suddenly melted.

Johnny held tightly onto the small of Elle's back with one arm. With his free hand, he caressed her between the legs and then forcefully shoved a finger inside her. Elle's body tensed. She tried to squirm away, but her limbs refused to follow directions.

Johnny kissed her neck. "You like?"

This can't be happening.

Elle attempted to scream, but her voice was silent.

Johnny jammed another finger inside Elle, more roughly this time. "Tell me you like."

Elle couldn't speak. Helpless, she looked to Mike. He interjected forcefully in Japanese, telling Johnny to stop, that Tak wouldn't approve.

Johnny looked at Mike and seemed to consider what he said. He turned his attention back to Elle, sneering. "I know you like." Johnny pinched Elle's insides, then removed his fingers and let her go. He lifted his hand to his nose and smelled his fingers. "Yes. Very nice." Johnny picked the towel up off the floor and threw it at Elle. "You dress now."

Elle stood in a daze. She was grateful Johnny had let her go, but she was still unable to move.

"Now!" Johnny yelled. To emphasize his order, he held his hand up in the air, threatening to strike her.

Elle made a conscious effort to walk. In a dreamlike state, she rummaged around the studio, grabbing the first clothes she saw: sweatpants with her sorority letters across the back and Mitch's Ramones T-shirt. The one he was wearing the first day they met at Narita.

Meanwhile, Johnny and Mike were haphazardly going through her chest of drawers and throwing things into her duffle bag. "Nice panty!" Johnny lifted several pairs of her white cotton underwear and laughed as he threw them into the duffle bag.

Elle hadn't worn anything but thongs in ages and had completely forgotten about her grannie panties.

Apparently satisfied he had packed enough, Johnny zipped Elle's duffle bag and lifted it over his shoulder. "Hurry! We go airport now."

The airport? Why were they going to the airport? So they could fly her to some remote location and kill her?

Elle reached for her purse, the Hello Kitty one. She considered the smiling kitten face. She had never seen anything so stupid, so juvenile, in her entire life. As Johnny thrust Elle toward the stairs, she grabbed a stack of photos from on top of the TV, hastily putting them into the purse as they left the room.

Johnny stopped at the bottom of the stairs to put his shoes back on. Elle slipped on a pair of clogs and considered how ironic it was that Johnny had politely removed his shoes before entering her home, like he was an honored guest. Elle tried to reach for her sneakers, but Johnny shoved her out the door and onto the street before she could get them.

Tak's black Mercedes was parked up on the sidewalk outside of the apartment, blocking the way for pedestrians and bicyclists. Tak frequently parked this way. At first this had impressed Elle—Tak was so powerful, so important, he could park wherever he wanted. Elle had loved being a part of this world; she found it intoxicating. She saw it all differently now.

How could I have been so stupid?

Johnny pushed Elle into the back seat of the Mercedes. It smelled so strongly of cigarettes, she gagged. Elle had driven in Tak's car hundreds of times before and never been bothered by the smell. How odd it would affect her so strongly now.

As Mike drove Tak's Mercedes out of her neighborhood, Elle slowly began to regain use of her brain—it seemed to have shut down for the last ten minutes. Or had it been an hour? She couldn't be sure.

Elle was a mess. The stale cigarette odor in the car worsened her dull headache, and from the persistent tingling on her lip, she knew the cold sore was going to be a nasty one. Her cheek stung and was no doubt puffy and swollen; she hadn't been given time to cover it with makeup. She hadn't even had time to comb her hair or put on a bra. At least she had grabbed Mitch's T-shirt. Elle could smell him on it, and that gave her a small semblance of comfort. She wished she could call him. Mitch would help her.

Speaking in Japanese, Elle asked Johnny and Mike why they were rushing her to the airport. It seemed pointless to continue pretending that she didn't understand their native tongue. Whatever advantages it had provided in the past were now long gone.

Johnny reacted to hearing Elle's flawless Japanese by turning his head abruptly toward her, and Mike looked in the rearview mirror with raised eyebrows. Elle took satisfaction in their shock. She still had the power to surprise them.

Even so, Johnny and Mike refused to acknowledge her question. Elle knew it would be futile to try and get more answers from them. She had been in Japan long enough to understand the Japanese could do silence. They were masters at it.

Elle couldn't stand the quiet. "Will you please turn on the radio?" She tried to sound polite, but it was difficult. Her voice was shaky and uneven.

Mike turned the dial up on the car radio, and Elle recognized the song immediately: Blue Oyster Cult's "(Don't Fear) The Reaper."

Oh, fuck. Fuck!

It had been nearly two years since Elle had relied on songs for direction, but she couldn't ignore this message. Music had never let her down. This was bad. Really bad. Elle shook uncontrollably. She needed a cigarette, something to calm her nerves. Try as she might, Elle couldn't heed the advice of the song. She *did* fear the Reaper.

Johnny told Mike to change the channel, he didn't like that song. Mike obeyed and turned the dial to a different station. Elle was hopeful. Perhaps the next song wouldn't have such a dire message.

The Ace of Base song "The Sign" came on. This was definitely a sign—the song title couldn't have been clearer. But what did it mean? Elle couldn't be sure. She was out of practice. She listened to the lyrics for more clues.

The lead vocalist sang out about seeing a sign and having her eyes opened.

Aha.

Elle got it. At some point over the past two years, she had stopped listening to the signs. She had become too confident, cocky even, and thought she didn't need them anymore. Elle was being punished for her hubris.

She should have known better. Music had never let her down. It had been foolish to ignore the signs. She wouldn't make the same mistake again. The song on the radio was right. Elle needed to open her eyes to the signs and to the situation she had gotten herself into. It was a bad one. All around.

As Elle was driven to a fate unknown, she brokered a deal with the gods of music.

I hear you. I understand. If only you will spare me from the Grim Reaper, I promise to never ignore you again. I will pay more attention. I will listen. Cross my heart and hope to die.

◆ ◆ ◆

3:11 p.m.

Johnny led Elle brusquely by the arm toward the TWA ticket counter at Narita Airport. She was thankful they had taken her there, rather than Haneda, the smaller domestic airport where Sugar Puss kept their plane. Elle had considered the possibility that Johnny and Mike were going to take her onto the band's jet and toss her out somewhere over the Pacific. Boarding a commercial flight seemed much safer.

Elle looked around the terminal at all the happy, eager faces. Children proudly wearing cow-shaped backpacks in eager anticipation of their first airplane ride. Friends excitedly discussing the waves they were on their way to master. Couples holding hands so tightly they were either embarking on their honeymoon or dreading the other's imminent departure.

How must she look?

Before reaching the counter, Johnny grabbed Elle by the chin. "You go Hawaii now. You no talk about Tak. You no come back Japan. Never. Understand?"

Elle's shoulders dropped, somewhat relaxed—they weren't going to kill her or hurt her after all. And the terms Johnny outlined would be easy to adhere to; it would be her pleasure to never mention Tak's name again. "Yes, of course. I understand."

As they stood in line, Elle panicked. "My passport—I don't have my passport!"

Johnny squeezed her arm tightly. More tightly than was necessary. "I have."

He had her passport? How? Tak must have taken it at some point. Elle again cursed her stupidity. She'd been such an idiot.

Johnny gave Elle her passport. She put it into her Hello Kitty purse and noticed that she didn't have any money. She had used all her cash paying for Mitch's birthday dinner the night before. Elle looked at Mike and Johnny, distraught. "I don't have any money."

They didn't respond.

Frantic, Elle looked through her purse, vainly searching for money where there was none. She was such a bonehead. Why hadn't she grabbed cash out of the Mitch and Elle's Adventure Jar before leaving her apartment?

At least she had her ATM card. If she could get to an ATM machine, she could access her savings from English First. Elle touched Mike's arm. "I need to go to an ATM and get some money."

Mike deferred to Johnny, who shook his head. "No. No time."

"Please, it will just take a few minutes, I promise. Please!" Elle's heart pounded. What would she do without any money? She tried a new tactic. "Look, I have a ton of money in my account. I'll give you guys half—half of all I have."

Johnny pursed his lips like he was considering the offer, but after a few moments he said, "No. We go."

"Please, Johnny! It would be around one hundred thousand yen for each of you. No one will know. It will be our secret." *"Our secret"*—What a stupid thing to say. Like it mattered. Still, Elle was desperate.

"I say NO!" Johnny grabbed Elle by the arm and pulled her close to him. She tried to squirm away, but he tightened his grip and leaned in close, brushing his mouth against her cheek. "You listen me. You be quiet. You leave, you no come back. I see you again, I fuck you like dirty whore."

Johnny loosened his hold and looked at Elle. A cold, hard look devoid of any feeling, except perhaps satisfaction. He had won. All the times Elle had spoken to him condescendingly, all the times she had ordered him around like an errand boy, none of that mattered. He was in control now, and they both knew it.

And really, what did Elle expect after the way she had treated him? A big hug and a teddy bear? No, she had brought all of this upon herself. She had really fucked up this time. There was no way around it.

Elle had gone to Japan in search of something better. Something more. A place where she wasn't the daughter of a single mother who worked in a bar and was poor. A place where she wasn't responsible for having a dead brother. A place where she could be the person she had always wanted to be; the type of person to whom others looked with envy.

But instead, Elle had done things she was so ashamed of she couldn't bear to acknowledge them. Lost in a time and place where consequences didn't seem to exist, she had forgotten what mattered. The one true thing Elle had found in Japan was her friendship with Mitch, and she had managed to screw up even this.

Elle was like

Tonya Harding when all she had wanted was to be Nancy Kerrigan. *What would Jimmy think of his big sister now?*

Elle returned Johnny's steely gaze. There was no sense in fighting or arguing or making a scene. She was beaten down and wanted to cry. She had nothing. Nothing but a hangover, a cut cheek, a cold sore, and a stupid Hello Kitty purse.

Elle held back her tears and willed herself to maintain the one thing she could control: her composure. She would not give Johnny the satisfaction of thinking he had broken her.

◆ ◆ ◆

3:41 p.m.

The ticket agent at the TWA gate announced the flight for Honolulu was beginning to preboard. Surprisingly, Tak had bought Elle a ticket in first class. She couldn't begin to fathom why—maybe he did still care for her? Regardless, Elle was thankful. She hadn't eaten all day, her stomach was beginning to rumble, and she had no money to buy food. At least in first class she would be well-fed.

Johnny stood up from his seat and signaled for Elle to do the same. Once again, he gave her a hard, ruthless look with not a trace of humanity. Was it possible he had no conscience, none at all? "Remember, no talk about Tak and no come back Japan."

Elle nodded.

Satisfied he had completed his job, Johnny turned to leave. Mike bowed slightly to Elle, turning to see where Johnny was. Noting Johnny's back was toward them both, in one fluid motion, Mike quickly thrust a wad of yen into Elle's hands.

She quickly took the money and stuffed it into her purse, regretful over her past behavior toward Mike. This was the second time that day he had shown her kindness and compassion. Elle wouldn't be able to properly thank him—at any moment Johnny might turn around—so she looked at him intently, hoping to silently convey her sincere gratitude.

Did he sense it? Elle hoped so. It was only a short moment before he, too, turned away from her.

Elle handed the agent her ticket and prayed no one would be in the seat next to her. She couldn't bear the thought of small talk. The only person Elle wanted to hear from was Mitch. He would know what to do. She would call him as soon as she landed in Hawaii.

As Elle boarded the plane that would take her out of Tokyo, she was grateful. Despite all the ways in which she had errored, the universe had been good to her. The gods of music had accepted her deal; she had been spared. It was her turn to give back. Elle resolved to make amends for all her poor behavior. Not only would she would honor her vow to pay attention, to listen and to learn, but she would also be the kind of person Jimmy would be proud of. And that meant no more drinking, no more smoking, no more drugs. It wasn't too late to start over. Elle would do better. She would be better.

Starting now.

TWENTY-EIGHT

JAMES BAY: "LET IT GO"

June 5, 2017
12:01 a.m.

Elle absentmindedly turned the slim straw in her martini around, taking in the bar as Win excused himself to go to the men's room. She couldn't remember the last time the two of them had gone out alone, but karaoke had been so fun that Elle decided to join her husband for a nightcap before going up to bed.

Elle rarely drank and was feeling the effects of the vodka from her martini. Everything seemed softer to her, slower and gentler. Why had she imposed such a strict stance on drinking for so long? Yes, she had abused alcohol when she was younger, but that was a long time ago. Elle was older now, wiser. Surely, she could handle a few cocktails.

In a strange coincidence, this was the very same bar Tak had taken Elle to on one of their first dates. It was decorated differently back then—very WASPy and preppy, like a country club on the East Coast, which was precisely why Tak would have chosen it. He had always been so enamored with everything American. At the time, Elle had also been impressed with the place. Surrounded by the air of wealth and prestige, she had felt important being there.

The bar retained its air of exclusivity but was now styled in a more modern design, all minimalist with clean lines and edges. Elle preferred this new look. The only remnant from the past was the piano in the corner bay window. A young Japanese woman sat behind it and was playing music softly, just as one had done many years before.

Elle allowed herself to think about Tak for a few minutes, something she hadn't done in a very long time. It was hard not to remember him here, in this bar, where after their date they had gotten a room and made love. Sex with Tak had been incredible, unparalleled to anything Elle had ever experienced before or since, but mind-blowing sex wasn't everything, not even for a young person. Tak was an asshole. She couldn't forget that.

Elle took a sip from the martini, concluding she should be thankful for Tak, for the experiences she'd had with him. Without them, she wouldn't be in the place she was now.

And where, exactly, was that?

"Are you happy, Mom? Are you living your dream?"

Am I? Sure, Elle was happy at that moment; the last few days had been fun. But was she truly happy?

No, despite having everything she thought would bring her joy, Elle wasn't a happy person. Not really. Maybe she couldn't be. Maybe it wasn't possible for someone like her. Maybe after everything with Jimmy, she didn't even deserve to be.

Still, she *had* been happy when she first lived in Japan.

Elle considered the piano player. Was *she* happy? How could she be, given her thankless job? Her hard work and skill weren't being appreciated—not one person was paying her the least bit of attention. It seemed of vital importance to Elle to acknowledge the pianist's efforts, to validate she was more than a prop providing ambience. Elle decided to give the woman her full attention until Win returned.

She turned toward the piano and strained to hear the music above the din of the guests engrossed in their own conversations. The soft notes sounded vaguely familiar, but Elle couldn't quite identify the song. Then it came to her. It was "Let It Go," the song from the Disney movie.

Of course. It had to be a sign.

Let . . . It . . . Go . . .

Elle had been convinced this song and "Shake It Off" were warnings about a confrontation with her past, but what if they were messages about her future? Could it be that the key to her happiness was letting go of the past? Finally, for once and for all, shaking off the devil that had been on her back since the cold December day when she had found Jimmy cold and lifeless next to her in bed.

Elle would never be able to fully forgive herself for her brother's death, but perhaps she could excise her other demons. Was that possible? What if the reason for her happiness in Tokyo had been because Elle hadn't hidden who she really was? She didn't pretend around Mitch. She allowed him to see her true self, and it hadn't mattered. He accepted and loved her for who she was.

Elle had belonged with Mitch.

To be happy in the same way again maybe, like the princess in the song, she needed to stop pretending. Instead of trying to be the mom, the wife, the friend she thought everyone wanted her to be, Elle needed to let go and simply be herself.

But who was that person? And would she be accepted?

"Are you happy, Mom? Are you living your dream?"

How could she be? Elle hadn't told the truth from the moment she left Japan in 1994. Well, not the whole truth anyway.

TWENTY-NINE

TRACY CHAPMAN: "NEW BEGINNING"

June 6, 1994
2:15 p.m.

A salesman wearing a cheap toupee and brightly colored Hawaiian shirt was on TV, shamelessly hawking junky used cars. His pushy tone and grating voice irritated Elle and made her nostalgic for the singsong, light, and innocuous sound of Japanese. She looked around for the remote to change the channel but couldn't find it. She tried jumping up to reach the buttons on the TV but was too short. Sweating profusely—the laundromat was impossibly hot—Elle sat down, dejected, on top of a dryer and watched the water rise in the washing machine in front of her. In a few minutes, save what she had on, all the clothes she owned would be swirling around in the warm soapy water.

After everything she had done to her escape her dismal past, to reinvent herself, Elle couldn't believe it had come to this. Here she was, once again, the pathetic and inferior girl in a self-serve laundromat.

Elle hated laundromats. Along with the bitter whooshing sound made when the door to a public transportation bus door closed—everyone else had a mom or a dad who could drive them to school—the hot, damp smell of laundromats was a visceral reminder to her of growing up poor.

Doing the laundry had been one of Elle's childhood chores. The apartment she had lived in was so crappy it didn't have its own laundry facility, so twice a month Elle had to schlep a rose-pink laundry basket to the laundromat several blocks away. To get there, she had to walk past a park her classmates frequented. Elle dreaded this part of the walk. She was terrified someone from school would see her with the laundry basket, and it would confirm what they already knew about her: Elle was poor. She didn't have a house with a backyard and a laundry room. Or a dad. Or a baby brother. She was different.

Elle's mom paid her twenty-five cents to do the laundry, and while her Holly Hobby sheets spun around in the water, she would use the quarter to buy a Coke out of the vending machine. She would then walk back to the park, sit on the grass across the street, and watch her classmates play. As they were pushed in the swings by their moms and accompanied down the slide by their dads, Elle would drink her Coke and wonder what it would be like to be one of them.

And now here she was, some ten years later, in another hot, damp laundromat with the same bad memories and an entirely new set of problems.

Elle had been in Hawaii for only a few weeks after being banished from Japan and was just now getting her life back together. For days, she had slept on the hard, fake-leather seats in a boarding area of the airport, using the pillow and blanket she had taken from the plane. Elle had been paralyzed, incapable of action. The only thing tethering her to reality had been the throbbing ache of the cold sore on her lip and the nausea. Elle had been physically sick. Perhaps a result of withdrawal from nicotine. Or alcohol. Or cocaine. Or all of them. She had been desperate for a cigarette but wouldn't allow herself one.

Elle had debated calling Mitch but decided against it. Though anxious to talk to him, she had decided it was best to wait until she had sorted herself out more. If she called in her current condition, she would break down in tears and that would only worry Mitch.

After three days, a security guard had finally approached Elle and in a polite, but firm tone, told her she was longer welcome at the airport. Forced to act, she had exchanged the yen Mike had stuffed into her hands for dollars. Grateful for his act of generosity, Elle had bought some deodorant and toothpaste in a gift shop and gone into a bathroom to wet her hair and brush her teeth with her finger. Satisfied that she was somewhat presentable, she had headed outside into the Hawaiian sun, unsure of what lay ahead.

There had been a billboard advertising an English language school outside of the terminal. It reminded Elle that a former student of hers from English First had moved to Honolulu to open a school of his own. He was an incredibly nice man; maybe he could help her. Elle found a telephone booth and looked in the Yellow Pages for a list of English language schools. Although she hated to spend thirty-five cents on a wrong number, she started at the top of the list and phoned each school, hoping to find the one owned by her former student. Luckily, it had taken only four calls—$1.40—to find her friend's school.

He remembered Elle as a good teacher. Fortunately, he had been a student at the beginning of Elle's tenure, before she had started drinking so heavily. When she had explained her situation, he immediately offered her a job, asking when she could start.

Elle had then used the Yellow Pages again to find the address of a youth hostel. After taking a bus there and checking in, she walked to a nearby drug store. Johnny and Mike hadn't done a very thorough job of packing her belongings, and she was missing several essential items. Mindful of her limited resources, Elle had bought only what she deemed absolutely necessary: an ill-fitting bra (there weren't many choices), a pair of flats, and some makeup to cover the bruise on her cheek. Even though it had been against her better judgment to spend money frivolously, in honor of Mitch, Elle splurged on three pairs of red thong underwear. Hoping her condition and circumstances weren't completely obvious, she had started work the very next day.

This was Elle's first trip to the laundromat. To save money, she had put it off for as long as she could, hand-washing her bra and underwear in a bathroom sink at the hostel. As Elle watched her clothes tumble in the machine, she craved a cigarette. Quitting smoking had been incredibly hard. Still, Elle was determined. She had changed. There was no going back to the mess she had become.

Elle thought of Mitch. She missed her best friend terribly and longed to talk to him. She had tried calling him several times, but he never answered. Elle would try again later. She wanted to hear all about his evening with Kenji, to explain what had happened, to make sure he was okay.

Ting, ting.

The bells on the front door rang. Elle looked up. A young guy around her age walked in carrying a full pillowcase on top of his shoulder. He wore a gray T-shirt, athletic shorts, and sneakers. He was sweaty and seemed slightly out of breath. From his short, cropped haircut, Elle guessed he was in the Navy or the Marines. There were military guys everywhere in Oahu.

He set his pillowcase down and pointed to the washing machine next to her. "Is this one taken?"

Elle shook her head. "It's all yours."

"Nice." He dumped the contents of the pillowcase into the washer. "All the machines on base were being used, and my stuff is rank." He smiled widely. "And besides, I wanted to go for a run anyway."

Elle considered the stranger. He was good-looking in a very American way: the boy next door who plays baseball and is an Eagle Scout. Elle realized she missed this sort of guy and was grateful her cold sore had finally healed.

Laundry started, he turned and jumped on top of the machine next to Elle, extending his hand out to hers. "I'm Win, by the way."

Elle turned to return his handshake, then remembered she wasn't wearing a bra. The only one she had was currently being washed. As Elle shook his hand, she tucked her shoulders forward. She was wearing Mitch's Ramones T-shirt, which was big and baggy on her, and she hoped it would conceal her bra-less boobs. *What sort of freak walks around without a bra?*

"I'm Elle," Here, Elle paused. She was going to do this right. She had learned. "Actually, my name is Michelle. I just go by Elle."

"Nice to meet you, Elle. My full name is Winston—no offense to my grandpa, but I'm sure you can understand why I wouldn't want to go by that name."

Elle smiled. She was at ease with Win. He had bright, twinkling eyes and a relaxed, easy manner. He oozed authenticity. He was someone who shoveled his elderly neighbors' sidewalks when it snowed and stopped to help stranded motorists change their flat tires. Win was the type of guy who would have volunteered to play Legos on the living room floor with Jimmy. He would have let her brother sit on his lap and drive around the block in his pick-up truck with him.

Win looked at Elle's T-shirt and lifted his chin. "The Ramones. Good band. 'Blitzkrieg Bop' is a killer tune."

Impressive. Win had good taste in music, too. Elle would have taken him as more of a country music kind of guy. She tucked her shoulders in even further, hoping he wouldn't be able to tell she was missing a bra.

Win sensed her unease and mistook its meaning. "Hey, look, I'm sorry. I didn't mean to bother you. I've been on a carrier with sixteen hundred dudes for the last six months—I'm a little rusty." He smiled, apologetically.

"No, it's fine." Elle found his humility refreshing. "I get it. I've been living in Tokyo for the past few years. I'm a little rusty, myself." Elle realized this was the truth. When was the last time she had flirted with an American guy? She couldn't remember.

"Tokyo? Cool. I was supposed to deploy to the Pacific, but Saddam Hussein had other plans, and we ended up in the Persian Gulf. What were you doing in Japan?"

Win's question flustered Elle. How should she answer? She didn't want to lie. She had done enough of that already. "Um . . ."

Win looked at Elle expectantly. She was taking too much time to answer. It was a simple question. *Get it together, Elle.* "Sorry, I seem to be having a hard time thinking in English . . . I was an English teacher." That was the truth. Well, sort of.

"Nice. What was that like?" Win leaned in closer to Elle.

Again, she wasn't sure how to respond. She hadn't thought this through, explaining her life in Japan. It was too soon. Elle wanted to direct attention away from herself. "Um, it was fun. Not nearly as intense as being in the Gulf, that's for sure. Are you in the Navy or the Marines?"

So the conversation began, lasting longer than the time it took to wash and dry their clothes. Win made it easy for Elle. He was warm, funny, and engaged. For the first time since leaving Tokyo, Elle was relaxed and having fun—a reprieve from what she had been through.

Laundry done, Win stopped Elle at the door as she was leaving. "So, some of us guys are having a bonfire at the beach tonight. You should come—that is, if you don't have any plans."

"Yeah, sure. That sounds fun."

Elle took down the details of the party and promised to meet Win later that night. As she walked back to the hostel, Elle was excited about the possibility of seeing him again.

But by the time she made it to the entrance of the hostel, Elle's confidence had waned. Who was she kidding? She couldn't meet Win. Sure, she had gotten away with not revealing too much of what had happened in Tokyo, but how long could that last? Win wasn't the type of guy who would understand—let alone condone—someone who had behaved the way she had. To him, people who used drugs would be losers, like the stoners he had gone to high school with—guys who smoked a bowl before playing Black Ops in their basements with a bag of Cheetos, while he and his friends had the balls to go out and face the enemy themselves. The way real men did.

No, it would never work. Win was cute and nice, but it was futile to expect anything could ever come of it. Why waste her time getting her hopes up?

Elle walked through the door into the hostel, depressed about her situation. Blasting from the radio in the lobby, she heard Mariah Carey's "I'll Be There." Elle stopped. Was this a sign? *I'll be there.* Maybe she *should* go.

Elle was confused. Her gut told her that she had no business meeting up with Win; he was out of her league. Still, this had to be a sign, and Elle had promised to pay more attention.

She would go. She had to.

Elle looked at her bag of clean clothes with the three pairs of red thong underwear in it. They had been worth the splurge. She would wear a pair to the beach that night—Mitch would be proud.

THIRTY

TALKING HEADS: "THIS MUST BE THE PLACE"

June 21, 1994
7:17 p.m.

It was a sublime Hawaiian summer night. Ukulele music was playing against the backdrop of a perfect sunset across the ocean. All around, families in matching Hawaiian-print shirts took pictures with their disposable cameras to properly document their dream trip to Waikiki Beach.

Win had invited Elle to a luau dinner with his parents. He had missed them on his long tour away and had purchased tickets for them to come and visit. Elle was nervous; it was critical that she make a good impression on his family. Despite her fear that it would never work, Elle and Win had gotten serious rather quickly—she didn't want to mess things up now.

Elle liked the person she was around Win. He challenged her intellectually, and she remembered she was smart and had interesting opinions and ideas of her own. Together, they went for runs on the beach, made dinner in his officers' quarters, watched movies, and talked until dawn. Elle was so comfortable with Win that she had even opened up to him about Jimmy's death.

Elle hadn't provided *all* the details—like how she had taken her brother out of his crib, put the stuffed animals around him, and her pink blanket on top of him—but she *had* been honest about how devastating his death had been. Win had listened with perfect understanding and sympathy. He made it easy for Elle to live up to her vow to be a good person. She wanted to be better for herself *and* for him.

Though Elle had worn her thong underwear on their first date, she and Win had not yet had sex. He had been a total gentleman, stopping after kissing and heavy petting. Elle was glad; being chaste gave her more time to erase all her wrongs. She would cleanse herself of all her mistakes and be pure again for Win.

Yes, Elle would be the kind of girl Win deserved. The kind of girl he wanted to introduce to his parents. That's why this night was so important.

Win looked across the table to his mom, Sue. "You should order something to drink, Mom. You're on vacation and it's my treat."

It was clear Win adored Sue. Elle suspected she was the consummate mom, the one who proudly displayed macaroni artwork, who taught Sunday school, and who, when stopped at a red light in her station wagon, protectively stuck her arm out in front of the child next to her.

"Yes, dear. Get something." Win's dad, Winston Jr., whom everyone called W.M., seemed equally suited in his role of patriarch. He had kind, gentle eyes. The eyes of a dad who didn't need to raise his voice when disciplining his children. His disappointment in them would be punishment enough.

W.M. placed his arm encouragingly around his wife's back and winked conspiratorially at Elle. "I just might get something tropical myself."

Elle felt like she had been placed in the middle of an episode of *The Brady Bunch*. The way the Martins spoke kindly to each other, sharing one silly anecdote after another, made them seem just like the sitcom family on TV. With her short ash-blonde hair and in her pantsuit, Sue even looked a little like Carol Brady. "And then mother got icing all over her face!" *Cue laugh track.*

Indeed, the Martins laughed easily. Not the snarky laughter gained at the expense of others that Elle was accustomed to, but a laughter of sincere and uncomplicated happiness.

Do people like this really exist?

The Martins—a quintessential American family—were a first for Elle. Growing up, she had spent most nights alone with her radio, savoring every bite of the chocolate brownie dough she took out of her Swanson's TV dinner before microwaving it. "Family dinners" came on the rare Sunday nights that Bobbie didn't go out on a date. Even then, men were rarely in attendance.

Sure, Bobbie dated, but her boyfriends came around almost exclusively late at night after the bar closed. Elle considered the parade of men who spent the night in their sad little apartment: the one who grew up in pre-Castro Cuba and channeled Jim Morrison with his messy hair and tight leather pants; the one who was a conspiracy theorist and believed in UFOs; and the one who broke it off with her mom by playing her the song "Free Bird" on their stereo which doubled as a TV stand. Elle barely spoke to any of them, but she deduced from the jackets left by the afghan on the couch that her mom was not alone in her room. A new jacket meant a new "friend" and there was a new Members Only or leather one every few weeks. Elle grew up accepting that men never stayed long. Least of all the ones who only were babies.

So while years at the bar and her work at the Big YAC had honed Elle's ability to make small talk, sitting here with the Martins—the nicest, most welcoming family she could imagine—made Elle uncomfortable.

She was out of her element and wished she could talk to Mitch. She still hadn't been able to reach him despite numerous attempts. What was he doing right now, at this very moment? Was Mitch missing her as much as she was missing him? Elle hoped he was with Kenji. She pictured him at a table off to the side, observing her as he had at the Big YAC. What would he make of the Martins? Of Win? Would he approve?

Sue clapped her hands in delight. "Oh, okay. I guess I *am* on vacation." She turned to the waitress wearing a grass hula skirt. "I'll try a piña colada."

W.M. motioned toward Elle. "What about you, young lady? Can we tempt you with a piña colada? Or how about one of those daiquiris?"

True to her promise on the plane ride, Elle hadn't had a drop of alcohol since leaving Tokyo. Even so, she considered ordering something now—a cocktail would certainly help ease her nervousness. And besides, a daiquiri wasn't really a *"drink,"* was it?

Elle looked at Win. He smiled broadly and winked at her in the same way his dad had. No, she wouldn't drink. Staying sober was a key element in her plan for self-improvement. "Sure, I'll have a strawberry daiquiri, but can you make it a virgin?" Elle turned toward W.M. and Sue, explaining, "Alcohol and I don't mix too well."

Alcohol and I don't mix too well. This was the version of the truth Elle had become comfortable with, and what she had told Win their first night together at the bonfire when he had offered her a beer. Win had accepted her explanation without hesitation. Would his parents?

Elle hoped they wouldn't disapprove, but if her relationship with Win was going to work, she had to be as forthcoming as possible. Elle saw no reason to divulge *all* her past, but she didn't want to start with blatant mistruths. After so many lies in Japan, it felt strange to be honest, but good and necessary.

"You know, that's a great idea. Make mine a virgin, too." Sue smiled at Elle. "Heaven knows I don't need the calories!"

That was it. No looks of confusion or disapproval. Elle didn't drink. *Okay.* If she didn't drink, neither would they. Elle shouldn't have been surprised; Mike and Carol Brady weren't the type to pass judgment.

"So, tell us about your family, dear." W.M. directed his attention toward Elle, leaning slightly forward over Sue.

The question caught Elle off guard. *Her family?* She hadn't given Bobbie much thought since her arrival in Hawaii. She had successfully locked away the devastating circumstances of her mom's death to deal with when she was in a better place.

What should I say?

"Well, I was raised by a single mom . . ." Elle paused to gauge the Martins' reactions. W.M.'s and Sue's faces didn't register any negative emotion, so she continued, "Her name was Roberta, but she hated that name and went by Bobbie. She . . . um . . ."

Elle pictured Bobbie behind the bar, cigarette in one hand, laughing her deep, throaty laugh at something a customer said. She wanted to remember her mom this way, not lying mangled on the hard asphalt. Their relationship had been wrought with misunderstanding and disappointment, yet her Grandma Jean had been right. Bobbie was a good person. She didn't deserve to die so young, in such a tragic, violent way.

My mom is dead. How could Elle say it out loud, when all this time she had pretended it didn't need to be acknowledged?

"She was, um . . . killed in a motorcycle accident." Tears swelled in Elle's eyes and her shoulders began to shake. She couldn't bear to look at Win's parents and focused her attention down on her plate. Teardrops formed in a small puddle on the bright-orange fish-shaped dish. Win draped his arm around her, but she didn't dare look up. Elle grabbed the napkin off her lap and tried to graciously excuse herself. "I'm sorry. I . . . um, excuse me for just a minute."

Elle stood and clumsily left the table. She needed to get away before she completely broke down. As she hurried toward the bathroom, Win caught up with her. He gently held his fingers under her eyes, drying her tears. "Hey, are you okay?"

Elle rubbed the napkin across her eyes and nose. She was embarrassed. Humiliated, really. How had she let herself lose control? "I'm so sorry. I don't know where that came from. I—"

"Look, you have nothing to apologize for. I had no idea about your mom. I'm so sorry." Win put his arms around her shoulders. "I can't imagine how horrible that would be."

Elle sniffled. What had happened to her mom *was* horrible; she just hadn't really internalized it until now. It took being with Win and his *Leave It to Beaver* family for Elle to realize not only what she didn't have, but also what she had lost.

Bobbie might not have been the kind of mother she had wanted or needed, but she had done the best she could. Losing a child was the cruelest of punishments. That her mom had gotten up and out of bed everyday was enough. It had been unfair of Elle to fault her for not knowing, not understanding, not being tormented by the need for more, the way she was. Bobbie didn't question, didn't yearn, didn't feel sorry for herself. She simply got on with it and expected Elle to do the same.

Why can't I?

Elle took a deep breath and tried to compose herself, although she implicitly understood she didn't need to be embarrassed in front of Win. She trusted him. "I just haven't talked about it too much, I guess. I'm okay."

Win cupped his hands around Elle's face, the way Tak used to, the way Gustavo had. She didn't feel the same intense physical attraction to Win as she had with those two, but it didn't matter. What Elle had experienced with Tak and Gustavo wasn't authentic—she had been someone entirely different then. Someone living a make-belief life, in a make-believe place, fueled by drugs, alcohol, and pretense. It felt better with Win; it was safer. It was real.

"It's going to be alright. You'll see." Win kissed Elle on the lips. Gently. Sweetly.

Elle kissed him back, wallowing in his warm, kind lips. Could he be right? Despite all the ways she had fucked up, could Elle still find redemption? Could she be like the Martins? Elle wanted what they had. She wanted Win. She wanted this.

Win wouldn't leave. He would be the dad playing with his children in the park.

Elle was desperate for a sign. All she could hear in the background was the soft ukulele music of the luau. What else could she use as a sign, an indication it was going to be okay?

The date. It was June 21st—the summer solstice. The summer solstice was a day of new beginnings. Surely that was a good sign. Elle would take it.

Win was her chance at normalcy. At happiness. Elle would do anything to make it work.

THIRTY-ONE

Sara Bareilles: "Brave"

June 5, 2017
12:09 a.m.

Elle finished her martini, satisfied. *Message received.* She would no longer hide her past. She would be more honest with herself and her family. Then, like Princess Elsa in *Frozen*, Elle would get her happy ending.

Win returned from the men's room and took a sip of Glenfiddich from the highball glass on the table in front of him. The strong, pungent smell of Scotch reminded Elle of the Big YAC and how she had encouraged clients to order the most expensive bottles available.

"Aah . . ." Win set down his glass and leaned back with his hands interlaced behind his head. "Karaoke was fun!"

"Yeah, it was," Elle agreed. "We need to spend more time together like that."

"You're right." Win nodded and then sat up straight, noticing Elle's hand around her martini glass. "You're wearing your old wedding ring?"

Elle looked down at the simple gold band on her finger, the ring Win had proposed with. It was unusual for her to wear it. For their tenth anniversary, Win had upgraded it to a platinum one with a five-carat ass-cher cut diamond. "Yeah, it seemed safer to travel wearing this one." Elle looked at the ring. "Don't get me wrong, I love the other ring—it's beauti-ful—but I think I might actually like this one more."

Elle *did* prefer the simple gold band. When it came right down to it, she didn't want or need the private plane, the suite at the Four Seasons, the $2,500-a-plate dinners. It was days at the park as a normal family that she had longed for.

"I always loved it on you." Win scrunched his eyes slightly and looked playfully at Elle. "I like seeing you here. You're in your element."

He was right. Away from the constant anxiety over whether she was doing and saying and wearing the right thing, Elle was at ease. She hadn't been concerned about what Aubrey was or wasn't saying or anything else for that matter. Her dreams had been gloriously free of cats and dogs gnawing on feminine hygiene products. "You know, it's strange. Being back here has been so . . . I don't know . . . cathartic, in a way. It's like being away from everything back home makes me realize none of it is important. Except Duke, of course. I miss him desperately."

"Has Angela been sending daily reports and pictures?"

"Well, she has sent a few pictures, but believe it or not, I haven't been worried about him."

Win turned serious. "It's good to see you so happy."

Elle panicked. *What does he mean?* Did Win suspect the truth? She thought she had been convincing in her portrayal of a perfectly content person.

Elle considered her resolution—here was her chance to follow the signs and be honest. She took a large sip of her martini for courage. "Do you ever wonder how we got to this place?"

"Well, if I remember correctly, I think it was on an airplane."

"Exactly. Not just an airplane—a private jet. How did that happen?"

Win shrugged his shoulders. "There are worse things."

"I know. It's not that, it's . . ." Elle didn't know where to begin. She wasn't accustomed to expressing her true feelings. She decided it would be best to be direct—ripping a Band-Aid off in one swift movement was always less agonizing than the alternative. "Why did you want to marry me?"

Win jerked his head back in confusion. "What do you mean, why did I want to marry you?"

"I don't know—what was it about me, about us, that made you think this was it?" Elle sat back, nervous. What would he say? Was she ready to hear it?

"Your succulent ass might have had something to do with it."

"Very funny! I'm serious, Win. Why me?" Elle was resolute. She needed answers.

Win regarded her question for a few moments. "Well, there were lots of things. You were so different from any of the other women I had dated, so independent and strong. Determined."

Independent, strong, determined? Elle thought back to the time they met and didn't think she had been any of those things. Quite the opposite, she remembered being scared, confused, and uncertain about her future. "You thought I was strong? I remember feeling rather unsure of myself back then."

"Well, that's what was so attractive. You obviously had guts. Not many college coeds pack up and head off to Japan by themselves. I admired that about you. At the same time, having lost your mom and all, you were sort of vulnerable and not afraid to show it. It was endearing."

Elle's heart sank. This was precisely what she had always deep down been afraid of. After Win's long tour away he was anxious for female companionship, and she had been like a mutt at the pound, sweet and doe-eyed and orphaned. Win had wanted to rescue her. It was only after he took her home that Elle's true nature was revealed. She was damaged. Broken beyond repair. But by then, it was too late. The pound had a no-return policy. Win was stuck. He saw the real Elle and knew he had been duped, but he was too good of a person to admit his disappointment. He'd had no choice but to carry on. To make the best of it, knowing deep down he shouldn't have made the rash decision to bring the mutt home. He should have waited for the show dog with superior breeding.

"And of course, you were smart. Smarter than me, that's for sure. And so funny. We had so much fun together. Remember?"

Elle nodded, trying not to cry. They *had* had fun together. That was real.

Win took another drink. "Where is this coming from?"

Elle looked down to hide the tears welling in her eyes. How could she admit the truth to Win? That maybe he fell in love with a girl who didn't exist. That she had lacked the courage to show him her true self because she feared he wouldn't, or couldn't, love that person, flawed as she was. Elle had never even had her own mother's love. How could she deserve his?

Win reached his hand across the table and touched Elle's arm. "I also knew you would be an incredible mom, which you are."

This was classic Win. Always finding the best in everyone—even her. Elle couldn't stop the tears. She looked up at him, her lips trembling.

"Hey, what's wrong? What is it?" Win slowly stroked her hand with his.

"It's—" Elle couldn't get the words out.

"C'mon, let's get out of here." Win stood, reached into his pocket, pulled out several 10,000-yen notes, and left them on the table. He gently grabbed Elle's hand and led her out of the bar.

Win placed his arm protectively around Elle as they stood in silence in the elevator. She struggled to maintain her composure and wished she hadn't drank the martini. There was a reason she had quit drinking; Elle didn't like not being in control.

The elevator moved rhythmically, past one floor after the next, as it made its way to the penthouse suite. Somewhere between floors 39 and 42, Win looked down at Elle, held her chin in one hand, and kissed her. It was a gentle, tentative kiss. Elle received it hungrily. She didn't flinch, nor recoil.

By the time the elevator doors opened to the penthouse, they were locked into each other, kissing passionately. Win reached into his pocket for the suite key as Elle unbuttoned his shirt. Still kissing, they stumbled into the suite and their bedroom where their frantically made love on the king size bed.

◆ ◆ ◆

12:51 a.m.

Elle rubbed her fingers along Win's chest. Being with him felt natural and easy in a way it hadn't in a long time—too long of a time. She felt safe and was ashamed of being so afraid of sharing a bed with her husband.

Elle had spent the last few years so consumed by her own insecurities, she hadn't considered Win's feelings. It occurred to her that perhaps he was experiencing the same weariness about their lives as she was. That Win, too, was trapped in a role he wasn't sure he wanted.

"Are you happy, Win?"

"Are you kidding me? Yes! That was awesome."

Elle punched him affectionately in the stomach. "No, that's not what I meant. I mean, are you happy? Does all this deal-making bring you fulfillment?"

"I suppose so, but maybe not as much as it used to."

"You've done enough, you know. More than enough. You've given me a life I never dreamed of." Elle meant it. She hadn't expected all this. She was lucky.

"Thank you. That means a lot." Win turned toward her. "What about you? Are you happy?"

Elle's instinct was to answer, "Yes, of course I'm happy." Why ruin this perfect moment? But she remembered the signs, the indications to let it go, to shake the devil off her back. Elle needed to be more truthful.

"Yes, and no." Elle paused. What could she say? That she was exhausted from all the pretending? That she wasn't the person he thought she was? How could she explain those things? Elle started again slowly,

"I'm lucky, I know I am. I love our family, it's just . . ." Elle worried she might cry, but she had to continue, "I don't know. I feel . . . tired."

Win pulled Elle close to him, lifted her head, and kissed her slowly and deliberately. It was a kiss of understanding and compassion. He moved on top of Elle and they made love again, this time more carefully and patiently, as if they wanted the moment to last.

THIRTY-TWO

JOURNEY: "DON'T STOP BELIEVIN'"

June 5, 2017
8:11 a.m.

"Good morning." Win woke Elle with a kiss on the cheek. He was already dressed for his day of meetings in a smart navy bespoke suit and the simple red tie Elle had packed for him.

"Mmm . . . morning." Elle stretched out lazily and turned in bed toward her husband. His kiss had sent a warm and exquisite tingle down her spine.

Sex with Win after the elevator ride had been amazing, more passionate than it had been in years. Elle worried it was a result of her lack of inhibition from the alcohol. What would happen when she was sober? Would she tense up and recoil from his touch again? But when they had made love again later, it had been even better. Perhaps it hadn't been quite as fervent, but it was powerful and wonderful all the same. Elle felt an undeniable connection to Win, maybe because in being honest she had allowed herself to be vulnerable, to feel something real and true.

Elle and Win had stayed up late the night before, their sexual intimacy opening the door for a more candid conversation than they had had in years. They discussed their children, agreeing it was important for

Brynnie to know that they supported her, regardless of her sexual orientation. They promised to be harder on Four, acknowledging that at times they had spoiled him. Elle even admitted to questioning the integrity of her so-called friends, and Win surprised her by responding that he was glad to hear it—he found them vapid and their husbands flaccid. He had tolerated them only because he thought they made her happy; he much preferred the company of his old Navy buddies.

Encouraged by Win's responses, Elle had opened up to him more truthfully about her life in Japan, sharing stories about Mitch and how anxious she was to find her old friend. She briefly even considered confessing to her guilt over Jimmy's death, but it was still too painful to admit to. *Baby steps.* It could wait.

Win sat on the side of the bed and ran his fingers through Elle's hair. "I was thinking about what you said last night, about the private jet, about how we got to this place."

"Yeah?" Elle sat up and leaned against the pillows.

"What is it you would want to do, if you could do anything, anything at all?"

"Are you happy, Mom? Are you living your dream?"

"That's the million-dollar question. I'm not sure . . . I should probably do more for the SIDS Alliance. Beyond that, I don't really know. I liked being a social worker, so probably something helping others. I'd like to give back."

Win nodded. He was in work mode now, presented with a problem and thinking of a solution. "Ok. What kind of help, specifically, and to whom?"

"Well, my favorite clients were always young women at risk. Maybe I should go back to work at a shelter full time, but I don't know if it's enough."

Win rubbed his chin thoughtfully. "Enough for you or enough for those who need help?"

"Both, I suppose."

"Okay. You want to help young women at risk, and you want it to be meaningful. What about opening a shelter for at-risk female teens?"

"That's a great idea, but I don't think I'm qualified to do that."

"Well, what if we did it together?"

Elle was taken aback by Win's use of "we" and skeptical of its meaning. She knew how hard he worked at Martin Global, how little free time he had. "That would be a huge commitment. How could you possibly fit it in?"

Win answered quickly, like he had already thought about it. "The way I see it, I need to give this deal the next six months. It's gonna take at least three months to get everything in place and then another three for me to fully transition out. If you got things started on your own, by spring of next year I could be all yours."

"What are you saying? You would do this with me?" Elle hadn't expected this.

"Absolutely! Look, I thought a lot about what you were trying to get at last night. You're right. We should spend more time together. Do something that matters."

"Really?"

"Why not? How many more deals can I broker?"

"Oh, my gosh, yes, Win!" Elle gushed. If her heart could smile, it would be beaming.

Win kissed her on the lips. "We'll talk more about it later. I should get to my meeting."

"Okay. Good luck with your negotiations."

"Thanks. I'll need it. This Akimoto can be a real stubborn S.O.B." Win was frustrated with the Tsugunai president. The previous day, his lawyers had presented Martin Global with a new contract, different in its terms than those originally agreed upon. Last minute changes like these were unprecedented and difficult to negotiate through.

Elle rubbed her husband's back. "I have no doubt in your ability to win him over."

"Actually, I'm counting on you to use your charm on him at the party tonight."

"I'll do my best." Elle smiled wanly. She didn't want to think about charming Japanese men; it was a little too close to the part of her life in Japan she didn't want to remember.

Never mind that. Elle wouldn't let anything ruin this moment for her.

"I love you." Elle had never meant it more. She *did* love Win and hadn't been fair to him. She had expected him to save her, to bring her happiness, to give her life meaning. When he couldn't, she had become resentful, hence the physical coldness.

Elle wouldn't allow that to happen again. She understood what she needed to do now. She had listened to the signs. It was still going to take time and work to make her marriage successful—they weren't Jonathan and Jennifer from an episode of *Hart to Hart*—but it could be done.

"And I love you." Win kissed Elle, put on his suit jacket, and walked to the door. He turned back toward her before leaving. "I hope you have some luck tracking down Mitch. Let me know if you want me to put someone on it."

"Thanks. Good luck with your meetings." Elle watched Win leave. She had been right about him; he was a good man—the kind of man who understood the subtle perfection of saying "*And* I love you" over the more pedestrian "I love you, too."

She lay back down on the bed considering where she would start with her search, when Win's head suddenly popped back in the door. "One more thing—since we're shaking it up a bit. How do you feel about quitting the club when we get home?"

"Yes! Let's!"

"Good. I'm getting tired of playing golf with those assholes. They cheat!"

Elle smiled. *At last*, she was happy. If only she could find Mitch, her life would be complete.

◆ ◆ ◆

9:51 a.m.

Elle chewed on her piece of toast, thinking it was the best toast she had ever had—nice and hot, which was impressive, considering it had made its way to the suite via room service. French bread toast with apricot jelly—not typical for a Japanese breakfast, but delicious.

Elle couldn't help feeling everything was headed in the right direction. That anything and everything was possible again. How ironic that she had been so afraid of returning to Japan, only to find herself more optimistic about her future than ever.

Elle would now focus on finding Mitch. Hotel pen and pad in hand, she made a list of places to visit. The first few were obvious: the apartment she and Mitch had shared (she had the key in her purse), the mom-and-pop grocery store they had frequented, and The English First school where they had worked. Elle wasn't sure going to any of these places would yield any results—it *had* been over twenty years—but it was a start.

What about Samantha's? Elle was uncomfortable with the idea of seeing the club again, it was the site of so many of her poor decisions. Still, she should go there. Kenji was the last person she knew of who had been with Mitch. It was highly improbable that the club was even still open, let alone that Kenji would still work there, but she would try.

What if Samantha's *was* still open? What if Tak still owned the club? Elle shuddered. She had promised to share more of her past with Win, but maybe she didn't have to tell him everything . . .

Elle put the pen in her mouth and thought of other ways to find Mitch. Perhaps she should ask the hotel concierge to do a Google search in Japanese for him. Was there even such a thing? She would ask Brynnie.

Elle heard a door open and looked up from her notepad to see her daughter enter, freshly showered and wrapped in a soft, fluffy white hotel robe. "Good morning, sweetheart. Perfect timing. Room service just came. No kombucha sadly, but I did get you some green tea and a bowl of fruit."

"No kombucha! Here I thought this was a luxury hotel . . ." Brynnie grabbed a mug of tea off the table, stopping first to give her mom a hug. "Green tea will be great, thanks."

"Is Four awake? I ordered him an omelet and some toast."

"Yep, but he's skyping with his *bae*, so he'll be awhile."

"His bay?" Elle was confused. She tried to keep up with her teens' lingo, but she had never heard this expression before.

"B – A – E. Before anyone else—it's slang for your significant other." Brynnie was matter-of-fact, free from the condescending tone that often accompanied her attitude when explaining things to her mom. Things *were* better.

"Oh, got it." Elle took a drink of coffee. "I like Tabby; she's a sweet girl."

"Yeah, she is. What she sees in Four, I'll never understand."

"Brynnie!"

"I'm kidding!" Brynnie took a piece of toast from Elle's plate. "But you know what I mean. He's a good kid and all; he's just got a bit of growing up to do."

Elle nodded, she had reached the same conclusion with Win just hours before. Their conversation fresh in her mind, Elle decided to broach the subject of Brynnie's sexuality. *Why not?* Her new mantra was all about honesty. "I remember most boys in high school as being pretty immature. Maybe that's why you've never found anyone you've wanted to date."

Brynnie shrugged her shoulders. "Yeah, maybe."

"There isn't anyone at school you like, no one you're attracted to?" Elle chose her gender-neutral words carefully.

"At Country Day? Are you kidding me? No!"

Elle decided to just come out with it. Brynnie was a straightforward kind of person. She would appreciate her directness. "Sweetheart, you know your dad and I love you, more than anything, and . . ."

"And what?"

"Well, if it turns out you prefer . . . if you are, you know, attracted to women, it's fine. We just want you to be happy." There—she said it.

Brynnie's head popped back in surprise. "So, you and Dad have discussed this?"

"Yes." Elle sat back. She wanted to give Brynnie time.

"You're telling me if I were a lesbian, you guys wouldn't be at all disappointed, embarrassed even?"

"Embarrassed, no!" Elle answered truthfully. "We would never be embarrassed or ashamed of you. I'm so proud of you—you must know that. We both are."

"I get that with Dad, but what about Aubrey, all your tennis ladies—wouldn't it be hard for you with them?"

It stung Elle that Brynnie didn't question Win, but her own allegiance was in doubt. How could her daughter believe she would care about what others thought?

Because she did. Elle couldn't deny it. Brynnie could detect the truth in the same way she could. She saw her mother's weakness.

And maybe Elle *did* care too much about what others thought, but not regarding Brynnie. She loved her daughter unconditionally. "Fuck them. If they don't like it, they can go to hell."

"*Mom!*" Brynnie choked on her green tea.

"I'm serious, Brynnie." Elle meant it. She wouldn't abide her so-called friends mean-spiritedly gossiping about her daughter. In fact, Elle was planning to confront them all about their behavior once she returned home.

"Well, as much pleasure as I know it gives everyone at Country Day to think otherwise, I'm not a lesbian."

Elle felt relief, then guilt about the relief. Why would she feel relieved?

Brynnie continued, "Though I do enjoy making people wonder. It kinda lets you know right away where you stand, know what I mean?"

"I do." Elle nodded sympathetically. She considered Aubrey's cruelty toward Brynnie and understood that her initial reaction of relief was not due to prejudice, but the realization that being straight meant her daughter would be spared the callous judgment of ignorant people. As self-assured and confident as Brynnie was, it would still be difficult to be openly gay. "Dad went as far as to suggest you bring a female date to the deb ball."

"Really? That would be hilarious. Can you imagine? All those tight-asses wouldn't know what to say or how to act."

"Yeah, I can picture them all practically tripping over their Jimmy Choo stilettos at your grand entrance. That might be worth seeing."

"I'm sure a cosmos or two might be spilled." Brynnie laughed, then looked at her mom thoughtfully. "Since we're having this Hallmark mother-daughter moment, I've got to say, I'm happy to see you eating normally."

Elle was startled. "What do you mean?"

"C'mon, Mom. You never eat carbs, and you've had rice all week. And you just ate toast. *White* toast!"

Again, Brynnie's observations were keen. Without a scale, Elle hadn't been obsessively weighing in every morning. She hadn't even given much consideration to what she was eating. And here Elle thought she had been so smart, so careful all these years. Adamant that Brynnie would not grow up with body-image issues, she had never mentioned the word *diet*, never restricted what Brynnie ate, never complained aloud about her own weight. Careful as Elle had been—or thought she had been—it hadn't been enough to mask the truth.

Elle conceded, admitting, "I suppose you're right."

"It's good. You seem more relaxed, happier."

"Do I?" Win had said the same thing.

"Yeah, you do. I like it."

"Me, too!"

"So, tell me more about Mitch . . . about our plan for today."

Elle began to answer when Four bounced into the room, naked, spare a pair of navy-red-and-green plaid boxers—the same type Elle had wanted Mitch to wear instead of tighty-whities.

"Morning!" Four hugged Elle.

"Good morning! I ordered you some breakfast."

"Awesome. I'm starving." Four grabbed his plate of food and hopped enthusiastically onto the couch across from Brynnie, sitting down cross-legged.

"Ew! I can see your nut sack!" Brynnie turned away.

"Impressive, right?"

Brynnie shook her head in disgust. "At least tuck them in or something. Really—I'm trying to eat."

Four ignored his sister and took a bite of the omelet off his plate. "Mmm, this is good. That food from last night didn't sit so well . . ."

Brynnie shook her head. "You're so gross."

"Speaking of gross, I wouldn't use our bathroom for a while."

"Four, really? Is that necessary?" Elle tried to be patient.

"I'm just warning you, that's all. I told you that shabu-shabu didn't sit well. It's a good thing there's a normal toilet in there. I coulda been in big trouble if I had to squat through that one."

Elle frowned, concerned. "I hope it's not the same thing you had on the plane."

"Nah, it was just that shabu shabu. I'm good."

Elle noticed Four give Brynnie a furtive look. She briefly wondered what it could mean, but dismissed it as inconsequential. She had more important things on her mind. "So, I was just talking to Brynnie about looking for my friend Mitch today. Do you want to come with us?"

"Mitch—is that the gay guy you were talking about?"

Elle was angry. More at herself than anyone else. Four's attitude and ignorance were her fault. She had given him too many passes. It had to stop. Treating him with kid gloves wasn't going to bring Jimmy back. It was her responsibility to teach her son to be a more thoughtful and empathetic young man. "Four, you have to stop categorizing people. It's ignorant and shameful."

"Sorry, sorry!" Four held up his hands.

"I'm serious about this. Don't be that guy. You know better." Elle looked to Brynnie. Had she been firm enough? She added for emphasis, "Really, I mean it. It's not acceptable."

Brynnie didn't say anything. Elle took this to be her tacit approval.

"Okay, you're right. I got it. Sorry."

Elle hoped Four meant what he said. She would no longer condone his flippancy. "Do you want to join us?"

Four stretched out lazily. "The thing is, the hotel lobby is a major Pokémon Go hotspot and I'm in the hunt for Tauros. You good with me staying here?"

Elle tried not to be disappointed that Four was more interested in playing a video game than spending time with her, but as Brynnie had pointed out, he was still young and immature. It would be fine. They would probably have a better time without him anyway.

"Yeah, sure. Just be ready by five-thirty. That's when the car is coming to take us to dinner."

Four held his thumb up. "Got it."

Pleased, Elle stood and turned to Brynnie. "Alright, I'm going to go get ready. Let's plan to leave in about half an hour." Elle was excited and optimistic. "Operation Find Mitch is officially underway."

THIRTY-THREE

Golden Earring: "Twilight Zone"

June 5, 2017
5:22 p.m.

Elle studied herself in the full-length mirror with distaste. She looked ridiculous, but what could she do? In the Japanese tradition of gift-giving, the Tsugunai President, Mr. Akimoto, had presented her with a gown ahead of that night's formal dinner. It would be rude for Elle not to wear it.

Still, the dress was beyond awful. It was hot pink, strapless, and too body-hugging for someone her age. Plus, it had sequins. *Sequins!* If Elle had a corsage, she would look perfect for her high school prom.

Mr. Akimoto's other gifts had made more sense. There had been a welcome bouquet in their hotel suite of Elle's favorite flowers, yellow Gerber daisies; Brynnie had received a leather-bound book on Buddhism; and Four a popular gaming system which wasn't available in the States.

Yet inexplicably, Elle had also received a Miss America gown and a tube of ruby red Christian Louboutin lipstick. (There was *no way* she was putting this on—the gaudy gown was bad enough.) Elle sighed. *Oh well.* It was the thought that counted, and she needed to get over her aggravation with the dress. Tonight was important for Win, so Elle had to make the best of it.

Win. What would he think of the dress? Would he be as horrified by it as she was? Elle hadn't seen him all day. His meetings had run late after another snag in negotiations, so he had been unable to come back to the hotel. Elle and her children were going to meet up with him at the Tsugunai offices.

Elle dreaded seeing Win in her current get-up. And then there would be the cameras at the event, capturing for all of eternity her fashion disaster. Ainsley, wearing a minimalist Calvin Klein or Ralph Lauren gown which showed off her perfect breasts, would probably smirk. *Joy.* Elle had that to look forward to. At least there was nothing between the young producer and Win. He had assured her of as much the previous night.

For the first time since arriving in Tokyo, Elle was irritable. Up to this point, she had been uncharacteristically at ease, not prone to her usual mood swings, but wearing this dress annoyed her. That and a lingering sense of sadness that her search for Mitch hadn't yielded any results.

Full of hope, Elle had carried the apartment key to her old neighborhood, but it turned out the block was no longer residential; it was now a business park. Even the small grocery shop she and Mitch had frequented was gone, replaced by a Taco Bell. This last discovery had, at least, brought a smile to her face. The absence of Mexican food in Tokyo was something Mitch often bemoaned, especially after a late night out drinking. It was nice to see the chain had finally made it to Japan.

But then there had been more bad news. English First was out of business, as was Samantha's. Elle had been naive to think she would somehow stumble upon her old friend in a city of over thirteen million people. She would talk to Win about hiring someone to find Mitch when they returned home. Being in Tokyo had brought back to life so many happy memories of her old friend, it was important to her that they reconnect.

Elle looked in the mirror one last time, grabbed her purse, and walked into the sitting room of the hotel suite. The car to take her family to dinner would be there any minute. As Elle entered the sitting room, neither of her children looked up from their phones. She had to speak to get their attention. "What do you think?"

Brynnie lifted her head. Seeing Elle, she placed her hands over her mouth, her eyes wide in disbelief.

"Wow." Four followed, his fingers split in shock against his face.

"I know! I know!" Elle shook her head with a playful smile. The whole thing was so absurd.

Brynnie stood up from the couch. "You look like someone on *Dynasty*."

"Well, at least I haven't crimped my hair. The sad thing is, I would have worn something like this back in the day."

Four cringed. "That woulda been a bad day."

"Yep, I had a lot of those." Elle pulled at the top of the dress. "What do you think Dad will say?"

Brynnie shook her head. "I don't know, but I think we should take a picture and text it to him as a warning, so he'll be prepared."

"That's a good idea. Let's do that. Four, can you take a selfie with your phone?"

"Only if you promise to never say selfie again!"

Four and Brynnie surrounded Elle. She looked at her children with approval. Four was debonair and handsome in a fitted tuxedo with a madras plaid cummerbund and bow tie. Brynnie had taken the unusual step of applying lip gloss and a touch of mascara, and she looked radiant in the simple, understated white pantsuit she had also worn to her high school graduation. The three huddled together and Four extended his right arm with the phone in it. "Here we go . . . one, two, three, cheese!"

Elle snuggled in close to her children and smiled. Forget the stupid prom dress. She was happy. Jimmy would have been proud of the family she had created. Even her mom might have been, too.

◆ ◆ ◆

5:33 p.m.

"So, what is it exactly that we are going to tonight?" Four sat across from Brynnie and Elle in the limo taking them to the headquarters of Tsugunai.

"Well, from what I understand, they are going to unveil the technology Dad's company bought. It's a sort of lifelike robot that can think for itself." Elle honestly didn't know any more than that. Win had explained only enough for her to be able to give the opening remarks at the press conference the next day. He wanted her to be surprised by the product's introduction along with everyone else.

Brynnie was skeptical, saying, "I'm not so sure about the wisdom of artificial intelligence. Who knows what it could lead to?"

"You're right, sis. I'm sure it's some sort of conspiracy by corporate America to take down the indigenous people of Malawi. I think it sounds cool. Maybe I can teach it to play lacrosse."

"It will be able to teach *itself* to play lacrosse, that's the scary part."

Elle tried to be diplomatic. "Or the exciting part. I suppose it depends on how you look at it."

Four put his pinkie to his lips. "As long as we keep it away from Dr. Evil, we should be good." He gestured to the bar along the side of the limo. "How about a glass of champagne to toast Dad's accomplishments?"

A glass of champagne? Elle was shocked by her son's request. "No. I don't think that's such a wise idea."

Four shrugged. "I don't know. I figured it was a special occasion. Besides, we're in Tokyo. It seems different."

Elle understood Four's logic. All too well. She had felt the same way twenty years ago. It *was* different being there. The rules didn't seem to apply. If no one you knew saw you, it didn't seem to count. It was just this type of thinking that had gotten Elle into so much trouble. She decided to cede a little. "How about this? If they have champagne at the party, you can have a glass."

"Alright, cool."

Brynnie reached for a bottled water. "I'm not into champagne; it's too sweet."

What? When had Brynnie tasted champagne? How did she get the alcohol? For someone who prided herself on seeing the subtext, Elle worried she had missed some fairly significant information. She would pay more attention.

As part of her honesty pledge, she should also talk to Brynnie and Four more openly about the dangers of drinking. Elle could minimize her past behavior all she wanted, but she had had a seriously bad relationship with drugs and alcohol. What if, along with the genes for being short and fat-assed, she had also passed along to her children a proclivity for substance abuse? Brynnie and Four needed to know what they were up against, she owed them that. Elle couldn't possibly abide another death she could have done more to prevent.

How much was she prepared to give away?

Elle remembered all the mistakes she had made while she had been wasted on alcohol or high on cocaine or both. How could she possibly admit to her appalling behavior?

She couldn't. Not to her children. Elle decided she would simply cop to her overdrinking, but not now. She needed time to prepare, to think through exactly what she would say. Besides, it wasn't the right time. Today was about Win and his groundbreaking deal. She would talk to Brynnie and Four when they got back home, when Win could also be there. Yes, that would be better.

The limo pulled to a stop in front of a large, impressive high-rise glass building on a busy street in Ōtemachi. It stood in contrast to the older, prewar buildings surrounding it; its boldness and modernity imposing its will on the entire block. Light from the evening sun flickered off the glass, like a spotlight, further highlighting the building's dominating presence.

As the driver opened the door for Elle, she saw Win approach. He seemed in a hurry to get to her. This was uncharacteristic; he was always so calm and deliberate.

Win kissed her on the cheek. "Man, am I glad to see you."

Something was wrong. Win looked tense and uncomfortable. He hadn't even noticed her dress. Concerned, Elle asked, "What's the matter?"

"This has been a hell of a day. Akimoto went Dr. Jekyll and Mr. Hyde on me."

"What do you mean?"

"I don't know what happened! We were ready to sign the deal, and then—out of nowhere—he became irrational, with a whole new set of demands. I've never seen anything like it."

"I'm sorry." Elle rubbed Win's shoulders as Brynnie and Four got out of the limo. "Will you be able to work it out?"

"I think so. I'm just glad you're here. I'm counting on you to work your magic on him."

Elle bristled at Win's choice of words. She was uncomfortable; everything was off. She had never seen her husband so frazzled before; it worried her. She thought about her day—had she missed a sign?

Win greeted his children and hurriedly ushered them and Elle toward the main entrance of the building. In the bright light, Elle could see the outline of a Japanese man holding the door open for them. She pulled her dress up again. On top of everything else, she was going to have to make sure her boobs didn't spill out all night. They reached the entrance, and out of the sun's glare, Elle could see the man holding the door open more clearly.

The sensation of cold, steely metal in her mouth returned.

It can't be.

But it was. Elle was sure of it. She couldn't forget that face. Those inhumane eyes. He was older, with gray hair and a slight stoop, but there was no mistaking it. The man holding the door open for her family was Johnny.

He looked at Elle and sneered, revealing his broken front tooth for a flash. He then bowed so deliberately, Elle was convinced he was mocking her. She couldn't move and couldn't think. Wasn't this the same man who had threatened to rape her if he ever saw her again?

How can this be happening?

Elle's cheeks warmed and droplets of sweat formed under her armpits. Speechless, she allowed herself to be led into the building and onto the elevator. Win and her children were talking, but she couldn't follow their conversation. She didn't giggle along with them as the elevator rose quickly to the 110th floor, making their stomachs drop. Elle couldn't feel anything but the warmth of her skin.

The elevator opened onto a breathtaking scene. They were atop an expansive outdoor rooftop decorated in shades of yellow. There were Gerber daises and candles and twinkle lights everywhere. U2 was playing softly in the background. The Imperial Palace and the lush gardens surrounding it were visible in the backdrop.

Everything was perfect. Elle wouldn't have changed a thing if she had designed it herself. A crowd in the center of the balcony dispersed as the Martins entered. Elle reached for Win's hand. That's when she saw him.

In the center of it all, standing next to a young, attractive woman with platinum-blonde hair down to her waist, was Tak. He, too, looked older but retained the same domineering presence as the day she first met him at the Big YAC.

Tak, in command.

Of course. How could Elle not have guessed it would be him? The signs pointing to a collision course with her past had been there all along. How had she missed all the clues?

The name Akimoto. The same hotel where she had been with Tak. Her favorite flowers in her favorite color. The bright red lipstick. And the dress. Most of all the dress. It was almost identical to the one Tak had purchased for her many years ago.

Elle's body temperature rose again. Her cheeks were on fire, and the perspiration under her armpits were now like pools of sweat. She remembered the last time she had seen Tak, hungover and vomiting in his bathroom. His final command was that she never return to Japan.

What am I going to do?

THIRTY-FOUR

Ozzy Osbourne: "Crazy Train"

June 5, 2017
8:02 p.m.

"How long have you lived in Japan?" Elle turned toward the woman with the impossibly long platinum-blonde hair who had been standing next to Tak when they entered the patio. She had been introduced as his wife, Tiffany. Except for being taller, she bore a striking resemblance to a younger version of Elle. Apparently, Tak still preferred blondes. Did he run his fingers through Tiffany's hair the way he had with hers?

Elle hoped her voice didn't betray her utter horror with the situation. How could she be in the same room as Tak? His warnings had been clear. What would he do to her?

Tiffany leaned in conspiratorially toward Elle. "Don't tell Tak. I'm not supposed to say anything . . ." She seemed unsteady and was slurring her words. Elle suspected she was either drunk or high or both. "I know all about you two, how you were going to get married and have a baby . . ."

Get married? Have a baby? What was she talking about? She was high for sure. *What should I say?* Elle needed to be extra careful. Ainsley and her team were filming the event, along with several Tokyo-based TV stations. Evidently, Tak was a big deal in Japan; Elle couldn't afford to slip up or make a scene. She tried directing the conversation toward something that would be easy for Tiffany to discuss. "So how did you and Tak meet?"

"I know everything!" Tiffany was emphatic, her head wobbling as she spoke. She struggled to stand up straight. Elle felt sorry for her. Tiffany seemed sweet, but she was clearly in over her head. Perhaps that's why she had chosen to get high, to help her get through the night. Elle remembered feeling the same lack of control and had a sudden urge to protect Tiffany, to save her from herself. Yet how could Elle possibly help her? She was having a hard-enough time maintaining her own composure. It was like the instructions for using the oxygen on an airplane—Elle needed to focus on getting her own mask on first.

As Elle struggled to find her voice in this increasingly strange set of circumstances, Tak approached. "Tiffany, please, I think you should go sit down now." He nodded toward a large dais under some lights at the edge of the patio where a long rectangular table had been set up. It reminded Elle of the sort of table a bride and groom would sit at during their wedding reception.

"Sure, sweetie pie, whatever you say." Tiffany leaned in to kiss Tak, but he stealthily sidestepped her advance and pushed her away, toward the table. It struck Elle as incredibly rude. She was right to pity Tiffany; Tak was still an asshole.

As Tiffany walked away on unsteady feet in impossibly high heels, she turned one last time to Elle, put her index finger to her lips, and mouthed a silent "Shhh."

Elle nodded her head kindly, hoping Tiffany would understand this to mean she wouldn't betray her confidence. Elle had no idea what she had been talking about in the first place, so it wouldn't be difficult to keep anything from Tak.

This whole night was confusing. And disturbing. This was not a scenario Elle had ever imagined. Sure, there had been signs indicating a confrontation with her past, but this! What were the chances?

It was bad enough to see Johnny again. His broken tooth and ruthless smirk harrowing reminders of his cruelty at the airport, his brutal threats, and his hands violating her on her that final day. Elle couldn't stand to think of any of it, but at least she could easily avoid him.

It was much more complicated with Tak; she couldn't exactly ignore him. At least he had pretended not to know her when Win made their introductions. Still, it made Elle uneasy to be around him. What would he say to her now that they were alone?

"I apologize for my wife. She was nervous about this evening, and I'm afraid she might have had too much to drink."

"Oh please, don't worry. It's fine." Elle hoped she appeared calm. Inside, her stomach was in a tense knot and her mouth was parched. She took a drink of champagne out of the flute she had been offered when they entered the party. Elle knew better than to drink very much—she certainly needed to have her wits about her now—but she needed something to combat the uncomfortable dryness in her throat.

Tak stood in silence and looked her over. "You look very beautiful. As stunning as the first night I met you. Do you like the dress?"

The knot in Elle's stomach tightened more. She didn't want to acknowledge the dress Tak had given her or how she looked. She was uncomfortable with the way he was eyeing her. It felt invasive. Unsure of what to expect, Elle tried to be cheery. "You speak English so well now."

It was true. Tak spoke elegantly and accent-free, like a native English speaker. Quite a contrast from the halting English he had spoken when Elle had known him years before. Tak was also still very handsome, although much more conservative in appearance. Gone was the small diamond earring and gaudy pinkie ring. His dark black hair was no longer in a ponytail but cut short and sprinkled with just the right amount of gray. With his tanned face and in his tuxedo, Tak looked like a Japanese James Bond ready for a night of high stakes gambling at a casino in Monte Carlo.

"Thank you." Tak bowed slightly. "I'm glad we have a moment to be alone. There are some things I have been waiting a long time to tell you."

Oh, no! What is he going to say?

"Okay." Elle nervously bit her lip and looked around for Win. He was talking with a few other Tsugunai executives and Ainsley. As Elle had predicted, the producer was wearing a Ralph Lauren gown; it was arctic blue and floor-length giving her the appearance of a guest at the event rather than a paid employee. Elle tried to get her husband's attention, but she was distracted by Tak's hand brushing against her arm.

"Elle, I want to apologize for the way I treated you. It was wrong, and I'm deeply ashamed. I am not that man anymore."

Oh, thank goodness! Elle had been terrified Tak was still angry with her and intent on making her pay for her past mistakes. Still, she had no desire to discuss their shared history. She held her hand up in protest. "Please don't. It's not necessary. It was a long time ago. Let's not talk about it."

Tak gently grabbed her hand and led it down to her side. "Don't worry, Elle. I have no intention of embarrassing you in front of your family. I won't reveal anything to them about our past."

"Thank you." Elle was assuaged by Tak's promise. She had vowed to be more honest with Win about her life in Tokyo, and she would be—but it needed to be on her terms.

"You must know how truly sorry I am. Do you know what the Japanese word 'Tsugunai' means?"

"It's atonement, right?"

"Very good." Tak smiled. "Yes. It's atonement. I have spent the last two decades atoning for my sins against you. I hope you will accept my apology, and that we can start our relationship anew."

"Apology accepted. Please, let's have no more talk about it."

Tak bowed deeply. "Thank you, Elle. I've made it up to you—you'll see."

Why was Tak being so dramatic? It made Elle nervous. She again looked over at Win and was finally able to make eye contact with him. He excused himself from the group he was with and made his way toward her.

Win approached and put his arm around Elle. "I'm glad you two are having a chance to talk, Akimoto-senpai. Did you know my wife used to live in Tokyo? She taught English here back in the early nineties."

Elle sensed an immediate change in Tak's body language around Win. He stiffened and held his arms tightly at his side, his hands clenched into fists. Elle guessed it had something to do with all the last-minute negotiations on the deal. Win had said it had been difficult. She also noticed Tak didn't correct Win's use of *senpai* at the end of his name. Win was Tak's equal, not his inferior; he shouldn't be required to be so formal.

It was important to Elle that she tackle the situation with Tak with some honesty. She turned to Win. "You're not going to believe this, but I actually know Ta—, Mr. Akimoto." Elle quickly corrected herself. "He was a student of mine."

It wasn't the full truth, but it was a start.

"Really? How incredible!" Win directed his attention toward Tak. "Well, I have to say, my wife was a good teacher—your English is superb!"

Tak looked at Elle with a glimmer of curiosity, but he also smiled, perhaps gratified by her willingness to acknowledge their past relationship. "Please, both of you, call me Tak."

"Ok, Tak." Win squeezed the small of Elle's back, giving her full credit for Tak's change in attitude.

"Yes, Miss Elle was an excellent teacher. I must admit I had a very large—what is the English word? *Crush?*—on her. She was very beautiful then, as she is now."

"That she is." Win looked over at Elle, pride gleaming in his eyes. "If it's not too much trouble, perhaps you can find a way to incorporate this coincidence into your opening remarks for tomorrow?"

"Of course. What a great idea!" Elle forced a smile. This was all happening so quickly; she didn't have time to process it properly.

"Although I am eager to reminisce more with Miss Elle about her time in Tokyo, I think it best we go find our places at the table and begin the presentation." Tak held his arm out and led Win and Elle toward the dais.

Elle was grateful for the distraction. She needed time to figure out her next move.

◆ ◆ ◆

9:15 p.m.

Elle was unable to eat. When she noticed Brynnie eyeing her full plate with suspicion, she tried to force down a few bites, but it was difficult. She was too consumed with trying to figure out exactly what was going on. Had Tak somehow known she was Win's wife all along? It seemed impossible, but how else would he have known to gift her with yellow Gerber daisies? And the lipstick. And the dress. He *must* have known.

When did he find out? And how?

Elle took a sip of water and tried gleaning more information from Tiffany. It was challenging; the tall blonde wasn't making much sense. The only thing Elle could gather was that she had been married to Tak for a little over a year, and together they had an infant son. Tiffany had shown Elle pictures of him on her phone, explaining how Tak was thrilled their son had, against all odds, inherited her light-colored hair and eyes.

In one picture, the pink-faced, chubby-cheeked baby was swaddled in a blue blanket, and he reminded Elle of Four. And then of Jimmy. She was glad Tiffany at least had him; someone capable of returning her love.

Tak stood and clinked the side of his glass to get everyone's attention. Again, Elle had the sensation of being at a wedding, with a toast to the bride and groom forthcoming. The Tsugunai and Martin Global employees in attendance all quieted.

Tak straightened his shoulders. "Thank you to everyone from Martin Global for making the trip to Japan to be with us here tonight." Tak turned and bowed politely toward Win, who stood and graciously bowed back to his host in acceptance of his thanks. The crowd clapped politely.

Tak nodded his head until the applause subsided. "We appreciate the opportunity to work with you and are excited about our collaboration. Tonight, I have the great pleasure of giving you all a first look at the revolutionary technology we have created here at Tsugunai, before we launch it at our worldwide press conference tomorrow. I cannot emphasize enough what a labor of love this project has been for me." Tak paused, then turned and looked at Elle for a moment before continuing, "We have, through incredible innovation with artificial intelligence, created the first robot with the ability to interpret data and make decisions on its own. Our partnership with Martin Global will allow this groundbreaking technology to be shared with unlimited applications. One day soon, what I am about to show you will be in every house, like a TV or computer, forever changing the daily lives of millions of people."

Tak walked over the to the side of the dais where a yellow silk cloth covered the Tsugunai invention. He looked directly at Elle and held her gaze for what felt like several long minutes. *Why does he keep looking at me?* She hoped no one else noticed. There was no reason for Tak to direct his attention toward her. She had nothing to do with any of this.

"Ladies and gentlemen, without further ado, I give you . . . Blondie!" Tak removed the cloth. Elle was expecting a robot, something mechanical and steely gray. Instead, what she saw was more like a mannequin: a woman with long platinum-blonde hair and blue eyes. It was incredibly lifelike. So lifelike, it could be her twin.

THIRTY-FIVE

PINK FLOYD: "WISH YOU WERE HERE"

June 6, 2017
10:23 a.m.

Mitch looked exactly the same: long eyelashes, mischievous eyes, and a warm smile. Elle was thrilled to see him. Even though the sun was shining brightly and it was very warm outside—hot, even—Mitch wore a camel-colored lambskin coat. This was not his typical style, it was too conservative, more like something Win would wear. Mitch preferred black and leather. He was carrying an axe loosely in his right hand, and—curiously—he was barefoot.

Elle was worried his feet would get hurt. "Where are your shoes?"

Mitch said nothing.

Elle became more worried, frantic almost. "You need shoes. Let me get you some shoes."

Mitch smiled. Although he didn't say anything or move to greet her, she could tell he was happy to see her. He seemed peaceful, content.

Elle reached her arms out to hug him. "I've been looking all over for you!"

Again, Mitch smiled, but he didn't return her embrace. Instead, he turned and walked purposely toward a large, lone tree a few feet away. There was something under the tree, but Elle wasn't sure what it was. A car seat maybe? That didn't make sense.

Why wasn't Mitch as excited to see Elle as she was to see him? Where was he going? To cut down the tree with his axe? To get the car seat?

Knock–knock–knock.

Elle awoke to the sound of a loud rapping on the door. She sat up in bed, disoriented.

Where am I?

Dazed, Elle looked around. Noting the unfamiliar duvet cover, she realized with dismay that she was in her hotel bed. She must have been dreaming. Elle couldn't shake the hazy feel of everything, the aftereffect of the Ambien. She had been so upset the night before, she had taken two pills, as if a deep sleep would make it all go away. Elle was depressed by the realization she hadn't actually seen Mitch, and horrified by the events of the previous evening.

Tak and Johnny. Thinking about them made her nauseous. Just when she was starting to feel so hopeful about her future, she had to see them again.

Had there been signs?

Of course, but Elle had misinterpreted their meaning, naively believing that being more honest was enough. Thinking her life could somehow be compared to that of a princess in a Disney movie had been ridiculous. Colossally stupid. Elle should have paid more attention, heeded the warnings more seriously.

She needed to talk to Win. Elle had intended to tell him more about her relationship with Tak when they returned to the hotel, but Tak had insisted Win and the other Martin Global executives stay and work through some last-minute preparations for the press conference. Elle had taken two Ambien, hoping that rest would clear her head and provide her with better perspective to talk to Win in the morning. *Where was he?*

Elle looked at the clock on the bedside table: 10:25. *Geez.* The Ambien had really knocked her out. Win must be gone already. Should she try calling him?

Knock–knock–knock.

There it was again. Had Brynnie or Four ordered room service? Elle got out of bed, wrapped herself in a hotel robe, and went to the door. She couldn't shake the melancholy that seeing Mitch had been an illusion. It had seemed so real. Elle had been so pleased to see him again. She wanted to hold onto that feeling of happiness for as long as she could.

Elle opened the door to see the hotel concierge. He bowed deeply, apologizing, "I'm very sorry to disturb you, Mrs. Martin, but there is someone here at the hotel who wants to see you."

Someone to see me? Who could it be?

Elle crinkled her eyebrows. "Do you know who it is?"

"He said he was a friend of yours from years ago. Of course, I would never give out your room number, so I took his picture to show you. He was quite insistent about seeing you." The concierge handed Elle his phone. Her heart skipped a beat. *Could it be Mitch?*

Elle looked at the picture and instantly recognized Kenji. It wasn't Mitch, but it was a good lead. *Finally!* "Yes, I do know him. Where is he?"

"He's downstairs in the restaurant. I told him to wait there until I talked to you."

"Okay—wow." Elle took a few seconds to process this information. "I need to get dressed. Tell him I'll be down in a few minutes."

"Very well." The concierge again bowed several times.

Was Elle supposed to tip him? She decided it wasn't necessary. Instead, she offered several rushed bows in return. "Thank you. Thank you so much."

Elle closed the door and hurried back to her room to change, her mind racing. She still needed to talk to Win; she should check her phone to see if he had left a message. And what about Brynnie and Four? Were they still sleeping?

Elle picked her phone up off the nightstand and was surprised to see she had over thirty texts. *Something bad must have happened.* Panicked, she read the first message. It was from a series in a group text including all her Country Day parent friends. From what Elle could gather, it had been discovered that a popular biology teacher had been accused of molesting students at another private school he taught at in the late eighties. Although this news was distressing, Elle wasn't interested in the details. Impatient, she skipped over all the messages from the group.

Next, there was a single text from Aubrey asking how Elle was doing. It was ironic, given Aubrey's behavior in the past few weeks, that she even bothered to keep up the charade of pretending to care about Elle. Elle deleted the message without responding and hurriedly read the next text; one from Angela reporting that Duke was doing well and that the leak in the sprinkler system had been fixed. Elle again regretted having previously doubted her housekeeper's intentions. *Angela* wasn't the problem. Elle would give her a raise when she returned home.

At last, Elle got to a message from Win, at six o'clock that morning, when she would have still been deep in her Ambien-induced sleep: *You were a rock star last night! Your charm finally wore down Akimoto a bit, but still working through some details. Headed to his office. Didn't want to wake you. Try to call later. Car is coming at noon. They have a room for you to get your hair and make-up done in. Love You.*

Elle hated to think of her husband negotiating with Tak. His body language around Win had been so antagonistic. *Why?*

There was one final text. It was from Brynnie: *4 and I are going to Tokyo Disneyland. Daddio gave us the green light, we didn't want to wake you. We will be at press conference on time. Don't worry. xo*

Don't worry. Did Brynnie mean Elle shouldn't worry about her and Four, or had she sensed her mom's panic the night before and understood the position she was now in?

THIRTY-SIX

SIMPLE MINDS: "DON'T YOU (FORGET ABOUT ME)"

June 6, 2017
10:45 a.m.

Elle adjusted her hair into a loose knot above her head as she walked out of the elevator and into the hotel restaurant. In her rush to meet Kenji, she hadn't brushed her hair or put on any make-up. With her luck, she'd probably run into Ainsley... *So what?* Elle no longer cared; she had more important things on her mind.

Elle saw Kenji sitting alone in a booth toward the back of the restaurant near a window. He looked just as she remembered. Dressed in skinny jeans and a tight black T-shirt, he could have still been a young man of twenty-one. It was remarkable how he hadn't aged. Seeing Elle approach, Kenji stood and bowed profusely to her.

"Kenji! Oh, my gosh, it's so nice to see you!" Elle wanted to hug him. Was that appropriate? Not sure, she settled on an awkward bow of her own. "I can't believe I'm seeing you after twenty years. How are you?"

"Prease, Erre-san, sit." Kenji motioned to the empty seat across from him; his hand was shaking.

Poor thing, he's nervous.

"You want coffee? Prease." Kenji pointed to the silver carafe on the table.

"Sure, thank you." Elle sat down and wondered where to begin. She had so many questions. "How did you know I was here?"

"I see you on TV news. At big party . . . with Tak. I know I must find you."

At the mention of Tak's name, Elle's stomach tightened. Did Kenji still work for him? Was that why he was so nervous? What did he know?

Elle tried sound cheerful, saying, "I'm so glad you did. I'm anxious to get caught up with you! Are you still in touch with Mitch? I'm trying to track him down."

Kenji shifted uncomfortably in his chair. "You no know about Mitch?"

"No, I haven't seen or heard from him since I left in 1994. I'm dying to hear what he's up to. Do you know?"

Kenji looked down at his plate, then up again, his voice shaking. "Yes, I know."

Oh no. It must have been a messy breakup. Too bad—they would have made such a great couple. Still, Elle was thrilled he had information about Mitch. "Tell me everything!"

Elle took a sip of coffee and settled into her chair, anxious to hear what Kenji had to say. After her horrible night, she was looking forward to some good news.

THIRTY-SEVEN

VANCE JOY: "MESS IS MINE"

May 11, 1994
11:47 p.m.

Mitch

Mitch blamed himself for Elle's situation. She had been coked-up the previous night; he could tell. He should have insisted they stay away from Samantha's. Elle was in no condition to see Tak, especially as she was planning to break up with him.

But Mitch had wanted to see Kenji. Worse yet, he was so over Elle's relationship with Tak, he had kind of encouraged her flirting with the incredibly tasty Brazilian soccer player. But his most egregious mistake had been leaving without even checking in on Elle or saying good-bye. *Selfish prick.* He had been so distracted by the fantasy of what he and Kenji were about to do, he hadn't even thought about his best friend. Mitch was racked with guilt. He should have been there for Elle. He would make it up to her now.

Mitch was discouraged to find Elle wasn't at their apartment, and there was no sign she had ever made it back there. She must have crashed in Tak's office at Samantha's.

Mitch headed to the station to take a subway into Roppongi. How could he best help? *Maybe it won't be that bad.* Elle was incredibly charming. Perhaps she had already talked her way out of the situation.

It was hard for Mitch to concentrate; he couldn't stop thinking about his mind-blowing night with Kenji. He couldn't wait to see him again. Consumed with fantasies about the slender and pretty bartender, the subway ride went quickly.

Mitch exited out of Roppongi station and walked the two blocks to Samantha's. At this time of day, the streets were quiet. Quite a change from the previous evening, when there had been a long line of young people clamoring to get into the club. The front door was propped open, so Mitch walked in. A cleaning staff was inside mopping the dance floor.

It was strange to see the inside of Samantha's during the day. In the daylight, it was uninteresting, sterile almost, except for the lingering smell of alcohol. The club was so quiet and lonely now that it seemed unfathomable that it was regularly the scene of young men and women lustily grabbing, grinding, and fumbling with each other, all in search of some sort of connection.

Mitch waved to the cleaning staff and sauntered up the stairs to Tak's office. He knocked lightly on the door.

No answer.

Maybe they were still asleep? Mitch looked at his watch and considered the time—12:07. *Fuck it. It's past noon. I'll go in.*

Mitch opened the door and saw Tak sitting glumly at his desk with his head in his hands, a bottle of rum in front of him. It appeared Elle had already given him his walking papers and he was drowning his sorrows.

With rum? Really? What kind of guy goes on a bender with fucking rum?

Tak looked up as Mitch entered. "What you want?"

Mitch could tell by the redness in Tak's cheeks that he was drunk. He was such a lightweight. Always had been, which is probably why he started in on the coke.

"I'm looking for Elle, is she here?"

Tak made a fist and hit it against his desk. "Why you look Elle?"

"Relax man, I just wanted to make sure she was okay. She was pretty fucked up last night." Mitch was teed off by Tak's attitude and behavior. *He thinks he's such a tough guy. What a fucking dick.* He hoped Elle had let him have it. *Asshole.*

"She go. She your apartment."

Shit! Mitch must have just missed her. "Alright, thanks." He couldn't wait to get out of there. In fact, he hoped he never saw this prick again. What had Elle seen in him? At least it was over now. *Good fucking riddance.*

As Mitch turned to leave, Tak added, "She there with Johnny and Mike."

At the mention of Johnny and Mike, a chill went down Mitch's spine and the hairs on the back of his neck stood up. This wasn't good. Those guys were Tak's goons.

Mitch turned back to Tak. "Why are they with her?"

"You know what Elle do?" Tak tried to stand, but he was so drunk he wobbled.

Mitch paused before responding. He needed to be careful here. What did Tak know? Mitch wasn't even sure himself how far it had gone with Elle and the Brazilian.

Tak didn't give him time to answer. "She fuck another guy! Here, in my club!" He slammed his drink down on his desk, shattering the glass into pieces.

Fuuuuck. This was the worst-case scenario. Mitch was now very concerned about Elle. Tak was completely unhinged. Irrational. Who knew what he was capable of?

Mitch tried to stall, desperate to come up with a game plan. "Wait a sec, that's not exactly right." *Shit, Mitch, think of something, anything.*

Tak had grabbed the bottle of rum and was now drinking directly from it. "It true. I find rubber package in cloakroom where they are together."

A rubber? Mitch was glad if Elle had gotten it on with the hot Brazilian, but this was bad.

Tak looked at him expectantly.

Mitch extended his forearm and opened the palm of his hand, hoping to appear conciliatory. "Here's the thing. She didn't have sex with him. They only kissed, and she realized it was a mistake . . ."

Tak shook his head. "No, I see empty wrapper."

Mitch needed to come up with something better. He considered Tak. He would forgive Elle. The real issue here was his pride. Someone would have to take the fall so he could save face. Mitch would be that guy. "That's mine. We were in the cloakroom together."

Tak cocked his head to the side. Mitch had his attention. He needed to make this good. But how?

"You know it was my birthday, and I was pretty hammered. We went into the cloakroom, and, I don't know, I thought I had a chance with her . . ." Tak wasn't stopping him. *This guy is so fucking stupid, this just might work.* "I got the rubber out and she totally shot me down. Swear to God, nothing happened." Here Mitch thought he should add something about how sorry he was, but Tak was such a dick, he couldn't bring himself to do it.

"Why Elle no say this to me?"

"She was trying to protect me."

Tak nodded slowly. "Ah so . . ."

He's buying it. Mitch's confidence grew.

"But Elle say, you like boy—you gay."

So Elle had told him the truth. *Good.* Pleased with this news and his ability to spin such a successful tale, Mitch became a bit cocky. "Well, I could go either way, but you've seen Elle's tits—they're perfection."

Tak hurled the bottle of rum directly at Mitch's head. He felt a sharp sting and fell back, hitting his head along the corner of a file cabinet on his way down.

◆ ◆ ◆

2:15 p.m.

Mitch was groggy. He remembered feeling like this once before, when he was eight years old, playing in his first tackle football game. He had gotten the ball and started running, the way his dad had instructed, when he was hit by a much bigger kid. Hard. He had fallen to the ground, his head snapping against the grass. Mitch felt now as he had then: dizzy, confused, and not at all sure what had happened.

He could see the outline of Tak but couldn't quite focus on him or what he was doing. His head hurt too much—was it bleeding?—and he was overwhelmed by the smell of rum. Mitch was nauseous and worried he might throw up.

Tak had his arms. What was he doing? Was he tying his arms to something? What was going on? Nothing made sense. Mitch couldn't concentrate. Better for him to just close his eyes and rest a little.

◆ ◆ ◆

7:25 p.m.

Mitch smelled rum again. Then he heard voices. Men, speaking Japanese. Then there was the pain. A sharp, stinging discomfort on his forehead accompanied by a dull and throbbing ache on the back of his head. Mitch vaguely remembered Tak throwing the bottle at him. That would explain the smell of rum and the soreness on his forehead. But why would the back of his head hurt?

Mitch tried to reach his hand up to check the sources of his pain, but he couldn't. He tried again. His arm wouldn't move. It took incredible effort to open his eyes, but Mitch was determined to figure out what was going on. Although they appeared blurry and out-of-focus, he could see Johnny and Mike hovering above him. Mitch tried to sit up, but they shoved him back down. He again tried to lift his arms, this time in protest, but he couldn't. They were tied down.

What the fuck?

Mitch smelled rum again. Tak was leaning over him. What was he saying? It was in Japanese and Mitch couldn't summon the concentration to translate the foreign words. He was too preoccupied with trying to figure out why his arms would be tied down. Had Tak said something about giving him a drug to make him relax? That didn't make any sense.

Mitch struggled to focus on what Tak was trying to communicate. If only he weren't speaking so quickly. Tak kept saying over and over what a bad man he was. Mitch was confused. Who was the bad man Tak was referring to? It was a lot to take in, and Mitch gave up trying to understand.

There was a prick in his arm. It made him twitch slightly, though it didn't really hurt. Was it a needle? Mitch hated needles. He was terrified of getting shots.

Warmth—Mitch experienced a rush of warmth, like he had been wrapped in the softest, most wonderful blanket.

Then he was sick. Horribly sick. He threw up in his mouth.

Someone held him up. Was it Johnny? Mitch vomited violently, convulsing in agony.

Then he was warm again—floating, completely and utterly relaxed, in a state of contentment he couldn't understand. The throbbing aches in his head disappeared.

Mitch was back in his childhood home in Iowa. He was in his twin bed, wearing his favorite pajamas. The one-piece zip-up ones made of fleece and decorated with *Star Wars* characters. He loved these pajamas. He saw the American flag needlepoint his mom had made in celebration of the Bicentennial hanging on the wall.

Everything in his room was the same way Mitch remembered; only now, he was no longer a confused and lonely little boy. He was calm and incredibly peaceful. David Gilmour was kneeling next to him in bed, rubbing his forehead softly and singing "Comfortably Numb" directly into his ear. His voice was divine. So very beautiful, every note exquisite in its clarity. Mitch was perfectly in sync with the song. He could feel each guitar chord coursing through his veins, a part of him.

Mitch soared, transcendent. He *was* music.

Mitch was experiencing such an unparalleled sense of the sublime he didn't wonder why his pants were removed. Or his underwear.

Japanese voices again, this time telling him not to move. Then it was English. Broken English. "Mitch! Mitch!" Tak was shaking him.

"Just nod if you can hear me."

It was Roger Waters. Or was that Tak? Mitch couldn't be sure. He didn't care. He didn't want to leave his twin bed or this feeling of bliss.

"Very important, you stay relaxed. You no move. Understand?" Tak shook Mitch violently.

Mitch opened his eyes and nodded. *Move? Why would I move?* He was suspended in the air. He closed his eyes, grateful to return to the twin bed in his Bicentennial room. Nothing else mattered. Nothing but David Gilmour's voice and the feeling of utter contentment, understanding and belonging. Then came the pain between his legs, so excruciating Mitch immediately lost consciousness.

THIRTY-EIGHT

BIG AUDIO DYNAMITE II: "RUSH"

June 6, 1994
10:03 a.m.

Mitch

Mitch second-guessed his plan. Maybe he should still go with his initial idea: a jump into Tokyo Bay off the Trans-Tokyo Bay Highway. Would that be better?

No, this was the way to do it. Who knew how long it would take his waterlogged body to drag up on shore and be found? And what kind of condition would he be in? Would the salt in the water preserve him, or would he be grossly decomposed? Whoever found him should be spared from that type of unpleasantness.

This way was less traumatic. Things would be resolved quickly and neatly.

Mitch removed the heroin from the plastic bag inside a small red balloon and emptied it onto a spoon. As fucked up as it was, considering the circumstances, he couldn't help but feel a bit of gratitude toward Tak. Of course, what he had done to Mitch was beyond reproach—the work of a complete sadist and sociopath—yet Tak had given him the heroin to get the job done. Not out of guilt—Tak didn't have the capacity to feel guilt. No, Mitch supposed it was because Tak had understood his intentions and wanted to help him, believing it was the honorable thing to do. A Japanese samurai performing hara-kiri.

Was it honorable?

It didn't really matter. Honorable or not, it was the only choice Mitch had.

There were those people who, when faced with extreme adversity, found an inner strength and drive they never thought possible. The news loved to broadcast these types of stories: the paraplegic who started a wheelchair basketball league; the refugee who escaped political per-secution and started a foundation for his homeland; the amputee who donated prosthetics to children who had lost limbs walking into land mines.

Mitch wasn't one of these people. He was too weak to overcome the hand that had been dealt him. Sure, he would heal physically—at least Tak had known what he was doing. Perhaps Mitch wasn't the first person he had castrated—but he would never get over the shame of what Tak had taken from him. Bitterness would color his every waking moment.

Then there was the heroin to consider. Mitch's life was forever changed the moment Tak had chosen to anesthetize him with the drug. Heroin had gifted him with such a sublime sense of contentment—the feeling was too damn good; the sole antidote for his tortured soul. Having experienced it once, Mitch wouldn't be able to go on without accessing that place of joy again and again. He *needed* the sense of belonging heroin gave him. He couldn't live without it, nor would he want to.

Mitch would become an addict. He would lie, steal, do whatever it took to obtain the incredible high again. Mitch couldn't let that happen, he was smart enough to recognize there was no silver lining to heroin addiction. No graceful exit. Better to leave now, on his own terms, before his hedonistic dance with the drug became his everything.

Mitch was confident in his decision. Still, as he added water to the heroin with a syringe, his heart ached over leaving Kenji. Sweet, adorable Kenji. Mitch could fall in love with him. Perhaps he already had.

Having your lover gets his balls chopped off the very day you have sex with him for the first time. What a way to start a new relationship. Poor Kenji—he couldn't have been more attentive to Mitch over the past few weeks, taking great care of him and even offering to change his disgusting, blood-soaked bandages. But it couldn't last. Kenji would stay merely out of a sense of obligation and pity, and Mitch couldn't abide that.

He regretted Kenji would be the one to find him. It seemed a rather morbid good-bye, but Mitch couldn't think of any other way to assure the money from the Mitch & Elle's Adventure Jar got into Kenji's hands. There was a shitload of yen in the jar—the equivalent of almost $10,000. Mitch certainly had no use for it and there was no way of getting it to Elle. Kenji deserved the cash, a sort of payoff for all his trouble.

If all went per Mitch's plan, Kenji would arrive at the apartment around six o'clock and find a note next to the jar instructing him to take the money and to call the police. Kenji would be confused and knock loudly on the door, shouting for Mitch several times. When no one answered and he discovered the door was locked, he would have little choice but to do as Mitch directed. The police would come and break down the door, and all Kenji would see was Mitch's body covered with a sheet.

Would he be sad? Perhaps a little, but Kenji was young and attractive, with his whole life ahead of him. Mitch would be remembered as nothing more than an asterisk in his story. The American he lost his virginity to. A nice memory, but in the bigger scheme of things, a teeny tiny piece of his life.

And what about Mitch's family? How and when would they find out? How would they feel? Sure, his mom would cry, but her tears would be accompanied with profound relief. She wouldn't have to worry about her son anymore. His dad and brother would simply shrug their shoulders, spit out their chew, and concede, *"Welp, he always was diff-rent."*

They would accept casseroles and Jell-O salads, pray for his soul, and life would go on.

It was more complicated to think about Elle. Mitch had asked Tak about her several times, and all he would say was that she was safe in another country. Maybe she had gone back to the States? Or off to London? Wherever she was, it was better she was gone. Elle desperately needed to escape Tokyo.

She had gotten in over her head with Tak, with the drugs, and likely at the Big YAC. Mitch was suspicious about how she had could afford first-class plane tickets and suspected the money was from a client at the Big YAC. Had it been payment for an exchange of services? Was that why she had quit her job? Mitch hadn't had the courage to ask Elle about it; he worried it would be too humiliating for her to admit the truth.

He could only hope Elle was doing well and was happy. How would she find out? When? She would be crushed when she heard the news. She would feel responsible.

Mitch couldn't leave Elle with that guilt. It was imperative that she know he was not desolate and in need of rescuing. To this end, Mitch had written her a note explaining his decision. To convince Elle that he was in a good headspace, Mitch purposefully used paper he had stolen from English First and even slipped in a reference to his balls. Elle would get it. She would understand he knew exactly what he was doing, and there was nothing she could have done to prevent his death.

To further drive his point home, Mitch had signed the letter with his given name, Wayne. Elle would take this as confirmation he had accepted who he was and what his fate must be. Over time, she would forgive him and understand that he had had no choice.

Mitch didn't have any regrets. He would do it all over again if given the chance. Protecting Elle from Tak was an honor. She was the first person to love him unconditionally. Without Elle and her friendship, he may have never fully recognized his sexuality.

The sacrifice was worth it.

A happily ever after wasn't in the cards for Wayne Mitchell Carpenter; he had always known it and understood it would come to this eventually. But it was different for Elle. She was destined for great things. She would be happy for both of them.

Mitch was at peace with his decision. Life had granted him a few moments of pure joy. He had experienced the ecstasy of physical intimacy with a man. Elle had given him the gift of unconditional love. It was enough—more than he ever expected.

Mitch took in the apartment one last time. All his belongings were in three cardboard boxes carefully stacked on top of each other. He wasn't sure why he had bothered with this extra step—everything would probably be trashed—but it seemed important he leave things as neat and tidy as possible.

Have I forgotten anything?

Mitch considered spraying himself with some more aftershave. He was worried about the stench of death and had taken the extra precaution of not eating anything for the past two days. The last thing he wanted was to shit himself. He considered peeing one more time but knew his bladder was empty. He had tried to go about five minutes earlier.

Mitch decided against more aftershave. He was ready.

He flicked his red lighter on and placed it under the bottom of the spoon, lamenting for a moment that he couldn't use a match to heat the heroin. He would have enjoyed the sound and smell of a match striking one more time. That, and perhaps the taste of one more Burrito Supreme with extra hot sauce. He *would* miss Taco Bell.

Satisfied with the consistency, Mitch soaked up the heroin from the spoon with a cotton ball and extracted it with a syringe. He used his favorite tie—a purple and black paisley designer one he had splurged $100 on—as a tourniquet around his left arm. Tak had explicitly warned Mitch that the heroin was pure and extremely potent. Still, for extra insurance, he swallowed a handful of prescription sleeping pills, choking them down with his saliva.

The final step in Mitch's plan involved music. It was key to have pre-cisely the right song for the occasion. He put in his earbuds and pushed play on his Walkman. U2's "Bad" was queued up. Mitch loved this song. He always had a visceral reaction to it that was so intense it was beyond understanding.

Mitch now understood why. The song explained everything. It just had to be "Bad."

Mitch put the needle in his arm. Why had he always been so afraid of getting shots? It really was no big deal. He lay down, pulled the sheet over his head, and closed his eyes. As the heroin explode through his veins in concert with his favorite song, Mitch was content. After a lifetime full of want, he was perfectly, sublimely, exquisitely at peace.

At last.

How very underrated.

THIRTY-NINE

U2: "40"

June 6, 2017
11:24 a.m.

Elle sat in the corner of the shower, her head between her knees. She had turned the cold-water knob off, allowing only hot water to come through the large rainfall showerhead on the ceiling. The scalding hot water burned her back. Elle welcomed the pain.

Kenji's story had gutted her. What Mitch had endured was beyond comprehension.

And for what? For me? She wasn't worth the sacrifice.

Elle banged her head several times against the wall of the shower. *Not again!* How could she be responsible for the death of another person she loved?

Kenji had also blamed himself. If only he had told Mitch right away, when he first saw her kiss Gustavo. Mitch would have interceded. Elle wouldn't have gone into the cloakroom. None of this would have happened.

Elle knew better. What happened to Mitch was solely on her shoulders.

Let them burn.

Her actions were unforgivable. Worse even than they had been with Jimmy. With her brother, there was always the smallest possibility—the tiniest of chances—that maybe, just maybe, he still would have died, even if she hadn't brought him into bed with her or placed the blanket and all the stuffed animals over him. But there was no question with Mitch. He would be alive if it weren't for her stupidity.

Elle sobbed. *She* was the one who should have been punished. Why hadn't she insisted on talking to Tak when he called her apartment that fateful day? She could have explained the truth. Mitch would have been spared. Elle had been so wrapped up in her own troubles, she hadn't considered the danger Mitch would be in.

So selfish. And she still was. Elle hadn't even lived up to Mitch's dying wish.

Kenji had given her Mitch's suicide note. He had presented the folded square paper to her in a very Japanese way, solemnly, with outstretched hands. It was faded and fragile and so very small—too small for something delivering such profound news. Curiously, it was written on paper from an English First notepad. Elle noticed the date: June 6th—right around the same time she had first met Win in the laundromat.

June 6, 1994
My darling Elle,

Thanks for my b-day present. It was fucking awesome! (Literally.) In a word: UNDERRATED. I would have never had the balls to pursue Kenji on my own. For your help in this endeavor, I am eternally grateful (as is my penis). I know you're sad, confused, and a bit pissed off at me right now, but don't be. This was the inevitable end. I have always known it would be this way. There was nothing you could have said or done to stop me, to change this outcome. Really. I mean it. If you were here right now, nothing would be different. Not a single fucking thing, so absolve yourself right now of any feelings of guilt or responsibility. You have been the best friend I've ever had. You loved and accepted me for who I am, which has meant everything to me, you must know that. It's your time now. I am commanding you a happy ending. Go on that adventure. Live a life of unadulterated joy. You owe it to yourself. And to me. I have no regrets. Don't you. (By this, I mean, for the love of God, ditch the grannie panties!)

Time for the Scooby Doo ending.

XOXO

Wayne

The letter was classic Mitch. Wry and sardonic to the end—he had even made a joke about having "balls." Elle found it strange he had chosen to sign it as Wayne. He loathed that name. Signing it that way was purposeful. Why would he do that?

Why did Mitch do anything he did? Why did this have to happen? *Why?*

In his suicide note, Mitch spoke of Elle's unconditional love for him. He had given her the same gift. He was the one man in her life she had allowed to see the full truth of Michelle Simpson, and Mitch had accepted her wholly for who she was.

And look at how I reciprocated.

Elle had boarded a plane and left Tokyo while Mitch was castrated. She flirted with Win in a laundromat, relishing her chance at happiness, while he sat broken and alone in their apartment—a needle and some drugs his sole companions. Elle had forsaken her best friend at the precise moment he needed her the most.

She couldn't live with that guilt. Something had to be done.

Elle willed herself out of the shower. She wished Duke could be with her; he would understand. Feeling weak and unsteady, it took considerable effort for Elle to dry off. She wiped a towel over the fogged-up mirror and looked into it, closely examining her face. She considered every line and each wrinkle.

Who was she? What had she become?

Elle felt empty—barren from a life based on fear, hubris, and narcissism. Fear of saying the wrong thing, looking the wrong way, not having the right friends, not being accepted. Hubris in her belief that she was too smart, that she knew better, that she could control everything. And narcissism in only thinking about herself and how things affected her.

"Are you happy, Mom? Are you living your dream?"

What a joke.

Elle's phone beeped on the bathroom counter. It was a text from Win reminding her that the car to take her to the Tsugunai office would be there soon. It ended with *"I love you."*

That was just perfect. Her husband was across town doing business with a complete sociopath. Elle had endangered yet another man she loved. What was wrong with her?

Elle looked at her iPod. She should have listened to her gut on what the signs had been telling her before coming to Japan. Instead, she had told herself what she wanted to believe. "Just be more honest." *Yeah, right.*

Could music save her now?

Desperate, Elle grabbed her iPod off the bathroom counter and put in her earbuds. Should she go to one of her favorite playlists?

No. She would trust the music.

Elle pushed play and closed her eyes.

Don't fail me. Please.

U2's "Bad" began.

Thank you.

Reassured, Elle dropped her shoulders and let out a long, deep breath. She loved this song; it always touched her in a way she couldn't quite understand—she had cried tears of joy when she heard it played live. It would be the perfect song to listen to. As the music played, Elle tried to quiet her brain and to give in to the moment. She felt the ecstasy in Bono's voice, the passion in the Edge's and Adam Clayton's guitar-playing, and the devotion in Larry Mullen Jr's relentless drumming.

Elle did as she was asked. She let it all go; she surrendered.

As she sang along to her favorite song with unabashed abandon, a tingling sensation raced through her body and she felt a rush of energy, like a wave had passed over her. Not a dangerous, frightening wave that threatened to pull her under, but a gentle wave, one that embraced her with compassion, hope, unity and even love. Yes, most of all, Elle felt love.

She welcomed this energy—this feeling of connection—and yielded to its power. Swaying in concert with the music that always brought her peace, Elle got it.

Finally, after all the years looking for signs where there were none, the correct message was received. The one that had been trying to reach her all along, but that she had been too selfish and self-absorbed to accept. Embracing the light, Elle was filled with gratitude, joy, understanding and peace.

She was wide awake. She was no longer sleeping.

Profoundly thankful, Elle was brought to her knees in humility. She was sorry. So very sorry. For everything. All of it.

Forgive me. Help me.

FORTY

PHIL COLLINS: "IN THE AIR TONIGHT"

June 6, 2017
1:15 p.m.

Let the games begin.

Elle sat on an uncomfortable wood chair in a room near Tak's office at Tsugunai headquarters. The team assigned to do her hair and makeup had just finished their job and left her alone. The press conference would be starting soon.

There was an abrupt knock on the door. It was authoritative and impatient. Elle stood and took a deep, drawn-out breath as she opened the door.

Tak was by himself, as she had requested. "Hello, Elle, you look beautiful, as always."

"Thank you." Elle stood aside and made way for Tak to enter. The room wasn't large, and it suddenly felt awkwardly intimate with the just the two of them in it. Elle moved away from Tak, creating as much space between them as she could.

"I hope you have found everything to your liking." Tak surveyed the room and straightened his tie.

"Yes, it's perfect. Thank you."

"Good, good. What can I do for you, Blondie?"

Elle had never liked this nickname and now with the unveiling of the creepy mannequin, it was even more unsettling, but she pretended it didn't bother her. "Being back in Tokyo has brought back so many memories."

Tak nodded agreeably and sat against the edge of the dressing table, relaxed.

Elle forced a smile. "We had so many good times together. Do you remember?"

Tak reached over and gently rubbed Elle's arm. "Yes, of course I remember. How could I forget?"

Elle moved closer to Tak and placed a hand lightly on his knee. His face reddened at her touch. "We made a great couple, the two of us."

Tak reached for Elle's hand, brought it to his lips, and kissed it. "The best."

Elle's instinct was to pull her hand away, but she allowed the contact, continuing, "And look how you turned out, such a successful business-man." Elle paused. She needed to be careful with what she said next. "I'm proud of you. I mean, what a change from owning a club with gambling, and the drugs—there were so many drugs."

Tak dropped Elle's hand. He looked stern, although not necessarily angry. "I don't know what you're talking about."

"Oh, c'mon, Tak. We did mounds of cocaine in your office at Samantha's."

Tak stood up. "Honestly, Blondie. I have no idea what you're talking about. Are you feeling quite well?"

Elle saw she wasn't going to get anywhere with this approach. Tak wasn't going to admit to anything. She might as well get to the point. "You know, I've been thinking a lot about Mitch. Do you remember him?"

Tak shook his head and straightened his back uncomfortably. "No, not really."

How dare he not acknowledge Mitch. Elle tried to remain calm. "Well, let me remind you. He was my best friend. The best friend I've ever had."

Tak shrugged his shoulders dismissively, indicating the topic was of little interest to him.

How can he be so cavalier?

Although it hadn't been part of Elle's strategy, she couldn't help but reprimand Tak. "Really? I would think you would remember castrating someone."

"Castrate someone?" Tak reached out his hand toward Elle. "Blondie, where did you get such an outrageous idea?"

Elle withdrew from his touch. She was incensed by his blatant lies and cursory disregard for Mitch. "How dare you lie to me! I was there! I know about all of it! The drug dealing, the beating up of innocent people. And Mitch! I can't even begin to think about what you did to him."

Tak's cheeks were now a bright, angry red, the way Elle remembered them being when he was drunk or in a particularly foul mood. "I don't know why you are saying these things, Blondie. I told you last night I was very sorry for the way things ended between us. The Tak you speak of is gone. There is no trace, no proof of anything you are saying." Tak's posture softened, as though he decided on a different approach mid-thought. He reached out and touched Elle's arm lightly. "Let's focus on the future, not the past."

Elle pulled away, undeterred. "What about Johnny and Mike? They saw you do all those things. They know the truth."

Tak laughed. "*Johnny?* He's my most trusted friend. As for Mike—I took care of him years ago. He was weak. He couldn't stomach what needed to be done."

"What do you mean, you took care of him?"

"He couldn't be trusted to keep the situation with Mitch quiet. He suddenly grew a conscience."

What did that mean? Mike had been a good person. He had shown Elle compassion and kindness when she had been at her most vulnerable. This was all so wrong—worse than Elle imagined—yet Tak seemed incredibly calm, given what he had admitted to.

Tak rubbed Elle's shoulders softly. "Is this all you wanted to talk about? Let's not dwell on the past. Our future is more important."

Our future? He had said that before. What was he talking about? How could he possibly think they had a future together?

Elle needed to finish this. She took a deep breath to calm herself. Resolved to hide her disgust, she again touched Tak gently on the arm and softened her voice. "First, I need to know the truth and that you're sorry. You owe me that, at least. You of all people know how much Mitch meant to me."

Tak shook his head. "I can't do that. I'm not the least bit sorry. In fact, it was a great moment for me, seeing Mitch cry like the little girl he was. I enjoyed it immensely."

Elle felt like she had been punched in the gut. Her entire body ached and she couldn't breathe. "How can you not be sorry for what you did? You took away the most important aspect of any man. It's your fault Mitch is dead."

"*My fault?* I didn't expect him to go off and kill himself. I thought he would have been quite happy as a eunuch."

Elle lifted her hand in anger, but Tak grabbed it before she could hit him.

"If you are upset with anyone, it should be with yourself. Someone had to pay. If you hadn't gone off with that soccer player, everything would have been different. We would still be together."

Tak was right—not about them still being together, that was crazy— but Mitch's death *had* been her fault. Elle could feel tears beginning to well in her eyes. She choked them back; she would not give Tak the power to make her cry.

Elle jerked her hand away from Tak's grip. "You talked about atonement last night. You must atone for what you did to Mitch. I won't let you get away with this. He deserved more."

"Sorry, Blondie. I have no intention of ever discussing that homosexual again. He got exactly what he deserved. You need to move on."

Move on? How could he possibly say something so appalling? They were discussing her best friend's life. It wasn't something one simply got past. Elle had tried her hardest not to cry, but she no longer had control. Tears streamed down her face.

"Now, now, don't cry." Tak approached her again. "You don't want your makeup to be ruined for the cameras."

Elle extended her arms to keep him away, but Tak was unyielding. He pulled her head close to his, roughly, with both hands. "You know what the best part of all of this was? When I was designing Blondie, I had a special one made, just for me. An anatomically correct one." Elle tried to get away, but Tak's hold on her was too strong. "She was good, just the way I remembered you. Nice and tight." He licked Elle's face. "Do you remember sex with me? Do you remember how you couldn't get enough? How you always wanted more?"

"Get away from me!" Elle was finally able to break free. She wiped her hand across her face where Tak had licked her. "And just so you know, that *most trusted friend* of yours—Johnny? He put his finger inside me. If Mike hadn't intervened, he would have raped me. That's some friend."

Tak straightened his shoulders. His cheeks reddened again. Elle could tell this news bothered him and she was glad to see him hurt. He rotated his head slowly in a circle, then cracked the knuckles on his right hand before saying, "I'm a little disappointed with this attitude, Elle, but I see you're not ready yet. I've waited over twenty years. I can wait a bit longer."

What is he talking about? He really was crazy. Elle needed to warn Win.

"I'm going to leave so you can compose yourself. You will want to look your best for this press conference. The whole world will be watching. I'll let you finish getting ready."

"Finish getting ready? You and I aren't finished. Not at all." Trembling, Elle walked past Tak to a closet door in the back of the room, which was slightly ajar. "You can come out now, Kenji."

Kenji stepped out from behind the door, so thin he didn't need to open it further to get out. His hands were shaking at his sides. Elle saw beads of perspiration across his brow. She was sorry he was nervous

293

and was intent on remaining strong for the both of them. "Do you remember Kenji?"

Tak furrowed his eyebrows, confused.

"Let me remind you. He was a bartender at Samantha's. He was Mitch's friend. A witness to what you did."

Checkmate, asshole.

"Ah, yes. Yes. I remember Kenji." Tak nodded slowly. "You have him. So what? You aren't going to do anything." He looked Elle in the eyes and spoke with remarkable calm. "If you reveal my past, you reveal yours."

"I don't care."

Tak laughed. "*You don't care?* Michelle doesn't care about her true identity being revealed? That's rich. I saw how you were with your daughter and that handsome young boy of yours. Do you really want to tell them Mommy was paid to entertain married men? That she sold them drugs? How do you think your husband will feel knowing you carried cocaine for me inside you?"

"It doesn't matter. You have to atone for what you did to Mitch. We both do."

"Mitch, Mitch." Tak waved his hand. "You always were so sentimental about him."

Elle began to cry again. "Mitch can't have died for nothing. I won't allow it. His story will be told."

"I am quite confident you won't be telling any such story. You don't want to ruin your perfect little life, do you?"

"I said I don't care. The truth has to come out."

Tak lifted his index finger in the air like he had just remembered something important. "Should I remind you of the lawyer—what was his name? Sato?—the one you met at the Big New York Apple Club? The one you rode in the town car with? What do you think your husband will think of your behavior with him?"

Elle's face flushed. Of all her mistakes in Japan, this was the one she regretted most. How could Tak possibly know what had transpired in the town car? She dropped her head in shame.

Tak directed his attention toward Kenji. If he was at all concerned about Elle's threat, he gave no indication of it. He spoke indifferently, in the tone of someone placing an order to a waiter, "Kenji, I have nothing against you. In fact, I remember you as being a very fine employee. I also understand you don't realize what you are getting yourself into. Elle can be quite persuasive. I'm going to give you two a few minutes alone to talk, after which I'm sure you will realize this entire conversation is best forgotten. I'm confident you don't want any trouble."

Kenji didn't respond. Tak stared into his eyes for several protracted seconds, as if daring him to blink. Kenji shifted his weight from one side to another then he, too, hung his head down in defeat.

Tak walked over to Elle and lifted her chin, gently cupping it in his hands. "I know this has been difficult for you, Blondie. Please trust me when I tell you how truly sorry I am for the way things ended between us." Tak held Elle's head firm in his hands, forcing her to look at him. "I have made it up to you. You'll see."

Elle was cold. Her heart skipped a beat. Then another. She worried Tak might kiss her.

Tak tenderly rubbed Elle's cheek with his forefinger and then dropped his hand. "It's best I get to the conference room. I'll see you in a few minutes." Tak opened the door to leave, adding, "And, Elle, remember, this is a great moment for you, for your family. For us. Don't forget to smile."

FORTY-ONE

The Police: "Every Breath You Take"

June 6, 2017
1:55 p.m.

Tak

Tak brusquely brushed his wife's hand away. What was she doing? She was such a stupid woman. Something would have to be done about her. Soon. Tiffany had served her purpose. Tak had his perfect baby boy; the one he was meant to have with Elle. With his light hair and eyes, no one would ever question who his real mother was.

He would have Johnny take care of Tiffany. Then he, himself, would take care of Johnny. Tak was outraged that one of his most loyal and trusted friends could betray him in the way Elle had described. Johnny's punishment would be severe.

Tak looked toward the entrance of the conference room. He was eager to see Elle again. To have her walk through the door and announce how excited she was about what *he* had created.

Elle must understand this was all for her.

Tak considered their meeting in the dressing room. He had underestimated the deepness of Elle's friendship with the homosexual Mitch. And Kenji? He had been a surprise, too, but Tak wasn't worried about him. He had dropped his head in shame within seconds of being challenged. No, Kenji wouldn't do anything. He was weak in the way all gay men were.

Elle was all that mattered, anyway. Tak was confident she still had feelings for him. Why else would she have admitted to her husband that she had known him? And then there was Elle's rage in the dressing room. It meant that she still cared. That he could still get such a strong reaction out of her excited Tak. When she had tried to hit him, he remembered her passion. A passion that in the past would have led to an explosive and exquisite lovemaking session.

Sex with Elle had been unforgettable. Better and more satisfying than with anyone else. She made Tak feel like a real man. He needed her. It was the memory of their intense physical bond that kept him going, gave him the strength to go through with his plan. It hadn't been easy. It had taken time, but Tak would do whatever it took to get Elle back.

He had immediately regretted banishing her on the plane to Hawaii. Furious that she had taken the Brazilian soccer player into the cloakroom at *his* club, Tak had acted impulsively and made a mistake. This wasn't how it was supposed to go. He had taken Elle's birth control pills. She would be pregnant soon. They were going to have a family and be together forever.

Tak had nearly gotten on a plane the next day to retrieve Elle, but knew he needed to make some changes first. He had behaved badly, and Elle would expect better. He decided to get serious. He stopped the drug use, sold Samantha's, and with his dad's help, got a good job. The single relic from his old life he refused to give up was Johnny.

After several months of rebuilding, Tak was anxious to show Elle how he had changed; how he was now a successful and well-respected businessman. Elle would be impressed, she would forgive him, and they would have sex again. Lots and lots of mind-blowing sex.

Tak had thought of nothing else on his flight from Tokyo to Oahu, where he knew Elle was teaching English. He had contacted all the English language schools with Japanese owners on the island and offered to pay Elle's salary if they would give her a job. Tak knew exactly where to find her.

His plan would have been perfect if it hadn't been for Win. Tak hadn't expected Elle to fall in love with someone else. The stupid fool Tanaka, the head of the English language school where she worked, had neglected to tell him Elle had a boyfriend.

By the time Tak arrived in Oahu, it was too late. Elle had left Hawaii, a married woman. He had missed her by only a few days. Tak had been livid. Tanaka paid the price for his ineptitude.

Dejected, all Tak could do was return home and come up with another plan. Another way to win Elle back.

His scheme had taken time. More time than Tak had wanted, but seeing Elle again and experiencing the intensity of her emotions had made it all worthwhile. Elle would return to him. Tak couldn't wait for the moment when he would be inside her again.

Tak looked at Win who was sitting to his left. *What an arrogant man.* Win thought he was so smart, having his lawyers slowly explain the terms of their contract. "Is the meaning of this clause perfectly clear, Mr. Akimoto? Martin Global Industries will own all future use of the technology you created." Like he was stupid. Like he didn't understand.

Tak knew exactly what he was doing. It was all integral to his plan. Let Win have the technology. It would be his undoing. Embedded in the code he was selling Martin Global was a virus so complicated and sophisticated that it was impossible to detect. But it was there, and, over time, everything Martin Global produced with Tak's technology would be disrupted. Win would stand by helpless as all his innovations failed. There would be chaos. People would die.

So, yes, Win. I am quite sure of what I am doing. I have been developing this plan for years. I am smarter than you'll ever be. I, Takeshi Akimoto, will win. Tak smirked, realizing the connection to his winning and his nemesis' name. Ironic.

It would serve Win right. He didn't deserve Elle. He was too focused on his career. He didn't put his wife on a pedestal the way Tak would, the way she deserved. It would be fitting for Win's obsession with work to be his downfall. Elle would be happier without him. He wasn't a man she would ditch her underwear for.

After more than twenty years, Tak's moment of triumph was near. Remembering Sato, the lawyer who had come to see him shortly after Elle left for Hawaii, had been lucky. Something untoward had happened between the two of them, Tak was certain of it. Sato had been agitated and nervous when asking about her. Whatever it was, Tak had correctly guessed that Elle didn't want to be reminded of it.

So, no, Elle wouldn't say anything other than what had been planned. She would protect her family and her reputation to the end. She would play along and then, when everything fell apart for her husband, Tak would be there waiting to pick up the pieces.

It had been a mistake to send Elle away. Tak had been young, and careless, and foolish. But he had made amends. He had been patient, and he had been smart. He had bided his time well. Tak was ready for the payoff. She would walk through the door at any moment.

FORTY-TWO

X Ambassadors: "Renegades"

June 6, 2017
1:55 p.m.

Win

Win looked toward the doors leading into the conference room, impatiently awaiting Elle's arrival. Strange how Akimoto had insisted she enter alone. This whole deal had been bizarre. Win couldn't figure Akimoto out. He had been such a pain in the ass the past few days, making last-minute demands on seemingly trivial points, like the name of the robot—Blondie. Win was convinced it was some sort of homage to Tiffany, whom the robot seemed to have been modeled after, but it was a terrible name. It was limiting in scope, old-fashioned, and highly unoriginal, yet Akimoto had, for no logical reason, insisted on keeping it. It was almost like in getting Win to concede on the name, Akimoto had won some sort of important battle. *Odd.*

At the same time, on the most important piece, Akimoto had seemed less concerned. Nonchalant, even. It made zero sense. The changes

Akimoto had insisted upon gave Martin Global the intellectual property rights to the artificial intelligence technology used to create Blondie. Granted, the purchase price for these rights was astronomical—Akimoto was going to be a very rich man—but the technology he had created was groundbreaking, its applications widespread. Win would be able to develop some of the most exciting and innovative products imaginable because of it.

It was unfathomable to him that Akimoto would give this up. So unbelievable that Win had taken the extra step of making sure his lawyers explained it clearly to him several times. Akimoto still hadn't cared. *Crazy.*

At least things would end on a high note. Win had read Elle's prepared remarks. They were clever, intelligent, and sincere, just like she was. And there was no doubt she would nail the delivery. Elle was the most charming woman he knew. She had the uncanny ability to connect with anyone—from the housekeeper and gardener to lawyers and CEOs. His wife had even worked her magic on Akimoto last night. Yes, the crowd would absolutely love her. That she could speak Japanese was icing on the cake.

Win was proud of Elle. She was a good wife. Things hadn't always been perfect between them, but what marriage didn't have ebbs and flows? Could their sex life have been more robust? *Sure.* Could Elle have been more engaged in his business? *Most definitely.*

Win thought about Cheryl, his former VP of Finance. A Wharton grad, she understood the way his brain worked in a way no else could, and the two of them shared a special camaraderie. Whereas Elle often seemed bored by his many business ventures, Cheryl found them all fascinating and had interesting suggestions and ideas of her own. Yet Win had still been shocked when Cheryl told him she wanted more out of the relationship. He would never leave Elle. Win had made a commitment to her and to their family, and he would see it through.

It was the same with Ainsley. Elle had confirmed his own suspicion that she seemed inappropriately attentive toward him. Flattering as it may be, Win was not tempted. Sure, the idea of multiple young and attractive sex partners was appealing—he was, after all, a normal, red-blooded male—but cheating on his wife and potentially destroying his family was something Win would never consider.

Infidelity was dishonest. Dishonesty was unacceptable—a refuge for the weak.

Perhaps he and Elle *had* rushed into things a bit with their whirlwind courtship—it wasn't unusual for guys returning from long tours away to get engaged quickly—but Win knew with certainty Elle was a good choice of life partner in all the ways that mattered most: she was honest, faithful, trustworthy, kind, and generous. Most of all, she had been an excellent mother to his children; in this area, his wife was beyond reproach.

It made perfect sense as to why Elle was now feeling a bit lost—her job was ending. Their children were nearly grown and didn't need her as much. Perhaps she was even going through menopause. He should have realized all of this and been more sympathetic to her situation.

Now that Win understood the problem, he could fix it. If opening a shelter for teens would make Elle happy, he would support her one hundred percent. Just talking about the idea had energized her. She seemed happier. She had engaged with him in real conversation with real meaning. And the sex—it had been amazing. As passionate as when they had first married. In this respect, Win wished he had paid more attention to what Elle had been feeling. The happier she was, the more sex they would have. He would remember that.

Win reflected on his children. Yes, Elle had been an exemplary mother. He was proud of them, too.

Brynnie was driven, independent, and smart. Smarter than he had ever been. He couldn't wait until she came to work with him at Martin Global. Sure, it wouldn't be right away. As with so many young people before her—hell, he had even considered joining the Peace Corps—Brynnie was armed with a naive idealism that made entering corporate America anathema.

So be it. Let her go plant vegetables on an organic farm and build a house with Habit for Humanity. Brynnie's unflinching adherence to her convictions would eventually fade and everything wouldn't be so black and white to her. In due time, she'd start shaving her armpits again, grow out her hair, and get a nice boyfriend. (He had to admit to being relieved when Elle reported she wasn't a lesbian.) So, yes, Brynnie would sow her oats for a bit and then come to work at Martin Global with him. Together, they would do great things.

Win next considered Four. He was a good kid at heart, but maybe they *had* been too easy on him. He would benefit from a little hardship and discipline. Win certainly had. A bit of a momma's boy himself, the Naval Academy had made him into a man. It would be the same with Four. Yes, the Naval Academy would be perfect for him. Playing lacrosse there would also be ideal. Win trusted the coach; his son would be in good hands. After his stint in the Navy, Four could join Brynnie at Martin Global. He'd be a natural in sales. Satisfied with this plan, Win made a mental note to follow up with the Navy lacrosse coach when they returned home.

Home. Win couldn't wait to get back. His head was spinning with ideas on applications for the newly acquired technology. He hadn't been this invigorated by work in years. This was his chance to leave his mark, to make a *real* difference.

Win had promised Elle he would give up work within six months, but this would no longer be possible, not with these new developments. Elle would understand. The technology Martin Global had acquired would change lives. Besides, he would live up to his commitment to fully support her in creating a new shelter. He'd provide contacts, funding, anything she needed. Win would also make another hefty donation to the

SIDS Alliance in Jimmy's name. He would do whatever he could to keep his wife happy.

Win couldn't sit still. He wanted to get this dog and pony show over with. He had work to do.

FORTY-THREE

Kid Cudi: "Pursuit of Happiness"

June 6, 2017
1:55 p.m.

Four

That fucking robot was so jacked. Maybe it was because he was so high, but it looked *exactly* like his mom. She was staring right at him like she knew he was stoned and didn't approve. Four usually didn't get paranoid after smoking pot, but it was tough with edibles. You never quite knew how the high would play out.

Fuck. Whatever was in those THC-laced chocolate bars had been some serious shit. It was almost like Four was shrooming. Going to Tokyo Disneyland baked had been like entering an alternate universe, similar to the place where the *Teletubbies* lived. Especially in Minnie's house. That was wicked.

Four's phone beeped. A text had come in. It was the night before back in the States and all his friends were at Tate's house—his parents were in Europe and he had the place all to himself. As they could all spend the night, everyone had raided their parent's medicine cabinets and a massive pharming party was in play. Prescription pill parties were always insane, and from all the Snapchat stories Four was getting, he could tell some wild shit was going down.

The text was from Mercer: *How's the sushi, bro? We're missing ya*

Four looked around the room to make sure his dad wasn't watching and texted back: *I hear you're the one that's been eating some sushi of late*
Beep.

Mercer texted back: *?*

Brynnie elbowed Four. She must have heard the beep. He better turn the ringer off. He looked around again. No one seemed to be paying attention to him.

Four stealthily typed at his phone with two fingers: *I heard about your Netflix and chill with some blonde piece of ass*

Mercer: *Fuck man, I wish. You're thinking of Thatcher*

Four: *Thatcher? Really? Who's that scrub fisting?*

Mercer: *IDK some pubie skank. She's blowing him 24/7*

Four: *Gotta love a pubie—country day chicks would never service you like that*

Four was bitter. It sucked ass to miss all the fun with his friends. Sure, the past week or so hadn't been all bad. Ainsley was a fucking dime—getting sucked off by those lips would be something else. And he had had some laughs with Brynnie. Once she had dropped her judgey attitude she was much more fun to be around. Even his mom had been more chill.

Still, Four needed to be more careful around his mom moving forward. It had been a stupid call to ask for champagne in the limo. He had been massively hashed and hadn't thought it through. Elle was sure to be onto his drinking now. Four didn't think she was the type to snoop around too much, like Grayson's mom, Aubrey—she was all up in his grill, reading his texts and stalking his social media accounts—but he'd need to take some more precautions.

It shouldn't be hard. It's not like he had a problem. Sure, he partied on the weekends—everyone did—but it wasn't like he was one of those guys who lit up every day. Four didn't *need* the weed, that was for sure.

It was just a bonus for when things were boring. And he knew better than to smoke during lax season. That shit would come up on a drug test. In season, he limited himself to drinking or shrooming.

But Four would make sure to be more careful. Like he wouldn't risk traveling with THC again. He had figured no one would search the private jet of a wealthy American, so when the guy in the uniform had come onto the plane he had almost shit himself. He was sure he would be caught, and all he could think to do was run to the bathroom and flush his supply down the toilet. It turned out the guy was just sent to help escort them off the plane, which had been lucky. His stash was safe. But still. *Fuck, that was close.*

Brynnie was right: bringing the edibles had been a twat move. From now on out, he'd curtail his use around his parents. It would be hella bad if they found out about his extracurricular activities. Win and Elle would rage.

Four felt his phone vibrate.

It was a text from Mercer: *Fuck man, just found out Thatcher in trouble again. That pubie—she's saying he like assaulted her or something. IDK will let you know when I hear more.*

Shit. That sounded serious. Thatcher could be such an idiot. Why would he trust a public-school girl? That was stupid. Four wouldn't tell his mom about this. She was already a Thatcher hater. Anyway, Thatcher's dad would get him out of it, just like he had with the Snapchat to Jacinda and that whole deal when he sold his Adderall.

Four was ready to text back when a picture popped up on his screen. It was from Tabby: a shot of her boobs in a bright-yellow string-bikini top. They were slammin. Perfectly round and perky. *God, I miss those tits.*

Four missed Tabby. More than he thought he would. And not just the sex, though it had been a long ten days of going without. He missed being around her. She was prime.

Four looked at the picture again. Tabby's boobs were luscious. He could feel himself getting hard.

Fuck me. Four shifted uncomfortably in his seat and tried to think about something else. Anything. He even looked up at the freaky fucked-up robot, but it didn't help. It was too late. He had a full-on boner. What did he expect? Tabby always did it for him. Four crossed his legs, covered his crotch with his hand, and hoped no one would notice.

He texted Tabby back: *1 more day miss u*

Four thought of all the guys at the party. Tate would probably try to make a play for Tabby in his absence. He was a dick in that way. Should he text Mercer and ask him to keep an eye on Tate? *Nah.* He trusted Tabby. Plus, he had seen from the pictures that Hadley and her crew of field hockey players were at the party. They were always thirsty. Maybe Tate would just bone one of them. Then again, Tate could be a real douche. He should protect Tabby.

Four shot a quick text to Mercer: *Tell that narp Tate to stay away from Tabby*

Remembering the news about Thatcher, he added hastily: *Keep me posted on Thatcher*

Brynnie elbowed Four again, trying to get his attention. He lifted his head. His dad was looking right at him. *Shit.* Had he seen him texting? Did he see his chub? As the two made eye contact, Win winked at his son. *Nice.* He hadn't seen anything.

Four didn't want to disappoint his dad, not ever. He respected him way too much. Still, he needed to figure out a way to get him off the Navy kick he was on. The Naval Academy? *No fucking way!* That was the last place Four wanted to go. It wasn't even like going to college, with all the rules, regulations, and what not. No, the Naval Academy was not for him. Four wanted to go somewhere near a beach so he could surf.

What could he do? Maybe the best bet was to go ahead and commit to play lacrosse for Navy. The coach had made an offer already, and it would only be a verbal commitment. Verbals didn't mean shit. Guys changed their minds all the time.

Yeah, that's the way to go. He would commit to Navy when he got home. It would be perfect— he wouldn't have to go through all the recruiting bullshit like everyone else. He could go out and party after games with all the other committed guys. What would it matter if he were tired and played like shit the next day? It wasn't like he would need to impress any coaches. And there was no way in hell he was going to do a PG year. *Fuck that.* Besides, it would shut up any of the dickweeds who thought he wasn't crack enough to play DI. *Fuckers.* It's not like any of them scored four goals in the state championship game. *Skrrrt!* And his game-winner was filthy—not many other players had the hands for that many fakes.

The best part about committing would be that it would buy him almost two years to get out of it—plenty of time to win his parents over. Maybe Brynnie would help him. She had passed on Brown. His parents had survived. They would be okay with it.

Four felt better. He smiled back at his dad. That was a money plan. Even better, all the thinking about the Naval Academy had taken care of his hard-on.

Four nodded his head toward Brynnie in thanks for the heads up that their dad was looking at them. It was a legit move. She was probably a dyke—but whatever, he didn't care. Maybe she would hook up with a betty. That would be something.

Four wished he could see more of Tabby's boobs. No, he shouldn't think about her anymore. There would be no privacy on the plane, no place where he could rub one out. Four lifted the front legs of his chair, and leaned back. He hoped the press conference wouldn't drag on forever. He couldn't wait to get back home. Back to lacrosse. Back to the parties. Back to his friends. Back to Tabby.

FORTY-FOUR

LADY GAGA: "BORN THIS WAY"

June 6, 2017
1:55 p.m.

Brynnie

Brynnie slowly turned her head from side to side as she considered "Blondie." The name offended her—it implied blonde hair was somehow superior and should be celebrated. It was 2017, for Christ's sake! It would piss her off even more if she weren't enjoying such a killer high. The chocolate bars must have been made with synthetic weed—she'd only eaten two squares and was stoned out of her mind.

Brynnie had been shocked when Four told her about bringing the edibles on the plane with him. It certainly explained why he ran off and hid in the bathroom when the security officer boarded the plane. *What a complete dumbass!* She enjoyed pot as much as the next person, but seriously, had her brother not thought through what would have happened if he had been caught? *Idiot.*

As Four had pointed out, he *hadn't* been caught, so after scolding him for a bit on his stupidity, she agreed to imbibe with him. Going to Tokyo

Disneyland high would be a blast and there was no point in wasting what he had. Besides, Brynnie wanted the chance to bond with her brother. She had decided it was her responsibility to make Four a better person. To teach him to see outside of his box of white privilege and entitlement.

Brynnie laughed thinking about how surprised her brother had been to learn she had gotten high before. He was such a simple person. Maybe it explained why her parents, especially her mom, always seemed to give him a pass. But that was okay, Four was going to be her next project and Brynnie never failed.

She considered Blondie again. The robot *did* look like her mom, there was no denying it. Too much so to be entirely coincidental—or was it the THC creating irrational thoughts? No, there was more to all this. Brynnie was sure of it.

Her mom had been so shocked to see Akimoto. She had tried to mask her surprise, but something was up. Elle was impeccable in social situations; she could talk to anyone. But not Akimoto. She had seemed uncomfortable around him all night.

What was the story there? Had they dated? It wouldn't be surprising. Tak carried himself in the same confident manner of her dad, and Brynnie guessed her mom was attracted to all that hyper alpha-male energy. She would ask more about it later, when she could be alone with her mom. Elle would be honest with her. Over the course of the trip, Brynnie and her mom had regained their connection. Things between them were back to the way they were before—easy, trusting.

In her mellow THC-induced state, Brynnie admitted she had been hard on her mom, and it hadn't been entirely fair. After all, she *was* a good mom. She really was. It just frustrated Brynnie beyond belief that she got caught up in all the bullshit of her stupid-ass society friends. Brynnie couldn't stand any of them—a group of vacuous, anorexic blondes prancing around in their tennis outfits, proudly announcing to everyone their utterly useless existences. *"I have nothing better to do than play tennis."*

Aubrey was the worst. The type of woman who would relate most to the character of Amy in *Little Women*. Oh, but that's right, Aubrey didn't read—*she didn't have time. WTF?* What kind of person thinks not reading is an attribute? And busy? Doing what? Fixing imagined problems and creating drama where there was none because she had nothing better to do?

Aubrey didn't have a clue. There were problems in the world, many of them to be sure, but not a single one involved women who relied on spouses with seven-figure salaries to bankroll their meaningless lives.

There was so much important work to be done, so many ways these women could be making a difference. Instead, they poured all their time and energy into ensuring their children would be admired by others. It was the highest form of narcissism—their children were reflections of themselves, so it mattered what they wore, where they went to camp, what grades they got, and where they went to college. Country Day moms toted their children around like they were nothing more than expensive accessories to show off.

It was disgusting. At least Elle allowed Brynnie to make her own decisions, albeit at times begrudgingly. Still, she couldn't understand why it was so important for her mom to have the Country Day crowd's approval.

Her mom was better than that. She had a master's degree in social work. She was smart. Empathetic. She cared. Brynnie understood all of this and had even called her mom out on it, asking her if she was happy, if she was living a fulfilled life.

Maybe it had been unkind, but it had to be done. To a certain extent, Brynnie thought it had been effective. Her mom had been a different person on this trip, away from all the Country Day tennis moms. She was more relaxed and easy-going. She was even eating like a normal person. Yesterday, she had mentioned going back to work. This pleased Brynnie. She would even forgive her mom the fillers she had recently gotten. It was an incredibly vain thing to do, but at least she had done it sparingly.

Brynnie saw her dad smiling at her from up on the dais. She elbowed Four as a warning to stop texting and pay attention. Doing so, she noticed a bulge in his pants. *Seriously? So fucking gross.* He must have gotten a picture from Tabby.

Men and their penises were so elementary. Women and their sexuality were so much softer and *waaay* more intriguing. You had to work for it. Brynnie thought about the conversation she had had with her mom a few days before regarding her own sexual preferences. She wasn't surprised it had come up. Her parents would have to be idiots not to wonder.

Brynnie *had* been honest with her mom, for the most part. She didn't consider herself a lesbian. Not really. Brynnie believed all humans had both feminine and masculine sides. She recognized both these parts of her being and was open to experiences honoring each of them. She sought not male or female, but *human* experiences—intimacy didn't have boundaries. It could be with a man, or a woman, or both at the same time. Who cared? Attraction was too complicated a thing to be explained and given a label. Gay? Straight? Bi? Her sexuality couldn't and shouldn't be defined.

No matter how evolved her mom thought she was—"my best friend was gay. It doesn't matter to me"—she still wouldn't be able to completely understand Brynnie's perspective. Besides, the look of relief on her face when Brynnie told her she wasn't a lesbian had said it all. No, her mom wasn't ready for the truth. And her dad? *Forget it.* He'd want to understand and he'd try, but as much as he was at the forefront of innovation in the technology realm, at his core he was still irrevocably tethered to his middle-class, middle-America upbringing. He couldn't possibly understand the idea of accessing his feminine side.

As supportive and progressive as her parents were and strived to be, they were still products of their stilted generation. They just wouldn't get it.

Brynnie had been right not to try to explain herself more. It would only bring up additional questions. It needed to wait. More pressing was how she was going to explain her decision to defer her admission to Reed for a year. Brynnie didn't want to go to college yet. She had the opportunity to work at an all-girls school in Liberia. It seemed so much more fulfilling.

How to tell her mom and dad? It would need to be explained in precisely the right way. Brynnie was skilled at manipulating her parents. She could easily come up with an effective explanation, one they wouldn't protest, but she didn't want to think about it now. This had been such a good trip. This was such a fresh high. Brynnie didn't want to ruin it.

Yes, she had been hard on her mom, but today, Brynnie was proud of her. This was Elle Martin's moment to shine. To show everyone she was more than the spouse of Win Martin, CEO of Martin Global Industries. She was intelligent, and articulate, and engaged. Her mom deserved this moment, and Brynnie would support her wholeheartedly.

FORTY-FIVE

FLORENCE + THE MACHINE: "SHAKE IT OUT"

June 6, 2017
1:55 p.m.

Elle was alone in the dressing room. She had asked Kenji to give her a few moments by herself. She looked in the mirror. With her hair in a perfectly coiffed French twist and in her pearl earrings and subdued makeup, she looked the part she was supposed to play: elegant wife of important man.

Was this how the wives of her clients from the Big YAC had looked?

There was a gentle rapping on the door. It was one of Tak's assistants. "Mrs. Martin, we're ready for you."

Elle stood and straightened her suit jacket. She had chosen a watermelon Chanel suit for the occasion. With its Peter Pan collar, three-quarter-length sleeves, large buttons, and knee-length skirt, it was very Jackie O. Despite being made of the finest material, the suit was scratchy and a little snug. Elle had been eating so freely, she must have gained weight on the trip.

She looked in the mirror again, turning to consider her backside. Even though the skirt was stretched tightly across her bum, there wasn't a panty line to be seen. The hotel concierge had been delighted to fulfill Elle's last-minute request for a pair of red thong underwear. She hadn't worn a G-string in so long it felt unfamiliar, but it was worth it. Elle gave herself one final look-over and took a deep breath in preparation for the cameras which would be waiting outside the dressing room door.

Elle walked out with as big a smile as she could muster. The camera lights were bright on her face—glaring and hot. Beads of sweat developed under her arms and around her neck. She wished Win could be there to greet her. Seeing him would steady her, but Tak had insisted she enter the conference room alone. It seemed pointless, but she couldn't argue. Elle tried to ignore the heat and smiled wider as she followed Tak's assistant into the conference room.

The room was full, more crowded than Elle expected. A red banner with BLONDIE in bold white letters hung on the wall. The U2 song "Beautiful Day" was playing in the background.

Bono's voice sounded like that of an angel and was reassuring. While Elle now understood that it had been a mistake to place blind faith in music, she would never deny its role in connecting her to what really mattered—a truth larger and more wonderful than she could have ever imagined.

She searched for Win and saw him standing up ahead of her on a dais next to Tak and Tiffany. He looked as handsome as ever. Tall, masculine, and safe.

As the crowd politely applauded her entrance, Elle walked up to the dais. She allowed herself to glance at Tak for a moment. He smiled back at her. If he was at all nervous about what she was going to say, he didn't show it. It was so Japanese of him—stoic until the bitter end.

Win approached and led Elle to the podium, lovingly placing an arm around her shoulder. She turned and looked at him, holding his gaze for several seconds more than was usual. His eyes conveyed warmth, love, and absolute confidence in her. He gave her a playful wink before returning to his place next to Tak and Tiffany.

Win loved her. He did. And Elle loved him. He was a good husband, a good father, a good man. The *best* kind of man—she had known it from the moment they first met. This trip had shown her that their marriage could work.

Will it survive this?

Elle adjusted her suit jacket and again felt hot. She worried her cheeks were burning red. Camera lights seemed to be everywhere, making it difficult to see. She looked to the front row and her children.

Four offered a sweet, genuine smile. He was so handsome, so charming. Elle understood his eternal optimism; everything would be easy for him. Four was the type of guy who rolled into Millionaire Acres ahead of everyone else in The Game of Life, his car game piece effortlessly filled with a gorgeous wife and beach-kissed-tan kids, having picked up a prestigious job and a portfolio of profitable investments along the way. Isn't this what she had wanted, what she had hoped for him?

Elle spotted Four's iPhone surreptitiously hidden in his hand under his navy Brooks Brothers sport coat. He had probably been playing a video game or texting Tabby and would likely start again the minute she began to speak. Yes, Four was young and immature, but there was still time. She could teach him to be a better person, to make a difference.

Will he listen?

Elle next focused her attention on Brynnie. As she had with Win, Elle held her daughter's gaze a few extra beats. Brynnie had ignored Ainsley's suggestion that she wear an emerald green sheath dress—"*That color with your hair? Perfection.*" Instead, she looked somewhat like a wandering gypsy in a brightly patterned flowing skirt and peasant blouse, with a large scarf around her neck.

Elle was impressed with her daughter's confidence and independence. In Brynnie, she had done something right. Something genuine and pure. Brynnie was the person Jimmy would have been if he had been given the chance.

Brynnie gave Elle a warm, expectant smile.

"*Are you happy, Mom? Are you living your dream?*"

Her daughter's words had been a slap in the face a few months ago. But now Elle understood. She *could* be happy. She was right on the doorstep to the fulfilled life she had always desired.

Tucking a stray hair behind her ear, Elle reached for the microphone in front of her. The G-string she wore remained uncomfortable, but she was glad for the reminder of Mitch.

Elle closed her eyes and thought about everything that led her to this exact moment in time.

Sweet Baby James: Jimmy smiling, reaching up for her; Jimmy snuggled against her chest; Jimmy, eyes open and cold next to her in bed. *Devastation. Guilt.*

Fleetwood Mac, The Doobie Brothers, The Eagles: paper dolls, coloring books, a black Sony AM/FM radio; her dad, quarters, a glass of maraschino cherries, and a sunburn; Mrs. Whannel in a denim pantsuit, going to the playground hungry, walks to the laundromat. *Loneliness. Shame.*

U2, Sting, INXS: high school, homework, scholarship applications; fraternity parties, pizza, sorority sisters with credit cards and unlimited funds. *Determination. Pretending.*

Nirvana, Pearl Jam, Soul Asylum: Japan; Tak, Johnny, and Sato; cigarettes, booze, cocaine, and violence. *Escape. Shame.*

Green Day, Coldplay, Matchbox Twenty: Win, the Martins, the salesgirl at Nordstrom; graduate school, volunteering, work at a shelter; two beautiful babies and a loyal dog. *Redemption. Hope.*

The Fray, Mumford & Sons, Imagine Dragons: Country Day, board memberships, society galas, and tennis at the club; the Three Wise Men and Aubrey; feral cats and dogs gnawing on used feminine hygiene products. *Fear. Reckoning.*

Elle saved her final thoughts for Mitch. He was in a category all his own.

Dear sweet Mitch.

The Ramones, Queen, U2: laughter, adventure, late-night talks and confessions. *Acceptance. Sacrifice.*

Elle loved Mitch. She owed him this.

Elle pulled her shoulders back and cleared her throat. In the back of the room, she saw Ainsley whispering directions to a cameraman. Everything she was about to say would be documented on tape for eternity. Elle faltered, turning to look at Win behind her, and then back out to her children in the front row. They all smiled at her encouragingly.

Family. Future.

Elle thought of Mitch again. He *wanted* her to live a life of unadulterated joy, to be happy for them both. Hadn't he demanded as much in his suicide note?

Elle would honor Mitch's last request. *I* will *be happy.* She wouldn't let her best friend down. Never again. She would wear sexy underwear until the day she died.

Elle took a long, deep breath and exhaled calmly. *Yes. This is what Mitch would want me to do.* She cleared her throat and looked directly into the eye of the camera. Confident it was the right thing—the only thing—she could do, Elle smiled as she began to address the crowd.

All she had ever wanted was love.

The Beatles: "The End"

Made in the USA
San Bernardino, CA
16 June 2017